SMOKE PORTRAIT

TRILBY KENT

ALMA BOOKS

ALMA BOOKS LTD
London House
243-253 Lower Mortlake Road
Richmond
Surrey TW9 2LL
United Kingdom
www.oneworldclassics.com

Smoke Portrait first published by Alma Books Ltd in 2011
© Trilby Kent, 2011

Trilby Kent asserts her moral right to be identified as the author of this work in accordance with the Copyright, Designs and Patents Act 1988

This is a work of fiction. Names, characters, places and incidents either are the product of the author's imagination or are used fictitiously, and any resemblance to actual persons, living or dead, business establishments, events or locales is entirely coincidental.

Cover: Rosanne Cooper

Printed in Great Britain by CPI Mackays, Chatham ME5 8TD

ISBN: 978-1-84688-129-9

Smoke Portrait

In daily life we never really understand each other; neither complete clairvoyance nor complete confessional exists. We know each other approximately, by external signs, and these serve well enough as a basis for society and even for intimacy.

— E.M. Forster, *Aspects of the Novel*

1

When my father heard that Krelis was dead, he went up to the gatehouse with a bottle of Westmalle and the family Bible and told me to go home.

"But this is home," I said – because the gatehouse is actually just a landing between our house and the de Bruynses'. In olden times it was part of a watchtower, but now there's nothing to watch besides ducks on the canal. My father didn't hear me.

In the kitchen, Mrs Lekaerts and Aunt Marta were making coffee. Mother sat by the Leuven stove, exactly where she'd been when the message arrived that there had been an accident at the fulling mill. When Aunt Marta heard me come in, she whispered something to Mrs Lekaerts. Mrs Lekaerts slid me a look the way you do a spider in the bathtub – hoping it won't notice you until you're dressed, so you can squash it – and whispered something back.

"He doesn't understand. Leave him," said my mother.

So I went upstairs to my bedroom, where I had been reading *Bahlow's Book of Birds* when the news came about my brother. Actually, not reading: trying to peel apart the pages that Mother had glued together when I was little and easily frightened. I had just managed to separate two leaves when a mill worker arrived with the news, and then there had been so much commotion that it had become impossible to concentrate.

The picture was of a black eagle and her two chicks. The mother bird was flying off in the distance, and the chicks were fighting. The caption read: "The older chick begins its persecution as soon as the second egg hatches. In most cases, it kills the younger sibling in a battle commonly known as the 'Cain and Abel' scenario".

The picture had given me nightmares once. The larger chick was stabbing at the little one with its hooked beak, snaring it in the eye, while its little brother or sister wrestled on its back with its pink tongue poking out in a futile scream. Its skull had been punctured and glistened with fresh brains, but both eyes were still open – watching me as I watched it die.

I turned onto my back and wondered what my father was doing on the other side of the wall. I would need the Bible before long: it was already Friday and I'd still not begun reviewing the lesson for Sunday. We were supposed to be studying Acts, but I was preoccupied with different questions, such as, "If God didn't create the sun and the stars until the fourth day, how did he separate light from darkness on the first?" Or, "If the serpent was condemned to crawl on its belly for tempting Adam and Eve, how did it get around before that?" And, "If Adam and Eve were the first people, where did Cain's wife come from?"

They were good questions, reasonable questions – questions I could ask Mr Hendryks, who served with me at Mass in Sint-Janskerk. Mr Hendryks had a high, bald forehead and the eyes of a robber fly, and was the only person I knew who hadn't been born in Mechelen. He was from Diksmuide, but had come to our town after the war to work for the Railway Authority, although he'd been retired for as long as I'd known him. Being retired seemed like a very dignified thing to me: it meant you could do nothing all day but walk to and from church and still hold your head high. When I'd said that I thought I would like to be retired one day, he'd smiled and told me that I should start saving up now – which was another way for him to say that our country was going to the dogs. That's what most of the grown-ups in our town believed, though Mr Hendryks took great pains never to admit as much to me. But his eyes, magnified by his spectacles to resemble enormous, blinking beetles, said something different. It felt wrong to watch him lie, so I'd changed the subject to ask why the statue of St Bartholomew in our church was smiling, despite the fact that he was holding his own skin after being flayed alive. This was the sort of question Mr Hendryks liked best, and even though I already knew the answer, I had listened like an obedient schoolchild while he explained that the statue was meant to be St Bartholomew in heaven, and the skin in his hands was just his earthly skin.

I rolled back onto my stomach and considered the picture of the eagle chicks once more. I wondered if snakes got to be reunited with the skins they'd shed during their lifetime. Did they go to heaven, even though they didn't get baptized and couldn't atone for their sins? If what Pepijn at school said was true, most species that ever lived on Earth have long since gone extinct. Only the well-adapted ones – the ones closest to perfection – survive. Like humans and black eagles and boa constrictors, who can produce up to seventy babies in one go.

Krelis was perfect. My parents had never understood him; his brilliance had bewildered them almost as much as his disappearance into the river. Mother had stopped school at fifteen to become a seamstress, and Father wasn't much older when he went to fight in the war, so Krelis knew more than all three of us put together. He won the Poetry Prize three years in a row and played football and hockey better than anyone else. His mathematics teacher used to set him extra assignments, but soon Krelis was the one coming up with formulas that even the headmaster couldn't unravel.

He had been working at the fulling mill for six months now. Kurt Bokhoven had talked him into taking the job the week they graduated, and he had already made many friends there. After clocking off, the young men would smoke behind the mill in surly, reflective pairs with their collars turned up against the wind and their chins tucked into their chests, so that they resembled a huddle of brooding generals. Sometimes I would wander down at the end of the day and listen to them talk disparagingly about the old men who oversaw them, and once Kurt had pressed a few pamphlets into my shirt and told me if I let anyone catch me with them I'd be sorry. One of the pamphlets was titled *What Is to Be Done?* and looked as if it had already been read by many people. I didn't understand most of it, but I forced myself to read it right to the end, flicking impatiently through the greasy pages covered with dense rows of jagged text. The following day, I'd handed the pamphlets to my brother and told him to give them back to Kurt. "What did you think?" Krelis asked me. I told him the tiny words made my eyes hurt, and he just grunted, folding the pamphlets into his pocket. "Perhaps you're too young still," he said, in a way that made me wish I'd tried harder. My brother had a knack with people like that: we were always desperate to please him. Krelis could have had a new girlfriend every week if he'd wanted, but the worst part of it was that he was kind and noble and rather old-fashioned. He even looked like a knight: sun-bleached hair perfectly parted to the side – tanned, broad-shouldered, sweet-smelling. Mother used to say that his skin still smelt like babies' breath, even now that he was a man.

He had been perfect, but now he was gone.

* * *

By the time I woke up, my room was shrouded in half-light. Blue shadows filled the corners where the ceiling met the floor, and on the trunk next to the wardrobe my accordion had turned into an armadillo withdrawing its head beneath scaly armour.

I closed the book and returned it to its shelf between the mattress and the bed frame. Then I stood up and went to the window that looked out onto the brick step gables of the houses on the other side of the street: flat red-and-brown façades with tiny square attic windows just like mine. Further down would be mossy gargoyles and arched doorways, ironwork curlicues in the windows and sunken stone steps that melted into the cobbles. But from where I stood, the houses were so close that it was only possible to see a few rooftops stricken against a leaden sky. I liked their tidy angles and the way the layers of brickwork had been tamed into orderly rows, each one shortening by half a brick's length the higher they went. The gables were just and precise, pointing heavenwards.

No one had called me for supper. It must have been almost eight o'clock, and yet I could hear none of the normal evening noises downstairs – the clatter of dishes, the hissing of a kettle, the scratching of the wireless being tuned by my father. I straightened the bedclothes and inched through the darkness towards the sliver of light creeping beneath the closed door. I never let myself look around in the dark: that was how I would miss things in my path and stumble, or get drawn into black holes in the corners. There were particular floorboards that had to be avoided, ones which creaked, ones which I knew to be unlucky. The rules in my room kept it safe. (Don't make detours on your way to church, because God must never come second. Put your right shoe on before the left, but always wash the left foot first. Spit on nail parings. And so on.) Mr Hendryks thought that this was why I was so interested in science – because there are rules everywhere. In natural science there are, anyway. I once asked him if there's such a thing as *un*natural science, and he looked at me strangely before giving the sort of sensible answer I'd come to expect from him.

"Unnatural science means breaking the rules," he said.

On the landing, I noticed that my parents' bedroom door was closed. No light seeped through the joins, and the stillness was uninviting. To my left, Krelis's door was ajar – but his room, too, was dark.

I crept downstairs, encouraged by the glimmer of a gas lamp on the kitchen table. But no one was there. Aunt Marta and Mrs Lekaerts had disappeared, and I realized that Mother must have gone to bed. Three cups sat in the sink: two empty, one half full with tepid, milky coffee. All that was left of the bread was a dry heel and a scattering of crumbs. I opened the icebox: a knot of giblets was the only remaining evidence of a hare Krelis had trapped the previous autumn.

Suddenly, I was very hungry.

Father would have to give me money to run down to the tavern for some bread and cheese. Someone at De Kraan might take pity on us, offer me a hot meal and invite Father in for a drink on the house. Encouraged by the prospect of a creamy *waterzooi* bubbling with chicken fat, the soft chunks of potato bobbing like floating islands in the carrot-thick waters, I ducked outside.

The entrance to the watchtower was in its own little alcove between our kitchen door and the de Bruynses' carriage house. The walls had been painted with whitewash that my father dyed with bull's blood – in those days the colour was more brown than red. When we were much younger, Krelis and I had used the alcove as a last resort in games of hide-and-seek, although we rarely went all the way up into the gatehouse itself. According to Krelis, a young woman had been found hanged there shortly after the war. My friend Nijs said that this must have been because she'd done it with a German soldier. Every time I heard the starlings that nested in our roof making their strange, bleating cries, I imagined that they were mimicking the sound of the creaking rope. No one else ever talked about the hanged woman, so I sometimes wondered if Krelis had simply made the story up just to frighten me – but once an idea is born, it's just as alive whether it's true or a lie. I never liked the thought of going there alone.

Putting my shoulder to the door, I edged myself into the vestibule and peered up through the gaps in the staircase that wound around a stone pillar, right to the top. A wan light flickered on the landing.

"Father?"

Gripping the iron railing, I pulled myself up several steps before stopping halfway. I leant into the eye of the staircase, resting my head against the cool stone column. "Father, are you there?"

A chair dragged across the floor overhead, sending particles of dust trembling through the floorboards. I knew by the hollow thud of glass on wood that the bottle was empty.

"Are you there, son?"

"It's me, Father…"

"Krelis?"

I stopped, the top of my head just inches from the trap door. In dreams, I was able to leap down staircases in one bound, skimming the ground with the floating grace of a bird landing on water. But there was no room to drop between the railing and the stone column.

"It's Marten, Father."

"Who?"

The trap door slid open, and my father's enormous head appeared, eclipsing the weak glow of a guttering candle.

"I'm hungry. Mother's asleep, and there's nothing to eat…"

"Oh?" A hand plunged through the darkness, but I was no longer small enough for him to lift me easily with one arm. I struggled, landing with a bump on the edge of the floor.

"I thought we could go to De Kraan, Father. Buy you a drink."

My father's shirt was loose and streaked with moisture. Staring at me with poached eyes, he took my face between two hot, clumsy paws and shook me gently.

"Where is Krelis?" he said.

The room was empty but for a table and stool. A decayed starling nest had partially descended from the rafters, quivering with brittle feathers and bits of crumbling bark. "Where is Krelis?"

"He's dead, Father."

"Dead?"

"Yes, Father."

He rolled back onto his haunches and allowed his head to loll on one side. "You want to eat, then?"

"I'm hungry."

"You're hungry."

"Yes, Father."

"Then we shall eat."

He began to search his pockets – trousers, shirt, inside one sock – and produced a few coins.

"It's not going to be enough for both of us, Father. Enough for some bread, maybe. Or a little soup…"

"You must eat, Marten," he said, pressing the coins into my hand and bending my fingers into a fist. "You can't fight your body. Times are hard."

"Yes, Father."

"Life's a struggle, Marten. In the desert, on the mountain…"

"A struggle with the Devil, Father?"

He smiled approvingly, extending a wavering hand to stroke my hair before realizing that he was too far away to reach me. "With the Devil, that's right. You fight to stay alive. You fight, and you fight, and you fight."

"Yes, Father."

"Just like I did. Remember that, Marten."

"I know, Father."

11

"Why'd I fight the German scum, Marten, eh? For what?"

"For a free Flanders, Father."

"And what did we get instead?"

I shook my head.

"What did we get?"

"We got… we got…" I gulped for words, and he nodded with grim satisfaction.

"You see?"

"Yes, Father."

He levered himself onto his back with a groan. "Get yourself something to eat, Krelis."

"Marten, Father."

"Is that Lekaerts woman still downstairs?"

"No, Father."

"Good."

When his breath became gravelly and slow, I edged myself through the trap door and carefully picked my way back down the winding steps. By the light of the candle overhead, it was possible to make out the dim silhouette of the letter box at the back of the alcove. I lifted the catch and felt inside. Empty. But as I brushed it closed, something fluttered to the ground, skirting my bare knees. The envelope was smooth, and fat, and cool.

Pieter van Houten
2, 812
Melkstraat 6
Mechelen
Belgium

Melkstraat 6 was my house, but I didn't know anyone called Pieter van Houten.

I tucked the letter into my pocket and went inside.

2

Gnawing on a pencil stub, Glen considered the bundle of paper still tied up with kitchen string, all but the top corners clearly un-thumbed. It was her eleventh rejection: a form letter on Curtis Brown stationery, not even signed. So that was that, she thought, with something approximating relief. And yet, shoving the type-script in the bottom drawer felt inadequate somehow: like the tell-tale heart, it would still be there, insistently alive. For now, she tossed a newspaper over the offending title page, so she wouldn't have to look at it. Then she stood up and began to pace the room.

The telegram that had arrived from her mother two days ago rested, unanswered, on the mantelpiece. Still chewing on her pencil, Glen paused to consider, reflecting that she had never received a telegram which didn't convey bad news – telegraph wires the world round hung heavy with looming catastrophe. Still, she couldn't help but suspect that her mother's tone had been designed to intrigue her.

```
Annabel  again  another  bout  of  madness  always
terrible  luck  with  men  Tully  home  this  weekend
do come Mummy
```

The mention of her brother filled Glen with the same queasy anxiety she remembered from mornings before school: a sensa-tion she had come to associate with the chafing, damp-warm itchiness of wool stockings pulled over barely dry skin after swimming lessons. But her curiosity had been piqued. The heady rush of liberation from any hopes she might have invested in the poems wouldn't last for ever, she told herself, so she might as well capitalize on it now. She reached for her purse: there was still time to catch the 6.45 to Tisbury, and it wouldn't be too late for the boy to meet her with the car at the station. She scribbled a note for Emily, explaining that she would be back by Sunday evening with a basket of fresh eggs and cream scones, and asking if she'd make her apologies to Harry if he called.

As it was a warm evening, and still light, Glen decided to walk to Waterloo. It was a compensating benefit of living on the wrong side of the river that her escape route was never far off, and tonight the girl felt so energized by the act of leaving the building in a different direction that she began to whistle softly to herself – a meandering, half-remembered tune. Her daily trek to the bookshop took her south, through some of Southwark's less salubrious neighbourhoods. She had only walked along the river once in six months.

Six months. Half a year since graduating, and what did she have to show for it but a dozen rejection letters and a part-time job in a shop where second-hand paperbacks passed as "antiquarian"? Well, it was her own fault for indulging in such silly delusions of literary grandeur. She realized now that her First-class degree meant very little in the scheme of things: those with poor Seconds had found jobs at the *Times*, while one who had scraped a Third was now an artist's model in Paris. Most of the varsity boys were working in the literary reviews – apart from Laurie, still reading Italian in his ascetic's set on the Turl – and any bluestocking worth her salt would be putting her brain to good use. Nine-hour days surrounded by frowzy, dog-eared pot-boilers, self-published collections of earnest poetry and justly forgotten nineteenth-century novellas provided little encouragement for an aspiring writer. Most of the shop's passing traffic was limited to enquiries for the A–Z or directions to Waterloo Bridge. In between queries Glen passed the time furtively reading *The Sexual Life of Savages* and trying to decipher the notes another reader had pencilled in the margins, or else composing mental responses to the less than charitable letters she'd received from literary editors.

She followed the pavement around a curve of boxwood, brushing gently against crackling leaves to allow a suited man to pass. He strutted ahead with the hasty bounce of a schoolboy trying not to run, coat tails flapping against his backside, the cuffs of his trousers – too short by an inch – catching inside his shoes. Perhaps he, too, was after a train to the south. But no: he disappeared up the next road, towards Blackfriars.

Observing other people always led to a certain self-consciousness on her part, and only now did Glen realize that she was not wearing a hat. She glanced at her watch: twenty minutes to go. Well, her mother would have to live with it: an inky-fingered, hatless daughter – and one in flannel bags, at that. With any luck, the wardrobe at home would turn up more suitable attire for tea.

Tea! Proper tea, for once. Dining at the flat rarely involved anything more elaborate than Marmite on toast. More than once Emily had announced her intention to join the next hunger march on Hyde Park, a comment which Glen couldn't help but feel was in slightly poor taste. Having developed an aversion to Ovaltine, she now subsisted on the water that trickled from a limy tap, which was only marginally clearer than the fusty stream that splattered from the pipe at the bookshop. Little wonder that she kept full dehydration at bay only by traipsing after Harry on the weekly party circuit. Did the lemon in a Horse's Neck count as fruit? Succumbing to scurvy in this day and age really would be the final insult.

She didn't even enjoy the parties all that much. Of course, in the early days going out with Harry had been an easy way to forget her loneliness, and she'd convinced herself that evenings at Ciro's and the Monseigneur would provide fodder for her art. But how boring it had all become, and how quickly: watching grown men behaving like schoolboys while their dates affected indulgence and gossiped about the same people, night after night… The truth of the matter was that she was tired of the parties, tired of Harry's friends, tired of driving around London into the small hours only to wake up on Sunday afternoon in no state to write.

Only a few nights ago they'd attended a do in Hampstead at which the guest of honour had been a striking German girl – Gerda? Gertrud? – whose Teutonic self-possession had made Glen feel clumsy and hopelessly juvenile in a way she hadn't since schooldays, when she had fawned over a certain prefect until a public telling-off had forced her to retreat to the San for an entire week to nurse her shame. It wasn't simply the fact that this Gertrud was said to be a political exile, possibly even an anarchist (a detail which only added to her allure): she had been wearing a fur coat that seemed to weigh on her slender frame in a grizzly bear's embrace, and rumour soon spread that she almost certainly hadn't bothered to put on anything else underneath. "The Krauts have a word for lovelies like that," Harry had whispered admiringly in Glen's ear: "*Natürlich.*" And yet, when Glen had finally worked up the composure to introduce herself, the remarkable creature had stared straight through her before turning to accept another gin sling. Glen had returned home that night feeling inexplicably chastened, unable even to channel her feelings into a poem, and declined Harry's invitation the next day to join some friends on a drive to show the German girl the delights of the English countryside.

The real rot of it, she thought now – detaching a corner of soggy newspaper stuck to her heel – was that one writes to be *understood*. What was there worth understanding in her life? Others had already covered the indignities of renting in a city bedsit, the strap-hanging army and the soul-destroying realization of semi-genteel failure. She couldn't bear to succumb to such pitiful self-loathing. Narrative-hungry, that's what she was. Not just for a story, but for *her* story. And yet look at her, rushing home to be consoled by Mummy and Pa.

"How *are* you, Miss Phayre?"

The voice belonged to an elderly gent peering up at her from behind the flower stall with gimlet eyes. How did he know her name? She must have told him. Six months ago, one of the first things Glen had done on arriving in London was to buy a bouquet of sweet peas for the flat. That afternoon she had collapsed onto the bed, imagining herself a sadhu on a board of nails as the wire coils pressed into her shoulders through the thin mattress, and tried to picture how the room would look to her in a few weeks' time. By then, no doubt, it would feel properly hers. She would memorize the scratches on the window and the spaces between the peeling wallpaper – brown and mustard flowers against a background of floating spots that might have been bugs – and the plaster ceiling: she would no longer notice the damp smell of the quilted bedspread or the greasy reflection in the washstand mirror; she would fill a jam jar with shillings for the gas meter. She had put up pictures from the summer of a yellow beach crowded with families, where bodies jostled for space amid striped changing tents, wayward umbrellas and picnic baskets that belched bottles of lemonade, packed sandwiches and sunning foil. The Studland peninsula had never felt so far away. And so she had wandered out to do something practical, to take her mind off of these things. Handing over the bouquet of sweet peas, the little old man at the flower stall had winked at her and said, "A girl who buys herself flowers will never be lonely. Miss Phayre," he added, "the fairest of 'em all."

Glen smiled and pointed to some foxgloves. "Those are lovely. Will they survive a train ride? My mother loves violet."

"Of course, Miss."

It wasn't as if her parents would be short of flowers at this time of year. Her father's dietary experiments with every species of vegetable, seed and blossom was a quarter-century strong, and their sprawling garden would be bursting with more variety than Kew. Still, arriving with a house present might make her feel slightly less a child.

Waiting in the queue next to her was a woman rocking a perambulator. A small, round face glowered up at Glen who, trying not to look over-interested, looked back at the baby. Though just an infant, it had the stern features of a ballet mistress's little daughter from long ago – a solemn, silent creature who used to pace up and down the rows of pliéing girls with her tiny hands clasped behind her back, judging the students' turnout and the lines of their *battements tendus*. Even then, Glen had marvelled at the ability of a child barely out of nappies to make one feel quite so small. Now she smiled at the memory: a smile which she tried to transform into an expression of tenderness for the infant. But the surly little thing only twisted its features in discomfort, and Glen averted her gaze lest the baby started to bawl.

17

"Your flowers, Miss."

"Thank you." Glen dropped two coins into the seller's dust-caked palm and took the bouquet, wrapped in newspaper and baking parchment. The latter was a "quality" touch. The newspaper she would save for later.

* * *

For as long as Glen could remember, the tall library bookshelves had been covered in netting to keep the swallows off. This extension had been her grandfather's creation – a cross between a conservatory and a smoking room, where writhing ivy crept through the window panes and dark niche shelves creaked and sighed under the weight of so many books. Mottled glass cast dapples of light across the sloping floor, creating a shimmering reflection of the ceiling's remarkable *trompe l'œil* of birds in flight.

An umbrella stand in one corner supported what looked like a dead cormorant, which, along with everything else in the library, was covered in a thin coating of dust. More than a decade had passed since Glen had taken her final lessons here before being sent off to school, but the room evoked memories as vivid as the moving pictures on a cinema screen: herself as an infant, grimly chewing on a piece of blotting paper as she studied the engravings of suffering martyrs in a tattered copy of Butler's *Lives of the Saints*; her sister playing nurse to a row of invalid dolls; her brother lining up armies of tin soldiers with obsessive precision along the windowsills, his brooding features darkened by the usual thundercloud. Though most boys had outgrown such games by his age, reports filtering in of the Artois-Loos Offensive only deepened his interest in military strategy, and he had quickly become unresponsive to any conversation not relating to the "Big Push". They had been fierce and dreamy children, but Tully had always been the more inclined to saturnine moods. Glen remembered seeing him being smacked by the girls' nanny for some impertinence or other and knowing even then that he would harbour that humiliation for the rest of his life, storing it away so that a small part of him would remain forever locked in that moment.

Each had had their cross to bear – in Glen's case, a stubborn child-hood lisp; in Merle's, hip dysplasia, which had committed her to a harness for the first ten years of her life – and make-believe play had provided their escape. But of the three, her brother had al-ways been the one to embrace his roles with the fiercest devotion to accuracy. On days when downpours reduced the tennis courts to soup bowls and the children's blackened socks would have to be draped, eel-like, over radiators that rattled and clanged, Glen and her sister would play at being white slaves, casting Tully as the sheik. As raindrops bulleted against the bevelled glass and the sweating walls filled the room with the sweet smell of damp wood, he would mutter and fret over his assembled army while his sisters cowered beneath the writing desk and plotted their escape across the sand dunes.

Although she was the youngest, Glen had been perhaps the first to realize that a healthy imagination required constant feeding. Almost by instinct, by an early age she had become expert at peering through keyholes, listening at doors, loitering on stairs. She had taken for granted the secrets with which they'd grown up – Tully's first, a blooding at their uncle's hunt, an experience which his sisters were allowed to spy only at a distance – as well as the make-believe games that often felt more real than their everyday lives. The gap in their ages (a ten-year lacuna between Tully and Merle haunted by the spectres of three siblings lost to miscarriages and stillbirth) only heightened this sense of matters unspoken, yet to be discovered. Envy of the things her brother got to do later led Glen to invent a male alter ego for herself: it had been Chester's fault, she remembered insisting to her mother, that the milk-glass horse had lost its tail. She now found herself observing the remaining figurines – there were six in total, clustered on a shelf that was furry with dust – before reaching for the one in the shape of a pig. It was heavy and strangely cold to the touch. It had no eyes and no tail. A pink flower had been painted on its pot belly. Funny, she thought, how one can be whipped back into childhood by such a silly thing. A cord relaxes, snaps at its lowest point, and plunges you into a time and place that you've come to associate with someone else...

19

An almighty crash shook her from the daydream, followed by a breathless stream of curses that rumbled through the wall as fine puffs of dust burst and drifted along the trembling shelves. Startled, Glen picked her way across a threadbare Persian rug and emerged into the hallway, where she became gradually aware of a curious smell – musty and warm, with a distinct carbon edge that made her suspect that something, somewhere, was burning. She poked her head into the next room, and drew a sharp breath of surprise.

Her father was standing on the dining-room table with a steaming iron in his hand. All around him strips of hand-painted silk wallpaper, brought back from China by Glen's grandmother, curled to the floor.

"Glynis!" Murray Phayre returned the iron to the grate and sprung from the table with the agility of a young man to embrace her. Glen laughed as she felt the air crushed from her lungs.

"Careful, Pa!" she gasped. "The flowers." Then, casting her gaze over the drooping tatters – here an exquisitely painted lily, there a little bird perched on a cherry blossom – she added, "What *are* you doing?"

Her father's gentle face crumpled into a smile. "It's all part of the redistribution process, my love."

"I beg your pardon?"

"I've had a good offer for this paper from a fellow in town."

"What kind of offer?"

"You should see what I've done next door…" He hooked one finger, led her outside with the enthusiasm of a loyal hound. If he had a tail, Glen thought, it would be wagging. "Behold!"

It was as if a fault line had split the study in two. Almost every precious floorboard had been torn up, the panels of maroon stinkwood and fine yellow sapwood striking tortured poses around a gaping black mouth which now yawned at the centre of the room.

"How'd you manage this, Pa?" Glen shook her head in disbelief, running a hand along one of the boards. The wood was tough, as durable as teak, and she felt a ripple of disgust pass through her. As children, they had played skittles in this room: the memories crystallized in the face of such ridiculous destruction. "I don't understand…"

"They're worth a lot of money, you know."

"But why?"

Her father sank into an armchair. "Household finances. Everyone's been tightening their belts since the Crash. Nothing to worry your pretty head about." He leant forwards. "Speaking of which, what in Heaven's name have you done to your hair this time?"

The usual complaint. Her brother and sister were dark, like their mother, and Glen's golden colouring was a point of pride to her father.

"It's the fashion, Pa. You've seen it before."

"Before it was feminine. It reminded me of Louise Brooks. Now you look like a goatherd – like the lad from the dairy…"

"I always thought he was rather scrummy."

"None of your cheek. Anyway, I thought you were interested in that swot."

"Which swot?"

"You know the one – up at Oxford. Bookish fellow, kept apart from the bright young things…"

"Laurie?"

"That's the one."

"Laurie's a dear, Pa. But possibly not interested in girls."

"Ah."

Glen placed the flowers on the sideboard and lifted a corner of protective sheeting from the sofa. She enjoyed these silly conversations with her father, a comradely relationship that he should have been able to share with Tully – poor, vulnerable Tully – but couldn't. Where there had always been a mutual shyness between Glen and her mother, Murray had found a way to appreciate his youngest daughter's obstinate, coltish nature. It was from him that she had learnt to adopt defiant gaiety in the face of family tension, from him that she had acquired a pair of boxing gloves at the age of eleven, to her mother's trumpeted disapproval. Infancy and adolescence had embarrassed Murray Phayre, but now that his daughters were grown, they had begun to rediscover the easy camaraderie of those long-ago days.

"How's the diet going? You were on dandelion tea the last time I visited."

Her father grunted. "Did wonders for my arthritis, but it's a laxative – *and* a diuretic. I spent six weeks on catabolics before deciding to experiment with raw foods. Doctor Patterson informs me that kelp is an excellent source of iron, and it's something that I can collect with my own fair hands when we visit Lulworth."

"And has Doctor Patterson told his wife about your latest fad?" The Phayres' neighbours inhabited a comparatively conventional world of Clarice Cliff, Ouija boards and games of hunt-the-slipper.

"Couldn't care less what he tells the old biddy," smiled her father. "As long as he continues to take my blood pressure every Thursday before tea, the good doctor will have served his purpose." He nudged a dejected floorboard aside with his toe, and the smile faded.

"Where's Mummy?"

"At a recital in Salisbury. Fauré." He tugged the watch from his waistcoat. "Should be home by midnight."

"Apparently there's been some new drama with Aunt Annabel."

Her father laughed. "Isn't there always a drama with Annabel? You'll have to get your mother to tell you about it. The last I heard was that the marriage was on the rocks." He tucked the watch into his pocket. "I think Mummy's secretly rather pleased."

"Surely not, Pa?"

He only shrugged, although she detected a wicked glint in his eye. "Ask her in the morning. She'll be up first thing, preparing for your brother's arrival."

"I was hoping that Betty might make us scones tomorrow." From her father's expression, Glen knew that something had changed. "Is Betty no longer here?"

A wisp of a sigh. "As part of the…"

"The redistribution process?" Glen lowered her voice and spoke firmly – the tone in which a stubborn child is warned for the final time. "How bad is it?"

But her father only raised his palms in surrender: and with that gesture she saw that he had become an old man.

Later that evening, Glen ran a finger along the faded spines that lined the nursery bookshelves: tales of adventure and intrigue, stories that had convinced her from an early age that she would grow up to be anything but ordinary. It was still too early to give in to the creeping fear that she might not be good enough to make it as a poet, but while she waited for inspiration she could perhaps turn her hand to something new.

Journalism was surely the fastest route to significance, she thought, spreading out the salvaged newspaper on the school desk. If she didn't yet have her own story to tell, perhaps she might capitalize on someone else's. The idea appealed to her interest in watching people, a hobby she had cultivated since childhood, observing tense conversations in tearooms and bland chatter in post-office queues. Lately, she had been keeping track of a man who caught the bus outside her flat at the same time every morning – he appeared to be permanently stuck at the halfway mark in *Vanity Fair* – and now kept a journal of ticket stubs, magazine scraps and transcripts of snatched conversations covertly jotted down from behind the counter at the shop. Glen had always searched for symbols in her life, auguring the future from the happenstance of burnt toast or a shiny penny discovered on the pavement, but all too often these symbols seemed fabricated in retrospect, irrelevant to her banal reality. The now-defunct poetry collection had been pompously titled *Scenes from Away* – and yet where had she been, barring a bicycle holiday in the south of France and two soggy Christmases in Wales? Perhaps travel was the answer.

As she unfolded the newspaper sheet, which was still partly smudged and damp from the cut flowers, her gaze fell upon a box of text two-thirds of the way down the classifieds section – a goldmine for ephemera-hunters.

Be a Ray of Hope
  Christian Women's Union seeks correspondents for pilot letter-writing scheme to improve the language skills of inmates in medium- to high-security prisons across Europe. Anonymity guaranteed. Details of participating offenders available upon request. Box 7339.

Glen read the advertisement twice before reaching for a pencil.

3

Mrs Maes told me that our lesson would have to end early because her husband was going to his first finching competition that afternoon. He'd trapped his own chaffinch – the prettiest little thing, she said, all orange and grey, with eyes like black caviar and the most exquisite song, which is why it's always worth trapping a wild one if you possibly can – and he'd even built it a special cage.

I'd been to a *vinkenzetting*, once. About a dozen boxes were lined up along Begijnenstraat, and inside each box was a male chaffinch. Every time a bird sang its song, its owner would chalk a notch on a wooden stick, and the bird with the most songs in one hour was the winner. Many of the owners were old men who had fought in the war and been blinded by the gas, whose only consolation was that they could still listen to birds singing.

I was glad that our lesson was cut short. I'd not practised very much that week, and I hated it when Mrs Maes tried to be encouraging through her disappointment – that was worse than getting hit on the knuckles, which is what would happen at school. Our school was not like the schools I read about in English books: there were no tennis courts or hacking trails, and no one drank mugs of steaming cocoa or ate rice pudding. When you were little you were taught by nuns, and when you were older you were hurled into a world of men: red-faced masters and sour-smelling older boys. In her dark-green dress with the crocheted collar and dainty house slippers, with her silver hair pinned in tight curls around her temples, Mrs Maes was the only teacher I'd ever felt guilty about disappointing. My melody side was good, but I didn't like touching the black notes, in the way that some people can't stand the sound of nails on a blackboard. When I had tried to explain this to her, she looked confused and said that if I didn't play the black notes I could only ever learn pieces in the key of C, which wasn't very interesting.

We didn't have that conversation today, though, because we were short of time. As she put on her coat and checked her lipstick in the mirror, I asked Mrs Maes if it would be all right for me to leave my accordion in the school overnight. I told her that I was going to make a detour on my way home and didn't want to carry it. She said that that should be fine, as long as I remembered to collect it the next day, as there wouldn't be anyone to open the classroom for me over the weekend. Then she turned and looked at me strangely, and asked if everything was all right and how my parents were coping: she'd heard that they still hadn't recovered the body…

"They're fine," I said. "We're all fine." And I wished her good luck for the finching competition.

Once in the corridor, I could barely keep myself from running: past the rooms where the carillon students had their lessons, around the crooked vestibule housing spare parts for the bells, across the inner courtyard where Father Vandyk tended his herb garden, and into the street.

I followed the canal to the fringes of town, across an industrial development and along the mud flats that were being covered in concrete. For as long as I could remember there had been a bomb crater there, left over from the war. Years ago, after a heavy storm, the hole had filled up and some kids had decided to go swimming. One of the smaller ones got tangled in some netting that had been left behind after a football game, and by the time his sister noticed he was gone it was too late. That afternoon, after the body had been retrieved, Krelis had taken me there, but by then all there was to see was a big hole filled with dirty water. We'd come home down the alley that smelt of potato and oatmeal sausages, where cats gathered to wail for scraps. At supper that night I had snivelled into my jumper sleeves and said I didn't want to eat, which made Father chuck the plate of *stoemp* onto the floor because didn't we realize that beggars can't be choosers. Krelis had explained why I wasn't hungry, that we'd been to see the hole where a little boy had drowned, and then Father was silent for a long time. Because what do you say when your boy is crying at the table and you've just thrown a perfectly good meal on the floor?

When I reached the second field, strewn with weeds and scattered building debris, I broke into a sprint – over a fence and across a meadow, where the grass was long and sharp enough to cut through skin and a few cows paused to look up at me with sad eyes. Following the towpath as it curved away from the river, I headed straight for my safe spot in the forest. Crouched low to the ground, I would listen for the scrabbling of rabbits and imagine myself as one of them, burrowing in the forest floor with twitching nose and beady eyes, peering up at the vast sky and canopy of branches, nibbling on the bending willows that bordered the riverbank. Through the leafy gloom, I watched a goshawk slice between the treetops on its after-noon death cruise, cutting across a string of wire that had been pegged along the opposite bank to prevent cows from wander-ing into the stream. In the summer, Krelis used to settle himself in the crook of a tree that scooped out of the riverbank and let his bare feet trail in the cold water while I scouted for lost treasures in the shallows.

Every year in these parts there were rumours of wild-boar sightings: a mother seen lumbering through the undergrowth with her piglets, or a lone male rooting for tubers. But most had died out in the war, killed by the Germans for their meat. Once, I thought I'd heard one: a rustling of leaves, an almost human grunt. A pair of wood pigeons had scattered in alarm at some-thing which I could not see, but which I knew was there.

Leaning against the log pile that never seemed to grow or shrink, I pushed my feet against the empty frame where hunt-ers hung the bodies of trapped hares. Sometimes I would watch the animals being skinned. The carcasses let off steam, the warmth from their lifeless bodies escaping like tiny souls into thin air.

I had lost track of the number of times I had read the letter. A week had passed, and still I had not decided what I was going to do. A part of me didn't want to decide. So I read it again:

Dear Mr van Houten,

I'm afraid that the Christian Women's Union (CWU) sent me your details without explaining your level of English. If you do have any difficulty understanding this, I hope that you might be able to find a warden who would be willing to translate. I was once told that the Dutch are taught very good English from an early age, so with any luck you won't struggle to read my letters and I shall be able to help you refine yours.

The information I received about you was rather sparing in detail. I know that you are serving fifteen years in a prison in Machelen, which I understand is somewhere near Brussels, and that you are thirty-six years old. You must forgive my lamentable knowledge of Belgian geography – Waterloo is just about the only place I know, apart from Bruges, which I am told is very beautiful. I hope you will be able to educate me about your country, which I can't help but think of as an old man, even though it is really so very young in the scheme of things. I would also very much appreciate learning more about you, Mr van Houten.

In the meantime, I suppose you'll want to know a little bit about me? I grew up in the English countryside with my parents and two siblings – a brother and a sister, both older than me. My parents are retired, as is – in a manner of speaking – my brother, who had some rather frightful experiences in the war; my sister is happily married with two small children.

For my part, I am currently plotting an escape from a life of drudgery in London. I have considered going to Spain, or possibly to Romania, where I hear the locals practise bear massage. It sounds, to quote my friend Harry, "positively savage" (by "savage" we mean splendid), although I imagine the travel would cost a packet.

I don't suppose I'm remarkable to look at: fair, with short hair and a long neck, a slight overbite and eyes that are more grey than blue and might be described as "deep-set". I have a rather low voice, which I used to abhor but now I'm grateful for it (my sister is rather shrill). I should like to be a writer, but I don't know that I'll ever be good enough.

You must let me know if I've made myself difficult to un-derstand. They say that tyrants like simple language, so I feel it's almost a moral imperative to be as complex as possible in this day and age. If you'd like to respond I promise you shall always have a sympathetic ear in me—
Yours in eager anticipation,
G.P.

She mentioned Machelen in the letter – Machelen, near to the capital – but had addressed the envelope to Mechelen. Same street as mine, same number.

From my earliest days at school, Father had insisted that I would not waste my time learning French. As a result, I had taken up English, and my knowledge of it was good – almost as good as that of Mr Hendryks, who had spent a summer in a place called Purbeck when he was a boy. Although many of the words in this letter were a mystery to me – I could only guess what "drudgery" and "savage" might mean – I was fairly certain that Spain was the same as *Spanje*. This Christian Women's Union sounded terribly official. Perhaps she was an evangelist?

The letter was far too interesting to be thrown away. The easiest thing might have been to show it to Mother, who would want to send the letter to Mr van Houten with our apologies, even though it wasn't our fault. I wondered what crime he had committed to end up in prison.

Hearing voices from across the clearing, I folded the letter and stuffed it into my pocket before wriggling closer to the log pile. I flattened myself against it like one of those shiny grey bugs that can squeeze into spaces you'd never think could take them. There were three people: one was breathing heavily while the other two spoke.

"That was too easy."

Pepijn. I knew his froggy voice and recognized the awkward lurching of his too-long body. Pepijn was taller than anyone else in my class, and his legs were already covered with a jungle of golden hairs.

"He *made* it easy. Didn't you?" I didn't recognize this voice. "I said, didn't you?" A soft thud, followed by a grunt and more wheezing. At last, the third boy spoke.

"Can we go back now?"

There was a gap in the log pile just above my eye level. Carefully, without breathing, I drew up to it.

The boy who had asked the question was crouched on the ground with his back to me, the curve of his spine heaving up and down. I didn't recognize his voice, but I saw that he had a bad cut on one leg. Bits of dirt and bark, and even a tiny green leaf, stuck to the scarlet stripe that glistened from his knee all the way down to his sock.

"What happens when a Trapper catches an Indian, Arend?" asked Pepijn.

"The same thing that happens when an Indian catches a Trapper. The point is, he was caught."

The older boy, the one called Arend, was wearing a version of the local scouting uniform, with a red armband and a badge on his cap that was decorated in the Dutch colours. I looked at my own school coat – the piping was coming loose at the cuffs, and there were holes picked in the flannel where my mother had sewn Krelis's swimming badges – before trying to get a better look at the insignia on Arend's cap. He was almost as handsome as my brother, with a square face and severe jaw, and eyes as bright as glass. I'd never seen anyone stand so straight.

"It won't happen again, Arend," snivelled the boy on the ground. "Can we go back now?"

"Get up." Arend turned to Pepijn with a swagger. "We haven't got room for weaklings, understand? I don't care how clever he is. The brainy ones are always the weakest."

Pepijn nodded with dumb exuberance.

"Pain isn't weakness – admitting pain is." Arend scanned the ground around him, and I ducked. He halted a few feet from the log pile, and from the rustling of leaves I could tell that he had picked something up. "We just need to find out how weak he is, Pepijn, before we decide if he can join."

There was a pause, followed by the sound of something slicing through the soupy evening air. A heavy sound – not like the crack of a whip, but something blunt and flat and hard. It was followed by a snapping noise, and a shudder.

"You must be fast as a greyhound, understand?"

"Yes, Arend…" The younger boy was crying now, groaning and rocking back and forth, like a buffoon. Arend's head shone golden in the sunlight as he raised his arm for a second time. There was another splitting noise, followed by a dull thud, and a grunt.

"You must be tough as leather…"

And again.

"Hard as steel…"

"I promise, Arend!"

The boy had rolled over to one side, his bony shoulders quivering as he drew his knees up to his chin. He was very pale, with dark hair and freckles. He couldn't have been older than eleven or so. His long, black eyelashes glistened with tears.

"You see how we do it, Pepijn?"

"Yes."

"Good. Take him back to the campsite. You can show the others next time."

As soon as they were gone – Arend striding ahead, Pepijn supporting the limping dark-haired boy – I decided that I didn't want to stay in the forest any longer.

When I got home, I went straight to my room and dug out an empty jotter. It was one I'd stolen from infant school, with a picture on the cover that showed three children sitting by a fireplace, listening to a story being read by an older girl in a pink sundress. Opening the notebook to a blank page, I decided to compose my letter in Flemish first and wait until I could borrow an English dictionary from school to translate it.

Dear G.P., I wrote.

What to say? *My name is Marten Kuypers and I am thirteen years old. I live in Mechelen, which is not the same as Machelen. My best friend at school is Nijs, and my best friend outside of school is Mr Hendryks at church. There is also a girl I like called Mieke, but she is two years ahead of me and probably fancies my brother, who's dead.*

That wouldn't do. I started again.

You shouldn't feel sorry for Belgium. Did you know that of all the foreign armies he met, Julius Caesar said that the Belgians were the bravest?

It looked so silly on the page.

My father was also in the war. The only people he talks about from then are the French, and how they shot Flemish soldiers who didn't understand their orders. That's the French for you.

No – I shouldn't bring Father into this.

I chewed on my pencil for a while, then ripped the page from my book and crumpled it into a ball. How wrong was it to lie? Jesus said that St Bartholomew was incapable of deceit.

What if I got caught?

Dear G.P., I wrote. *Thank you for your letter. Life in prison is hard, but I can tell you about it if you like.*

4

In 1924, showing a rare interest in life beyond his garden idyll, Glen's father had taken his children to see the British Empire Exhibition at Wembley. Glen had been eleven at the time, her sister thirteen. Tully had already started university, but Glen could remember the gleam of fascination in his gaze as they had watched a dramatic reconstruction of the Zulu Wars. British soldiers dressed in scarlet tunics, glengarry caps and pith helmets fired blanks at Zulu warriors in animal skins. Brandishing shields and assegais, the Africans chanted ferocious war songs and hooted with rapturous delight when the white men fell.

According to Merle, their brother had been cruelly snatched from the real war and robbed of his right to fight with honour. Young though she was, even then Glen had known that opportunities to die in glory were now few and far between.

"What's Tully been up to lately, Mummy?"

The broad rim of a battered straw hat obscured her mother's face. Squatting amid the basil and rue, sleeves rolled halfway up her slender arms, her shirt tails trailed in the freshly raked soil as she jabbed at the ground with small, punctuated huffs. Her garden was the one place that Sylvia Phayre would ever be caught in such an undignified posture. Now particularly, it provided a welcome escape from the destruction being waged indoors.

"Visiting the Cheshire cousins." She indicated the basket resting at her daughter's feet, and Glen passed it to her. "Pa thought that William might convince your brother to give the Civil Service a go." She deftly snipped a few clippings of lavender balm and handed the basket back to Glen.

"I suppose that will mean examinations."

"One has to eat, darling," she said, darting a pointed glance at her daughter's boyish frame, which Glen pretended to ignore. "Speaking of which, what do you do for food in London?"

"Emily and I can cook, Mummy."

Sylvia snorted.

"We do toast and things."

"Well, you certainly are looking lovely and slim, darling." Sylvia began to pull the gloves from her hands, finger by finger. "I worry about you two, that's all. Merle is the only one who's doing something sensible with her life."

"Merle got married, Mummy."

"Exactly, dear heart."

"Well, what if I don't want to get married?" said Glen.

"I'm not saying you should, darling." Sylvia wisely decided not to pursue the point. "There was a letter from your aunt the other day," she said. "You really must see the drawing that Althea sent – it's too dear. Such a clever little girl. And such an imagination."

When they were little, the Phayre children would gather excitedly to hear the latest news from their mother's youngest sister. Tully would read the letters in clipped BBC tones, recounting their uncle's tactic of placing ping-pong balls among the eggs to trick the cobras or the chaos that ensued when their aunt stumbled into the middle of a lepers' strike in Colombo. After one report of a hunting expedition ("…my blood ran cold at the terrifying sound of a disembodied growl…"), the children had spent days pretending to be on safari in pursuit of a faceless monster.

"What's the matter with Annabel, then?"

Sylvia resumed her assault on the flower bed, stabbing at the earth with renewed vigour. "Uncle Ray has left her. Apparently he's planning to join the Planters Rifle Corps. It was just an excuse, of course – he's an utter scoundrel, that Ray Moodie. I told her that when she married him, but would she listen? This Planter Corps business is just an excuse."

She stopped to peer up at her daughter from beneath the rim of her hat, assuming the air of a disappointed schoolmistress. "You know I would never say a word against my sister, darling, but I do worry about her *habit*."

"Oh really, Mummy!"

You're being just like Aunt Annabel. That had always been the last word in chastisement when the children were young. The mysterious woman who appeared occasionally in letters and photographs from the other side of the world – who only ever became a subject for discussion late in the evenings after Glen's parents had uncorked the port – was almost invariably spoken of in gently disparaging tones. It had never been entirely clear why, although over the years Glen had accumulated a number of possible explanations. Annabel had declared her atheism at the age of seventeen, shortly before eloping to Ceylon with a man described as "entirely unsuitable" by her older sister. Unsuitable, Glen gathered, for reasons of age, class and reputation – the latter a convenient catch-all for the faintest whiff of moral or fiscal laxity – although in the photographs he looked a dashing character. It had been his idea that they should run a tea plantation together. To the rest of the family, it remained unthinkable that Annabel should stoop to managing labouring coolies in that tropical heat.

"There's Althea to look after, and the plantation, of course… and now I hear she's adopted a little boy."

"Oh?"

"It's typical Annabel: taking on far too much, just as her life is falling to pieces. Not only is it unbecoming – it's unhealthy." Sylvia sighed wearily. "I'm going to tell her that she should come home."

"Why on earth would she want to do that?"

"Well, she would have *us*, for one thing." Sylvia ignored her daughter's doubtful expression: it was too easy for the girl to sympathize with an idolized aunt she had never met. "Her letter was a cry for help. She'd never admit it, of course – far too proud, far too stubborn. But family is family."

"Why on earth would she want to come here?"

"Honestly, Glynis! What's wrong with England?"

"It's wet and depressing, to begin with."

"Oh, don't be so contrary."

Glen twisted a piece of straw from the basket, working it back and forth until it finally splintered in two.

34

"You do know what they say about the place, don't you?" she said.

"Hm?"

"Don't bother stopping. Just Sail-On."

"Very droll." Sylvia had begun to brush herself down, and Glen extended one hand to help her mother to her feet. "I suppose Annabel would have to adjust to a more modest lifestyle if she came back. By the sound of it, the commonest folk live like aristocrats out there."

Out there. On an island shaped like a pearl – or a teardrop.

Glen discovered the letter on her way in to lunch. Her little cousin's drawing was, admittedly, very accomplished for a girl of ten. A jolly jade man sat cross-legged in a jungle grotto, eyes splitting into numerous laugh lines, belly overflowing, jewels circling his neck like gentle rolls of fat. The portrait had been signed by the artist – *Althea Moodie, Beulah Lodge, January 1936* – and was underlined with a child's ambitious flourish.

* * *

She found her brother on the far side of the ha-ha, smoking a cigarette. The ditch was retained by a wall that ran the length of the estate, drawing the boundary between the far end of the garden and the grounds beyond, and sunk so as not to obscure the view from the house. "To preserve the prospect," their mother had explained to the children, when they had wondered aloud at this curious subterranean barrier. Although they had often been told that it was intended to prevent roaming cattle from entering the garden, Glen had always assumed that its true purpose was not so much to keep livestock *out*, as to keep them *in*.

"Hiding, are you?"

The man jolted, then looked embarrassed when he realized that it was only her. It had been a struggle, as always, to entice him back into the family fold.

"For Heaven's sake, don't let them see you standing there. Come on – there's plenty of room down here." He tapped a spray of ash into an empty flowerpot by his feet and edged to one side.

She dropped into the ha-ha next to him. As a child, Tully had always shown little interest in trying to leap over the trench as his cousins did, instead preferring to lower himself into it to stare up at the narrow ribbon of sky overhead. Later, he would explain to Glen that it gave him a worm's-eye view of the landscape: an opportunity to observe nature from the ground up. During those awful months of waiting during the war – when it was already clear to Glen that her brother could not return home, not because he was dead, but because of something too shameful to discuss – the girl would sit in the ha-ha and try to imagine the crump of distant shellfire, the smell of smoke and blood.

"No one could find you after tea."

"It's always this way, coming back." Tully stubbed out his cigarette on a stone, twisting the butt hard.

"Mummy says you've been visiting the Cheshire cousins…"

"William's trying to talk me into some ghastly civil-service job."

"Oh dear. I hear the examinations are rather horrid."

"There aren't going to be any examinations – it's all a nasty rumour concocted by Mummy," sniffed her brother. He pressed his back straight against the wall with a brittle smile. "Ingeniously orchestrated, of course. A proper pincer attack: Mummy on the one side, and Uncle Will on the other. *Get the boy sorted. It's time for a fresh start.* But I won't stand by and watch a fresh batch of young chaps sent off to the same horrors."

She watched her brother's smile fade. "Well, I suppose they only want to help. It's Mummy's way, isn't it?"

"Mummy wants to save face." He laughed – a cough framed by that same boyish smile – and met her gaze for the first time. "The things we have to believe in to survive, eh, sis?"

"Dinner's going to be ghastly. I can feel the guilt creeping up on me already…"

"Darling girl, what have you to feel guilty about?"

"Being overeducated and unmarried. For starters."

"I'll bet she'll say you're too thin."

"She already has."

He laughed again, properly this time, and Glen was filled with sudden, tender warmth for her brother. "We shall endure it together," she said, giving his hand a squeeze. "The important thing is to show no fear."

They stopped to watch a nightjar cruise overhead, its pointed wings tracing the curve of sky like a compass.

"You've heard about Annabel, I assume," she said at last.

"I'd be surprised if half the county hadn't heard about dear Aunt Annabel!"

Glen turned to face him, serious now. "I don't see why she should have to give everything up just because Uncle Ray did a runner."

"Well, who says she must?"

"According to Mummy, the children are growing up semi-feral."

"Sounds rather jolly."

"It does, doesn't it?" Glen plucked a dandelion from the verge and traced the jagged leaves with one finger. "You know, I could offer to tutor Althea for her entrance exams – give Annabel one less thing to worry about." Her brother looked at her. "There's nothing keeping me here, Tull. And now Pa's talking about selling the house…"

"Running away isn't the answer, sis." There was no smile, no hint of irony.

"But it wouldn't be running away. I'm looking for somewhere to *go*. Throwing myself onto the world, rather than waiting for it to come to me. There's a difference."

Someone had begun to call their names from across the lawn, summoning them to dinner, and Glen groaned.

"Did you know that birds migrate along magnetic fields?" Tully was still watching the nightjar. "Makes you wonder, doesn't it? If they have any choice in the matter."

"I shouldn't think they spend much time worrying about it." She took hold of her brother's lapel and worked the dandelion through his buttonhole. "They just go, don't they? They know when it's time."

"I can already hear the wheels whirring inside that pretty head of yours. And I don't suppose there's the slightest thing I or anyone else can do to stop them."

"It must be the birds churring that you hear," she said, heaving herself onto the grass. "Noisy bunch, aren't they?"

* * *

Harry's reply arrived on the same day that she booked her berth on the *Amphion*.

> *Listen, dear girl: I think the idea sounds positively hideous. I don't know what could possibly be less appealing than the combination of snotty-nosed children and insects the size of a man's head, but that's only my humble opinion. I hope it goes swimmingly for you – just please, for Heaven's sake, don't come back chewing betel.*

It was typical of him, she thought, to adopt such a narrow view of things.

> *Children, darling! You've never shown any interest in the little rotters. What will the native staff make of a golden-haired* garçonne *working below stairs, you dizzy girl? Don't be surprised if they mistake you for a widow – or, even better, a holy man.*

Alone with his letter, Glen felt herself blush. Of course it was a preposterous idea – of course she wouldn't belong. Silly, self-absorbed girl! But then, out of nowhere, she felt a rush of righteous frustration flood her from head to toe. How dare he mock her? The very thought filled her with enough annoyance to crumple the letter and toss it in the waste-paper basket. Was that really what he believed – that she was such an amateur? That she wouldn't go through with it? That, at best, she would only be another vapid English girl adrift in the Orient: blushing and innocent, unwittingly courting corruption?

Mummy had taken some convincing, although a tactical suggestion that the colonies might be just the place for introductions to the right sort – military types with staff appointments, at the very least – had done the trick soon enough. Her mother had never fully approved of Harry, anyway; she thought him idle, which he was, and too easy with money. Pa had simply wanted to know if Glen wouldn't mind sending him a few samples from the island. "You know that Mr Gandhi survives on a diet of fruit and nuts, don't you?" he'd told her, his voice tinged with admiration. And to Sylvia, "The girl won't be missing anything here. If there's to be a war, perhaps we'll follow her out there in a year or two."

Standing alone at the station, waiting for the London train, Glen felt herself teetering on the brink of momentous change. How silly to be anxious! Behind her lay an old house besieged by silent armies of carpet beetles and moths; ahead, an exotic paradise, purpose, inspiration. It was as if she had glimpsed a secret passageway, beyond which her old reality had already begun to dissolve. This, *this* was the beginning of her story.

At the far end of the platform, a couple were embracing. Glen couldn't see the woman's face, although she noted an exemplary waistline and a rather lovely pearl bracelet circling one dainty wrist. Her arms were clasped around the man's shoulders, and his hands rested gently on her hips. The man wore a fedora, pushed to a jaunty angle as he received the kiss. The couple were oblivious to everything around them, completely absorbed in each other. Glen tried to remember when she had last participated in a moment so fully. She almost succumbed to a pang of envy – but then her attention was distracted by another gentleman hovering nearby, just in front of the schedule board. She had not noticed him before. His features were not so fine as those of the Japanese students she had met at a party in Oxford, but he was most certainly of oriental extraction. *I wonder if he feels himself alone*, she wondered, trying not to stare. *Adrift in a foreign place, with no lovely young girl to fling her arms around his shoulders, to whisper in his ear.* And suddenly, not for the first time in her life, she felt strangely divorced from the scene before her. The lovers and the oriental gentleman were not incidental characters in her story, but players in stories and lives that would never concern her.

It was a strange thing, this realization, and instinctively Glen reached into her carpet bag to feel the crisp edges of the letter that had only today arrived from Belgium.

5

My best conversations with Mr Hendryks always took place in the vestry. We couldn't talk during the service itself, when I followed him around the church with the incense, helped him to light the candles and stood next to him to catch the crumbs when Father de Wit broke the bread. Sometimes, if the sermon was very long, he would wink at me from across the altar. One time Mother saw this and remarked that it wasn't very godly behaviour.

A few weeks after the memorial service, he told me that people no longer believed in God. I thought that it was a strange thing to say, seeing that we were buttoning our surplices for the nine o'clock service at the time.

"Your poor brother," he said. "Even he had stopped believing in God."

"You mustn't say that," I replied. I should have been angry, perhaps, but curiosity got the better of me. "How do you know?"

Mr Hendryks pressed his lips together, creasing the loose skin around his mouth and making his jowls bulge. He looked at me with eyes like blue jellies.

"You're right, Marten: I don't know. I'm sorry."

"So why don't people believe in God, then?"

Mr Hendryks had finished straightening his gown, and he stopped to peer at me through wire spectacles. Mr Hendryks's eyelashes were so white they looked as if they were coated with frost.

"Because they've started believing in something else."

"What?"

"Governments. Powerful men. I don't know…" He reached for the crucifix. "It's a kind of make-believe. Everyone pretending together."

"Pretending what?"

Mr Hendryks turned the crucifix between knobby fingers, casting eddies of light across the dim vestry walls.

"Pretending that they can organize an untidy world."

"But we've already done that."

He stopped turning the crucifix. "Have we?"

"It's what prisons are for. And courts, and mental hospitals."

"I suppose you're right, Marten. I suppose that people just don't want to have to think about those places. We all need distractions."

Our church, Sint-Janskerk, was not very large. It was short and squat, like a lot of Flemish churches, with fat stone columns and bow arches. Inside, there was always a strong smell of incense and beeswax floor polish. It was packed full of paintings and statues and relics – my brother called it a holy junk heap – but the best thing about it was the pulpit.

It was about ten feet tall and over four hundred years old, carved out of a single oak. The canopy was a thicket of branches and leaves filled with birds and insects and, of course, harbouring a serpent. The base was a grotto scene, with a lamb and some frogs and a pretend fountain. Creeping around one side was a human skeleton, pointing a bony finger down to Hell. On the other side was a woman, completely naked, serene and unaware.

During the sermon, after counting all the creatures on the pulpit (there were twenty-seven in total, not including the skeleton and the woman), I turned my attention to Jesus. He was nailed to a cross that had been suspended at an angle from the ceiling, so it looked a bit as if he was flying over the congregation. Girlish curls framed his face, which was tilted meekly to one side, and his fine features had been gaudily tinted – rosy cheeks, pink lips – as if Our Lord was one of the women that hung about on Keizerstraat behind the railway station. Father de Wit had once told us that we should nail all our fears to the cross, which sounded like a strange idea given that Jesus seemed to be struggling enough as it was.

After the service, I told Mr Hendryks that I had decided what I wanted to be when I grew up.

"Oh, yes? What will you be, then?"

"A zoologist or a priest."

We were waiting on the bench outside the church for Mr Hendryks's wife to meet him. My parents had not come to the service, as Mother was having one of her bad mornings.

"Well, I think that's a fine idea."

An elderly man was walking a small black poodle on a lead, and we stopped talking to watch it. The dog was sniffing furiously at some weeds poking out between the paving stones. Cataracts made its eyes look like radiant pearl buttons.

At last Mr Hendryks noticed his wife emerging from the church, and he stood up. "Would you like to come to our house for lunch, Marten?"

"No, thanks. I'm supposed to help Father clean out the chimney this afternoon."

"I understand. You'll pass on my regards though, won't you?"

"I will. See you next week."

When they had gone, I cut through the Klapgat on my way to the postbox. The passage was shady and usually deserted; I had never noticed anyone using the gossips' gate before. So it came as a surprise to see someone sitting on the wall, watching me as I approached.

It was the dark-haired boy from the forest.

"Hello," he said.

I wasn't used to being spoken to by people I didn't know.

"Hello," I said. "Are you allowed to be on that wall?" It was a silly question, but he looked so young that it would have been strange for me not to boss him a little.

"There's no rule, is there?"

"What are you doing up there?"

"Watching."

"Watching what?"

He shrugged. "People. You." The cut in his lip had begun to heal, but a corner of his eye was still stained with a mussel-blue smudge. "My name's Adriaan."

"I'm Marten."

42

"You're the boy whose brother died. My parents were talking about it – they said he drowned."

I stiffened. "So?"

"I've heard people say that it seemed strange there wasn't a body. The river isn't that deep."

"It's none of their business."

"That doesn't stop people gossiping. They said—"

"I'll cut your tongue out if you don't shut up." I tried to remain calm, hoping that the tremor in my voice sounded like Father's growl. "It's none of their business. You tell them I said so."

Adriaan seemed happy to let the subject drop. But he wasn't finished with me yet. "So, you're friends with Nijs."

I scowled. "What do you care?"

"I'm about to meet up with him. Do you want to come?"

"Why should I?"

I hadn't meant to sound quite so aggressive; now he looked a little frightened.

"No reason. Only if you wanted to… I was going to show him how we use secret codes."

"Who's 'we'?"

Adriaan cast around lamely for an answer.

"It's… it's a kind of club."

I snorted. "What school do you go to?"

"Yours. I'm in the third year. My family moved here from Brussels last month."

"And you've started a club?"

Adriaan shook his head vigorously. "No, not me. It's older boys, mainly. They asked me if I had any friends…"

"And do you?"

"My father has been doing the accounts for Nijs's dad. I met Nijs last week, that's when I told him about it…"

I nodded slowly, trying to look bored. Who was this Adriaan, anyway? And what was he doing courting my best friend? Did the "club" have anything to do with the boys in the forest?

"Are you friends with Pepijn?" I asked, feeling bold.

Adriaan flinched. "Not really, no… I… he's in our group, too, though."

43

"He's an idiot."

To my surprise, Adriaan nodded. "I know."

I didn't have a watch, so I pretended to think carefully about the time.

"I've got things to do today. I can't mess about for long."

Adriaan's face lit up, and he scrambled from the wall. "That's all right. I said we'd meet him in five minutes."

* * *

We found Nijs on the steps leading down to the canal, behind the derelict brewery. He was not doing a very good job of looking as if he was meant to be there. Nijs was a little bit taller than I was, and looked older, but he was actually a bit of a mother's boy. Doing things that he wasn't supposed to – like mucking about behind an abandoned brewery on grimy canal steps – was not really his strong point. He was good at making owl noises, and getting teased by girls. That's about all that could be said about Nijs.

"There you are," he said, with relief. He was speaking to Adriaan. "I was right, wasn't I? He was at church?"

Adriaan nodded, squatting by my friend against the damp stucco wall.

"What's this all about, anyway?" I asked.

"Adriaan says that we can join his club," replied Nijs. "Do you know anything about it, Marten?"

I shook my head. "Is it like the Scouts?" I asked Adriaan. "Doing activities in the forest?"

Adriaan screwed up his nose.

"It's not just *activities*," he said. "It's more like training."

"Training for what?"

Adriaan frowned. "For in case." And then, as if it would make a difference, he added, "We get our badges and ties from the VNV."

In Mechelen, you had three choices: you could be a Catholic, a communist, or a member of the VNV, the Flemish National Union. Being a communist was dangerous, because it meant you didn't believe in God. Being a Catholic was all right, although it left a lot of questions unanswered and involved hours of sitting still and keeping quiet. I didn't know much about the VNV, apart from the fact that they'd just won an election.

"Why should we be interested?" I asked, glancing at Nijs. He was looking at the cut on Adriaan's knee.

"Because it's worthwhile. Not like prancing around church in a dress."

"It's not a dress, you idiot. It's a cassock. And it's not prancing." This Adriaan was getting on my nerves. "Who are you to talk? Are you a Yid, or something?"

Adriaan looked at me with a funny expression – scared, but also proud, as if he knew something I didn't.

"Marten's right," said Nijs. "What's so great about your club?"

"It's not my club. It's bigger than that. It's bigger than all of us."

"How big?"

"Massive. Huge. It's like… it's like the pyramids."

"What?"

"You know, the pyramids. In Egypt."

"Of course I know. What about them?"

"They're what made the pharaohs immortal."

I snorted. "Of course they weren't immortal. There's no such thing."

"Eternal, then."

"What, like the Ouroboros?"

"The what?"

"The serpent that devours its own tail."

Adriaan's expression darkened. "That's clever, Marten. Really clever." I could tell that he was getting impatient. "So you're happy to believe that when you die there won't be anything left?"

Nijs had begun to look concerned. "What do you mean?"

"If you were to die tomorrow, it would all be over. Only your parents will remember you, and a few friends, until they die, too." Adriaan shoved his hands in his pockets, casually crossing one foot over the other. "Unless you'd been a part of something bigger. Then you'll be remembered."

"Remembered for what?"

"Whatever you want. I'm going to go to the Olympics."

Nijs smiled indulgently, the way he did when we teased his little sister. "In what?"

"Long-distance running." Adriaan folded his arms, gazing onto the murky water. "You'll see."

"So what does this have to do with anything?" I said. "With your special club, for instance?"

Adriaan unfolded his arms and looked me in the eye. His irises were hazel, flecked with black.

"It's big. We learn all sorts of things, survival skills and stuff. Things they don't teach you in school, or in church."

"Teach us something, then." Nijs slid down from the edge of the wall, closing in on the smaller boy. Nijs had never won a fight in his life, but Adriaan wasn't to know this.

"How about this?" The boy pulled a blank piece of paper from one pocket. From the other, he withdrew a matchbox. "See anything?"

Nijs peered closely at the paper, so that his nose almost touched it. He shook his head.

"Stand back, now."

Adriaan removed a match from the box and struck it. He raised the flame to the paper, but not so close as to set it alight. After a few moments, as if by magic, writing appeared.

Told you so.

"It's invisible ink. I made it myself."

"With what?" Forgetting to be nonplussed, Nijs tore the paper from Adriaan's hand and touched the writing with his finger.

"Milk, egg whites. It's easy when you know how." For the first time, Adriaan allowed himself to smile. "We could have our own secret codes, you see."

"What else have you learnt, then?"

"Morse code. How to make matches waterproof."

"How do you do that?"

"You dip them in wax."

Nijs's smile faded.

"What do you think, Marten?" Adriaan was watching me closely.

I looked at the paper, the matches, the invisible ink. Then I remembered the letter in my satchel. In the last few days, writing had changed from something that I'd only ever associated with punishment into an activity of surprising promise.

"All right," I said. "What do we have to do?"

6

For the third time that day, Glen opened the feather-thin envelope and gently slid the folded page from its nest. The paper was greasy, almost translucent, and had been creased with remarkable precision.

Dear G.P.,

Thank you for your letter. Life in prison is hard, but I can tell you about it if you like.

As you know, my name is Pieter van Houten. I have been imprisoned here in Mechelen for a long time.

I've done some terrible crimes. I'm not sure that a nice lady like you should hear about them. Some have been very gruesome. Mostly, this was not my fault. I only wanted to do the right thing, but now I am sorry. Like you, I am a Christian.

I imagine that you are very pretty. I am not so handsome. My hair is yellow, almost white. My eyes are green. I am not very tall. My family is poor. My father was in the war but I don't know if he met your brother.

You want to know about prison. Well, here there are many rules. I like rules: I like knowing that you don't start eating your supper until the Boss has finished his, and you don't get to read a letter if he hasn't received one that week. Other rules are: only one book allowed from the library at a time (not including the Bible), no swearing, keep things tidy, lights out at nine.

My life here is quite boring. From my little window, I can see across the rooftops all the way to the river. Once I tried to count all the shingles until my eyes started to hurt. I got to 674, although it is possible that I counted a few of them twice.

That's all for now. I hope that you will write again soon. It
would be nice to have someone to talk to.

Pieter van Houten

It was a charming letter, if somewhat abrupt. His style, beyond
the simplicity forced upon it by the language barrier, suggested an education cut tragically short by forays into the criminal
world. This was only to be expected – but she must disabuse him
of the notion that she was a Christian as quickly as possible; no
use getting dragged into requests for prayers or rosary beads...

There was little to read on board the *Amphion*, aside from
what could be found on a shelf in the Captain's mess constitut-
ing the "library". Its scant offerings included a pencilled copy of
1066 and All That, *The Joy of Cooking* and an unbound Book
of Common Prayer. As a farewell gift, Laurie had posted her a
slim volume of Petrarch's poetry, but in a thoughtless moment
Glen had packed it in a trunk destined for the cargo hold.

And so she read – and reread – her letter from Flanders. It
had arrived a few days before her departure, shortly after a reply
from her aunt had rat-a-tatted in from a telegraph office half a
world away. She had reacted immediately to the telegraph, re-
serving a berth on the *Amphion* the following week. The letter
she had saved for later.

After three weeks on board a twelve-passenger freighter, Glen
found herself settling into a kind of transitory inertia. The *Am-*
phion was no pleasure craft: broad-bottomed and thunderously
noisy, it boasted no swimming pool or ballroom, and only three
deck recliners. The other passengers kept mostly to themselves.
Two Indian gentlemen returning, freshly qualified, from the
Inns of Court; a rigidly taciturn governess chaperoning young
charges home from school; a couple of sea cadets; an elderly
couple returning from an extended visit home; and a melancholy
Dutchman who had warned her that whistling on deck would
bring bad luck.

"Reading again, are we?"

Strawberry-nosed Mr Walsh beamed at her from his view-
ing post across the deck. Mr Walsh fancied himself something

of a seaman, and spent a few minutes every hour taking notes from his lookout. As usual, Glen could see little that warranted remark. The sun glistened on innocuous peaks of water that crested and dived, crested and dived, slapping against the sides of the ship, thousands of them – millions, an infinite number – disappearing into the horizon. It had been days since seabirds drew wide, drunken arcs in the sky overhead – weeks since the last sighting of land as they left Suez behind them.

"Just thinking, really. I don't suppose I'll have much time to think a few days from now."

"You could get a lot of writing done on board. Gandhi finished *Indian Home Rule* in just ten days on the way back from London to South Africa: he wrote with his left hand when his right hand got tired."

Mr Walsh snapped his notebook shut and shoved it into his back pocket. His khaki shorts reached almost to his armpits, snug around a belly that trembled like jelly in a mould. His knees were pink, speckled with freckles.

"That's impressive. Writing with both hands, I mean."

"It's not a long tract."

"Oh?"

Mr Walsh grinned. "Not long enough, anyhow. India's finally coming to her senses: non-cooperation's run its course, the Mahatma's parted with the Bolshevists..."

"Is Mr Gandhi a communist, then?"

Mr Walsh let out a bark of a laugh. "No, but he's a damned good performance artist. The Salt March business, the hunger strikes... all smoke and mirrors, of course, but it's been a marvellous show. Shame you missed it."

"I heard one of the cadets say he was mad."

Mr Walsh's little eyes gleamed. "Quite the contrary, my dear, quite the contrary. The Mahatma is very, very cunning." He leant heavily against the railing, and Glen briefly entertained a vision of a pair of pink, freckled knees shooting into the air as their owner toppled overboard into the spangled water. "You know, there's a great tradition of rational argument in Indian philosophy. It's not all airy-fairy gods and monsters." Mr Walsh withdrew a handkerchief from his pocket, daintily padded his brow. "The problem is, when it comes to politics, they don't know their own interests. The Congress would like to be another Ireland, but it will never happen."

"Never?"

"Our Empire can do without Catholics, but the Raj is different."

Glen watched him tuck the handkerchief into a pocket. Older people always seemed so sure of themselves, of the world, despite everything. "One of my tutors used to say that every country needs a revolution of its own. We had one, after all."

Mr Walsh snorted. "Out here, dear girl, it would be the blind leading the blind. The continent would fall to pieces without us."

"Ceylon, too?"

He gave a nonchalant shrug. "Why try to fix something that isn't broken? We've got the best of both worlds: a nice, gentle, anti-colonial colonialism." He smiled broadly. "We're all friends who have agreed to play by British rules – Indian Tamils, indigenous Sinhalese, Kandyans, Buddhists, Hindus, Muslims, Christians…"

"All of those people, on such a tiny island?"

"Not to mention the Dutch. Half-castes, admittedly. They think we're awful snobs!"

Glen wasn't sure why this was meant to be amusing, but she smiled anyway. "I hear that the English live like kings."

"It's not a bad life. The men have all kept their wartime titles – Captain This, Major That. You'll see everyone turn up for the races a few times a year. We've just missed the Monsoon Meet. You'll have to wait until the Nuwara Eliya Cup in August, now."

"Nuwara Eliya – I think my aunt mentioned it. Her plantation is nearby."

"Wouldn't surprise me. We pale folk keep better up in the mountains!" Mr Walsh laughed again. "What's your aunt's name?"

"Annabel. Annabel Moodie."

"Doesn't ring any bells."

"I imagine the family keeps to itself. She's divorced now, has two children..." Glen sensed that she might be revealing too much as Mr Walsh's eyebrows inched further up his forehead.

"Divorced, eh? How very sad."

"Oh, not really. The plantation is small, but quite successful."

"Glad to hear it." Her companion consulted his watch. "You will join us for tea, won't you?"

* * *

Only moments ago, the two figures at the edge of the dock had been little more than an indistinct blur on the horizon. As Glen watched, the blur had stretched, bulged, and finally split into two small blobs like a reproducing amoeba. Two grey dots, one slightly larger than the other, fuzzy around the edges and appearing to shimmer like tiny dark flames. A spot and a speck. The larger of the two lengthened – a hand raised in greeting – while the other remained still.

Yet when it was time to disembark at Colombo, the two figures were promptly swallowed by a crush of human bodies. Cattle clip-clopped lazily among the human mass, while shrieking three-wheelers careened past street merchants hawking spices, tin wares, and fluttering crates of wild-eyed kitchen birds. Beyond the loading dock where Glen received her luggage, crumbling colonial façades squeezed the humid air into small squares of blue sky.

Never mind the stink of sweat and urine mixed with the salty spray of the sea – never mind the camphor and dung, or the black soot spurting from spluttering exhaust pipes. As if anyone could have the appetite for it here, there was the smell of food – local dishes to which the girl knew not a single name, but would in time: spicy crab curry and steaming hoppers, sweet jaggery sauce and cooling buffalo curd, fried brinjals and pappadams, tamarind and mustard oil. Her hand shot to her mouth as she noticed streams of blood trickling from the steps leading off a butcher's. The steaming contents of silver tiffins met the sickly smell of trampled pineapple, jackfruit, mango and overripe pawpaw – squashed pulps hosed off the ground while their intact counterparts competed to enchant passers-by with bright, juicy flesh.

Smoking sticks of patchouli and agarwood, bags of rice, pastries stacked in pyramids. Brooms, tools, kindling, clay jugs brimming with murky water, teak ornaments inlaid with ivory and mother of pearl. Women carrying baskets of flatbread called out to one another, haggling with shopkeepers who wore dhotis and sarongs, chastising children who scampered among wagon wheels and fruit stalls. Suited men loitered in small groups in shop fronts and alleyways, watching half-naked labourers as they hauled heavy containers from the ships to collection stations dotted along the harbour front.

Something tugged at her sleeve, and Glen discovered a grubby child of indeterminate sex peering up at her with large brown eyes. Its greasy hair sprang in all directions, and a trail of sticky moisture dribbled from its nose to its upper lip. With some disgust, she noted a thin trickle of drool meandering from the edge of its mouth, collecting in a glistening drop from the tip of its chin. When it put out one hand it became clear that no part of the urchin was uncontaminated by stickiness.

"Shoo!" She pushed the child away despite herself. "I haven't anything for you. Run along, now. Shoo!"

"Miss Phayre!"

A man with a face like a peach stone had emerged from the crowd, craning his neck and waving frantically to attract her attention over a multitude of heads.

"Do I know you?" She took his outstretched hand and smiled gamely. He was uncannily dark, and could have been anywhere between forty and sixty years of age.

"You are meeting Miss Annabel, isn't it?"

"That's right. I'm Glynis. Glen."

"Micah. Let me help you, please. A coolie will take your trunk. Miss Annabel is waiting outside Cargills. Not so many crowds there – it isn't far. You see the Grand Oriental Hotel? Big stone building, yes? We go that way. Sssk!" The man swiped at a ragged figure behind them. "There are many, many pickpockets about, Miss – pay attention on that, yes? Please to follow me, slowly-slowly."

So Glen allowed herself to be led through the crowd, turning occasionally to keep an eye on the halting progress being made with her trunk.

"Do you know Annabel very well?" she called after Micah's lurching shoulders. A crisp white shirt billowed over his lanky frame.

"I have been working since five years for her – as gardener, as porter, as driver." He counted the functions on slender fingers. "As police, too!" This last was followed by a proud wobble of the head. "She is a very fine lady, very good to my family."

"I've never met her, you see. We only ever received letters and photographs."

"Ah, but she knows how to recognize *you*, Miss."

In the end, Glen needn't have worried. Her aunt was identifiable by a shock of auburn hair and a heavy bone necklace that the girl recalled from one of her photos. Her kohl-smudged eyes – were they damp with humidity or tears? – grew large as Glen approached, and her mannish chin dropped with a small howl of delight.

"Glynis, darling!" Annabel's bangles jingled a private cacophony as they embraced.

"Auntie Annabel, it's so good to see you."

Words Sylvia Phayre used to describe her youngest sister included "stubborn", "flippant", "careless" and "a terror". Glen would have added "fearless" to the list: in her small case she had packed a framed studio portrait of Annabel freshly arrived in Ceylon at just nineteen years of age, reclining on the back of a leopard in repose. Tully and Merle had often bickered over the tactics employed to ensure their aunt's safety in such a position. Perhaps the leopard had been drugged, or perhaps it wasn't alive at all; perhaps the photograph was just a clever trick, and Aunt Annabel had never been anywhere near a leopard. But Glen knew better. Who but Annabel would attempt such a striking pose and manage to look so handsome in the process? Ash-blonde curls framed a pretty face: painted lips coy, violet eyes that seemed to laugh at the camera. Glen would recognize those eyes anywhere.

They sparkled as her aunt continued the giddy introductions. "Glen darling, meet Hollar."

Glen hadn't noticed the boy, nudged gently forward by Annabel, until now. His eyes were wide and dark, deeply set below straight, black eyebrows; his nose was long but delicate, and his nostrils flared sideways in imitation of ears that were still slightly too large. His mouth was a perfect archer's bow, his hair a disconcerting shade of russet-black. Two cowlicks refused to be tamed: one at the front grew in a diagonal tuft, while another sprouted atop his crown like the upturned tail of a surprised lark. Bony legs were tanned and dirty under pale khaki shorts, white socks and sandals.

"Hello, Hollar. It's jolly nice to meet you at last."

The boy stared at his feet. In one hand he clutched what appeared to be a brass spoon. Annabel pulled an arm around his shoulders.

"Hollar is a collector – he has a new favourite object every day. That's from the Chinese ink set, isn't it darling?"

Hollar nodded, pressing the spoon into the folds of his shirt.

On the train, the boy slept. Micah sat in the next cabin with Glen's luggage, and the ladies were able to chatter freely.

"Micah's a funny name for an Indian, isn't it?" said Glen, hungrily spooning apricot jam onto a strangely flat crumpet. A plate of bread and preserves trembled precariously on the fold-out table between them.

"His forebears were baptized by the Portuguese centuries ago. Micah is a *devout* Catholic."

"He said he has a family?"

"Oh, Perdita's a gem! They have two little girls, six and ten. Althea bosses them about dreadfully."

"She sounds a marvellous child – Althea, I mean."

"She'll adore you!" Then, with an admiring look: "Your hair really is something else, darling. Very modern."

"Pa loathes it."

"I wouldn't mind him. But the locals won't know what to make of you – they're used to old biddies in floral prints."

"Really, Annabel!"

"No, honestly. I can't wait to see their faces! Shouldn't blame them, really – if I had legs as nice as yours, I'd walk on my hands."

As Colombo receded behind them, the land became overwhelmingly green, emerald treetops reflected in the still waters of lakes glimpsed through silver gum forests and mangrove keys. Dogs appeared out of nowhere to run alongside the train, their long pink tongues lolling out of spittly mouths, before falling back when they sensed that they had strayed too far from home.

Past smiling paddy fields, gullies and escarpments, through viridian forests and pitch tunnels, the train carried on its journey. A parade of boulders edged along the horizon: water buffalo herding towards a water hole, oblivious to the hum of steel tracks that echoed through the valleys.

"We'll get off at Nanu Oya, then take a van the rest of the way," explained her aunt. "The hills are too much for these old engines – it would be more effective to haul the blasted things up with rope, really."

"But it's so beautiful! And we call England a green and pleasant land."

"According to legend, Adam and Eve were banished here when they were turned out of Eden." Annabel considered the racing countryside with a small, satisfied smile. "Not much of a punishment, to my mind."

"A perfect exile, I should have thought."

"That's what we think whenever we hear the news from Europe. That ridiculous little German stirring up trouble on the Continent, and you poor people poised on the fringes…"

"If there's to be a war, I wish that the powers that be would get on with it," said Glen, licking the last traces of apricot jam from her finger. "I imagine that life in wartime shall be very liberating. Living for the moment and all that."

"That's what you're after, is it?" Her aunt arched an eyebrow.

"Pa says now's the perfect time to embrace change, what with the world being the way it is."

"And to do something out of the ordinary."

"Quite. As it is, Mummy and Pa have more to worry about than they're willing to let on – 'reduced circumstances', Mummy calls it. Penury doesn't suit her."

Annabel snorted. "Your mother was never suited to letting go. You should know: you children were always little extensions of her." The smile faded as she pressed out the creases in her napkin. "Poor woman. Somehow the challenges that confront us later in life don't seem quite as beguiling as the adventures we seek out when we're young." She considered the child curled up like a cat in the seat next to her, his breath condensing on the window glass. Beyond him, a family squatted by the railway tracks, selling vegetables in straw baskets. "Listen to me, waxing maudlin. Ray always used to say that running a plantation is by far the best life for an Englishman out here, and I'm determined to make it work. Demand is as strong as ever for high-grown tea. With the economy beginning to recover a bit—"

"But you're not running the business on your own, are you?"

"Who else would?" A look of genuine amazement melted into gentle scorn. "I won't be imprisoned in my bungalow zenana like a snotty memsahib, darling. I never was content to endure the heat of the day in solitude, like the other wives – oh no!" She shook her head stoutly. "I seize the day, every day. No use wasting time on regret."

"Well, I'm sure it's not all for nothing. They do say that one finds strength in adversity."

"Does one?" Detecting the trace of a smile, Glen sensed that perhaps her sentiment had sounded hollow, if well intentioned. "Yes, I suppose one does. Perhaps that is the only choice we have."

7

The next letter arrived a few days before the May Procession of St Peter and St Paul.

Dear Pieter (may I call you Pieter?),

How good it was to receive your letter. I am pleased to hear that you can see the river from your window: for some reason, I have always found it comforting to be near moving water. However, I am almost certainly made of sterner stuff than you (very considerately) implied. Perhaps you could give me some clue as to what led you to your current situation. You say that you intended to do the right thing: is it reasonable to venture that this might make you a political prisoner?

I should tell you that I am not, myself, a practising Christian. I do however try to live by the Golden Rule and have always respected the solace which faith seems to provide for so many people. I hope that you will also take some comfort from our letters.

For my part, I shall endeavour always to be entirely honest with you. I do subscribe to the modern belief that it is our duty to record the small truths of our experience, so that history may remain in the hands of the multitudes and not be corrupted by politics. Fiction may be my hobby, but my letters to you will not fictionalize: disguises are merely a way of hiding from ourselves, don't you agree? In time, you shall come to know the whole truth of me – and, I hope, will feel that you can do the same.

Having said that, I write to you now with some very exciting news indeed. The postmark must have given you some clue to this already. I have embarked on a grand adventure, Pieter, and you – lucky thing! – shall be coming along with me. My aunt has offered me a fine escape from the woes I described in my last letter: for the next few months, home shall be a plantation house located high in Ceylon's central hills. My main role will be to help with her two children, while she attempts to run the family business single-handedly.

This will be an adventure to go down in the history books – I can feel it in my bones, even though I've not the foggiest idea as to what awaits me here. I only know that before I was set on a route to becoming one person, and now I am about to become another.

I have been here for two days already. I won't bore you with details of the journey, which was dreadfully dull – no storms or pirate attacks – suffice it to say, I was only seasick once, and managed to befriend a dear old English couple who have lived on the subcontinent for years.

My aunt's house – that's Beulah Lodge, where you must write to me – is too, too splendid for words. Not grand, admittedly, but it has all the charm of those old aquatint postcards we used to collect of Her Majesty's colonies. It is a long, low building that stretches lazily for the shade of a magnificent jacaranda tree. The lawn is very much coarser than our lawns at home, but the garden makes up for it with rhododendrons, arum lilies and hardy lavender. We are quite isolated – the nearest homestead is several miles away, and the labyrinthine tracks through the hills triple most journeys in these parts.

Clucking about at large are half a dozen silkie hens (my aunt keeps them as pets, but she refuses to have a rooster), which are dear little things: not at all like normal, scrabbling hens, with lovely feather pantaloons and surprising dignity for flightless birds. That is, when Nuisance isn't about (he's the requisite dog – a terrier of some sort).

The house is full of teak, rattan, calamander, bamboo and cane, just as one would imagine. I look out over miles of sleepy green valleys dotted with tea pickers who carry baskets slung from their heads. From here it really does feel as if one is on top of the world. On the drive past Nuwara Eliya, we passed the most glorious waterfalls, and our car had to proceed very slowly around several hairpin bends that hug the mountain, at times taking us within inches of the precipice.

My aunt has suffered terribly, I think, though she puts on a brave face. But herbs, "though scentless when entire, yield fragrance when they're bruised". Perhaps she has come into her own at last. It is not easy work, running the plantation alone, but somehow she manages. She's always up before sunrise to receive the morning reports at the factory; from there, she takes a horse into the tea fields to inspect the coolies. After breakfast, she sees to her paperwork – paying the men, signing off sick workers and so on – then pays a second visit to the field in the afternoon. The nice thing is that the late afternoons tend to be left free – apparently my uncle used to play lawn tennis at the Club between four and six o'clock every day – and in the cold season, only one outdoor inspection is necessary.

My aunt's little daughter is a character. When we arrived, the first thing she asked me was, "Would you like to meet my tortoise, Nikolai?" The creature lives in a pen alongside the chicken coop, and tolerates the costumes she designs for him with remarkable equilibrium. She is a bright if occasionally rambunctious child – more lively by far than Annabel's adopted son. Now he is a funny boy. Very quiet indeed – not at all as garrulous or sociable as his sister. I imagine he must be slightly older than her – twelve, perhaps – but one wouldn't guess it. Annabel said she felt the house needed new life in it, after Uncle Ray left, but I don't suppose she was counting on Hollar to be quite so withdrawn. I suspect I shall have to make some effort to draw him from his shell, although to be honest I fear he has a stubborn streak a mile wide. Boys of his age are a filthy bunch!

You said that you like rules, so here are a few I've gathered over the last couple of days. They were imparted to me by Perdita, our housemaid:

Avoid eating odorous food when you're on your own, as the devils will be able to smell you out.

Never step on bone, hair or human ash, as this is unlucky.

One must never show a mirror to a baby, as it will make the infant go dumb.

Travellers are advised to discontinue a trip if they encounter a cat, a snake, a monk or a widow along the way.

Groups of three are unlucky.

Goodness, I do go on! That's probably more than enough for now. I hope that my tales will inspire you, Pieter – and I very much look forward to hearing from you soon. Please do send a photo if you can, so that I can picture you when I am writing. Your English is very fine, by the way!

Yours truly,

G.P.

At first I was surprised – and just a little anxious. There was no indication that she had any suspicions about Pieter's true identity.

Dear GP,

It was very nice to read your letter. One day, when I am a free man again, I would like very much to go to Ceylon. I hope that you will be happy there.

I scanned her letter a second time. She had asked if I was a "political prisoner". The phrase reminded me of something that I had seen on the front page of the newspaper Aunt Marta had left in our kitchen. I dropped my pencil and raced downstairs.

There it was, still on the table. A quick check confirmed that I had remembered correctly: one of the headlines contained the all-important words: *politiek gevangene*. I pounced on the newspaper and took it back up to my room.

It is true that I am a political prisoner. They have not yet decided my sentence. This is very difficult for me. I am not allowed to discuss my case, but I am sending you an article about what has happened to many of my comrades.

The article was about Germany. "The President of Munich Police has announced that a camp designed to hold 5,000 political prisoners – communists and others who pose a threat to the security of the state – is to be opened near Dachau," it began. She would like that: her countrymen hated the Germans. They had forced their prisoners of war into hard labour – not just Russian captives, either, but British and French as well – which was against the old rules of war. Sometimes, for fun, they would line the captives up and shoot every fifth man. Any English girl would feel sorry for a prisoner like me.

It is hard for me to talk about what happens here, I wrote. *At night I have terrible dreams. Sometimes I wake up screaming, and then I realize that I am still alive. But that doesn't make me feel better. I am at war with myself all the time.*

Details. I must make her believe me with details.

Some days, we are put on half rations; other days, we do not eat at all. Often the electricity is switched off so we are without heating or light. Some punishments for bad behaviour are: getting hit with the leather strap, electric shocks and standing on a chair for many hours with no break. The guards like the last one because it does not leave any marks.

I knew about the electric shocks from Kurt Bokhoven, who said it was the best way to extract confessions from spies. As for the other punishments – well, what was good enough for the masters at school must have been good enough for prison wardens.

Then there is solitary confinement. They put you in a room where no one can see you and you can see no one. The walls are so thick that it is impossible to hear anything. After a while, you think that you are going mad, because humans are like dogs: we want to be in a pack, we want to move, we want to be told that we are good. When we can't have these things, the only option is to go inside ourselves.

I considered myself in the mirror, hoping that I would find myself eye to eye with a hardened insurgent. But I only saw myself: a boy of thirteen, blonde, scrubbed, square-faced.

I can't send you a photo, but I will try to draw a picture of myself so that you can imagine me.

I drew a man somewhat like Arend, with a hard jaw and a large chin, broad shoulders and shiny black jackboots. Thirty-six seemed old, but then I realized that Mr Hendryks was nearly twice that age. I decided that I shouldn't make the portrait look too angry, so I erased the heavy eyebrows and replaced the stern mouth with a smile. I added a scarf around his neck but decided against the armband.

Thank you for sending me the rules. I will add them to my list. Please tell me more about your aunt's children, especially the boy. You said that he is twelve. Does he know how to make invisible ink?

Please write again soon.

From,

Pieter

In the children's park on the other side of town, there was a giant map of the world that visitors could walk on, painted on sprung boards like a dance floor. After a few weeks, people stopped bothering to take off their shoes and socks, so the continents became scuffed and most of Europe turned a funny shade of grey. You could tell where most people liked to go – Belgium, the middle of Africa, and America – because those were the places where the names had worn thin.

We didn't have an atlas at home, and school was closed for the festival, so I went to the park to see if I could find Ceylon.

It turned out to be a lot bigger than I expected, like a pearl earring hanging off the tip of India. It was painted bright pink, and crisscrossed with red railway lines. I quickly found Colombo, but there was no sign of Nuwara Eliya.

Just as I had started to judge the distance between it and Flanders – about three long strides – someone called my name.

"Aren't you a bit big for that?"

It was Mieke. Her hair was in braids today, tied at the ends with a blue ribbon that matched her eyes. Mieke had perfectly square teeth and a nose that was a little round and turned up at the end. She often teased me, and I suppose in a way I liked it.

"There's no rule," I replied.

She set down the shopping bag and leant over the side of the low wall. I felt a bit like an animal in a zoo, being observed from across my enclosure.

"Looking for any place in particular?" Mieke asked. The way she was leaning, I could have seen right down her dress if I'd wanted to. She wasn't to know – pretty girls often don't realize they are vulnerable – and I didn't want to embarrass her. So I kicked aside some leaves and pointed to Ceylon.

"I don't know if it's part of India or not," I said.

Mieke hopped over the wall and strode up to join me. Planting her hands on slender hips, she peered down at the island.

"It's pink, like India," she said decisively. "It's British."

I nodded, trying to think of something intelligent to say. I had just come up with something really good – a question, I think, because girls like to be asked about themselves – when Mieke bent down and looked me square in the face.

"Is everything all right, Marten?" she asked. A small cleft had appeared between her eyebrows, the soft skin dimpling with concern.

"Everything's fine," I said. She looked away, then back at me.

"I miss him, too," she said. She bit her lower lip, turning the pink flesh white. "You poor thing."

I should have given her my hand, perhaps even put an arm around her and told her to be strong, like a movie hero. Then she'd realize that I wasn't just someone's little brother any more.

Instead, I retched. Mieke straightened like a jolt, the look of concern giving way to bewilderment and vague disgust. The sound had taken us both by surprise. Before I could apologize, a stabbing pain in my stomach caused me to double over with a pitiful howl – the kind of noise a dog makes, not a sound I'd ever heard from myself – and Mieke lunged to catch me as I fell.

* * *

The doctor told me it was worms.

"But we cook our meat properly," protested my mother. For some reason, she seemed in a hurry for the doctor to leave. "Are you suggesting that I don't look after my son?"

"Has Marten eaten anywhere else? At school, perhaps, or in a restaurant?"

"Father took me to De Kraan," I said. I didn't say that we'd eaten there most nights since the memorial service, as Mother no longer had the energy to cook.

The doctor smelt of snuff and mothballs. Although his head was as bald as an egg, thick white whiskers sprouted beneath his nose and from his ears. "Could have been," he said, getting up from his chair by the bed. "If we're lucky, a course of sulphate drops and castor oil will take care of it. The main thing is to make sure the parasite doesn't migrate to the appendix."

There was something rotten inside me, and I needed to know what it was. I knew about guinea worms – the ones that can live inside a person for up to a year before burrowing out through a blister they chew in the host's leg – but the doctor said it was very unlikely that I had a guinea worm. Mieke had asked if she could bring me anything, so I told her that I wanted to read about parasites. She seemed a little surprised, but brought me a book from the library the next day.

"*Tænia solium* and *Tænia saginata* are the most common varieties of tapeworm," began the chapter on worms. "Symptoms of infection can include abdominal pain, diarrhoea and nausea. Cysticercosis may occur when the parasite develops outside the intestinal tract to muscles, bone marrow and in some cases the central nervous system. The latter may lead to seizures and severe neurological problems."

Tapeworms have a hook for a head – that is how they hold on to the intestines – and absorb nutrients through their skin. All worms are both male and female, so a single tapeworm can reproduce all by itself. They sounded like very clever creatures, and I began to feel a little sorry for the one living inside me. The doctor's plan was to wage war on the tapeworm with medicine, because the grown-ups' hatred for foreign invaders didn't exclude invertebrates. He told me that, with any luck, I would go to the toilet one day and discover it there. It seemed a very humiliating way to die.

It wasn't long before Nijs found out, and of course he told Adriaan. We were supposed to have our initiation in two days' time, and he was worried that I might chicken out.

"Don't worry; I'll be there," I told him.

Sure enough, by Sunday afternoon I had begun to feel a lot better. There was still no sign of my tapeworm, but the medicine had done a good job of controlling the stomach pains.

Mr de Bruyns had invited my parents and Aunt Marta to join his family in the Grote Markt. Little Pieter de Bruyns would be carrying the papier-mâché figure of St Paul in the procession, and his father had reserved seats at the Café Royal – where Charles V had once watched wild boar and stags being hunted for show – so that they would have a good view for the flag-throwing.

Mother wasn't sure about leaving me alone when I was unwell, but as usual Aunt Marta had been quick to interfere. It was the first day in a long time that Father hadn't been too sad or too dumb with drink to face our pitying neighbours, and nothing was going to stop her from getting my parents out of the house – not even the chance that I might develop brain fever like little Hansie Joubert, who died because a parasite caused his nervous system to boil over like a kettle left for too long on the hob. "You can't coddle the boy now just because he's an only child," Aunt Marta said. "It's high time he learnt to stand on his own two feet."

I counted to three hundred after hearing the latch fall behind them, pretending to be asleep.

Adriaan had told us to meet him by the rail crossing, about a twenty-minute walk from the centre of town. Everyone in Mechelen was either in the Grote Markt or going there – I was the only person headed in the opposite direction. By the time I crossed the bridge on the northern gate, I was well and truly alone.

"Look, it's the invalid."

Waiting with Adriaan and Nijs was a boy who I recognized from the year above me at school. His name was Dirk. Pepijn was there also. He had brought his dog, a mutt that might have been half Laekenois. The dog had a thick neck and a broad snout and dopey eyes. Pepijn had wound its lead tightly around one hand, holding it taut as if the creature might attack at any minute, but the dog just looked bored.

"Don't," said Pepijn, as I reached to stroke it.

Dirk whistled, and the dog's ears pricked momentarily. Pepijn yanked the lead, hard.

"He doesn't look very dangerous," I said.

Pepijn flushed. "That's what you think," he snapped. "He's part wolf."

"Kuypers, is it?"

Arend. He strode towards me with a baronial swagger, thrusting his beefy palm at me as if it were a bayonet. I gripped it firmly, remembering what Mr Hendryks had told me about handshakes.

"That's right." No one had ever called me by my last name before, and I suddenly felt very grown up. I stood a little straighter and met his gaze.

"You're Krelis's brother." I nodded. "I didn't know him well; he was in the year above me. We kept to different friends. That fellow from the mill, Kurt…" Arend seemed to be thinking hard. "A strange sort to be mates with Krelis." He was still thinking, but in the end he seemed to change his mind about whatever it was he was going to say. Instead, he placed a hand on my shoulder. "It must be difficult, losing a brother."

"He'd want us to be brave."

"I'm sure that's true." He turned to Adriaan, who was looking very serious. "Your friends are all right," said Arend. "So many of the younger kids are just babies. The future belongs to the youth. You two are ready to grasp it, I can tell."

Nijs was watching me closely, but I ignored him. I was too busy concentrating on Arend's badge, which was inscribed with the words *Authority – Discipline – Dietsland*.

"You want to be a part of this?" he asked me, pointing to the badge. "It's a national movement for Flemish youth. The only one."

"Maybe," I said.

Arend laughed. "We only take the best lads, the strongest lads," he said. "Your friend tells me that you were unwell. It's nothing serious, I hope?"

"No," I said, willing my tapeworm to stay still. "Just an upset stomach."

"You must try to avoid infection, Kuypers. Healthy mind, healthy body."

"All right," I said, not sure how else to answer. My father used to say the same thing: he told me that I should do fifty press-ups every morning if I didn't want to grow up with arms like birds' legs.

"Let's get started," Arend said, turning to Dirk. "What time do you make it?"

"Three-oh-two," said Dirk, glancing at his watch.

"Good," said Arend. He pointed to Nijs. "You. Come here."

Shooting me one last look, Nijs joined Arend on the level crossing.

"Adriaan tells me that you two are top of your class. But we're not interested in what you know. We're interested in what you're made of."

Nijs nodded slowly. "So what do we do now?" he asked.

Arend hopped down from the crossing, indicating that Nijs should stay put. "Go and join your friend, Kuypers. One in front of the other, yes? Like this," and he pulled Adriaan in front of him, so that they would both be standing in the middle of the tracks.

I did as he instructed.

"That's right – now back up, so that you are ten feet apart. No, make it fifteen... there." Arend casually ran a hand through his sandy hair. "Adriaan has told you that all new recruits must pass an *ontgroening* – is that right, Kuypers?"

I nodded. I liked the sound of the word *recruits*: it sounded as if they had come looking especially for me.

"Well, then. It's very simple. We all must learn to obey be-fore we can lead. This activity is all about following orders.

68

Learning to listen to me rather than to the voices in your head. Understand?"

I nodded again, even though I wanted to tell him that only crazy people heard voices in their heads.

"Good. Both of you must stay put until I tell you to move. We begin... now."

For a while I thought that it was like a staring competition: trying not to blink, or move, or say anything. After a few minutes, I began to get a little bored. Pepijn's dog yawned loudly.

"Marten – look." Nijs pointed at something in the distance. I leant sideways, standing on tiptoe to peer over his shoulder. Black smoke trailed a question mark on the horizon.

"What is it?" I asked.

"Stay where you are," said Arend. Only now did I realize that he and Dirk had fallen back behind some bushes where the crossing signals were. Adriaan remained on the other side of the tracks, watching us. "Dirk has the controls; he'll drop the stop sign."

We waited. The plume of smoke rose higher.

"Why hasn't he dropped the sign?" I demanded.

"Be patient, Kuypers."

Nijs looked back at me. "Marten," he hissed, "do something."

"Who gives the orders around here?" barked Arend.

"You do," I said, glaring at Nijs. He could be such a baby sometimes.

By now the ground had begun to rumble as the train muscled towards us. Pepijn's dog barked twice.

"Marten!" hissed Nijs. The train was about two hundred yards away.

"My money's on Kuypers," said Arend, sounding bored. "Dirk?"

"Kuypers," agreed Dirk.

Now it was Nijs's turn to glare at me. "This is stupid," he said.

"If it's so stupid, perhaps you don't want to join, after all," said Arend.

"Of course he does," I said. I wondered how long it would take before Nijs started a nosebleed. That was often what happened when he got upset. "Everything's fine."

Adriaan was watching us with a detached expression, like a face peering through a one-way window. "Just listen to Arend," he whispered. "It's easy."

One hundred yards.

"That's it," said Nijs, turning around. "Marten, get off. Don't let him bully you!"

But I knew how to handle my father when he bullied us: I knew that it paid to be stubborn. "Shut up, Nijs," I snapped. My stomach had started to ache.

"Don't listen to him, Kuypers."

Fifty yards. A whistle shrieked.

"Stay put, Nijs!"

"Stay there, Kuypers... wait until I say..."

Thirty yards.

"Marten, don't be stupid! We'll get killed—"

"Are you in, or aren't you?"

"Hold firm, Kuypers..."

Nijs leapt, tumbling down the craggy bank and leaving me to confront the iron monster on my own. Another piercing scream: the driver's head appeared out of the side of the front carriage. He wore a red cap and was waving his arms.

The pain in my stomach clenched into a fist.

"Marten, get off—"

"Now, Kuypers, *now*!"

I jumped – or was I flung? Tossed aside on billows of sooty air – and landed hard on one shoulder.

The train thundered past, its whistle shrilling.

"Are you all right?" Nijs's tear-streaked face pressed towards mine.

"You deserted!" I screamed at him, in furious exhilaration.

"That was the stupidest thing you've ever done!" cried Nijs. But he was quickly pushed aside by Dirk and Pepijn, whose dog started licking my face with its long, rough tongue.

"I'm impressed, Kuypers." Towering over me, Arend offered his hand. He hauled me to my feet, cupped my cheek with a paw-like hand and gave two friendly pats.

Deep inside me, my tapeworm wriggled.

8

Up to her elbows in soapy water, Perdita kept one eye on her daughters as she commenced a fresh bout of scrubbing.

Miss Annabel said that her English niece had come to help with the children – to learn not to be a child herself, she surmised. That was all very well, but it was a shame the girl insisted on calling them by such ugly nicknames. Jayanadani had become "Jay"; Nimali was "Nim". Boys' names. Soon they would want to cut their hair short like boys, too.

Girls like Miss Glynis did not usually come out to Ceylon to look after children; there were plenty of local women for that. English girls came to find husbands. "The fishing fleet", they were called. Fishing for a suitable match with an officer whose Raj connections would secure a respectable income and invitations to the homes of the right sort of colonials. In short, a comfortable life: safely exotic, strangely familiar.

The English girl was not shy to ask questions, and Perdita could tell that she suffered the same giddy enthusiasm that others always did, before the boredom set in. They arrived expecting sandstone pavilions, smouldering princes and fire-worshipping Parsis, sniffing after the masculine odour of the desert, keening to hear the lonely wail of a *dilruba*. That was before they realized they had confused the island with Mussoorie and other hill stations, that here their lives would be regulated by the BBC World Service over breakfast, the *Times* crossword with lunch, and a brandy sundowner after supper. The Club on Saturdays, church on Sundays.

But who could blame them for expecting more? The British liked to believe what they were told, and it was always the high castes who did the talking. They created the myth, not the British. If this country was ever to achieve independence, it would not be the one that the Mahatma promised.

Perdita had already tried to explain this to the girl, but Miss Glynis – Glen, she had insisted they call her – was more interested in what could be seen, tasted, experienced. Someone she had met on the boat had told her about Swami Rock – Sammy Rock, the English called it – and she wanted to know if it would be possible to go there and back in a day. And she had asked about the Rock Veddas who lived in the mountains, only smiling when Perdita had insisted that they were savages, not people worth seeking out, certainly not alone. Glen was not so interested in the temples or the public baths – the few monuments that locals knew much about – but she had listened patiently as Perdita explained how Theravada temples might be distinguished from Hindu ones.

The girls were laughing now, thrilled at Glen's ability to wiggle her ears and trying, in vain, to imitate her. They had formed a cosy cabal in the shade of the banyan tree. Perdita's daughters were dark as coffee beans, with thick black hair tied back into plaits; Jayanadani was the spitting image of her mother, but Nimali's eyes were the colour of drenched grass, strangely translucent. Jayanadani was older, serious, conscientious, and it was a joy to see her enjoying herself for once. Too quickly the children grew up, grew old, like their parents.

"Your children are delightful," said Glen, wandering across the lawn strewn with spiky pink rambutan, while the girls bickered over the tap to wash their hands. Stray wisps of hair clung to her temples, and her cheeks were flushed, but still she would not complain about the heat.

"They are good girls," smiled Perdita. "You know, Jayanadani got hundred out of hundred on her final exam."

"Do they go to a village school, then?"

"Yes, not so far from here. The school now, it is run by the government, not like when Micah was a student – then it was all missionaries. The teacher is very kind, he encourages the girls to study." Perdita slapped the wrung sheet against the sink. "When I was their age, school was for boys only. You know what they told us? Too much study would drain all the blood from a girl's *voom* – how do you say it?" pointing to her stomach.

"Womb?" suggested Glen.

"*Achcha*. From a girl's *voom* to her brain. So we would be poor mothers."

"I've told Annabel that I'd tutor Althea for her entrance exams. Perhaps Jay and Nim would like to join us? I don't suppose the village school teaches Latin."

"But of course!" Perdita waggled her head, flicking a bangled wrist. "It is proper-proper English. Their teacher studied at London. He is very-very serious about English education. Come, you will be joining us for lunch."

"Oh, I wouldn't want to impose—"

"Impose, impose. The girls will like it, yes?"

For Perdita, it was a useful excuse to exercise some hospitality; young charges offered an occasion for rulers and ruled to interact, to play at being equals. The English girl was intrigued, she could tell. In the struggle between decorum and curiosity, curiosity won.

Although thatched with coconut palm, their white clapboard house was in many ways a miniature version of the bungalow – tidy, cool. But where the bungalow had many rooms, here there was only a kitchen and a living area, which Micah and Perdita shared with their daughters as a bedroom. The clay floor was neatly swept and soft to walk on. In one corner, the girls crouched on a bamboo mat as they distributed the plates.

"It's called *malu hodhi*," explained Perdita, spooning steaming chunks of white fish over a mound of red rice nestled in a banana leaf. "Salty-sweet, with coconut milk. And jackfruit, too." She smiled as Glen politely waited for the others to serve themselves. "Nimali, run to the house and bring a fork for Miss Glen."

"Oh, that's all right," said Glen. "I'll eat with my hands, too. It's better that way, I hear."

Nimali made a pincer movement with her forefinger and thumb.

"So your fingers can taste," she said, her voice a shy whisper.

"Sinhalese food is the best in the world," smiled Jayanadani. "But I would like to try... what is it? Black pudding. It sounds so strange."

They all laughed.

"Tell me about this schoolteacher," said Glen. "You said he studied in London?"

"That's right. His name is Ganan. A good boy from the village. His mother still lives there. His father was a tailor, pushed Ganan very-very hard. Jayanadani, Miss Glen is needing more chai, please."

As the girl scurried into the kitchen, Perdita lowered her voice.

"They all think he is the *bee's knees*. Very handsome. He teaches the boys the cricket and shows the girls how to draw. It's only a shame that his English is better than his Sinhala."

Jayanadani returned to pour the tea. "I'm glad he came back," she offered, in a soft voice.

"But why did he go all the way to London, just to become a schoolteacher?" asked Glen.

"His father wanted him to be a lawyer, but the exams, you know, they are so difficult. Ganan was not cut out for it. Still, he got to see the world, and that is what matters. In stories, the prince must always experience ex... how is it, then? Ex-ill?"

"Exile," offered Glen.

"*Ai-yoh*! Hindu mothers, they are doting all the time! A boy, especially, must learn to be independent."

"My mother would agree with you. My brother still doesn't know what to do with himself."

"Perhaps he will marry, no?"

Glen had to stop herself from laughing. "Tully would make an awful husband," she said. "He's far too spoilt, too infantile himself." She pushed the rice around her plate, moistening it with the curry sauce so that it would hold together. "He could be a jolly good father, though."

"Is he very handsome, Miss Glen?"

"Hopelessly handsome." The girl smiled at Jayanadani. "And an utter rogue."

"A *rogue*, Miss Glen?"

"Somebody who gets into trouble, darling." Her smile faded. "He made a mistake when he was younger, during the war. Or perhaps I shouldn't call it that – perhaps he did the only thing he could have done." She was met with an expectant silence. "He fled the front, you see. It's the worst thing a soldier can do."

"But now he is no longer a soldier," said Perdita.

"That's right."

"You like the curry, Miss Glen?"

"It's divine, darling."

"Is it 'positively savage'?" parroted Nimali.

Glen checked herself, registering Perdita's look of surprise. "In the best possible way," she replied to the beaming child. "*Positively savage.*"

* * *

From the servants' quarters, the bungalow loomed large. Green netting billowed over the veranda, keeping the mosquitoes out and creating a system of cool breezes inside. When the winds grew, doors would slam suddenly and loudly, making those indoors jump and giggle about ghosts.

The English girl watched as Perdita rinsed the plates under the outside tap. She had offered to help, although both knew that this was a preposterous suggestion. The Phayre children had been taught an obsessive respect for their parents' staff – required always to raise their hats to the pedestrian farmers they passed on riding excursions and trained never to call the servants by their first names until invited – but distinctions between employers and employed remained more deeply ingrained than Glen herself cared to admit. While Jayanadani and Nimali made dolls out of discarded corn husks, the girl contented herself with keeping the housemaid company as Perdita went about her work.

"Where is Hollar from?" she finally asked.

Perdita paused to observe her reflection in the spoon she was washing. Upside down, her face appeared elongated. She tilted the spoon for a more accurate reflection, wishing that the bridge of her nose was not so severe. Still, not a grey hair to be seen, not a wrinkle. She tossed the spoon back into the sudsy water and sighed.

"It is a very good question you are asking," she replied. Then, not knowing what else to say, she picked up the spoon again. "It's funny, no, how our reflection changes?"

Glen shrugged, began to look slightly bored. "I suppose so."

"My girls are dark, like their father," sighed Perdita. "Every week, I ask Jayanadani to use the rose clay, and every week she refuses."

"What does it do?"

"For lightening-whitening."

Glen nodded. In the last few days, delicate freckles had appeared across her nose – something that did not seem to bother her, much to Perdita's surprise.

"You see, I was wondering about Hollar's name..."

"That I do not know," said Perdita abruptly, shaking her head. "It is an ugly name."

"Do you think so?"

"Most definitely. But the boy is lucky; as we say here, 'he is eight *annas* in the rupee', and passing for an English boy, almost."

"I suppose his father wouldn't have to have been English. He could have been from any number of faraway places."

Perdita frowned at her. "What's that, missy mem?"

"Oh, you know – like the other white settlers. The Portuguese or the Dutch."

A light of recognition dawned. "*Achcha.* Further than Pondicherry, then."

"I saw him in a singlet the other day, helping Annabel plant peas in the garden. He's not at all dark, really. I was surprised, because when we went to the Club to collect Althea from her riding lesson, several people did seem to look at us – at him – in a funny way. We were on the balcony – you know where it says 'Europeans Only'?"

Perdita nodded, although she had never been to the Club.

"And it made me wonder: do people here see more than I do? When I look at Hollar, I see a rather miserable boy, but when others do..."

"He is not miserable. He is slow," huffed Perdita. "*Tuttu deke.*"

"Oh, I don't know about that."

"It is true. The boy never speaks." She sniffed. "I said to Miss Annabel, what you need to do is catch a thalagoya, the lizard with the hooked tongue. You cook the tongue, have the boy eat it. That is the only way to cure dumbness."

"I don't think that Hollar is dumb. He's just very shy. And... *particular*. He likes things just so. I think that must be why he's such a compulsive collector."

Perdita grunted. "He spends too much time alone for a boy of his age. Sits in his room, wanders about the churchyard..."

"But the church is miles away."

Perdita cocked her head towards the valley. "Not the one you go to – another one, you can walk to it in twenty minutes. It is ruins only; the building is not used any more." She lowered her voice, glancing askew to make sure that her daughters would not hear. "It is haunted, missy mem. Many bad spirits, many bad things happening. The coolies are all afraid of it. Only Hollar goes there. Last week I heard him tell his sister that he was meeting someone." The woman tapped her temple with a hooked finger. "The boy's not right in the head. He is a com-*pulsive* liar."

"Are his parents buried there, perhaps?"

Perdita looked up from her washing with wide eyes. "His parents? Oh, but he is not an orphan, Miss Glen."

"But I thought—"

"I know. But it isn't true."

At last Glen seemed to realize that this was not an avenue of discussion that Perdita wished to pursue, and she changed the subject.

"Do you know Mrs Cornish?" she asked.

"*Ai-yoh*! Everyone knows that woman," smiled Perdita. "She thinks she is a grand memsahib. Miss Annabel does not like her, she finds bridge and mah-jong boring-boring. I don't know, I never play these games. But Mrs Cornish is a rude woman, if you ask me."

"Well, she's coming for tea this afternoon, so I've been told I'm to be *at home*. Annabel says she was all a-flutter with news about some newcomer in the village – English..."

"An army man came to stay at the Burgher guest house last week. They say he speaks fluent Hindi."

"That might be the fellow. Annabel's become rather suspicious of army types, though, what with Uncle Ray and the Planter Corps business…" Glen rolled her eyes and allowed a pause in an attempt to lure some gossip out of Perdita – but none was forthcoming. "Anyway, I don't suppose he'll bother coming all the way up here, so we'll just have to rely on Mrs Cornish for all the juicy details. Annabel has said she's very keen to meet me, you know."

"She will be wanting you to teach her horrible son for no pay, Miss Glen. You be careful."

Movement from the veranda attracted their attention to Althea, who had emerged through the netting and was casting her gaze around the garden, shielding her eyes from the sun with one hand. Catching sight of her cousin at the bottom of the garden, the child tumbled down the uneven steps.

"What are you doing here?" she asked, auburn curls trembling loose from neatly ribboned plaits.

"What does it look like we're doing, silly? We're talking."

"Where were you at lunch?"

"Perdita very kindly asked me to join her and the girls for a curry. Perdita, I wanted to ask you—"

"You did what?" Althea's eyes grew round as saucers as a smile crept across her frank little face. "Whatever will Mrs Cornish say to that?"

"Is she already here?"

"She's been here half an hour, Glen. We thought you were in your room…"

"Rats!"

"I'd hurry up, if I were you." The little girl grabbed Glen's hand and began tugging her up the garden path.

The housemaid watched them disappear inside as Mrs Cornish's bossy laughter exploded from the drawing room. Perdita could almost smell the memsahib's rose perfume, could almost taste the lipstick that gathered wetly at the corners of her mouth. Pale eyes fringed with clumpy mascara never met the servants' gaze directly, but would slide after their retreating backs as they withdrew from the room. It was only proper to wait for privacy before resuming polite conversation.

Turning back to her work, Perdita noticed that her daughters were fashioning banana-leaf dresses for their husk dolls – just as she had done as a child, many years ago – and she wondered if Micah was right: if things were indeed beginning to change on the island. *Today, the English girl ate* malu hodhi *in my house,* she thought. Anything was possible.

* * *

In addition to the fruitcake and two yards of patterned fabric which she had brought for Annabel ("I order in from London every few months, so it wasn't any trouble really – and I had noticed that you could do with a pretty dress for the summer"), Mrs Cornish presented Glen with a written invitation to a party at the Club, arranged to take place that weekend.

"It's a young people's do," she'd explained in a voice like treacle, winking knowingly at the girl's aunt. "We do feel it's terribly important to give them something to look forward to – carefully supervised, of course, so the girls feel quite safe. The Women's Committee have great fun doing up the decorations. You really will be amazed at what we manage to come up with, darling!"

"And not a moment too soon," smiled Annabel, shooting Glen a conspiratorial glance that said, *Go, and we'll have a good old laugh about it afterwards.* "I'm quite surprised the poor girl hasn't perished of boredom out here already."

And so that Friday Glen was dropped off at her first club dance. She was surprised to discover that the event was held in a building shaped like a barn some distance from the main house.

"The dance hall," Micah announced proudly, as the car idled at the foot of the drive. "I'll be waiting here for you at ten, yes?"

The girl nodded, glimpsing in the rear-view mirror a party of youths trailing up the road behind them. "I suppose I'll join this lot," she said to Micah, hoping he would not hear the uncertainty in her voice. All of sudden she thought of the servants' quarters at the bottom of the garden and wished that she could be there instead, listening to Perdita's stories of haunted churches and the medicinal properties of lizards' tongues.

It's that old first-day-of-school feeling, she told herself. *Just go in and be cheery and only have a little to drink, and before you know it you'll have heaps of lovely new friends. That is what you want, isn't it?*

"You have a good time, Miss."

The group she latched on to seemed friendly enough, if rather younger than she'd expected. The men were all lean, boyish types; the girls wore day dresses that had been specially altered for the occasion: a bow here, a layer of chiffon there. In her silk crêpe gown, Glen felt something of an alien. The other girls cooed over her dress and when they heard that she was new to the area they called their friends over to make giddy introductions.

The dance, it transpired, was an eighteenth-birthday party being thrown in honour of a local girl called Ruth McDowall. Most of the guests had bussed down from Matale, which explained why Glen didn't recognize them from previous visits to the Club. The majority appeared to be no more than eighteen or nineteen, although a small group of older "marrieds" watched from the sidelines. There was a disparity between these groups, Glen quickly realized: a lacuna into which, almost twenty-four and single, she alone seemed to fall.

"Local, are you?" asked a voice in her ear – and Glen turned to find herself being offered a glass of something pink by a ruddy-faced young man. The first things she noticed were a rather impressive forehead – was it that, or a prematurely receding hairline? – and a strong smell of pomade, followed by laughing grey eyes and full, sensuous lips. A good nose, though; and he filled out his suit rather better than many of the young scarecrows bobbing about on the dance floor.

"Thanks," she said, accepting the drink. "Local, yes. I'm new here."

"You didn't strike me as a Wiltshire girl."

Glen glanced around the crowd. "Oh?"

"Not that Wiltshire," he teased. "It's our name for the Knuckles foothills. Most of this lot are from the rubber plantations round thereabouts. Ruth's is a tea family, though – she's a top girl."

"Oh, I see. You're from Matale, too, then?"

He extended one hand. "Douglas Brink. Dougie."

"Glynis Phayre. Glen."

"Do you dance?"

He was a competent partner. Glancing at the other couples jostling alongside them as they shuffled across the swept wood floors, glittering in the light of coloured tea lamps strung from the high beamed ceiling, Glen felt rescued. Dougie had a decent face, she thought; not swoonsomely handsome, but not unattractive, either. And yet she sensed something in his easy manner that suggested he didn't want her particularly. A young man like Dougie could spend the better part of his youth in these pleasant hills, passing his days at the Club, his evenings at young people's parties, working a bit perhaps, waiting for the right girl to come along, to marry with the same smiling ease.

The band managed quite well for a group of school lads. They played some Benny Carter, a little Duke Ellington, 'Honeysuckle Rose'.

"So what do you think?" Dougie grinned down at her, his breath smelling of grenadine.

"It's all very jolly."

"It won't last, you know."

"What won't?"

"These silly parties." His smile faded. "Yes, you do think it's silly – I can tell by your face, Glen."

She blushed. "It's a barn dance, that's all. I'm older than most of these girls – I mean…" She pointed to the bunting. "These are children's decorations. Don't you find it… well, I don't mean to be ungrateful…"

"You are a funny kid, aren't you?" he laughed, taking her by the waist as the band struck up a new song.

She pretended that she was seventeen again – *Be bright and silly*, she told herself, *or these people will never be your friends*

81

– but at the end of it she couldn't help pressing Dougie for an answer.

"What did you mean when you said it wouldn't last?"

"The fun. It's not real, of course. But you've seen through it already."

"So what do you suppose will replace it?"

He shrugged, looking bored. "Whatever came before." He indicated a group of young men standing in one corner, smoking cigarettes and gazing over the heads of the crowd with expressions of lofty indifference. "Those are the Edwardians. I call them that, anyway – the lads who lost brothers or fathers in the war, who go through life trying to live up to their memory. Laughing isn't something they do in public; they just turn up to these things out of a sense of duty." He cocked his head at the rest of the party. "The others – the girls, mostly – are simply playing the game. Affectation has become second nature to them."

"It's the only way they have to rebel," she said. "By pretending they don't care."

"Oh, but they do care: they care *dreadfully* about not getting left on the shelf. They care *awfully* about finding a husband who doesn't drink too much or gamble his family's money away, who will give them children to keep them occupied – until the brats get sent away to school in the Mother Country, that is – and who will allow them to settle down somewhere with silly dance parties to kill the boredom." He reached for a sandwich.

"But why? I mean, can't they see what's going on out here?" There was a smugness to his expression which filled her with a sudden desire to shock him into listening to her. "Have you read *Indian Home Rule*, Dougie?"

It was a gamble, mentioning a book that she, herself, had not read. Dougie sucked his teeth and shook his head slowly from side to side. "I hate to break it to you, kid," he said, "but if you thought you'd come here to see some charming demonstrations, you're going to be disappointed. That's all over now – everyone's fed up with Gandhi's religious experiments and all that twaddle rejecting modern civilization. His lot, just as much as ours." He brushed the crumbs from his fingers onto his trousers. "It's all kicking off in Europe now, and everyone knows it. These are uncertain times, Glen." He cast his gaze over the crowd and repeated, with some satisfaction, "Uncertain times, indeed."

"And so they dance?"

"And so they dance."

Is this what it comes to, she thought, watching Dougie wander off to greet some friends who had just arrived. *Edwardians and hapless maidens left on the shelf? Well: no, thank you.*

She danced with two others that evening and chatted for a while with Ruth, whose attention Glen sensed was focused rather more on a late-arriving group of men than on her female supplicants. The last half-hour she spent on the porch, waiting for the headlights of Micah's car to appear over the ridge.

"There you are!" Dougie dropped onto the step next to her.

"My ride will be here soon."

"That's all right, then." His top button was undone now; his expansive forehead shone with perspiration. "There's to be a party in Wiltshire in a couple of weeks – Holly Cash and Jim Fortescue have just announced that they're getting engaged. Jim's an old friend of mine. You'll come, won't you?"

Glen considered his broad, simple face and smiled tamely. "I'd love to," she said.

9

I carried her letter with me all day, waiting for the right moment to open it. I was halfway home from school before I realized that I was following the road to the fulling mill.

It was a Friday, which meant that Kurt and the other workers would have left early. The private road leading to the mill was empty. I remembered Kurt's face when I had snooped about here before, the way he had clutched me by the shoulders and whispered that if I told anyone I'd live to regret it. I ran a fingernail along the edge of the envelope in my pocket and kept going.

The mill was old: a square, brick building that had started to slump in the middle, like one of Aunt Marta's cakes that never rose. There were two turbines inside which connected to a big wooden wheel that turned in the current.

I couldn't go inside, as it was locked. But I had seen it all before: the groaning machinery and the network of creaking wooden platforms; the heavy fulling stocks, the swinging harnesses that beat the cloth. According to Kurt, my brother had been standing too close to the edge of the platform which ran along the outer wall. He was hit from behind by one of the stocks, which sent him toppling over one side. Some piece of his clothing – his braces, possibly, or a loop in his belt – had caught in the blade of the turbine, dragging him under water before anyone could notice what had happened.

Lots of people who knew the mill said that it didn't make sense: it was hard to imagine such a shallow current sweeping a body away, especially the strong body of my brother. But by the time the accident happened it had rained heavily for three days, so the current was strong and the waters deep and muddy. One of the younger lads admitted to having left the sluice gates open by mistake, which meant that there was no stopping the body once it had travelled far enough downstream. The current had swept any trace of my brother clean away.

It didn't feel haunted in the way that the gatehouse did. It felt peaceful. And so I settled myself on the slope against one side of the mossy wall and took out the letter. It had arrived only a day after I'd posted my last reply.

Dear Pieter,

I found myself with a little extra time after lessons today, so I thought I'd post you a surprise. Unfortunately the CWU says that I'm not allowed to send you any parcels, or else I would have posted some milk toffee or a lovely new sweater. But I hope this will be almost as nice.

Given the fact that you can't go outdoors, I thought I'd offer you the next best thing: I'm going to take you somewhere else. Are you confused? Don't be. All you must do is to imagine that the walls around you have fallen away; bricks and mortar and iron bars, the lot. You are no longer in a prison cell – or, for that matter, in a thronging canteen, or a caged exercise run. Close your eyes and you are here, in Ceylon.

I closed my eyes tightly, gripping her letter with both hands as if it were a magic charm. But all I could see were flashes of blue and white against the pink darkness of my eyelids. I could still hear the same birds in the trees and the sound of water tripping over stones in the shallows. I opened my eyes.

Look, there – do you see? A hanging parrot, just between those branches! You'll never see one of those birds touch the ground: they nest in the trees and eat there, and raise their young there, throughout their entire lives. It's a smallish thing, and I wouldn't blame you for missing it at first – the bright green of its wings gets lost amid the leaves. But you'll see when it moves – there! – that its head is stained blood red, and its back a bright orange. As if that wasn't enough colour for one little bird, his tail feathers are a stunning blue. Isn't he beautiful?

85

Now I shall take you down into the valley. A few monkeys are crying out, and a bird sings keloo-keloo! In the distance there is the sound of a crashing waterfall. Very occasionally, you may hear the trumpeting of an elephant, as he labours under human cargo to clear the jungle passes. All around us are rolling hills, carpeted with tea bushes. Smell that! The air is still, but soft and warm against your skin. Best to give the durian trees a wide berth – the fruit is ripening now, and from the right height a falling shell can brain a man. Watch your step, and keep an eye out for snakes – one of Annabel's workers was bitten by a viper just last week...

She led me as she might have led a blind man, through jungle paths and grassy hill country, up steep crags and into lush valleys, stopping now and then to point out the labourers or white folk she knew from their club. The place she described sounded to me like the Garden of Eden – right down to the Devil in a serpent's guise.

And then I realized what it was that she had done: she had delivered me from prison, just like the angel who delivered Peter. "Now I know of a surety, that the Lord hath sent his angel, and hath delivered me out of the hand of Herod, and from all the expectation of the people of the Jews." That's what Peter said when he found himself out in the world again, a free man.

We've come full circle, Pieter, and now we have arrived at Beulah Lodge. Perdita has given her daughters kalu dodol as an after-school treat, and she wants to know if you would like a little, too? It is made with coconut milk and sugar, which is cooked until you get something that looks and feels rather like cheesecake. Perdita adds cashews to hers. Go on, don't be shy – try some of mine, and see what you think. Ah, so you like it! I shall ask her to make some more for your next visit. Then I shall take you to Kandy to see the so-called "devil dancers", and the temple which houses a tooth that belonged to Buddha himself...

I was sad when the letter ended: I didn't want to leave that place, which was so strange and beautiful. But, more importantly, I didn't want her to leave me. My world – this world of crumbling corners, the empty mill silhouetted against a grey sky – was not magical. I folded the letter carefully into its envelope, and wondered what I could possibly write in reply.

* * *

A few days after I passed the test, Arend presented me with a badge. It was similar to the one that he wore, with the Flemish lion and an eagle and a crooked black cross enclosed in a motto: *Wie Leven Wil Moet Strijden.* Who wants to live must fight.

Our movement – I liked the fact that he called it a movement, rather than a club – was the junior wing of the Vlaams Nationaal Verbond. So far, all that I had learnt about the VNV was that the leader was a man called Staf de Clercq, who loved the Flemish language and hated the French almost as much as my father did. Mr de Bruyns and Mr Lekaerts were also members; I knew this because they both had election posters stuck up in their windows with VNV written in bold. I liked the way that the letters looked strong – fierce as teeth – and I remember comparing them to the letters *CWU*, which my lady writer had mentioned, and wondering if her group was anything like mine.

The VNV scouts' troop was something to occupy me after school when I didn't have church or my accordion lesson. On those days it was best to stay out of the house for as long as possible, because Mother needed the quiet, and I never knew when Father was going to be looking for someone to bully.

The troop met three afternoons a week, usually in the woods, but sometimes in a field by the railway tracks and sometimes in an empty classroom at school. The older boys would show us how to do things like tie knots, or bandage wounds, and then we'd run races or play games like Capture the Flag or sing scouts' songs. Sometimes we'd just sit around and listen to Arend talk about what it meant to be Flemish and how we could be better citizens.

Nijs didn't come to these meetings. Arend had offered him another chance to pass his initiation, and it looked as if he might have gone through with it, but on the day itself he hadn't turned up. Afterwards, when I found him at home, he told me that his father had forbidden him from joining.

"But why?" I asked. "Did you tell him that I'm a member?"

"Yes, and he said that if you had half a mind you wouldn't be. He says that they're a bunch of hooligans."

"Adriaan's not a hooligan. His dad's an accountant; he knows your parents."

"Father says that Adriaan is playing a dangerous game."

That was all that Nijs would tell me, and we didn't discuss the movement much after that.

So Adriaan and I went to the meetings together. I never asked him about the day in the forest when Arend had made him cry, as I would have landed in no end of trouble if Arend found out I'd been spying on them.

I still hadn't made up my mind about Arend. On the one hand, I was fairly sure that he wasn't the idiot that Pepijn was. On the other hand, he could be cruel. Every week, he'd ask Willem to show him the welts on his palms. Adriaan told me they'd been made with a knife dipped in boiling water, a bit like sheep branding. As long as Arend was satisfied that the scars were still there, he'd grin and pat Willem on the back as if they were old chums. I hoped for Willem's sake that the marks would never disappear.

For the most part, Adriaan and I didn't discuss these things. Instead, we talked about accordions, and religion, and natural science. I did most of the talking, because I knew about these things and Adriaan was a very good listener.

"The problem with the Jews," I told him as we walked alongside the canal, following our reflections in the inky water, "is that they think they're special. You know how Dirk told us that they call themselves the Chosen People? Well, I asked Mr Hendryks at church, and he said it's true. Can you believe it? The Chosen People: just like that, for no good reason. It's like a really exclusive club."

"Not like our club," said Adriaan.

88

"Yes," I said. "That's exactly it. In our club – in the movement – you're only in if you deserve to be there. If you're good enough." Which we were: we both had the badges to prove it. "It's an achievement, right? Whereas if you're born a Jew, I think you probably grow up thinking that the world owes you something, that you're better than everyone else. When things get a little rough – like your shop gets closed because you've not been paying your taxes – suddenly you're the victim." That's what happened to Mr Kreyn: his shop was closed, and Aunt Marta said it must have been because he was cooking the books. "But because the Jewish god is on their side, that excuses them from everything."

"Right," said Adriaan. Then, after a moment's thought, he added, "And the Torah."

"What?"

"The Torah, the word of God."

I pretended to know what he was talking about. Arend hadn't told us about the Torah yet. "What about it?"

"They – the Jews, I mean – they think it's immortal. You can't kill a book, can you?"

"Obviously." I thought of Arend's habit of tearing out the pages of schoolbooks as he read: he boasted that it was more efficient than carrying around dead weight. I wasn't sure why the thought of tearing pages out of books made me uneasy, because it was quite logical, in a way. "You can't kill a table, either, can you? It's an inanimate object."

"No." After a few minutes, Adriaan looked up and said, "So do you think that God was protecting you on the railway tracks?"

"I don't know," I replied. "I wasn't praying or anything."

"What were you thinking, then?"

"Nothing. I was excited." I kicked at a stone. "And a little scared, I suppose. Mr Hendryks says that fear stops people from thinking."

We reached the forest to find Arend and Dirk and Pepijn already setting up the afternoon's activity. Dirk was carefully placing tin cans along the top of a wooden stile, edging them further apart or closer together as Arend directed, while Pepijn was using his heel to dig a line in the ground several yards away.

"Are we doing archery today?" asked Adriaan, full of hope. We'd learnt how to make bows and arrows the previous week.

"It's better than that," grinned Pepijn. "You'll see."

The other boys in our section – Willem, Joos, Bastiaan, Pim and Theo – arrived soon after. Bastiaan was the only one not in our school; like Adriaan, he was two years behind the rest of us. The backs of his legs, white as a lamb's flanks, still bore the brandings of a painful initiation on the hot water pipes behind the ironworks.

Filip was the last to arrive. As soon as he saw me, his squint started to twitch as if there was a firefly trapped beneath the skin. "Kuypers!" he said. "You know they've found a body? About a mile downstream from the mill. A man."

I felt my breath catch in my throat. Before I could say anything, Joos butted in.

"An *old* man," he said. "I already heard about it. It's not Marten's brother."

"How do you know?" Filip turned to me triumphantly. "It's all bloated. Doesn't even look human. No clothes or anything – his skin was all blue."

"Were there eels?" gasped Bastiaan. "Is it true that eels crawl into corpses?"

"Sometimes," said Filip, looking bored. "There might have been some in this fellow, but you'd have to cut him open to tell for sure."

"Did you see him?" asked Pim.

"Not exactly, but I know someone who did. He said the eyes had started to rot—"

"That's enough, Filip," snapped Arend, who must have seen the colour drain from my face. "Anyway, Joos is right: the fellow was old. It was probably one of the tramps who used to sleep outside the Schepenhuis. I heard the police say so myself." He threw me a sympathetic smile, and in that instant I would have done anything for him.

"We've got a surprise for you lads today," he continued, once the others had quietened. "Thanks to Dirk. Or rather," he smirked, "thanks to Dirk's old man."

"Not that he knows anything about it," laughed Dirk.

"We're going to add another skill to your armoury," Arend explained to the group. "There are ten tin cans up there – one for each of us. And we're going to remove them with this."

Slowly, like a magician dipping his hand into the magic hat, Arend pulled an object wrapped in oily cloths from his satchel. He peeled back the layers of cloth to reveal something smooth and silvery.

"It is real?" breathed Willem.

"Of course it's real," sneered Dirk. "You think we'd mess around with toys?"

"Is it loaded?" asked Theo.

"Of course not," said Arend. "That's the point. You're going to learn how to load it yourselves."

"And fire it?" asked Willem.

"Do you think I stuck those cans up there for my own amusement?" asked Dirk. It was hard to tell if we were supposed to laugh at this or shake our heads. Fortunately, Arend interrupted.

"Who will be first?" he asked.

Willem immediately edged forwards. "I will," he said. "I've seen how it's done in the movies. You load it, and then you cock it."

Arend pressed a catch and withdrew the magazine. "There are seven rounds already in here," he said, holding it up to us.

Willem took the pistol from him and reloaded the magazine into the butt.

"See how he keeps the barrel aimed at the ground," said Arend.

With a flick of the thumb, Willem pulled back the toggle joint and let it snap forwards, and we heard the click of a cartridge moving into the chamber.

"Very good," nodded Arend. He took the gun from Willem and raised it so that we could see. "This is a Luger pistol. It's a semi-automatic gun, German design."

"My old man took it off a Kraut in the war," said Dirk, provoking a communal gasp of awe from our group. "He polishes it up every Sunday."

"Which is why we're going to take good care of it," said Arend. Then, without another word, he swivelled back on his heel and a loud crack rang through the treetops. Almost as if by accident, one of the tin cans reeled and fell from its place on the stile, hitting the ground with a defeated clatter. We all jumped, exchanging looks of bewildered surprise and amusement.

"Can I try?" asked Joos.

"Come and stand behind this line," said Arend, moving behind Joos and guiding his hands to support the pistol as if he was making a ritual offering. "Don't hold it too tight; that will cause it to quiver. You want to pull the trigger slowly so it doesn't jerk. Find your target first. That's it."

Another resounding crack, but this time no cans fell.

"Bad luck," said Arend, taking the Luger from a deflated Joos. He turned to me. "Fancy a try, Marten?"

I nodded. I'd never seen a gun before, let alone been offered a chance to fire one. The Luger was surprisingly heavy, the handle already damp from two clammy palms. I edged away from Arend, asserting my ability to hold it the way he had shown Joos without needing any help. I peered along the top of the barrel, lined up the viewfinder with the centre can...

The bang sounded louder when I pulled the trigger; the gun's recoil caught me by surprise, and I let go with one hand and I stumbled back a few steps. In the same instant, another can toppled to the ground – not the one I had been aiming for, admittedly, but the others weren't to know.

"Well done," said Arend, while the other boys clapped. I'd never been applauded before, and I allowed myself to smile as I returned the Luger to him.

Willem and Filip also managed to hit the target. Adriaan came close; Pim missed. Theo struck a tree, and we gathered around to peer into the hole where the bullet had lodged. Finally, only Bastiaan remained.

"Your turn," said Arend, offering him the pistol.

Bastiaan considered it with a funny expression, as if he were looking at a dead dog. Then he shook his head.

"I don't think I'm allowed to," he said.

Dirk snorted. "What do you mean, pipsqueak?"

"My parents say I'm not to use weapons," whispered Bastiaan. "It's in the Bible. Christians can't fire guns..."

"The Bible doesn't say that," I heard myself retort. Was I afraid that Arend might think we Catholic boys were weaker than the others? "Lots of people use weapons in the Bible... the Amalekites, for instance. And David, even. Anyway, there weren't guns in ancient times, so how could anyone say that we're not supposed to use them?"

Arend nodded in approval. "Marten's right," he said patiently. "It doesn't have anything to do with being Christian. Plenty of good Christians have fought in righteous wars, after all. Like the Crusades."

Bastiaan looked unconvinced. "I don't know..." he said.

"It's not as if you'll be killing anything," said Dirk. "It's only a tin can."

Pepijn slid down from his perch on a tree stump at the edge of the clearing. "What about in self-defence – is it all right to fight then?"

Bastiaan shook his head resolutely.

"Not even then," he said. "You turn the other cheek."

The corners of Arend's mouth pulled downwards. He nodded his head, gently cupped Bastiaan's cheek with one hand and then brought the Luger down hard on the other side of his face. Bastiaan screamed, jerking away from Arend and muffling his jaw in the crook of his arm.

"Your old man should talk," sneered Arend. "He's a traitor."

"He's not!" shouted Bastiaan, seemingly oblivious to the fact that blood had started to pour from his nose. "He's the regional secretary, he's a patriot—" Pepijn lunged after Bastiaan and pulled his arms tight behind his back. Bastiaan struggled, but the older boy was twice his size. The rest of us simply watched, fascinated to see how the game would play out.

Arend approached Bastiaan, raised the Luger high in the air and fired a single shot. Bastiaan flinched and began to struggle harder. "I'm not scared," he grunted.

"Show us, then," said Arend, thrusting the Luger in front of Bastiaan. He nodded to Pepijn to release the boy's arms.

Keeping his gaze on the troop leader, Bastiaan reached for the pistol. Taking it in both hands, he let it droop limply towards the ground.

"Hold it up," said Arend. "Point it at me."

Bastiaan did as he was told. His eyes were dry and clear. At first I thought that Arend was going to challenge him to fire – it was the sort of test that he set us all the time, a test that was more in the mind than anything else, despite what he said about brains being overrated. I had done well at these tests so far, but I couldn't account for Bastiaan. He was only a little kid, after all.

Then Arend moved aside, and Bastiaan was pointing the gun at a gap between me and Willem. If we'd stretched our arms out we might just have been able to touch fingers – that was how much space there was. Bastiaan was standing about ten yards away.

"Willem and Marten, stay where you are," whispered Arend, before turning back to Bastiaan. Willem and I looked at each other nervously. It was one thing watching another boy get taught a lesson, but neither of us had bargained on being used as props. "You see the hole in that tree? You're going to shoot at it. No one will get hurt. And we'll know that what you say about your old man is true." He indicated the knotted scarf around Bastiaan's neck. "Dirk, blindfold him."

The twisted black-and-yellow scarf was our troop's official uniform. Bastiaan kept the Luger raised at shoulder height while Dirk lifted the scarf around his head and tied it snugly around his face, covering his eyes and nose.

"This isn't fair," pouted Bastiaan. "The others could see."

No, it isn't fair, I wanted to say. But I was already a part of the exercise; if I protested it would only make me look afraid.

"Turn around," said Arend.

"But I won't know if I'm facing the right way," protested Bastiaan.

"Do it," said Arend. When the boy was facing the tree once more, Arend strode up behind him and gripped him by the shoulders. "Now it's just a matter of visualizing your target," he said. "Remember the tree. Aim for it in your mind. Then shoot." He glanced up at the rest of us. "In the heat of battle, the enemy can become invisible," he explained. "At those times, we have to trust our inner eye."

"Go on, Bastiaan," said Dirk. "Shoot."

"He's too scared," sneered Pepijn. A part of me wished that Bastiaan would aim at him.

"Come on, Bastiaan," said Adriaan, adding a sole note of encouragement to the chorus. "You can do it."

Bastiaan wavered, elbows locked, clutching the pistol with white knuckles. For the first time, I noticed how small his hands were.

"Are you sure I'm pointing it in the right direction?" he said.

"Positive," said Arend. "You're lined up for a bull's-eye."

"You can do it, Bastiaan," echoed Joos and Filip.

"Marten? Willem?" barked Arend.

"Come on Bastiaan," I beckoned. "You can do it."

In that moment, I learnt how easy it was to switch out of myself. With just a little concentration, it was possible to become someone else: a political prisoner pressed against a wall in front of a firing squad. I could protect myself like this, without seeming afraid. It was a good trick.

When the gun fired, a sudden fluttering exploded from the target tree. Bastiaan tore the blindfold from his head just in time to see a flock of wood pigeons burst into the air, climbing, climbing desperately to reach the safety of the sky while the other boys broke into raucous hoots and cheering.

I dreamt about the birds that night. I dreamt that I had been one of them, that I managed to haul myself out of the bramble and swim breathlessly through the air, climbing, climbing, until I was directly overhead and the members of our little party were as small and insignificant as pinpricks. When I looked up, my brother was there, waiting for me.

Extending one hand to pull me up into the heavens, with the other he thrust the Luger between my eyes, so that I was peering directly into the darkness of the barrel.

10

As the flock swooped in a bell curve from the treetops and up again – higher, higher into the blue until they resembled the powdery aftermath of a fireworks display – Glen leant back onto her elbows and closed her eyes.

"They do make a noise, don't they? Those parrots."

"They're lorikeets," said the boy.

Glen opened her eyes and peered up into the trees once more, pointing at the flutter of green wings. "What, those?"

"Those are barbets," he said.

Glen smiled at his solemn expression, pointed with concentration as he carefully folded his fourth sheet of paper. Hollar had only recently introduced her to his collections – wine labels and paper cranes, mainly – and it seemed a small victory that their conversation should have lasted this long.

"Well, I know what that is, anyway," she said, pointing to a peacock as it picked its way across the gravel path and disappeared into the overgrowth.

"Do you know what a group of peacocks is called?"

Glen shook her head.

"A muster."

"Are you sure?"

The boy nodded. He popped another crane into the basket. When there were enough, Glen had agreed to help him string a vast mobile together to suspend from his bedroom ceiling. "Do you know what a group of cranes is called?" he asked.

"Not an inkling."

"No, not an inkling." This was only the third time in as many weeks that she had seen Hollar smile. "A sedge."

Colonnades of palm trees crisscrossed the botanical gardens, charting a controlled course around artificial lakes, foliage and expanses of neatly trimmed lawn. Althea had insisted on choosing a spot as far from the path as possible – "Otherwise, we'll spend the whole afternoon being interrupted by people who know Mummy" – and so the trio had ended up in a remote corner behind the orchid house.

Glen had sighed with relief when they'd finally made it into the serenity of the gardens after navigating the busy thoroughfare that encircled the grounds. Battling through the thicket of rickshaws, street vendors and beggars had proved difficult without Micah's guidance. But she was glad to have achieved something on her own, at last. Never mind the unwelcome stares from men loitering outside the gates – businessmen and hawkers, and coolies crouched on the stone steps, waiting on their masters like hounds – to which the children seemed oblivious but which had made her feel suddenly, and acutely, a woman.

The weight of their gaze, she scrawled in the journal at her side, *bore through me like a die. It was not enough that I was acting as a chaperone to two children; to them, it must have appeared strange that there was no one to chaperone me. Now I feel foolish for having been embarrassed by it: if the gawkers had wanted something to stare at, I should have given it to them! Well – next time.*

Two weeks had passed since she had last written to Pieter, and already Glen was aware that she was storing up fragments for her next missive. Talking with Annabel was one thing, but her aunt was so robustly practical, and there were things that Glen could feel brimming about the periphery of her consciousness which seemed too trivial to bother her with – a nagging, uneasy sensation which Annabel would no doubt put down to unfamiliarity with island life.

But there was more to it than mere dislocation, and Glen couldn't help but suspect that it was a feeling which must be shared by her prisoner: poor Pieter, living outside of time and place, beyond the gossip and haggling of the market square, the simple patterns of domestic life. In his latest letter, he had responded to her island "tour" with a description of his own world.

The prison is laid out like a star, with five big corridors going out from the centre. This is so the guards can isolate us if there is a riot. Like breaking off a dead branch to save the rest of the tree. It is very clever, because if you don't know that the others are scared you are less likely to feel scared yourself. And if you don't think that the others will revolt, you are less likely to take that chance on your own. Prison makes us feel far away from people just on the other side of the wall.

Here, Glen had begun to understand a similar sensation of standing on the fringes, and she realized that her interest in Pieter was no longer merely the trawling curiosity of a would-be journalist. That voice, simple and halting, had become an anchor to her. It was the voice of someone who was even more lost than she was.

"What are you writing?" asked Althea, glancing up from Nikolai as the tortoise began to nibble the cabbage leaf in her hand.

"Just thoughts," replied Glen, closing the book and placing it by her head to lie down. "Nothing important."

As soon as she had caught whiff of the idea that Mrs Cornish wanted them to meet for tea at the Club that afternoon, Glen had offered to take the children on an outing to the botanical gardens. After the dance party, Glen had found herself avoiding the Club whenever possible. As if the young people's "do" hadn't been enough, Mrs Cornish seemed intent on inducting Glen into the Women's Committee teas – but the tearooms, with their pungent smell of dying flowers, were all too redolent of her mother's world. Round about now, she imagined, the other women would be picking away at petits fours and airily reproducing their husbands' views on rearmament. No comment or gesture would escape the steely gaze of a lithographed Queen Victoria presiding pudding-like over her ladies' empire.

Perhaps Glen had been a little harsh on Mrs Cornish, who never missed an opportunity to remind the other women of her husband's status as a medical officer. Glen had only recently learnt that the Moodie family, like railway workers and colonial merchants, were mere *boxwallahs*: a different caste altogether. It was one thing that her uncle had risen from being a lowly creeper to a *periya dorai* with his own estate in just a few years, but this fact meant little to his English peers. Now that he had flown the coop, it was surprising that Mrs Cornish deigned to associate with their family at all...

Glen awoke suddenly to realize that the children had disappeared, and a moment of panic jolted her into cold consciousness. Then she heard Althea's laugh, and turned to see two small figures playing by the edge of the pond.

"What are you doing?" she called – and was shocked to hear her mother in her voice.

"Teaching Nikolai to swim!"

Glen smiled, and reached behind her for her journal. It was only then that she noticed it: a piece of folded paper, thinner and whiter than the journal pages, discreetly inserted beneath the cover.

Unfolded, it revealed a picture, sketched in pencil, of a reclining figure. A gored skirt and the subtle peak of small breasts suggested it was a woman, though one might be forgiven for mistaking it for a princely youth from Greek mythology. The figure was deep in sleep, head angled slightly towards the viewer.

It was a picture of her.

Beneath the image, in small, careful letters, the artist had inserted four lines which she recognized from a poem studied in school:

> *The reason no man knows, let it suffice,*
> *What we behold is censured by our eyes.*
> *Where both deliberate, the love is slight:*
> *Who ever loved, that loved not at first sight?*

* * *

The children claimed not to have seen anyone come near her while they played by the pond. The only person to appear on the path, walking from the orchid house towards the eastern gates, was an elderly woman who moved so slowly she could never have crept all the way to the picnic blanket without one of them noticing.

"Well, did you see anyone else – anyone at all nearby?"

"There was an Indian gentleman sitting on that bench for a long time," said Althea, pointing to an empty seat on the pathway opposite the orchid house. "He was there when we arrived. I didn't see him leave, though."

"A gentleman? What did he look like?" The thought occurred to her that perhaps they were being watched even now, but the park seemed quite empty.

Althea scrunched up her nose in her effort to remember, enjoying the attention. "Tall, I think. Quite thin. Properly dressed – he was wearing a suit."

"No, he wasn't," said Hollar.

"Of course he was," huffed Althea. "A grey suit. And bicycle clips."

"Are you making this up?" demanded Glen.

"No!" Althea replied crossly. "Hollar's the one with imaginary friends—"

"I am not!"

Glen placed herself between them, looking Althea in the eye. "What did he look like? His face, I mean."

"Not as dark as Micah, but not fair, either," said Althea. "He didn't have a beard."

"Spectacles," said Hollar. "He had spectacles on."

Althea weighed the memory with a far-off look. Then she nodded. "Yes," she decided. "He was wearing spectacles."

The evidence was inconclusive, and as much as Glen begged the children to tell her if they saw anyone matching the man's description as they left the gardens, in the end their search was fruitless. She couldn't quite decide if she should be flattered by the mysterious note or offended – frightened, even – by the audacity of it, and so spent the journey home wondering if she had attracted a genuine admirer or merely been the butt of some silly joke. The handwriting was elegant, and the drawing very good – certainly a worthy candidate for her mass-observation album.

What better example of spontaneous, anonymous observation was there than an impromptu portrait? A token of how someone else had seen and described her.

It was the first of two brushes with mystery that week. The second occurred a few days later. Glen had opted to stay at home while Annabel took the children into town, thinking that she might use the time to quiz Perdita on any local gentlemen with a talent for drawing and some knowledge of Marlowe. But, since it was a Sunday, Perdita and Micah had already gone off to church with their daughters in the opposite direction, towards Our Lady of Peace in the village where Micah had grown up.

Finding herself alone, with an entire morning to herself and no means of leaving the plantation, Glen decided to investigate the church that Perdita had mentioned in their conversation about Hollar. It would be her own small concession to religion.

The church – she did not know if it had a name – was farther away than she had expected, about halfway down the only hillside on the estate that had not been cleared for cultivation. The incline was steep and the path heavily overgrown, and as she walked she tried not to think of snakes. When at last she reached a narrow plateau, granite slate underfoot provided the first signs of any human attempt to tame the craggy hill face and dense foliage. Closer examination showed that the tiles were, in fact, tombstones. Only four bore inscriptions that had not been wiped away by time and mudslides, and of those, three belonged to members of the same family. Two girls and a boy had died in 1872; the eldest had been only six years old. Pock-marked inscriptions revealed that they were the young victims of a brief but devastating cholera epidemic.

Gazing at those stones, the only earthly evidence of lives cut down too early even to have known the first bloom of youth – that was the phrase the poets used, wasn't it? – the girl wondered what sort of children they might have been. None would have been old enough to believe in their own deaths, that much was certain. Even Glen struggled to get her head around the thought of non-existence, and it was only at moments such as these that she tried to imagine a day when the sun would rise over these graves and she would no longer be there to feel the warmth on her skin. For that was what it must come down to, in the end: an easterly wind, tea-scented, and a headstone marked with her name and dates.

Oh, but how glorious it was to be alive!

Glen followed the gravel pathway that hugged the cliffside, marvelling at the distance that still remained between herself and the farthest depths of the valley. Looking up, it had long since become impossible to see Beulah Lodge, although a corner of Perdita's cottage remained just in view.

At last the plateau widened, opening onto a weed-strewn lawn that was at least relatively easy to walk on. And there, not ten yards from the precipice, lay the church.

The basic structure was a small, grey-stone affair in the Victorian style – similar to the village church that Glen remembered attending as a child. In almost every respect, it was unremarkable. Its uncanny location made it somewhat unusual – it was difficult to imagine what sort of congregation may once have convened here – but what struck Glen most were the walls.

They were constructed of sheer glass. One enormous pane fronted the end of the nave, while the six narrow windows on either side were entirely transparent: there was not an iron window pane or sliver of stained glass in sight. The effect was of a building less like a church than a greenhouse. From where she stood, trapped in its sad stare, Glen could see all the way down the centre aisle to the baptismal font that adjoined the entranceway: even from this distance, without having set foot inside the building itself, she counted ten rows of wooden pews.

A solitary figure – a man – sat in one of them. He was gazing out of the church: past the altar, through the window, at her.

Glen froze. Then, remembering her resolution not to be put off by gawkers – it made no difference that this man was a European – she steeled herself to meet his gaze. For several seconds, she watched him, waiting for him to avert his eyes. But he did not waver – he did not even blink. She began to pick her way across the growth-choked yard, stopping only when she realized that the man in the church was still staring in the same direction. Had he not seen her, after all?

As she tried the door, a dog began to bark from inside the church. Glen leapt back in surprise. The barking continued. By the sound of it, the dog was only small, probably no larger than Nuisance. Glen's limited experience with the canine species had led her to conclude that the smallest dogs were always the most vociferous, and she told herself that there was no reason to be afraid.

"What do you want?"

The door had swung open, and a tall man in khaki breeches and rolled shirtsleeves blocked the entrance, leaning stiffly on a Malacca cane. His drooping eyelids, angular nose and fault-line crease of a mouth made her think he looked Russian, but he sounded as English as she did. She guessed that he was about fifty.

"I was interested in seeing the church. I hope I've not disturbed you…"

Behind the man, a small white dog was pressing its snout between his master's legs to sniff out the newcomer.

"Hush, Pepys," ordered the man. His gaze remained trained somewhere over Glen's shoulder, allowing her to study the down-weeping left eye, the pockmarked cheeks and the thin, raised scar on his left jaw.

"I just wanted to see the church…"

"The church? No one wants to see the church these days," said the man, shifting his weight and tightening his grip on the doorway. "I'm the only one who comes."

"As it happens, I know someone else who comes here regularly."

The man squinted, and for the first time Glen noticed that his hooded eyelids were surprisingly bare, populated only by a sparse layer of fine, almost invisible lashes.

"A boy – my cousin."

"Your cousin?" For the first time, the man's voice betrayed interest. "Miss Moodie, then, I take it?"

Glen faltered.

"Phayre, actually," she said. "Glynis – Glen – Phayre. My aunt is Annabel Moodie."

"Ah." The man let his hands fall from the door, and he stepped back, revealing the faintest flicker of a smile. "Well, then this is virtually your property, isn't it?" His tone made Glen wonder whether this was meant to be an invitation or a challenge. But he turned around and retreated into the church, leaving the door open for her to follow.

Standing inside the building was very much like being outside. Even the roof was of glass, making the blue arc of sky a fitting heaven. There was no altar, only pews and a stone font which had long ago been built into the foundations.

The man was walking slowly down the aisle, running one hand along the ridge of pews while his dog trotted at his side. His slow pace only thinly concealed a subtle limp. At last he returned to the same seat he had occupied when Glen had first seen him, propping the cane between his knees.

"It's very beautiful," she said.

The man did not reply.

"How do you know my cousin?"

"Hollar, is it?"

"That's right." She sank into a pew across the aisle and began to wonder how a blind man could possibly have managed the descent along the hill face.

"We met here two weeks ago."

"Our housemaid says that the coolies think this place is haunted," said Glen.

"They are too afraid of silence."

Glen gazed about the glass shell. "It doesn't feel haunted. I'm sure Hollar wouldn't come here if he thought it was."

"He comes here to think, as I do. It turns out that we share an interest in history."

"History?" Glen smiled. "That's news to me. Hollar likes birds. He collects wine labels. He's never mentioned history."

"He's a living piece of lost history," said the man. "He's a conundrum."

"Our housemaid is convinced that he suffers from delusions." Glen flinched as the dog began licking at her ankles. "Your dog's called Pepys?"

"That's right. Don't worry, he won't bite."

"Unusual name for a dog."

"Rather like Nuisance."

"So Hollar has told you about the menagerie? His sister's tortoise?"

"Step-sister, I take it."

"That's right." Glen wondered why she had not begun to feel more uncomfortable by the man's uncanny familiarity with her family. "You haven't told me your name, though."

"Royce. Emil Royce." Glen fancied that the shadow of a smile teased his mouth. "*Captain* Emil Royce."

"You're in the Army, then?"

"I was. Recently decommissioned."

The girl smiled. "You must be the one Mrs Cornish was on about at tea the other day," she said. "No white person passes through Nanu Oya without her knowing. Is it true that you speak Hindi?"

"It is."

"You weren't stationed here, then? Nothing to do with the Planter Corps?"

"Alas, no – Central Provinces. A *barasaheb* for almost thirty years."

"A bara—"

"A big man – a *farangi* with power. I sat in judgement of villagers who participated in the dacoities." He reached down to fondle his dog's ears. "I'm glad to be rid of it."

"Dacoities? Peasant revolts?"

"The Indians would have called it a nationalist rebellion." Royce sniffed. "We English are slightly snooty about these things, you know. Nationalism isn't a word we like; it reminds us of French peasants braying for the guillotine." He lifted Pepys onto his lap.

"How did you sentence them? The peasants, I mean."

"Some were executed, others imprisoned. Many claimed to have had no interest in a rebellion; they'd been bullied into it, they said, or swept up in the fighting."

"They're not true Nationalists, then." Glen noticed Royce flinch. "I mean, that's just the kind of thing Mr Gandhi would hold against the British. Using vague ideas like Crown and Country to justify our rule over a country the size of Europe…"

"The Congress are no better," interrupted the Captain. "You mustn't be fooled by dear Mr Gandhi's rhetoric. His political homeland is equally bound up with religion and nationhood. *Ethnicity*." He spat the word with a sudden jerk of the head. "In twenty years, you see if Hollar is any more welcome here than in his father's country."

The girl perked up at this. "You know Hollar's father, then?"

"No." Royce gently removed Pepys, who had begun to struggle from his lap. The dog scurried on bandy legs to the east front of the building and peered out at a flock of wood hens emerging from the bracken.

"Do you know many people in the area?"

"Not many, no. I'm staying at a guest house run by a Burgher woman. I've met a few of the locals." He smiled again. "I don't make a habit of visiting the Club, if that's what you mean. It's all a bit Little England for me."

"I don't suppose you've met a certain Indian gentleman, then – well educated, with a talent for drawing?"

"That, I'm afraid, is something rather difficult for me to judge," said the man, and Glen was suddenly relieved that he could not see the colour rise to her cheeks. "Scarlet fever did it, six years ago. My sight, I mean."

"Yes."

"The most highly educated local is the schoolteacher, by all accounts."

Glen's stomach turned. "Our housemaid was telling me about a schoolteacher who's something of a local celebrity – Ganan, is it?"

"Oh, I don't know his name," replied the man with a dismiss-ive wave of the hand. "But I know his type: a good Indian boy, raised on fresh, full-fat cream from the family cow while his sis-ters went without. Hair oiled every day by a doting mother, a practice that ended when he was sent on a scholarship to an Eng-lish school. Now he wears a suit and round spectacles, cultivates a thin moustache, reads *The Times*. Affects no obvious interest in political matters and presumes to rise above talk of swaraj because to do otherwise would be to imply that he is in some way deficient, a second-class citizen. Gandhi he would dismiss as a fanatic; Nehru is slightly more to his taste. Jinnah and the Muslim League do not even cross his radar."

"You seem to know him well," replied Glen.

"Why do you ask?"

"Oh, no reason. Just a... a diversion of sorts."

"What need has a young lady such as yourself for diversions?" For the first time, the Captain grinned broadly. "I thought the white woman's burden kept one suitably occupied: baking cakes and paying visits to the local orphanage."

"I'm afraid that's not my cup of tea." Glen shifted in her seat, unsure as to whether Royce was awaiting an answer or simply playing with her. "I'm a writer, actually. Well – trying to be one. I collect stories."

"The latest story doing the rounds at my guest house is that the English ladies make a habit of playing tennis in their underwear. Is there any truth to that?"

Glen let out a laugh. "Surely that's not for me to say…"

They fell into a silence that seemed to last many minutes, and Glen soon began to wonder if the Captain had lost interest in her or had fallen asleep. As she rose from her seat, Pepys let out an excited yelp, and his owner turned sharply.

"Going already?" he asked.

"My aunt will be home soon," said Glen. Then, sparing any pause for propriety, "I don't suppose you'd like to join us for drinks sometime?"

11

By now, I was spending a lot of time thinking about my lady writer. When I wasn't reading her letters or composing my own, I would try to imagine her studying my handwriting, marvelling at my sentences and detailed illustrations. I could picture her sitting at a breakfast table in a sunny room, with a plate of toast and pots of jam in front of her on the table, a porcelain cup of Ceylon tea in one hand. Why did I imagine her hands to be slender, her fingers sticky with jam as she turned the pages torn from my school jotter? I pictured fresh crumbs falling into the crease, imagined her lightly dusting them from the paper, eager to preserve the feel and scent of something that had travelled so far.

Did she count the days since posting her last letter as I did? Did she wait, as I did, for the right moment to open the envelope, sometimes carrying it for an entire day because the anticipation of what lay inside was almost as exciting as the words themselves? Did she open the envelope as I did, taking care not to tear it? Did she raise the paper to her nose, feeling the imprint of inky writing through the page before unfolding it? I was sure that she did.

More and more, I wished that I did not have to lie to her. While I knew that the only thing which kept her writing was her pity for the prisoner, I wished that I did not have to cloak my words in Pieter's disguise. I began to hate him. Perhaps hate is too strong a word. I resented him, the way I had sometimes resented my brother. Teachers used to greet me at the beginning of the school year with warm smiles. *You must be Krelis's brother,* they would say. It was probably the same for Jesus's brothers – James and Joseph. No one ever talks about them, even though they're mentioned in the Bible. That's what it's like when your brother is the Son of God.

I wished that I didn't have to share G.P. with Pieter van Houten. I wished that he would let me have her all to myself.

Dear Pieter,

I very much enjoyed your letter, particularly the drawing! You are a fine artist. As I write to you now, I have your portrait pinned to the wall before me, so that I almost feel as if I am talking to you in person.

My aunt's foreman, who is of Burgher stock, was able to translate most of the clipping you sent, which I have now added to my scrapbook. We were both quite shocked by what we read. I am very pleased to hear that you have not had to face such ghastly treatment for your political views, whatever they may be.

I was, however, most disturbed by some of the punishments you described – electrocution! That really is beyond the pale. I sincerely hope that you have not been subjected to any such abuse. If, however, you have, I should like to write a letter to the prison authorities on your behalf. There are laws about these things, Pieter. Give me the word, and I shall lodge a complaint against the overseer that will make his head spin.

Almost at once, my heart began to race. No – no, she must definitely not attempt any such thing.

Dear G.P.,

Please do not write to the prison authorities. I have not been badly treated. You must understand: here it is very dangerous for anyone to stand out. We want only to fit in, to be invisible. Please do not write to complain. Write only to me.

Putting words to the page calmed me a little. Still, I must be more careful in the future.

I returned to her letter.

So: to happier subjects. You asked about my aunt's adopted son. Well, I can tell you that the lad is very clever, if painfully shy. He is what is crudely referred to here as a "half-caste", although he speaks perfect English and is not terribly dark. Like you, he sometimes has nightmares. I have asked him if he knows how to make invisible ink, and he says he does not. He is very interested in birds, however, and I enclose an origami crane which he gave me several days ago. I hope that you like it!

I may not have told you that it is my aspiration to be a writer. Well, my first and only collection of poems was titled Scenes from Away: *it now inhabits the literal and figurative bottom drawer at home. I had expected that being in a new place would inspire me, but at the moment I am completely frozen with terror at the thought of beginning something new, lest it not be good enough. I have been thinking quite a lot about my family – my parents and siblings at home, as well as my aunt's family here – so perhaps my next project shall be based on the subject of family relations. Some of the locals here, the Buddhists, practise ancestor worship. It is a strange concept in many ways – but I imagine that the further back one goes, the easier it becomes to forgive the errors of one's forebears.*

It does not always work so neatly between parents and their children. I used to enjoy solitary train journeys as a little girl, because they provided a sensation of freedom coupled with the cosy knowledge that there were always others I could turn to for camaraderie and protection: the kindly ticket collectors and my fellow travellers, happy folk with their lives bundled into a single suitcase. My family, our enormous house, the coterie of staff and neighbours and guests, was self-contained in a similar way, however without the same quality of exhilarating movement and freedom. Like yours, it existed according to its own laws – but sometimes these laws took on a life of their own, predators in their own right.

I rocked back on my chair the way we were told not to at school, balancing on two legs while I scanned the page for telling words. I knew *predator*. I tipped my chair forwards and picked up a pencil.

Can I tell you about bee wolves? They are insects, like hornets. The bee wolf's nest is a very strange thing. It looks ugly from the outside, but inside it is very complex and beautiful. It is strong, too, and I think the bee wolves must feel very safe when they are inside it. But do you know what happens if the queen is killed? The bee wolves start to eat each other until every last one dies. So, you see, the bee-wolf nest destroys itself, and all because of the mother.

I picked up her letter again, and wondered if I should rub out my last sentence. But no: *what I have written, I have written.* G.P. had continued:

As far as I can recall, home was Mummy: it was Mummy whom I wished to please more than Pa – anything that I did was good enough for Pa – and Mummy to whom I would eventually have to prove my independence, my selfhood. It was not, to use the old cliché, a "love-hate" relationship. It was a bond formed entirely of love – but self-love, grasping, stifling, controlling, guilt-inducing love, which sparked my impatience to flee as much as it enticed me to stay. Of course, I also felt that I had to escape from the shadow of my siblings – something that perhaps you can understand? But then I don t believe you have mentioned brothers or sisters – I'll admit that I have always assumed you were an only child, goodness knows why!

I now realize that there is so much about my own mother that I shall never know: little details of her girlhood, her first love(s?), her life as it was before we three (four, if you count Pa) crowded into it. It is hard to think that I will never know her long enough to understand her as she must feel entitled to know me. I do love her, Pieter. But you know how it is with one's parents: as one matures, one begins to see chinks in their armour...

Well, enough of that. Thank goodness for happy diversions! For a time, I had begun to wonder if perhaps coming out here had been a terrible mistake – that my hopes of adventure had been but a pipe dream, that life in the colonies should prove a terrible disappointment – but it seems I judged this place too soon. Intrigue abounds here, and what luck that I should discover myself at the centre of a mystery ripe for solving! I refer, of course, to the beguiling poem and drawing left for me at the botanical gardens – an item, based on what few clues I have managed to gather from the children and Perdita and a rather strange Englishman who visits our church, that can only be traceable to the local schoolteacher. My reasoning: he is an Indian, because the children saw no English person nearby save an elderly woman who most certainly could not have executed so sly a trick. If he is an Indian, he must nevertheless be reasonably well educated, and where we are only the schoolteacher can be said to fit this description. Yes, Pieter, it is very clever. But do you know the best thing – the thing about this that makes the tease anything but tiresome or, dare I say it, distasteful? He is, I am told, famously, swoonsomely handsome. Jayanadani herself is in love with him as only a young girl can be. Had he been an old man, I suppose I should have laughed it off with Annabel – but things now have taken on a rather more pleasing turn, and I intend to keep my investigations secret until an opportunity arises to claim my prize...

There was not enough time to translate the final paragraphs without being late for school. I returned the letter to its envelope – the paper on the inside was coloured a dusty pink, and I fancied that it smelt of tropical flowers – and slid it under my mattress with the beginning of my reply.

* * *

Latin lessons with old Mijnheer Barhydt tended to start off badly and improve as the hour progressed. Our teacher almost certainly didn't intend it to be this way: he always began by opening his book to a page of declensions and probably planned to move on to conjugations and a lecture on the ablative absolute before ending with recitations of mnemonic verse. But, inevitably, someone would ask a question – we would wait until he made a passing reference to something, anything, that might draw his attention away from gerunds and ordinal numbers – and, before he knew it, Mijnheer Barhydt was perched on his desk, beady eyes aflame, regaling the class with impassioned accounts of the crucifixion of 100,000 slaves after the Third Servile War, as well as Nero's goriest crimes.

"As stubborn as Cato!" he might exclaim, referring to a wayward student – and ten hands would shoot up, and someone would beg him to tell us who Cato was, and why he was stubborn, and what good did it do him in the end.

"Cato the Younger: the Stoic, boys! A man of highest moral integrity, scrupulously conscientious in a time of rampant corruption, who dared to oppose Caesar and his triumvirate allies – who can tell me their names?"

"Pompey and Crassus, Mijnheer!"

"Very good, very good." Mijnheer Barhydt would edge his left buttock up onto the desk, then his right, until at last he was perched like a *desem* loaf squatting in a baker's window. "Following the Battle of Thapsus – 46 BC, mark it in your books – Cato realized that he faced, at the very best, a life under Caesarean rule. Refusing to be pardoned by the man he distrusted most in the world, he took a knife to his stomach. But it doesn't end there, no, no." Here, Mijnheer Barhydt would lean forwards, wetting his fleshy lips and savouring our rapt silence. "A servant raised the alarm, and the doctors arrived in time to stitch him up. Now, what do you suppose Cato did next?"

"Tore out the stitches, Mijnheer?"

"Not only that, but his intestines, too – in order to be sure that no doctor could save him again."

I wondered if my tapeworm was listening to this.

"That's better than Seneca, Mijnheer," said Pepijn, and the other boys murmured their agreement. Seneca, we already knew, had responded to Nero's accusation of conspiracy by slitting his wrists. When he saw that his withered old veins would not bleed quickly enough, he jumped into a tub of hot water to hasten the flow. After all that, he ended up being suffocated by the steam.

Mijnheer Barhydt shook his head ruefully. "You boys – such bloodlust, it makes me worry. Sometimes I think you are no better than wild animals."

I resisted the temptation to remind him that some animals, such as bee wolves and black eagles, were actually very clever and didn't deserve to be compared to the boys in my class. But Mijnheer Barhydt had already moved on to something else. "*Mundus vult decipi*: who can translate that for me?"

My hand shot up. "'The world wishes to be deceived', Mijnheer."

"Commonly attributed to Petronius. Long before he came along, Plato noticed something similar. You boys know the story of Leontius, don't you?"

"No, Mijnheer," we chorused.

"Plato tells us that Leontius, passing by a pile of executed criminals, could not resist the temptation to let his gaze linger over the gruesome scene. He became inebriated on this vision of blood, and damned his own eyes for their greed."

"Then what happened, Mijnheer?" asked Pepijn. Surely Leontius would gouge out his eyes, at the very least? It seemed a suitably violent fate.

But for the first time, Mijnheer Barhydt had no answer. "Is that not enough?" he asked – before reaching for his book and instructing us to turn to a new chapter.

12

Returning to the servants' house to search for a darning needle, Perdita discovered that Nimali had forgotten her school tiffin.

"That girl is getting more forgetful every day," she huffed, re-entering the drawing room. "Well, she will have to go hungry. Perhaps Jayanadani will give her some *puttu* at lunchtime."

Glen let the darning drop to her knee. "Let me take it," she said.

Perdita eyed her suspiciously. "But it is too hot to walk to the school now," she said. "Anyway, the girl must learn her lesson."

"It's not that hot, Perdita. And it's horrid trying to concentrate with a rumbling stomach." Glen had already packed the darning away. "I'll be there and back in time for my own lunch. Where is the tiffin?"

"Inside, missy-mem." The housemaid clicked her tongue. "I would not be doing this, otherwise she will never learn. Here," – she reached for one of Annabel's sun hats – "wear this, or you will burn to a *crisp*."

Glen had never followed the road that led to the village school before, although she knew that there was little to it: a footbridge over a pretty stream, a red dirt track past a tea hut, and there it would be...

There it was. The schoolhouse was larger than she'd expected, and less rustic – Glen chastised herself for her patronizing presumptions – with a tidy garden around one side and a paved square marked out for games. A rather smart bicycle was propped against a neem tree that shaded the porch. The students were inside, and their voices carried breezily through an open window. *Two twelves are twenty-four, three twelves are thirty-six...*

She approached the open window and peered across the rows of dark heads – cropped hair to the left, braids to the right, seated in order of age from front to back. And at the front, presiding over this picture of sweet harmony, unity in discipline, a tall figure. It was obvious why Jayanadani blushed when she spoke of him. Dressed in white shirt and linen slacks, he held his pencil like a baton as he tapped time to the chorus of voices. *Five twelves are sixty, six twelves are seventy-two…*

She knew that this was a transgression: not only to spy, but to enjoy the spying. Examining the person who had only recently – and without permission – examined her.

"Missy-mem!"

Twenty-two heads turned in surprise as Nimali bounded towards the window.

"I'm so sorry," said Glen, barely bringing herself to look the schoolteacher in the eye. He had removed his spectacles and allowed the pencil to drop onto the desk. "Nimali forgot her tiffin…"

"Thank you, Miss Glen!"

Some of the students began to giggle, and at once their teacher resumed command.

"I did not ask you to stop," he said, striding across the room so that his back was turned to her. "*Eight twelves are ninety-six…*"

Glen retreated from the window just far enough so that the seated children would no longer be able to see her, but that he still might. Did she imagine that their eyes met for the briefest of moments? Did she imagine that the hint of a smile crossed that stern face? That a glimmer of amusement – at her, at himself, at whatever it was they now shared – entered his voice when he said, "And now I think we will turn our attention to some poetry"?

Perhaps she did. But this did not stop her heart dancing as she turned towards home.

* * *

Women could only ever be "permanent guests" of the European Club and, as Glen was without an escort, her presence in the Palm Room was conspicuous. Two ladies had already wandered by to interrogate her – an interrogation, yes, despite the polite smiles and gentle queries after Annabel's health – but the bland exchange had been thankfully brief. With fifteen minutes remaining before Althea would emerge from her riding lesson, the English girl had settled into a cane chair by the window overlooking the lawns. Two older men – military types, she surmised – were drinking brandies at the bar. Behind the closed doors of the Hall, an amateur dramatics group was rehearsing *The Pirates of Penzance*. Piano music tinkled down the corridor, interrupted now and then by sudden bursts of laughter.

The girl considered her reply to Pieter's letter. Correspondence was becoming a kind of meditation for Glen, who found the one-sided conversation far more satisfying than the usual struggle to extract the right combination of words for a quatrain or sonnet. Here, too, was the possibility that her words might one day graduate to a new life. Her sister had often spoken of a German pen friend she'd had before the war, a girl called Bettina who had been paired with Merle by the language mistress at school. The correspondence had ended abruptly two years later, and Merle still occasionally mentioned that she wondered what had come of Bettina in the war.

Dear Pieter,

What a relief it was to hear that you have not been harmed. I will, of course, respect your wishes and reserve any communication with the prison authorities until such time as you inform me of any change in your situation.

You may be interested to know that I have finally managed to catch a glimpse of my mysterious admirer – and, it pleases me greatly to say, I was not disappointed by the early indications. Does the thought scandalize you, Pieter, that a white woman may find a man of another race attractive? But some of the greatest romances of all time crossed boundaries many people would have considered insurmountable: why, just think of Anthony and Cleopatra; and, in our own time, the glorious Nancy Cunard and Henry Crowder. They don't care what others think of their transgression: they care only for art, and life, and love. This is what binds them, not the petty conventions of so-called high society and the politics of race and class.

It is easy to speak of these matters lightly from here; in Europe, I know, it is quite another story. I must admit, I'm not terribly up to date with political movements – but I do know that I wouldn't trust my shoddiest hat with most of the men who would lead Europe today. It seems to me that ordinary folk are caught between a rock and a hard place: communism or fascism? What a choice that must be.

The world needs clear thinkers, Pieter: people who can see through the wool that some would try to pull over our eyes. Tyrants desire to keep us ignorant. Stereotypes and generalizations are the recourse of extremists who wish to deny us self-knowledge, self-understanding.

Voices outside drew her attention, and she moved closer to the window. At the far end of the lawn, an Indian gentleman had been stopped by two English youths. A gentleman, surely, because he carried a set of cricket stumps under one arm and was dressed in white flannels, canvas plimsolls and a pressed shirt that was open at the neck. Lean but square-shouldered, he towered over the other two, who could not have been long out of school.

"You've not told us where you're planning to go with those, old boy," one of the youths was saying, in a too-loud voice. "Has your *mahatteya* sent you?"

The Indian gentleman raised himself to his full height, and Glen realized with sudden horror that it was the schoolteacher.

"You must have missed the sign," the other youth said, pointing to the entrance behind them. It took Glen a moment to realize the one he meant: a neatly printed panel that hung just below the plaque advertising the European Club's centenary. DOGS AND INDIANS NOT ALLOWED, it read.

Tiny pinpricks of anger and humiliation scattered up the back of her neck. She had never felt shame like this before.

The Indian gentleman must have said something impertinent then, as the two youths simultaneously made for him. One tore the cricket stumps from under his arm, while the other grabbed him by the shoulder, hissing: "Easy does it, old boy."

Glen froze with fury, at once wishing that she could do something and hating herself for thinking that this would only make things worse.

The youth who now held the cricket stumps dropped all but one. He twirled it playfully at the man, who had finally lowered his head to stare at the ground.

"Just another *sakkili*, aren't you?" laughed the first youth.

Glen remembered how the schoolteacher had looked at the head of his classroom: commanding and composed, adored by regiments of dark-haired children.

Again he said something, and the other two burst out in guffaws. "I do beg your pardon, sir!" chortled one.

How strange, thought the girl, to feel both pity and admiration for a person: to hate the indignity of his situation, and to love the singular pride and composure – the gentleness, the gentility – in the face of his tormentors.

At this point, the military men who had been drinking at the bar emerged onto the veranda. One of them called after the youths, who stole a final, contemptuous glance at the Indian gentleman before slouching off. The smaller fellow – the one who had twirled the wicket – sang as he went. "*Swaami – How I love ya, how I love ya…*"

When they were out of sight, the schoolteacher bent down to collect the stumps. As he straightened, Glen drew back from the window with a thumping heart. After several seconds, she gathered the courage to look again – but by this time, he was gone.

"Dreaming again, Glynis? *Coo-ee*!" Glen turned to discover Mrs Cornish waving at her from across the table. "I say, you were miles away!" She squeezed herself into the chair opposite the girl and tilted her head at the paper in Glen's hand. "Writing a letter home? You must be ever so lonely, Glynis, stuck all the way up on the estate with Annabel working all hours. You really should think of joining in our little production – this year we're raising funds for Aid to Spain…"

"I honestly shouldn't think I'd be much help."

"Do you know my great-uncle was the first musical director of a European Club show? That's going back seventy-five years, now." She winked. "Colonial service has been a family calling for a very long time. All the boys taken on their first tiger shoot by the time they turned three…"

"There was an Indian gentleman outside just now, in cricket whites," interrupted Glen. "Do they usually play here?"

Mrs Cornish pursed her lips and nodded significantly. "Oh yes – he'll be one of the local team. Strictly professionals only, you understand. They're allowed to use the far pitch one afternoon a week." She arched her eyebrows. "New rules. If you ask me, it's a mistake…"

"Glen?" Althea had appeared in the doorway, fresh from her lesson.

"Althea, darling, you've tracked in half the stables!" fussed Mrs Cornish, launching herself at once from the chair and clattering across the tiled floor to shepherd the girl outside. "Haven't you any other shoes? Doesn't Mummy send you with a change of clothes? Just look at the state of your jodhpurs!"

Glen hurriedly gathered the letters and edged into the hallway.

"We really must be off, Cee," she said, trying to sound apologetic. "If Althea weren't in such desperate need of a wash I would have suggested drinks. You are still coming round this weekend, I hope?"

"Wouldn't miss it for the world! We're so looking forward to meeting the Captain. Now remember what I said about the musical, hm? The chorus could still use a little filling out." As usual, Mrs Cornish's chirpy optimism belied her insistence on having the final word. "*Poor wand'ring one! Though thou hast surely strayed, take heart of grace, thy steps retrace, poor wand'ring one…*"

* * *

She returned to her letter that evening. Outside, the birds continued to chirrup in the trees long after the sun had set.

Reading over what she had written at the Club, Glen realized that there remained a fundamental imbalance in her relationship with Pieter which had nothing to do with the language barrier. The stormy, brooding idols of her girlish fantasies were men she imagined herself making less lonely, less vulnerable: the attraction seemed to lie in that imbalance. Did Pieter sense this? Did he feel patronized by her attention? Did he ridicule her letters in front of his fellow inmates; make crude comments about her to impress them? There was a humbling thought.

What I saw this afternoon made me realize how many things there are that we do not talk about here. Only the other day, I tried to ask Annabel about Hollar – where he had come from, what had prompted her decision to take him in – but she has always maintained that the house was simply too large for her and Althea once Uncle Ray had left, and she liked the idea of having a boy, a member of the family, to manage the place come the day that she no longer could. But Annabel, for all her warmth, still seems to keep a small part of herself closed off to me, and indeed everyone else. It is vexing, Pieter, and although I try not to resent her desire for privacy on what must no doubt be very sensitive matters, I could not resist pressing her by asking what she knew of the child's history. Even then, alas, the only reply I managed to extract was a rather curt "What matters is the present, not the past."

But Pieter, surely the past matters tremendously – and to try to convince ourselves otherwise is to be guilty of a grave deception?

Well, I suppose it would be a shame to end on such a down note, so I shall pass on a rather more light-hearted query from my little cousin, who hopes you might help her to settle a dispute she is having with Perdita. Althea asks: who do you think are wiser, children or grown-ups? (I don't suppose there's any need for me to tell you what she would like your answer to be.)

Ever yours,

G.P.

13

Once upon a time, Nijs had sung in the choir at school. Our teacher never tired of telling us that Nijs must thank God every day for giving him such a beautiful natural instrument. The year we turned twelve, however, Nijs's voice started to break: though he could still hold a tune, the purity of the sound had vanished for ever. One morning, on the walk to school, he told me that he would never forgive God for giving him something wonderful only to take it away. He called it a betrayal.

I thought of Krelis and wondered if I would ever forgive my brother for leaving us. I didn't tell Nijs this, because that would have meant explaining everything.

Instead, I asked him if he knew the song about the Flemish Lion.

> *Pity the mindless who, deceptive and treacherous,*
> *Feign to pet the Flemish Lion, only to strike him down:*
> *He sees their every moment,*
> *And when he is wronged, he shakes his mane with a mighty*
> *roar!*

Nijs didn't know it. I asked him if he wanted me to teach him the words, but he told me that he was never going to sing again.

"And even if I did, it wouldn't be a stupid song about a stupid lion that doesn't even exist," he said.

I could have told him that the lion was a symbol, but Nijs wasn't interested; he was probably still sore about not being in the troop. I didn't press him, because I knew that I would get to sing it later that afternoon with the others as we hiked across the fields to our meeting. The bigger the group, the better it sounded.

He hungers for revenge; he will not be taunted by their bait.
With blazing eyes, he launches towards the foe,
He tears, destroys, crushes, bleeds –
And when he has achieved victory, he laughs over his en-
emy's trembling corpse.

I got goosebumps just thinking about it. The other lion I knew about – the one the Prophet Isaiah said would lie down with the lamb – wasn't nearly as impressive. It was also obviously untrue, because lions are carnivorous, and killing is what they do best.

That evening, our group arrived at the clearing in high spirits. Arend was already there. We thought that he would join in the final verse with us, his strident baritone giving strength to our reedy voices, but he was too busy scowling over a newspaper that he held open upon one knee. As we finished the song, he folded the newspaper and considered us sternly. It was clear that something wasn't right.

"Miners' strikes and hunger marches: is this what our country has been reduced to?" Arend flung the paper to the ground and fixed us with eyes that seemed to spark, just like the lion in the song. "Sit down, and listen closely."

We did as we were told.

"A frightened child wants to run to his father: but what happens when that father is not there to comfort him?" He paused for effect. I thought of Jesus on the cross, crying out *Father, Father, why have you forsaken me?* but then I realized that Arend wasn't talking about God. "A nation that forgets its glorious past is like a drunkard who allows his family to wander about in rags."

Pepijn shot me a look, which I pretended to ignore.

"Who here wishes to inherit his father's life?" Arend turned to Filip. "You? Will you be like your old man, who has just sold his business to a German Jew who doesn't speak a word of Dutch?"

Before Filip could answer, Arend confronted Dirk. "Or yours, a drooling fool who would have done his family a service to die at Klerken?"

"Mind your tongue," snapped Dirk. I wondered if he was going to ask where Arend's father was – according to Pepijn, our leader had lived with an uncle ever since his mother died of tuberculosis in the epidemic – but he seemed to think better of it.

"A godless lout who will grope anything in a skirt?" Arend barked at Theo, who looked as if he might burst into tears behind his wire-rimmed spectacles. Arend pointed his finger at Pim and Joos and Bastiaan. "And yours: invalids, scavengers and syphilitics! Layabouts who drink the dole to forget the hungry eyes of their wives and children!"

I thought of what G.P. had written about ancestor-worship and forgiveness, but decided on balance that now probably wasn't a good time to mention my English friend.

"His dad's an accountant," Willem said, indicating Adriaan.

"Swindlers and embezzlers – that's all accountants are. Do you call that an upright profession, adding up francs all day?"

Willem shook his head triumphantly while Adriaan stared at the ground. Arend turned to me. "And you, Kuypers—"

I chewed my lip, praying that he wouldn't say anything against Krelis. Father was fair game – I was as ashamed of him as the other boys were of theirs – but if my brother's secret came out, I'd never be allowed to stay in the troop. I tried to switch myself off the way I had when Arend made Bastiaan point the gun at me, but it was hard to concentrate on becoming someone different with the troop leader waiting for an answer.

"What do you want, Kuypers?" Arend's voice was no longer so full of anger.

"I – I don't know," I mumbled. Then, I had a vision of Pieter van Houten – grimly returning his interrogator's stare across an empty desk, squinting in the light of a naked bulb angled towards his face. I set my jaw and added, a little more loudly, "A free Flanders."

"And?"

"And an end to communism and Jewry."

"You see?" Arend declared to the rest of the troop. "Here is a lad who will not settle for his father's life. Here is a lad whose respect must be earned. A lad who demands to be respected in turn."

Whereas moments before I had been terrified of the troop leader – terrified of what he could do to me and my family – now

I felt only gratitude and a strange, desperate yearning. Listening to him was different from listening to Father Goossens's sermons; Arend's words made me want to hear more.

"There won't be any activity today," he told us. "Go home, and think about what I have said."

* * *

I don't know about the others, but later the same evening I did just that.

> Dear G.P.,
>
> Here is what I know about politics:
>
> The Vlaams Nationaal Verbond is now the most popular party in Belgium, more popular than the Rexists or the Workers' Party. Why is this? Because the Flemish people are tired of being weak, and the VNV helps us to be strong again. It may not be perfect, but you have to belong somewhere, don't you?
>
> The VNV and the Church have a common enemy: communism. Why is communism bad? Because it is the communists who are killing the priests in Spain. Ask yourself, how can a Catholic support this? It would be like a cow going into a restaurant and ordering stoofkarbonaden.

I put my pencil down and reread what I had written.

> We must all make choices now. There are people here who are helping me to do what is right. Arend is the leader. I think he sees promise in me, like you do. Arend says that the war has already started. Not with guns and tanks and aeroplanes – not yet. But a line has been drawn in the sand.
>
> You asked me if I think the past matters. I don't know, but I think there are things we don't talk about because we want to think that the past is over and done with, when it isn't. We want to say: so-and-so died on this day; that is the end of it. But that's a lie. Death is a lie.

I stopped writing, and realized that my heart had started to pound against my ribs like a bird beating its wings against the bars of a cage. I had to wipe the pencil on my shirt to make it less slippery in my hand.

It is hard to think so much about these things. The others are like sheep; they don't worry so much. But sometimes I get tired of lying to everyone. Did you know that ants can carry objects many times their own weight? Lying feels like this, only it weighs about as much as a house. I like to think that carrying this weight will make me strong, because if I can prove that I am strong then Father will be proud of me. Perhaps I am not as clever as everyone thinks I am. Tell Althea: grown-ups are wise, but it is the youth who are brave. Now, more than anything, I want to be brave.

I read through what I had written so far, and decided that Arend would be proud to see that I was writing like a true martyr to our cause. Satisfied, I tucked the letter beneath my mattress to finish in the morning, whistling a little tune to myself.

They will never tame him, as long as a Fleming lives,
As long as the lion can claw, as long as he has teeth…

14

When Glen discovered her aunt bent double under the bonnet of Uncle Ray's jalopy, her initial reaction was to grab the locking wrench from Annabel's hand and hurl it clear across the garage. Her aunt was clearly losing the battle with the oil filter – an ongoing saga which had fuelled endless dinner-table rants and heated debates with Micah. She gently suggested that they call a mechanic to fix the problem once and for all, only to be received with gales of laughter.

"Are you offering to pay for that crook to haul his lazy backside up this mountain and fiddle with my car to replace one problem with ten others?" retorted her aunt. "Because if you are, then there really is no doubt in my mind that you are your mother's daughter." Registering her niece's affronted scowl, she smiled apologetically through a tangle of spark plugs and coil leads. "Honestly, darling, I just need to get this new filter to fit the gasket and we'll be away to the races…"

A roll of thunder silenced them both. Glancing up in surprise at the steep afternoon sky, streaked in yellow and pink, Glen realized that it was only the distant echoing of a skin drum dismissing the tea pickers from work.

"I'm sure that Micah said he knew what the problem was," she said. "Something about a belt…"

"Micah's at Mass," huffed Annabel. "He'd sooner participate in two thousand years of misery than do something useful."

"Whatever do you mean?" laughed Glen, leaning against the open door.

"The Crusades, the Inquisition, Puritanism, witch trials…" She darted Glen a significant look. "All in God's name."

"Oh, I see. *Church*."

"A footstool for tyranny and a mask for ignorance. As if there weren't enough wonderful, unexplainable things in life, someone felt we needed God, too." Annabel poked her head around the bonnet and indicated an oily rag at Glen's feet.

Glen tossed the rag to her aunt and cast about for something with which to wipe her fingers. "I suppose so," she replied, reaching for a towel that had been left on the patched-up seat. Not since university had she bothered herself with these sorts of debates; flippancy had become second nature, as if to replace the boxes of haughty, studiously crafted college essays that now gathered dust in her parents' attic. Lowering her voice, she said, "Do you know what Hollar asked me the other day? *How shall I go to Heaven knowing that Ranjit will be in Hell?*" Hollar was far too old for imaginary friends. "Who's Ranjit?"

Annabel rolled her eyes. "My manager's little boy, a Buddhist. I certainly didn't teach Hollar this twaddle. He must have caught it from the Mission Society." She disappeared behind the bonnet once more, and Glen assumed that her aunt had let the subject drop. But no. "A writer should be the last person to consider any book holy," declared Annabel into the engine's depths. "You of all people should know this. Your art is the art of deception: creating a world for readers to believe in. It's all imaginary, though, isn't it?" She let out a long sigh and closed the bonnet. "The irony is, books will always do a better job of opening men's eyes, and their hearts, than religion ever will."

"But simple faith—"

"*Faith*," grinned Annabel, reaching for the clean towel, "is no different from your father's diets: if it makes him feel better, fine. Superstition is a darn sight less dangerous than religion. You don't have to have lived here all your life to understand that, darling."

Glen allowed her gaze to wander beyond the open garage doors and across the valley. The tea fields below were still now, emptied of workers' bodies and the hum of human exertion for another day. Leaves fluttered; a monkey cried out. Then there was silence.

"Do we need anything else for this evening?" asked the girl, monitoring her tone carefully. There was no point in winding Annabel up with only a few hours to spare before their guests began to arrive.

"Can't think of anything. I'm dreading it."

"Oh, don't say that! I can't wait for you to meet Emil."

Convincing the Captain to come to their soirée had not been an easy feat; two days earlier, the English girl had plied him with promises of her uncle's finest spirits, which had remained untouched in the drinks cabinet for almost a year now.

"It won't be a ghastly sit-down affair," she had assured him. "Annabel doesn't go in for productions, and she's only invited the Cornishes out of a sense of duty. I could use an ally in there, you know, I really could. Oh, *do* say you'll come, even if just for a bit?"

"I'll come for a bit."

The afternoon sloped gently towards evening with the same grudging ambivalence. Glen, jittery at the thrill of prospective company, lingered over her choice of outfit for a good hour before helping Annabel to prepare the children for supper and bed. By the time the Cornishes arrived fresh from dinner at the Club, the sky had darkened to a dusty pink. The Walshes followed soon after. Having provided them all with drinks, Glen returned to the veranda to greet their final guest.

Although the Burgher driver had not been allowed to help him from the car, Royce's gruff protestations would not deter the English girl. She greeted him with a kiss on each cheek, brushing his scar with smiling lips, and guided him by one arm towards the garden path. Her tenderness silenced him.

"Oh, darling Pepys has come, too!"

The Captain smiled awkwardly, snapping his fingers for the little mutt to follow. "He doesn't like being left alone. And he can be a help in social situations."

"We shall introduce him to Nuisance. They'll be fast friends, I'm sure of it."

Glen led her friend up the steps and past the blind through the front door and stopped as they encountered Althea on the stairs, gripping the newel post.

"Shouldn't you be in bed, darling? Hollar's already gone up. It's almost nine."

"I'm waiting for Mummy."

Annabel appeared in the hallway, already the harried hostess. A smudge of grease remained on her chin from her recent battle with the car, and Glen marvelled at her aunt's carelessness. Annabel scooped an arm around her daughter's waist and smiled towards Emil. "Come and meet Glen's friend, darling, then say goodnight."

Althea's face betrayed disappointment at the sight of him. "Oh. I thought it might be the Indian gentleman."

"Who?" asked Annabel.

"The one from the gardens."

"No, Althea – this is Captain Royce," interjected Glen, hastily.

"Emil, please," smiled the Captain. He gestured at the dog lurking behind his legs. "And this is Pepys. He can be a little shy."

The little girl peered up at him, thoughtful. "Do you draw pictures, too?" she asked.

"What a strange thing to ask," said her mother.

"I'm afraid I don't," replied Emil.

"Say goodnight, now, darling."

"They were playing a game, you see…" persisted Althea.

"I'll take her, Annabel," said Glen.

"No, darling, you stay and introduce Captain Royce to the others. Come along, sweetheart."

"It was just a game, Mummy…" The reproachful look of a child denied access to adult company. "Goodnight, Emil."

As mother and daughter disappeared upstairs, Glen gently nudged her friend to continue through the narrow hallway. "The sitting room is on the right," she said, leading him. "Here we are."

The other guests rose with polite smiles as they entered. Glen noticed that Mrs Cornish did not seem to know where to look – could one meet a blind man in the eye? – so she hurried through the introductions. "Everybody, this is Captain Emil Royce. Of Jabalpur Division. Emil, this is Alice Walsh, and her husband Monty… and Cecily Cornish and her husband, Walter. And that was my aunt, Annabel, on the stairs."

"I'm very pleased to meet you all," said Emil stiffly. "I hope you won't mind that I've brought my dog."

"But of *course* not!" beamed Mrs Walsh, too eagerly.

Pepys remained crouched in the doorway, grumbling at the sight of Nuisance, who was hoovering up bits of rolled toast that Mr Walsh had brushed from his lap. After several moments, Nuisance trotted over, curious but not unfriendly, and sniffed Pepys from head to toe. The inspection complete, he returned to his search for crumbs. The human company took this as signal to be seated.

"Monty here was telling us that you met them on the way over," said Mrs Cornish to Glen. "It's strange that our paths hadn't crossed until now." She turned to Mrs Walsh. "But then, I suppose you *were* in Jaffna."

Mrs Walsh cast a polite smile. She was a small, girlish woman of about fifty, whose sweetly tolerant temperament struck Glen as the perfect foil for her bumptious husband.

"How did you two meet?" she asked Glen, indicating the blind man in the corner.

"Oh – chance, really. At the glass church." She registered their blank stares. "About halfway down the valley. It's just a ruin, really."

Emil coughed.

"What brings you this far south, Captain?" asked Mr Walsh.

"Personal business."

"On your own, then? No wife?"

Suddenly Glen realized that she had never thought to ask Emil if he had married. It seemed unlikely that he should ever have been anything but alone, unfettered by matrimonial appendages.

"No. Pepys here is all the company I need."

There was a danger that his answer would sound like a snub, although Glen was almost certain that her friend had not intended it to come across that way. Fortunately, at that point Annabel joined them, bearing a tray.

"More drinks, anyone? We should liberate another bottle at once. Walter, be a darling and pour Captain Royce a beer…"

"Or would you prefer whisky?" asked Glen.

"Whisky, please." The Captain straightened in anticipation.

"Something cold, anyway," said Annabel. "Oof! This heat."

It was not the most interesting thing she could have said, thought Glen. Annabel was capable of better than this – idle chit-chat about the heat and malaria season. But courteous company rattled her, and so she conformed to its petty rituals. There followed a brief conversation about temperature fluctuations, and Glen was reminded of the listless voices of the officers' wives at the Club: women riddled by boredom and self-doubt. Despite Mrs Cornish's repeated attempts to sign her up for membership, Glen had avoided being drawn in to her induction. The female twittering of the tea rooms appalled her: like her aunt, she stoutly refused to be implicated in the wives' communal disparagement of their husbands, their marital clichés and endless, empty chatter.

"Annabel tells me you enjoyed the dance party, Glen," observed Mrs Cornish. "I do hope you made some nice friends there."

Glen composed her features into a civil smile. "Yes, thank you," she said.

"I'm sure a few of the boys must have fallen head over heels for you, my dear! Such… *sophistication*. Our girls don't grow up quite so quickly out here, do they, Annabel?" But Glen's aunt was busy proffering a bowl of stuffed olives to the others. Not to be slighted, Mrs Cornish turned back to Glen. "So, did you dance?"

"A bit. There was a young man called Dougie – Douglas – Brink. He seemed pleasant enough."

"Brink… Brink…" Mrs Cornish turned to her husband. "Do you know the name, darling?"

"His family's from Matale," said Glen, with a sinking heart.

"I knew a Johnny Brink at the Knuckles garrison," said Walter. "There was a rubber connection, I think."

"Well!" beamed Mrs Cornish. "A good family, then."

She's worse than Mummy, thought Glen. *I've only known the boy half an hour…*

"I hear you've been busy writing," said Mr Walsh, reaching for the bowl of olives.

"Oh, lovely!" gushed Mrs Cornish.

"It's rather slow-going at the moment," said Glen. She wished that they wouldn't talk about it like this: her *hobby*.

"Glen is writing to a prisoner," blurted Annabel. "In Belgium – is that right, darling? We don't get to see the letters, of course. Wonderful fodder, I would have thought."

"A prisoner?" Mrs Cornish gawped. "But isn't that terribly dangerous?"

"Why should it be?" asked Glen. "He's thousands of miles away."

"Well, what did he *do*?"

Glen shrugged. "I don't know. We don't talk about it."

"Well, what if he's a rapist – or – or a murderer?"

Everyone looked at Glen.

"To be honest, I never thought of it that way," admitted the girl. "At the beginning I simply assumed that he was innocent. From what I gather he's a political agitator."

The group took a moment to absorb this.

"Well, as I said: it must be excellent fodder," repeated Annabel.

"I started to write a novel once," sighed Mr Cornish. "Real life got in the way, of course. Now that I've the time on my hands, I rather fancied I might finish the job. They do say that we've all got a story in us."

"Sometimes I fancy I might make a rather fine medical officer," replied Glen. Annabel laughed and poured herself another glass.

"I sometimes think the creative instinct is wasted on men," attempted Mrs Walsh. "It's a woman's instinct to create, isn't it? And a man's to destroy."

"Excuse *me*!" chortled Mr Cornish.

"How is work, Annabel?" asked Mrs Cornish, in a pitying tone.

Glen's aunt knocked back the last of her wine and adopted her best face. "Oh, you know," she began – it was perfectly obvious that Mrs Cornish did not, would never know – "it's been a challenge at times, but I think I'm getting the hang of it."

"Discipline!" bellowed Mr Walsh. "You, especially, must establish discipline over those workers, Annabel. Otherwise you'll wake up one morning to find they've run riot all over you. Nationalism is just another word for terrorism. They'll call it non-cooperation…"

"...or *civil disobedience*," sneered Mrs Cornish.

Glen watched her aunt reach for the tonic water.

"My workers have no reason to rebel," said Annabel. "It's different here. They don't face the same challenges as those poor people up north. That's where the real problems are."

"But what about us?" demanded Mrs Cornish, her smile vanished. "Why does no one want to talk about *our* problems: the white problems?" There was something about her tone that made Glen suspect these were opinions that had been expressed many times before – a predictable rant that was injected with new passion as circumstances required.

"I've been trying to find a copy of *Indian Home Rule*," the girl said to Mr Walsh, so that everybody could hear. "It's just that I wasn't able to find one at the Club..."

"Really, Glen!" Mrs Cornish turned quite red.

"Well, I don't suppose there's anything in it to corrupt the girl." Mr Walsh flashed Glen a comradely smile. "Someone of her intelligence would see through the quackery in an instant, anyway. A trumped-up catechism for the masses, that's all it is."

"But it can't always be about them, can it?" said Mrs Cornish. "They've got us on the back foot – they'd have us all slaughtered in our beds, given half the chance..."

"Now, Cee—"

"Don't, Walter. Don't say I'm overreacting. I'm not."

Glen considered Emil, who had dropped one hand to stroke Pepys. Was he checking that the little dog was still there – searching for something to do in a room where he was, once again, all but invisible to those he could not see? Then Glen saw that Pepys's ears were pricked, and he was grumbling again – low but insistent – at the sight of Nuisance nosing about his owner's legs.

"Nuisance, darling, come out of there."

"You must excuse Pepys. He's like a child who prefers the company of adults to other children."

The others looked at Emil as if surprised to see he was still there.

"Jabalpur, eh?" said Mr Walsh at last. "Bet you've got some stories to tell."

"Emil presided over some very important trials," said Glen. "The dacoities, you know."

"That was years ago," said Emil.

"Tell us about the Central Provinces," urged Mrs Walsh. "It must be very different out there."

"There is a fine sense of space. I used to hawk on the Malwa plateau – yellow plains and scrubland as far as the eye could see."

Mrs Cornish straightened her skirt and shifted.

"You trained the birds yourself?" Mr Walsh's white eyebrows inched further up his head.

"Absolutely. It's the only way."

"Emil trained them in the old style: holding a bird on one arm for three days and three nights until it fell asleep." Glen smiled proudly at her friend. "Jolly hard work, I should think."

"But worth it in the end," mused Emil. "The hand became the bird's natural home: he had no concept of freedom beyond it."

"How remarkable," murmured Mrs Walsh.

Annabel was watching Emil with a sleepy, enchanted gaze. By her mental tally, Glen judged that her aunt had already had two glasses of wine and a double gin and tonic – and that wasn't counting the beer they'd shared in the kitchen just before the guests started to arrive.

"I do think birds are beautiful creatures," said Annabel, cupping her chin in long, thin fingers.

"Watching a kestrel hovering over a plain…" Emil's voice trailed off; he swirled the contents of his glass. "I remember thinking that I had seen God in that moment. Just a small flash of something… something literally *graceful*. Full of grace."

"I wish I could fly," sighed Annabel.

"The kestrel could see farther than any of us could."

The party sank into an embarrassed silence. Glen considered getting up to collect the empty canapé plates as a means of stealing Annabel's glass away.

"So you're one of these fellows who prefers animals to people, eh?" barked Mr Walsh. Glen looked at her friend, who merely smiled as if at some secret amusement.

"People are cruel; animals don't know how to be cruel," he replied.

"You tell that to the villagers who lost two children to tigers last year," retorted Mr Cornish. "North of Sigirya."

"One of those tigers was lame," said Emil crisply. "There was a price on its head. By the time the men found it, the creature was already half dead of hunger. They broke its skull with stones and dismembered the unborn cubs they found in its belly."

"Just because animals don't have a concept of cruelty doesn't mean they're not capable of it," observed Mr Walsh, with a self-satisfied smile.

Glen felt her cheeks burn for her friend. "Pepys isn't," she gushed, humiliated by this last resort into female silliness. "Neither is Nuisance."

"Or Nikolai!" laughed Annabel.

"Who's Nikolai?"

"Althea's tortoise. Poor thing has a bit of a cold at the moment." Glen was relieved to detect a lightening of the mood. "Walter, your wife has told me that you are an accomplished pianist."

"Well..." Mr Cornish's head sank into his collar.

"Play us something beautiful," insisted Glen. "Please do. The piano looks so lonely over there, and no one in this house can play..."

It was a stupid thing to say; Ray Moodie had been the musician in the family. Glen tried to ignore Annabel's bitter smile, told herself that her aunt wouldn't even remember what she had said the next morning.

"Go on, Walter!" bossed Mrs Cornish.

"Oh, how lovely!" said Mrs Walsh.

"A song!" cried Emil, thumping one hand on the arm of his chair.

Glen leapt to his side. "Yes, a song."

"Well, then... let's see about this..." Mr Cornish eased himself onto the piano stool. He stroked a few keys, teasing out a series of chords. "*So long sad times... Go long bad times...*"

"*We are rid of you at last,*" crooned Mrs Cornish.

"*Howdy gay times, Cloudy grey times…*"

"*Now you're a thing of the past!*" Annabel sprung to her feet, steadied herself, swept over to join him.

"*Happy days are here again… The skies above are clear again… So let's sing a song of cheer again… Happy days are here again…*"

Annabel draped one arm around Mr Cornish's shoulder, using him to steady herself as she beat time on the top of the piano. She closed her eyes as she sang, head tossed back, conducting an invisible orchestra.

> *All together shout it now,*
> *There's no one*
> *Who can doubt it now…*

Glen noticed that the others had stopped clapping along and were now watching the scene with thin smiles. Emil clutched his glass in both hands, nodding in time to the raucous singing. Annabel's voice grew louder with each line.

> *So let's tell the world about it now,*
> *Happy days are here… a–gain!*

As drunk as she was, there was a strange lucidity to Annabel's voice – as if the song had released a sudden moment of clarity in abandon. But all that Glen could see was vulnerability, the gay brashness of one too frightened to stop singing.

"Come on, everybody! *Your cares and troubles are gone… There'll be no more from now on… From now on…*"

That was when Glen noticed Hollar standing in the doorway. He looked like a bleary-eyed ghost in thin cotton pyjamas, she thought. A lonely little ghost.

"Oh, darling, did we wake you up?" Glen shot her aunt a glance – Annabel had not noticed the boy standing there – and hurried him out of the room.

"I couldn't sleep. I was staring at the crack in the ceiling, it looks like a monster's mouth…"

"And you heard us making such a noise – I'm sorry darling. Come on, let's take you upstairs."

He had wanted to be near the adult laughter, she knew. But Annabel was in no shape to put him back to bed, and Glen was glad of the excuse to escape for a few minutes.

* * *

It had started to rain, and the house creaked under the deluge like an old ship. Glen switched on the lamp in Hollar's room and pulled the covers up to his chin.

"Tell me a story, Glen."

"Darling, I've got to get back to the guests."

"A short one, then."

"There once was a boy called Hollar who couldn't sleep because of a frightening crack in the ceiling. But actually the crack was only a crack, not a monster's mouth at all, and when he realized that he had only imagined it to be frightening, he felt much better and fell asleep and dreamt very happy dreams. The end."

"That's not a story."

"I say it is. If you think you can do better, you make one up yourself – I'll come back to hear it in half an hour." He would be asleep by then, of course. Glen closed his door and returned downstairs.

She arrived to discover Annabel padding Emil with a napkin, having managed to spill half her brandy over his chair as she crossed the room.

"How frightfully clumsy of me – really, I can be such a fool sometimes…" Her aunt's eyes were brimming with tears as she mopped his knee. Too absorbed in her efforts to notice Pepys, she speared the little dog's tail with the heel of her shoe. Pepys released an outraged howl, which set Nuisance into a barking frenzy.

Emil collected the little dog in his arms and said, "He's over-excited. We should go."

"I'll ring your guest house to tell them you're on your way," said Glen.

"Oh, but you can't go! Not yet, please not yet... I'm so sorry, I've been such a fool..." Annabel straightened. "We were having such a lovely time."

"You've been very kind. It was a pleasure meeting you all. Please don't all leave on my account—"

"It *is* getting late..." said Mrs Walsh, sliding her husband a look that indicated he should make their excuses.

"And we've got the ladies'-association brunch tomorrow..." added Mrs Cornish.

"We daren't keep Anjali waiting up," said Mr Walsh with a decisive tone, as if consideration for his housemaid was the most important thing.

"I do hope you'll come again soon," said Annabel, forcing a weak smile and looking at no one in particular.

Glen hurried about collecting stoles and purses and walking sticks, pausing by Emil to whisper in his ear. She was about to apologize for her aunt's behaviour when he raised a hand and touched her lips with gentle fingers. "Don't be ridiculous," he said in a secret whisper. "I had a smashing time."

She walked him to the edge of the lawn, where they waited together for the Burgher driver to do a turn in the rutted drive.

"She is a lonely woman, your aunt," said Emil, in a soft voice.

"She's not usually like this," replied Glen, her embarrassment making her voice sound snappish. "Most of the time, the divorce doesn't bother her. It's just when other people are around, and so full of pity..." She studied the ascetic face. "I suppose she *is* lonely."

"We all are, in one way or another," he said. His arm remained on hers; he squeezed her hand. "Please, thank her again for me."

* * *

Sleep came easily to Annabel that night, but not to her niece. At last Glen decided to make the most of her wakeful state, and so she switched on her lamp to reread Pieter's latest letter.

He had offered strong opinions on politics and God's eternal forgiveness, as well as a lengthy description of his duties in the prison chapel, where he was responsible for lighting the candles and carrying the incense and clearing the crumbs after Communion. He had less to say about his family.

I am also very far away from my parents now. They do not like to think about me, because I make them too sad.

When I was little, I told the boys at school that I was going to marry my mammy. They laughed at me for this. They didn't know that my father is a complicated man. Sometimes he is strong, and other times he is weak. When he is not sad, he is angry. Altogether, I do not want to be like him.

I would like to be like my brother, even though it is because of him that I am in prison now. I am here because I lied, and now that lie is all I have. You see, I thought it was my duty to protect my brother because I loved him. But he rejected Flanders, denied God, and brought shame on our family. That is treason: three times treason. I have not even told my parents the truth.

You say that you do not know what to write. I think that you should write about me. I can tell you about my life, and you can write it into a book. I do not always understand my life, because it is so messy. But stories are neat. Stories have rules, like beginning and middle and end, hero and villain, lessons. So, you can make my story better than real life. Would you like to do that?

I am sending you another article for your scrapbook. This one is about the rebels in Spain.

From,
Pieter

She found herself wondering about his family, parents who could no longer bear to face their own son, and she tried to imagine what sort of man he might be. For some reason, the image that presented itself to her was always of Captain Royce – a younger Royce, perhaps – and she wondered about the girl-friend that Pieter had once described, who no longer came to see him in prison.

If Glen was honest, there were precious few people whom she would visit after a fifteen-year sentence. Her parents, of course, and her brother. As a young girl, she had dreaded marriage – was it this that prompted her, at the age of four, to declare that she intended to become a nun? – and at eighteen she had spurned the coming-out ceremony that had been the highlight of her sister's school-leaving year. Even the word "husband" filled Glen with revulsion: it made her think of husbandry, of stockbreeding sheep and fattening pigs. And then there was the appalling pageantry of the wedding to consider. The long, lonely walk down the aisle with her father; the charade of being "gifted" to some other family. A part of her would vanish: the child that had flourished through rainy afternoons in the library, instructing her brother and sister – gutsy orphans like herself – on the plan to flee the workhouse… the girl who had pressed her ear to a gurgling radiator in the belief that a tiny man was trapped inside. Life would speed up: the ordinariness of marriage must lead, inevitably, to children. To the indignity of pregnancy, to the horrors of labour, and the mindlessness of motherhood.

She studied Pieter's letter once more: the self-consciously neat handwriting, the complete absence of rubber marks, which suggested that the prisoner drafted his letters in rough before printing a clean copy. There was something inherently good about him, she told herself. There was an eagerness to please, a modesty that appealed to her. Like Jean Valjean, perhaps he had been wrongly convicted; perhaps he was a good man.

Years ago, when Glen had been convinced that no one could ever live up to the fictional idols of her girlhood, her sister had tried to convince her of the value of a "good" man. The fellow destined to meet her at the altar need not represent a grotesque compromise of standards simply because he was not named Heathcliff. Merle had accused her sister of suffering "a fatal disconnection with reality". Byronic rogues, according to Merle, were a penny apiece in the real world. Good men, on the other hand, were rare. Dependable, loyal, hard-working, kind men were rare.

"So are treasure hunters, and Arctic explorers, and theatre impresarios!" Glen had protested. But a part of her knew – was ashamed to recognize – that perhaps the best way to be wild and free was to be anchored, provided for, loved unconditionally. Terrified of never making it as anything but a talented dilettante, she could see the attraction of marriage, the face-saving security of it. Grand romances were usually terribly all-consuming, after all.

Dear Pieter, she began at last.
Of course, I should love to write your story…

15

It's funny, Pieter, how you manage to say things at just the right time. Your suggestion that I should write about you is a very fine one, and I shall set myself to the project at once. But first you must tell me more about yourself.

How cruel of the boys at school who laughed at you. Children are capable of such wickedness – I think that we do tend to forget that as adults. Take my new friend, Emil, for instance. His father was a missionary whose posting to Africa was changed at the last minute. A lucky escape, as he put it. Emil was born in India, and his early years were as happy as could be, but at the age of seven he was sent to a rather grim military asylum where the bullying by both pupils and masters was really quite monstrous. I thought of you when he told me this. In some ways, it was a very progressive institution, with a vegetarian ethos where meals consisted exclusively of oat skilly and boiled sprouts. My father, who's a bit mad about diets, would find it fascinating – but I don't suppose it's quite the sort of thing that most little boys would enjoy.

At first, talking to Emil was a strange experience. It may seem an obvious thing to say, but one is utterly invisible to a blind man. Do you ever feel as if you're just pretending to live, Pieter? That your life is only an imitation of something real, a kind of pastiche or a digression from something more meaningful? At first, speaking with Emil made me feel like a shadow, strangely unsubstantial. I'm sure he would be devastated to hear this – but then, it does make me wonder if he ever feels the same way…

Well, you will be interested to hear that he has helped me to snare my Indian admirer at last. I had been wondering how I might go about introducing myself to him – I felt too ashamed

*to do so anywhere near the Club, with all its odious associa-
tions – but thankfully Emil provided the necessary tip. Leaving
after drinks the other evening, he revealed that Monday was to
be a festival day at which all the local children would walk to
Buduruwagala for a ceremony at the foot of some enormous
rock sculptures. Perdita's daughters were participating in the
procession, so she was only too happy to accompany me. I decided to bring Hollar and Althea along, and told Annabel that
it was to be an educational excursion for their benefit.*

*Among the crowds of locals staking their position near the
Buddha's feet was a small party of English sightseers crouch-
ing low to the ground, virtually prostrating themselves before the presiding statues in order to capture their vastness
on celluloid. I must have been smiling at the sight, when I
recognized a gentleman standing on our side of the perimeter who appeared to be sharing in my amusement. He cut
a debonair figure: linen trousers, a cream blazer that could
only have been from a London tailor and shining brogues.
Honestly, Pieter, he would have been right at home in a punt
on the Cherwell!*

*Of course, it was the famous schoolteacher, attending with
his students. Before Perdita could stop me, I sidled up to him
and said, "Amorous Leander, beautiful and young, I take it?"
He had not expected to be identified so boldly, and as he
fumbled for words I worried that perhaps I had overstepped
the boundaries. But he quickly recovered himself in time to
greet Perdita. "I take it Jayanadani is no longer struggling with
her mathematics?" he asked her, studiously avoiding my eye.
And then he introduced himself to Althea and Hollar, who
through a rather unsubtle combination of winks, smiles and
nods confirmed that he was indeed the man from the botanical
gardens...*

I didn't understand what was so special about this fellow. So he
had drawn her picture and left a poem: if I had done the same
for Mieke, she would have told me not to be so silly – but then,
my pictures weren't terribly good.

I placed the letter on my desk. There was too much here that I couldn't understand. *Asylum* and *pasty*, for instance. *Prostrating*, *brogues*, *punt*. And who was Leander?

Perhaps my English lady writer was losing interest in me. Perhaps I was not upholding my end of the bargain, to be the kind of prisoner that she wanted. Was I no more than a guppy in a fishbowl to her, swimming in circles and bumping against the glass – an insignificant pet only too eager to gobble up the titbits she threw me? Did I exist only as an object for her occasional contemplation?

But no: she had agreed to write my story, after all. Consoling myself with this, I tucked her letter in the drawer and reached for my scarf and badge.

* * *

The best kind of rule is one that you arrive at through sound reasoning. Arend didn't expect us to believe everything he said simply because he was the troop leader, or because he was older than the rest of us. No, Arend gave us more credit than that.

"If a horse mates with a donkey, what will the result be?" he asked us one day.

"A mule," answered Filip.

I put my hand up. "Mules can't reproduce," I said, not to be outdone.

Arend smiled. "That's right, Kuypers. And do you know why?" I shook my head. "Because mules are biological errors." He turned to the others. "Now if I were to tell you that the Jews are like mules, only they continue to breed – do you suppose this is a good thing or a bad thing?"

"A bad thing," we said, all at once.

"And so what is to be done?"

"We should baptize them," I suggested. "Like the missionaries do in Africa."

"Let me ask you this, Kuypers: can a goat become a horse?" I shook my head, worried that perhaps he was making fun of me. "A Jew will always be a Jew," said Arend.

I couldn't help thinking about what G.P. had written about the dangers of simple language. It seemed obvious to me that people are not like goats and horses.

"But in Africa—" I repeated.

"The only reason there are missionaries in Africa is that they are addicted to power. No priest truly believes that he can make a human of a Negro." Arend seemed to consider his words, as if he was about to break news that perhaps we were not prepared to hear. "Faith is not as powerful as science," he said. "Least of all the Jewish faith – and do you know why?" We waited. "Because there is no such thing. There is only a Jewish race."

I thought about this for a moment. "What if a Jew and a Christian had a baby?" I asked. "And the baby grew up and married a Christian, and they had a baby... eventually, there wouldn't be any Jews left. Everyone would be the same."

"But we would be a race of mongrels, and we would return to behaving like apes in the jungle," said Arend. "No: the only way to deal with the Jewish problem is to eliminate it completely. The Jew is a cancer on our country. We must cut out the cancer to save the body."

I must have looked downhearted, because almost immediately Arend took me by the shoulders. "You must be brave, Kuypers," he said gently. "In every revolution, some blood must be shed." I thought of what G.P. had written about life being messy, and I nodded to show that I understood. "We must be always optimistic, always hopeful! The English and the French are eternally gloomy, and with good reason: their countries are flooded with Jews and communists. But we can face the future with smiling faces, because we are going to build a stronger Flanders, better than ever before!"

We all cheered.

I would never admit this to the other boys, but when I listened to Arend I felt a little like I did when I was with Mieke – only, with Arend I didn't stammer or sweat so much. The rest of the troop sometimes grumbled that he gave me an easy time of it; he never made an example of me the way he sometimes picked on the youngest ones, like Adriaan or Bastiaan, or anyone who seemed to be getting too big for their boots, like Filip. For some reason, the more Arend frightened us, the closer we drew around him. We forgave him everything: perhaps because we were bored – that's how it is when you are thirteen – and Arend entertained us.

Once, he chose me to demonstrate the best way to drag a wounded man out of battle. I had to lie on the ground and pretend to be unconscious. Arend tied my wrists together with his necktie and looped my arms around his neck. He showed the others how to crawl with an injured man in this way, shielding me against imaginary gunfire with his body. Of course, the rest of the troop laughed at me a bit, but I didn't care. Arend smelt of Musgo Real aftershave, the same kind that Krelis used. I closed my eyes – I was pretending to be unconscious, after all – and concentrated on going limp. Arend's shoulders were as powerful as a horse's, and his hot breath fell on my forehead in short, moist bursts as he pulled me along the ground, like a bear dragging a helpless cub.

The next time I felt the heat of his skin was the day that he announced Dirk's promotion to Banner Leader. Someone high up in the department had sent a special pin for Dirk to wear, and Arend showed it to us before affixing it to Dirk's lapel. Then he withdrew the Swiss Army knife from the sheath attached to his belt, and asked Dirk if he was ready.

We didn't know what he meant, but Dirk evidently did. He rolled up his sleeve and offered his arm to Arend. That was when I realized that he was going to receive a scar, like the one that Arend had in the same place. It was the German cross, the one that looked like a broken wheel and was a symbol of our common destiny.

I watched Dirk's face as Arend flicked the blade across his forearm. He only flinched when he saw the blood bubbling up from the cut. Arend began to pick at the wound with the tip of his knife while the rest of us watched in silence.

"Does it hurt?" asked Joos.

The blood was smearing as Arend went over the cut again.

"Not really."

"It's easy having someone else do it for you." Arend rolled up his sleeve to reveal the raised white lines on his own arm. He deftly drew the knife edge along one healed welt, splitting the skin. He didn't even grunt. Then he grabbed Dirk's arm and pressed the wounds together.

"Blood brothers," he said. It sounded as if he was laughing, although he was staring into Dirk's eyes like a hunter.

It was a moment that shouldn't have been interrupted, but the words tumbled from my mouth before I could pause to think.

"I want one, too," I said.

"Go on then," grinned Pepijn, giving Arend a nudge. "But do him and Adriaan together. Blood *sisters*."

"No." I glanced at Adriaan, who was watching, wide-eyed, from the fringes. The tips of his ears were turning red. "Not with him. I'll only do it with Arend."

Arend didn't give the others a chance to jeer. He beckoned me with the knife.

"Come here," he said gently. "Give me your hand." I did as I was told. Arend's hand was warm and strong, and I felt a chill of anticipation travel up the back of my neck. Arend was watching me with a stern expression, but his eyes seemed kind. I didn't believe that he would hurt me. "Count to three," he said.

"One. Two—"

In an instant, a flush of warmth spread through my open palm. The pain came seconds later. I saw Krelis striding into the kitchen, and Mother falling into his outstretched arms: a sudden, vivid image that disappeared as soon as I became aware that I was trying to hold on to it, trying to freeze the sound of my brother's laugh. As the pain gave way to numbness, I realized that Arend was still holding my hand.

"Good lad." He squeezed his own scar to make the blood well up again, and smeared the cut in my palm with wet fingers. It hurt, but the worst thing I could have done then would have been to pull away.

"Thanks," I said.

"You're a new man today, Kuypers," announced Arend. "Fate has smiled on you."

I believed him. For all I knew, Father Goossens didn't even boil the water that went into the baptismal font – but this was different. I was sure that I could feel the new cells coursing through the red rivers in my body like an electric shock, making me stronger.

16

She had already identified an ideal writing corner in the parlour, where a cracked leather armchair overlooked the garden through a large bay window. A floor lamp loomed over the chair, its oversized shade fringed with mustard tassels that teased Glen's hair. In the early afternoon, watery sunlight dappled the stripped floorboards, and the girl would extend a bare foot from her armchair island as if to dip one toe in a rippling pond.

It was here that she decided to begin work on a story. Or, perhaps more to the point, here that she could *see* herself writing a story. For Glen tended to observe herself as if she were moving through the pages of a book – peering over one shoulder, tweaking and sorting and clarifying and polishing her life as if it were a piece of living art.

She had not written a thing since receiving the last rejection for *Scenes from Away*, and during this time she had resolved to do away with poetry and concentrate on prose instead. While she waited for Pieter to supply her with details for his story, she had decided to attempt something completely original: a book about Ceylon – because how many young women writers were penning such tales back in England? She must sound out her talents and quarry her experiences to create a novel for the times: richly exotic, but also raw with feeling and in tune with the spirit of modernity.

She decided to begin with a description of a family gathering for a meal. Anglo-Indian food would not suffice: it must be authentic, thoroughly indigenous, and *malu hodi* was the only thing of its kind that she had tasted so far. Seeing Perdita pass beneath the veranda, watering can in hand, Glen tapped sharply on the window to catch her attention.

"Perdita!" she called.

The housemaid looked up, and when she saw it was the English girl she smiled and set the watering can down. Slowly mounting the veranda steps, she gathered the folds of her sari in one hand and pushed her thick plait over one shoulder with the other. Glen made a mental note to record the combined gesture.

Pushing the window open, the girl leant across the ledge so that she could be heard over the whirr of the clattering fan inside. "Perdita, could you tell me what kind of fish you put in the *malu hodi*?"

"It's just fish, Miss. Local fish."

"I need to know the name, for something that I'm writing. Is it cod? Do you get cod in these parts?"

Perdita's smile faded into a mystified expression. "Cod, Miss?"

"Or some kind of trout? Bass?"

"No, no, Miss. Just fish."

So fish it would have to be. But after a few attempts to capture the precise flavour, the intangible aroma that altered on the breeze – how did cardamom smell? Could she even be sure that it *was* cardamom? – Glen threw down her pencil in frustration and tore off a blank page.

The reality was that she had no story. Not here, anyway; she lacked even the barest resources to paint a convincing scene, let alone bring a foreign world to life. She had always aspired to capture Truth, and yet had always been disappointed, reading through a completed story or poem, to discover that, once again, Truth had evaded her. These fruitless attempts always left her feeling exposed – vulnerable, irrelevant. Perhaps it was time to try something a little less ambitious.

A character sketch. At first she thought that she might try to describe Emil: to capture the shallowness of his gaze and the exact line of the scar which ran along one jaw – no war wound, it turned out, but the remains of an accidental burn suffered during a childhood tonsillectomy. When she told him that she was giving up poetry for prose, he had replied that the best novelists learnt the art of metaphor from poems. She searched for a metaphor for the Captain's proud shoulders and aristocratic chin, but none came: trite symbols were too reductive. Here, now, he was too alive to her, refusing to be frozen on the page.

And then, another thought: a character sprung, like some mythological creature, fully formed from the recesses of her consciousness. Within minutes she was embroidering a personal history, a fatal weakness, a path to redemption. She wrote with a quiet fury: crossing things out, scribbling notes in the margins, turning page after page until finally the last glimmer of sun had faded from the walls and she looked up in surprise to discover that the room in which she sat was almost completely dark. She switched on the lamp and then, cocooned in a pool of light, she set back to work.

The story was about a young man, a soldier. As a boy, he had thrilled to the rallying cry of a bugle when the hunt streamed across the hills near his home. To him, it was a call to arms: a romantic evocation of the standard bearer and drummer boys leading their troops into battle. Tin soldiers clutched in still-dimpled hands, he had imagined himself khaki-clad and pith-helmeted astride a rearing Arabian stallion, thunderously pursuing a band of natives across craggy dunes and thirsty bush. In his child's mind the enemy were dark – it did not matter whether they were African or Asian, Turks or Trobrianders – and their land was hot, parched and teeming with peril. A scorpion bite would fell a man's horse in minutes; leopard attacks made cholera and malaria seem like friendly killers. At bedtime, waiting for Nanny to bring cups of warm milk to the nursery, the boy imagined himself watching the troop celebrate their victory back at the encampment. While his men sang round the fire, he would pen glittering battle accounts to send home to adoring relatives who hung on his every word.

When that boy became a man, he was impatient to enact these battles in a real war and signed up when he was just seventeen. But northern France was very different from the bleached Asian steppes of his imagination, the vast expanses of wilderness ripe for the taking: the enemy was not an infantile barbarian but a cunning equal, a man with a gun like his, as well as tanks, artillery and gas. He could not have predicted the hours of numb boredom at the sentry post, severed by a jolt of terror as the trench next to his collapsed into a sighing morass of mud and limbs, stifling the suffocated cries of men being crushed beneath. Years earlier, he could not have imagined the horror of such a prosaic death.

And so, after weeks of cold, cloying mud teeming with slugs and frogs and horned beetles, and rats the size of badgers who gorged themselves on the staring eyes of the dead; weeks of itching from lice that bred in the lining of his clothes, warmed by the heat from his body; weeks of shellfire that rattled his bones and made his ears ring in fury; weeks alongside men who controlled their terror with drink and cigarettes, who trembled and stammered even when the skies were clear and silent; weeks spent watching the novices peer over the parapet into no man's land, only to be cut down by a sniper, swiftly, as if they were mere targets on a range; weeks enduring the stench of corpses and overflowing latrines, of gangrenous feet, rotting sandbags and chloride of lime – after all this, when he could bear it no longer, he fled.

They found his discarded uniform in the back of a supplies truck near Dunkirk, but they were not in time to intercept the ship that he'd boarded, posing as a member of an Australian regiment bound for home.

His battalion listed him as a deserter, and recorded that he should be executed on capture; later, his death sentence was commuted, and he was sentenced, *in absentia*, to six months of forced labour. A year would pass before his family finally received word of his whereabouts; by then, the war had ended, and he returned to England with immunity. Several years later, the death penalty for desertion was abolished altogether, in time for a new war.

She recognized him now, of course, although the process of creeping beneath his skin had made him strange to her, unknowable. Considering her notes, Glen mulled over the possibilities for the story's voice. The first person lent energy to the telling; but she aspired to gravitas, and the omniscient third person sounded somehow wiser. The voice would determine how it all ended, and until she knew how it would turn out – whether her soldier would reveal himself as a coward or a hero – she could not begin work on a fresh draft. Was it wrong of her to resist judging him? Was it cowardly simply to tell his story, without expressing an opinion on what was right or wrong, under the circumstances? Perhaps he *should* be shot at dawn – perhaps there was some nobility in that pitiful, lonely death.

There was an element of deception at work, she realized, as she plotted his fate. Writing was an act of memory, an outgrowth of her childish desire to freeze moments so that she might remember them for ever. *Write it down.* There was something redemptive about it, too. Perhaps more than other girls, she knew that people make up stories to replace the past, to protect themselves from the truth.

* * *

She showed her draft to the schoolteacher, whose name was Ganan, the next time they met.

This had not been her intention, but he had noticed the pages fluttering on one of the cane chairs, anchored by a stone from the garden, and asked about their contents. Her first instinct had been to bundle the story out of sight, but it seemed rude not to oblige, and in the end she handed him the manuscript with a casual bravado.

Her self-assurance began to waver as he was reading, and she had to return indoors to compose herself. *He's made an exhibitionist of me*, she thought. *First the picture in the park, and now this.* What had made her trust him, a complete stranger, with something so personal, and so deeply flawed? She watched him through the window, but it was impossible to judge his response at a distance. At last, she returned to the veranda.

"I never do this," she said, hovering behind him as he turned to the final page. "Let other people read my work before it's finished, I mean. I don't know why I'm letting you. I know that it's rubbish... You shouldn't have read it."

They were alone, and acutely aware of it. That day at Buduruwagala, which now seemed so very long ago, Glen had asked the schoolteacher to Beulah Lodge. Two weeks later, he had finally taken up the invitation. Annabel and the children were visiting an elderly friend in Nanu Oya; Micah had taken Perdita and the girls to see his sister's new baby. Glen had given little thought to what she might say if they were discovered: the prospect of passing an afternoon with a like-minded soul had quickly obliterated any consideration for social convention. To think, her admirer was an artist, a poet! An educated man who had tasted life beyond these shores, who had not been foisted on her at some club dance and whose solemn eyes spoke of a soulfulness that was strange and exciting.

At last, Ganan placed the manuscript in his lap and peered up at her. "I think that it is very powerful," he said.

"Oh, don't—"

"No, really. It is the tragedy of our times. It reminded me of 'Drummer Hodge'."

"You must be joking..." She dropped onto the step next to him, swirling the ice in her tumbler and noting that he had not yet touched his own drink.

"If you want to think that, you may. But I mean what I said." He considered his words carefully. "Of course, your soldier doesn't die. Still, I couldn't help but think of those lines: 'Young Hodge the Drummer never knew – Fresh from his Wessex home – The meaning of the broad Karoo, The bush, the dusty loam...'"

"But Hardy's soldier is a hero. Mine, on the other hand..." She took the pages from him and shuffled them impatiently. "You can't really call him that, can you? One doesn't keep secrets about one's brother if he's a true hero."

"'But who can judge him, you or I? God makes a man of flesh and blood who yearns to live and not to die.'"

"Well, aren't you a trove of poetical knowledge!"

Ganan shook his head, abashed. "It's nothing," he said. "Please, I was not trying to show off."

"I didn't say that you were."

"I learnt English by reading it, you see," he said, as if by way of an excuse. "I developed unorthodox inflections, because I saw the words on the page before I heard them out loud. There was guilt, I suppose, for falling in love with the language of the ruling race – no, not guilt: shame. Because it is a more personal thing, no?" He studied the patch of earth between his feet. "My mother only speaks Sinhala, and Appah wasn't much better: a little English, Hindi." He brushed invisible crumbs from his trousers. "The first poem I learnt by heart was Kipling's *If*. I was moved by it, even though I doubt that I understood it properly."

"Imperial tripe!" she said laughing, with a flippant wave of one hand.

"If you are just a boy, reading those lines for the first time with no knowledge of colonies, of nations, of jingoism or self-rule – then the sentiment is a fine one."

Glen smiled. "My mother would be pleased to hear that – she used to get so fed up with me for wringing poems to death." She tossed the manuscript onto a basket chair on the veranda, recognizing in her nervousness the old instinct to shift her embarrassment onto a family member. "That was the worst thing, you see, to take things too seriously."

"It is a particular type of Englishwoman who resists such rigour. It is seen as unladylike." He smiled. "And *drive* is so terribly middle class."

"I think she simply got tired of listening to me ranting and raving."

For the first time, she noticed how the schoolteacher's smile spread from his eyes – black as Pontefract cakes, fringed with a thicket of dark lashes – to the corners of his mouth. "I suppose there is that, too," he said.

Taking her cue from his expression, Glen leant back upon her elbows, stretching her legs straight out before her. She teased off her flat leather sandals one at a time by sliding a toe under each heel, and noticed how this motion made him cast his gaze in another direction.

"I've decided," she said, "that's it is my imperative as a woman to write about the margins of society. About disgraced soldiers and all that."

"And your colonial subjects," teased Ganan. "Perhaps you would like to write about me and my students?"

"I wouldn't know where to begin. I've tried to describe Perdita's fish curry, and that ended in disaster. Can you imagine what would happen if I attempted to write about a real person?…"

Once again, she was laughing alone; her companion remained pensive. "If a nine-year-old Sinhalese boy could feel what Kipling felt, then anything is possible," he ventured. "Those of us who grow up living on islands, perhaps we are more introspective than others. So we learn to develop our imaginations."

They sat in silence, enjoying the pleasant sensation of being alone at the top of the world. It was a Saturday afternoon, and the valley was empty of human activity: silent but for the whisper of a breeze through the trees, and the crooning of a button-quail crying out to its mate.

"You know, this is the first time I've felt *myself* here," Glen declared at last. "With you, I mean." She glanced at him out of the corner of her eye; when there was no discernible shift in his expression, she hurried on. "The kids I met at that party a few weeks ago – every person there was playing a part. The tragedy is *they knew it*. It seems to be my lot to feel detached from things – as if I was just a ghost, floating in and out of other people's lives. Does that sound ridiculous?"

"Not in the least."

"There isn't room for people like us here," she said.

"People like us?" He blinked, taken aback by the intensity in her eyes.

"You and I. We're both at odds with things, aren't we?"

"Are we?" He pulled out his lower lip, tipped his head to one side and then the other as if rolling the thought around in his head. "I think perhaps you have overrated my capacity for rebellion, Glen."

She blushed. "I didn't mean to suggest that we're exactly the same," she mumbled. "Obviously."

"Obviously."

She let out a nervous laugh, feeling quite disarmed by his gaze. "Ignore me," she said. "I say things without thinking – or think for so long I forget what it was I meant to say. That's probably why I spend so much time feeling an utter fraud." Her companion cast a quizzical expression, and so she added, "As a writer, for one thing. I don't create anything; I just steal from real life."

"That's what writers do, isn't it? That is what all artists do."

"But I can't help being so... so *aware* of it." She shook her head. "Besides, the world doesn't need another writer – if anything, the world needs more readers. It's clear that I'm not ready to write anything worthwhile."

"Of course you are. You are a remarkable girl, Glen." He noticed the way her eyes sparkled at this and caught himself. "You'll find what it is you're looking for. Once we find truth, it is impossible to turn our backs on it."

"You say that. But what do I know, really? A happy childhood, a bookish adolescence, two juvenile love affairs – if you can even call them that. That's not enough. And I desperately want to know more, Ganan: to experience all that life has to offer. To feel things that were impossible to feel at home." She held his gaze, willing him to understand. "That's why I came here."

"Then you must be patient. Wait a little longer." He glanced away, as if contemplating something that he dared not articulate. "You are so young. You have your whole life still."

She looked at him. "We've talked so much about me. I want to know about you."

Ganan shrugged, rubbing his palms on his lap. "There is nothing to tell," he said. "You could fit the entire story on a grain of rice. I was supposed to become a lawyer, but I was not clever enough—"

"Rubbish! Tell me what you thought of England."

"I was only there for a few months – oh, nearly ten years ago now." His gaze grew distant, filling with memories. "London is a lonely city."

"I suppose it can be, yes."

"In the end, I came home early. And I have been a teacher ever since."

"And an artist."

He shook his head. "My parents always saw it as a waste of time. But this is not the best place for someone who wants to draw." His smile broadened, and he added, "On those days when I find myself hating art, I try to remember why I started drawing as a child. Then, it was only for fun. I still like to invent new ways to create pictures. In that sense, the Futurists are a great inspiration to me – Mario Sironi especially. One day I'll show you."

"I'd like that."

Ganan watched as she rose to take the glasses inside. She walked barefoot into the house and returned moments later with two tumblers filled with a clear liquid.

She passed him one of the glasses. "Here – I made mine a single. I can plough through a few doubles, but they leave me utterly corpsed."

"Corpsed?"

"You know, tipsy. Well, more than tipsy." She clinked the edge of her glass against his. "It's a gin and tonic," she said, noting his bemused expression. "Purely medicinal, of course: a sure anti-malarial..." Then she gasped and said: "Oh rats, and now you're going to tell me that you don't drink!"

Her companion smiled. "On the contrary," he said, and downed the glass in a single gesture. Glen let out a howl of delight and drummed her feet on the step.

"You rogue!" she squealed. "Shall I get you another?"

"No, no – I think that is enough for now," was his reply. "I should probably go soon, anyway."

"Why don't you come back tomorrow?" she suggested. "For a proper tea – you know, with biscuits and things. Perdita adds a little curry powder to the egg and cress..."

Ganan straightened, pressed himself forwards as if to stand, then paused. "I will be at the school all day tomorrow, and this weekend is no good," he said. Rising slowly, he placed the glass at Glen's feet in time to notice her crestfallen expression. "But perhaps the Saturday after next? We could go to the Cinnamon Gardens."

"That sounds lovely."

"Well, then." He paused, and took her hand with a small, self-conscious bow. "Two o'clock, shall we say? By the butterfly house."

17

I don't know why Father remembered the Psalms when he did. Weeks had passed since we'd last eaten a hot meal as a family. Mother had only managed to slice some bread the morning he appeared in the doorway, Bible in hand, and declared, "What is this I see, Marten?"

I quickly withdrew my hand from the butter dish and pressed both palms together between my legs. The fleshy bit below my thumb ached where Arend had cut me.

My father lumbered into the kitchen, pulled out his chair – the only one with arms – and lowered himself into it. Book cradled in his sprawling lap, he began to thumb through the pages. He still smelt of drink from the night before.

Mother had already brewed the coffee. When Father arrived, she began to shuttle the cups onto a tray on the table, stopping midway to remove them all – cups and saucers and milk jug and sugar pot – and replace the tray with a piece of lace cloth that Oma Kuypers left us when she died.

"Stop fussing, woman. Sit down."

We waited for him in silence. Finally, Father found the passage that he had been searching for.

"Psalm 119, verses 81 to 88." He looked up at me, finger pressed so firmly to the page that the skin under his nail turned white. "That was what we agreed?"

"Yes, Father. But I memorized it before…" *Before. When we were four, not three, and Mother cooked a proper breakfast and I wasn't the only one who had to recite passages from the Psalms.* I rubbed my palms between my legs, eyeing the butter dish and the bread and the steaming coffee. "I'm not sure that I can remember it all."

"Grief shall not make gluttons of us." I recognized the tremor in his voice. "Stand up, and recite."

I did as I was told, wishing that my father could be more like King David, who saw the pointlessness of fasting after his son died. *I am going to him and he will not come back to me*, David said. But my father did not have the king's dignity.

Scanning the kitchen for some reminder of that elusive first line, I counted the painted tiles lined up above the fireplace, felt the cool flagstones through my stocking feet, pressed my thumbnail into the soft, woody flesh of my chair. Mother was watching me, trying to catch my eye, mouthing the words almost imperceptibly. "'My soul faints...'"

"'My soul faints with longing for your salvation,'" I began, "'but I have put my hope in your word.'"

Mother cast her gaze downwards, nodding in rhythm to the line.

"'My eyes fail, looking for your promise; I say, "When will you comfort me?" Though I am like a wineskin in the smoke, I do not forget your decrees.'"

Father was following the text closely, peering down his nose as if through invisible spectacles.

"'How long must your servant wait? When will you punish my persecutors?'"

So far, so good. Only four verses left.

"'The arrogant dig pitfalls for me, contrary to your law. All your commands are trustworthy...'"

And? It was as if Mother could sense my panic; she stopped nodding, but did not look up at me. Father's finger hovered in the same place. "'All your commands are trustworthy,'" I repeated.

"You've said that part already," whispered Father.

"'Help me, for men persecute me without cause—'"

"That is incorrect," said Father.

I felt my knees start to buckle beneath me: the bitter aroma of coffee and the smell of warm bread was becoming too much to bear. I tried again. "'They almost wiped me from the earth—'"

"No."

A final, desperate attempt: "'Preserve my life according to—'"

"Stop!" Father closed the Bible and placed it on his right-hand side. He pulled his chair closer to the table, clasped his hands in his lap and said to Mother, "Some coffee."

"The bread is fresh from Ankie's this morning," said Mother, glancing towards me. "She added cinnamon to it especially for Marten."

"Then it is a shame that he could not be bothered to learn his verses," replied Father, lifting the cup to his lips. His mouth puckered at the bitter taste; I watched the bulge in his throat leap and disappear again. "An empty stomach is like a heart that will not open itself to God's word. The hungry body reveals a hungry soul."

That was when it happened: the moment I allowed myself to imagine what he would taste like. His ruddy face crumpled like a bellows around the hinges of his jaw, chomping, grinding, chewing, sucking every last morsel through his teeth, turning each mouthful over with his tongue, wetting the bread, squeezing it, pressing it to the back of his mouth and forcing it through his throat – washing it down with hot coffee that rolled and gurgled in his cheeks, coating his teeth and gums and tongue and throat with silty grinds and a stale aftertaste. I realized that I could never bring myself to consume his head, but the muscle around his shoulders, sloping from his neck around the curve of his arm – that would be the sweet, dark meat. I would avoid his gut, but crack each rib like a wishbone before proceeding to the meaty thighs and taught, stringy calves. Could I countenance those tender buttocks? At that precise moment, with my stomach howling in agony and my heart thumping and my brain boiling and floating and swirling in my skull – at that moment, anything was possible.

There had been a time when I was little, when Father had flown into a rage at Mother in the kitchen. He hit her so hard across the face that blood flew from her nose and stained the floor. Later, she told me that it was because of the war. She said that the memories still haunted him, and sometimes he would panic – like a child who wakes up screaming from a nightmare. At the time, I didn't understand: I was too angry at him for striking her. I had grabbed the carving knife from the counter and pointed it straight at him. "Leave her alone!" I shouted. I remember being so frightened that the anger made me feel strangely calm. My father's face had changed, as if he'd just woken up or come out of a trance. I don't know what he thought then, seeing his own son threatening him with a knife. I was only seven or eight at the time. Mother had grabbed the knife from me and sent me to my room.

Now, watching my father gorge himself over his Bible, I felt myself fill up with the same rage. I could devour him whole. And when I was done, I would let Mother clean up the rest.

They ate in silence until only a little bread remained. When Mother reached for the last piece, Father asked what she was doing.

"I thought I would wrap it in a cloth, to save for dinner this evening," she replied, not looking at me. But Father must have known that it would become mine the instant his back was turned. He stretched out his arm, and Mother placed the bread in his hand.

"It will be better appreciated by the birds," he said. "There are hungry months ahead: best that we scatter it by the canal, so that the mother ducks can feed their families." He turned to me. "Perhaps you would like to help me, Marten?"

My darkest thought was that I might one day be like him. It seemed more likely to turn out that way than not. On that day, I would wake up to find that I had grown old and angry, with a wife and sons like pitiful paupers huddled around an empty table.

* * *

The next day was my brother's birthday.

Father stayed in the gatehouse while Mother and I went to church. Neither of us mentioned Krelis, although it was obvious that she was thinking about him when she handed me a franc for the collection plate and said, "We can afford it this once."

There had been nothing to eat that morning, and only a little *stoemp* the night before; but instead of filling me up, the Communion bread had made the hunger pangs worse. Afterwards, as we walked home, Mother told me that if I collected some wild garlic she would make a broth for supper.

There was a patch in the woods where bluebells grew that was sometimes good for garlic and even mushrooms. I filled my coat pockets with as many roots as I could cram in, and then I jumped across the stream to see if there were any blackberries still growing. There were – and even though they were small and hard and sour, I ate my fill until my fingers were stained purple and the bitter juice had numbed my tongue. Then I pulled myself into the crook of a big old tree that had been dead for as long as I could remember, and pulled out the letter from my trouser pocket. Unusually, the handwriting was irregular and looked agitated.

A rather unpleasant adventure today, it began.

The plan had been benign enough: to meet Dougie Brink and a couple of his friends at the cinema where China Seas *opened last week. It meant a trip into Colombo, where I haven't been since the end of the summer. Given the interlude before my next outing with the schoolteacher (on which point, more later) the timing couldn't have been better. I was quite excited to return to the city – the mountains are beautiful, but in recent days I had begun to find them oppressive – and as it has been months since I last visited a cinema, the prospect of a few hours in Dougie's company seemed really quite bearable.*

It was only after Micah dropped me off at the Elphinstone that I realized there had been a mistake: that Dougie had meant the Empire instead. A man at the box office explained that the latter was in Pettah, not Maradana – a short journey by hackery. Well, it was still early, and I thought the exercise might do me good. The directions seemed straightforward enough.

Only they weren't – and within ten minutes I was quite lost in the middle of a busy intersection. I had the impression of an approaching wall of noise – drummers and singing and raucous chants – and by the time I realized my error, I found myself surrounded by hordes of demonstrators – local men mostly, in white sarongs and red banians, but many women also, who wore red saris and white shawls.

Not to be put off, I ducked into a doorway and decided to wait it out. It was a remarkable spectacle, Pieter, and the excitement in the air was quite intoxicating, though to be honest I hadn't much idea what it was all about.

A flea beetle dropped onto the paper and froze, stunned, in the middle of the next sentence. After a moment, it started to crawl tentatively across the page. I watched it pause at the edge, feeling the air with its tiny, twisting antennae, before doubling back in the opposite direction. I flicked the paper hard, and heard the tap of its shell hitting the ground somewhere near my feet.

One banner was emblazoned with the words Lanka Sama Samaja *– another read* Suriya-Mal, *and was decorated with flowers not unlike the poppies we buy for Armistice Day. I gather, from what Annabel tells me, that both groups fall towards the political left; Dougie insists the LSSP are "a load of Trotskyists", although by the time we found each other I suppose I looked in such a state he must have taken fright.*

It was all rather exciting, you see, until the moment I realized there was not a single European face in the crowd. Far from petering out or moving on to another part of the city, the demonstration seemed to grow bigger and bigger until at last I found myself being jostled out of the doorway and into the thick of a densely packed mob. Amid a cacophony of rallying cries, I picked up the word gore, *which is here applied to any white person regardless of nationality. It is not a slur, as such – but hearing it, I was suddenly aware to be the sole representative of my race amid teeming hordes twenty or thirty bodies deep.*

Still, I did not panic. I knew it wouldn't do me any good if I did, and besides, I have always felt myself among friends here. One woman even handed me a rose – full-blown, sadly, so that the moment I was pushed to one side by the crowd, it lost half its petals to the wind. There were petals everywhere: on the ground, trapped in the folds of dhotis and shawls, fluttering over heads that shone in the sun…

I considered the reeds growing along the riverbank and thought of the paper roses that Gypsy women sold outside De Kraan. A single stem cost five centimes, but if you bought a bouquet they'd only ask for ten.

We jostled like that for some time, as if in a dance, and I had almost become accustomed to the rhythms of this heaving crowd when at last a cry went up, shrill and unintelligible. That was the first moment I saw something malignant – not in the crowd itself, but in the black tongue of a parrot swinging deliriously from a balcony directly overhead. The bird seemed to be in a wild state of panic, and it was using its dry, blunt tongue to feel the crossbar of the window below as if testing it for some chink in the fortress. That was when I noticed that all the other windows were barred, too, and I realized that the building was a hospital – not Colombo's stately general hospital (which is easily mistaken for a hotel), but a much sadder-looking institution, more like an orphanage or madhouse. The fact is, I was so preoccupied watching the terrified creature that I failed to spot the glint of stone slicing through the crowd – and then the shouts—

I felt something hit my head, and heard a heavy "clinck" strike the pavement. But when I looked down, the rock at my feet seemed to have nothing to do with the hot trickle on my temple. I was vaguely aware of a scuffle unfolding in the middle of the street, where several protesters had begun to grapple with a young man in a red lungi, but people seemed more shocked by the sight of a white woman with blood on her brow than such fisticuffs. One woman pressed a handkerchief to my head, while others began to call for the police – but most of the crowd around me seemed to drop away, as if they saw in me something dangerous, something unlucky. I suppose I was stunned, and a little embarrassed – I was in no pain – but after thanking the woman who had helped me I turned around and started to walk…

I don't know for how long. I focused on a belfry rising over the top of some tall buildings, and told myself that I would go

*there. The streets passed by me in a blur; I was walking away
from the crowds and towards the sea, but other than that I
honestly can't recall a thing about the route I followed. It was
only when I walked into him – quite literally into him; the
barrel of his chest beneath a white shirt and club tie – that I
recognized Dougie. He looked at me as if at a ghost; and then
I saw the stain I had left on his shoulder, and at last I allowed
myself to feel afraid.*

*He hailed a cab and took me directly to the hospital – the
main one, with the red roof and pretty awnings – and after
they'd stitched me up he said that he would take me straight
home. Well, we had missed the film by now, but I said I'd much
rather have a drink first... so we went to the Grand Oriental for gin toddies. His friends soon excused themselves with
a great deal of bluff and bluster about making whoever had
done this pay – but really I think they felt embarrassed by me.
Dougie, too. I let him take me home, after that.*

*So now I have a rather fetching scar, just above my hairline.
What do you think of that, Pieter?*

I felt the line in my palm, which was still pink and a little sore. In
the last day or so it had started to swell, and I wondered if perhaps I should try cleaning it with peroxide. Only I didn't want it
to heal too quickly, lest it disappeared altogether. I remembered
how Arend had reopened his own scar with the edge of his knife,
and I used the edge of the paper in my hand to trace the ridge
running between my thumb almost as far as my wrist. It stung a
bit, which I took as a good sign.

I folded the letter and tried not to think about what Krelis
would say.

18

Pieter's latest letter had arrived with an unexpected squiggle drawn over the crease of the seal. When Annabel removed the envelope from the stack she had collected from the box that morning, she drew a sharp breath before passing it to Glen.

"What is it?" asked the girl.

"Your fellow in Belgium," said her aunt, raising her eyebrows. "I suppose the prisons are a breeding ground for this sort of thing."

A ragged wheel – four broken spokes spinning endlessly, unstoppably, in mid-air – had been scrawled on the back of the envelope. Glen shoved the letter into the pocket of her dressing gown, wondering why she was the one to feel suddenly ashamed.

* * *

There was no time to read it before that morning's lesson. Although Hollar's Latin was basic, Annabel hoped that he might develop an ear for the inflections of classical poetry.

"*Nil me pa-pæniteat sanum patris hu-i-us…*" The boy hunched over the book so that his nose almost touched the page. "*Eoque non, ut magna dolo factum negat esse suo pars…*" He fiddled with the bit of spine that had come unglued, rocking gently, forwards and back. "*Quod non in-gen-u-os habeat claros-que parentis, sic me defendam.*"

"Lovely, Hollar. Althea, perhaps you'd like to tell us what Horace was saying?"

"'I could never be regretting…'"

"Ashamed."

"'…*ashamed* of such a father… nor do I feel any need, as many people do, to… to…'"

"Apologize."

"'...to *apologize* for being a freedman's son.'"

"Well done. Shall we attempt one of the Odes?"

The little girl had begun to stare out of the window even as Glen asked this. After a moment's silence, Althea's head snapped around and she glanced down at the book in front of her as if noticing it for the first time.

"We don't know who Hollar's father is," she said plainly, as if passing observation on the weather.

Glen had waited for the outburst: a book slammed shut, a chair kicked over, footsteps storming out of the room. But the boy merely stared across the table at his sister, tugging at the piece of spine that now hung from the book by a single thread of glue – until at last it separated and dropped onto a piece of graph paper, like an island drifting off the shore of a vast continent.

* * *

Pieter's letter was brief. He did not share her interest in the schoolteacher – *Arend says that teachers are people who failed to make something more of themselves* – and had been lukewarm in his response to her story.

I liked the battle scene very much. It would be better if your soldier found a Luger on a German body and used it to shoot the commandant. Also, he should not escape at the end. The penalty for desertion is execution by firing squad. This would be a better ending, because it is sad but it is also just.

Here is something I learnt today: when you look at a tree, your retina sees it upside down, so the roots are sticking in the air and the leaves are on the ground. Your brain has to send a message to your eye to reflect the image. This means that everything is actually the opposite of what we see.

It made me think of a time when I was little, when I liked to play with invisible dust. It was imaginary, of course, but when my brother told me that he had stolen every last piece from the box in my room, I cried and cried until our mother heard me and told my brother to show her his hands. They were empty, as you would expect. But our mother made him pretend to give me back my invisible dust all the same.

"God hath chosen the foolish things of the world to confound the wise."

* * *

She had not planned to bring the children, but on Saturday morning Annabel left early to meet with her managers, and her niece couldn't very well excuse herself for an entire day without asking Perdita to mind Hollar and Althea. So an excursion to the Cinnamon Gardens was arranged – and, she told the children, they were to have their very own dedicated guide.

"Who is it?" demanded Althea at once. "Is it the blind man?"

"You'll find out soon enough," came the reply.

"Does Mummy know who it is?"

"I don't suppose she does, no." Anticipating the inevitable follow-up, her cousin added, "But I'm sure she'd approve."

"So it's definitely a man, then?"

"Most definitely."

Ganan's surprise at being greeted by a pair of children – one in a blue cotton pinafore and ankle socks, the other in ticking shorts, smock shirt and straw hat, both undeniably English – was only temporary. He smiled as they rallied towards him with excited cries of recognition.

"They remember you from the procession," explained Glen, trying to contain the nervous excitement in her voice. Ganan wore the same linen trousers and cream blazer that had caught her eye the day she introduced herself to him at Buduruwagala; she noted with satisfaction that the brogues had been freshly polished. "Children, allow me to introduce Mr…" She stopped short and felt the heat rise to her skin.

"Dharmasena," said Ganan. "Ganan Dharmasena, at your service."

"Glen says that you're to be our guide," piped up Althea. "But I don't know anyone who can name more birds than Hollar."

"Althea…" warned Glen.

"I have no doubt that you are right," smiled Ganan, withdrawing a couple of short pencils from the breast pocket of his jacket. "My knowledge is of a cultural rather than biological nature. Perhaps we should hold a competition? You two write down the names of as many birds as you can find within the perimeter of the garden; Miss Glen and I shall do the same. In half an hour, we shall see who has won."

"Hurry, Hollar!" Althea grabbed a pencil and tore ahead. The boy looked up at Ganan and raised a finger in the air.

"One rule," he whispered.

"Of course," said Ganan.

"You can only have up to three mynah birds and three flycatchers. Otherwise your list could be all flycatchers."

Ganan exchanged looks with Glen, furrowing his brow in consideration. "All right, then," he agreed. "Only three of each."

When the children were out of earshot, Ganan shook his head ruefully. "That is that, then," he sighed. "I think that I can identify only two birds in the world: a peacock and a seagull."

"According to Hollar, there are over fifty types of seagull."

"Well, then, there you have it."

By the time the children had begun to complete their list, Glen and Ganan were sitting by the fish pond, observing the shimmer of brocaded carp gliding close to the water's surface.

"It's so beautiful," said Glen. She had been waiting for that moment to arrive when the air between them would lose its self-conscious edge, when they would sink into a comfortable silence of the sort shared by like-minded souls. After a while, however, the girl had realized that her own reluctance to speak might communicate a primness that she was quite determined to avoid, and so she rushed to fill the silence with appreciative comments about the landscape. "The light here is different, like the light of an Indian summer – only *greener*. Now I understand what people mean when they say that there is something timeless about this place."

"Timeless, but not unchanging," replied Ganan.

"Who are they?" she asked, pointing to a pair of figures carved into a stone column supporting one end of the butterfly house.

Each column was inset with human and animal figures, although this one – of a man and a woman, he playing a flute while she raised one hand in deferential greeting – was by far the finest.

"Krishna and Radha. He is the eighth incarnation of Vishnu, and she, a lowly milkmaid, is his consort. They were childhood friends who became lovers." Ganan leant back onto the grass, hands clasped beneath his head. "He had to leave her for many years, but still she remained true, until at last she was forced to marry another man. But theirs was an eternal love. You very rarely see depictions of her without Krishna."

"Poor girl. It sounds as if she had rather a lot to put up with."

Ganan laughed and rolled onto his side. Propping himself on one elbow, he said, "But Krishna is the Supreme Being. Would you not put up with quite a lot for the love of such a man?"

"Well, now…" She glanced at him out of the corner of her eye, admiring the smoothness of his skin and the noble line of his nose – not leonine, like Micah's, but long and angular, like that of a northern prince. "If Krishna was so busy fighting battles, or gallivanting with milkmaids, or whatever else he was doing… if I were Radha, I might begin to suspect that it was all just an illusion. That I'd fallen in love with an idea, rather than with a real person."

The schoolteacher considered her with smiling eyes. "But is that not always the way with love?" he asked gently. "I do not think it is a selfless thing at all. Love is only need."

"Well, now!"

"You think it's so ridiculous? But why then do people who are in love always seem to go about looking so miserable? Because it is a burden to them; it is not something to be taken light-heartedly."

Glen watched an overfed carp swim along the pond floor like a twisting silver muscle. "And in your experience?" she asked, avoiding his eye. "Is love such a terrible thing?"

"Lust, loneliness – these are things we must learn to live with. But I am not a sentimentalist." He peered up at her with a half-serious look. "Of course, I assume that neither are you. A modern woman cannot afford to waste her time on such bourgeois notions."

"No," Glen mused. "No, I suppose she can't."

What about the drawing, she wanted to ask – *what about the poem?* But it seemed silly now to ask if he did not believe in love at first sight. Perhaps she had been foolish to think that he had intended the verse to be taken literally. Was it not enough that he had made a gift of it to her?

Ganan tossed a pebble into the water, watching it bounce over jostling lily pads before sinking into the colourless depths. Then, nodding in Hollar's direction, he said, "He is clever. He is more clever than some of my older boys."

Glen turned to observe the child. "It's a shame that most of Annabel's friends don't see it that way," she said. "They look down on him."

"But they are only English."

"What do you mean, 'only'?"

He shrugged. "The whites spend so much time studying us, sorting us into categories – has it never occurred to you that perhaps we are looking back?" Ganan began to tear at the grass by his side, pulling each blade out by the root and splitting it down the middle. Glen recognized a part of herself in his voice: a young man's rage with the world; an itchy, irritable impatience to *do* something, to prove himself. Could she blame him for wanting more? "Of course, it takes imagination to appreciate this. That's why we so often fall back on easy labels: white, brown, Indian, English. But children like Hollar blur the boundaries; they disrupt the regular order of things. *Half-demon and half-child*, indeed. That's why they are feared."

"Feared?" She had not seen fear in the eyes of the bumptious military men who had tweaked Hollar's ear and ruffled his hair on their last visit to the Club. "Well, I wouldn't be so sure of that."

"I assume he won't be sent to school in England, unlike his sister."

"Only because he has an awful lot of catching up to do. And Annabel is rather hoping he'll take an interest in running the estate…"

"Well, then."

"Well, what?"

He looked away. "These are things that maybe you cannot understand."

"Help me to understand, then."

"I don't want to lecture you."

"I want to know. I want to make it better."

Ganan laughed. "Of course you do! That is why your aunt adopted the boy in the first place." His voice was gently teasing. "You women are all the same: you make pets of foreign children so that they will not grow into foreign men. They will be like you, moulded in your image. The less foreign they are, the less threatening they seem."

The girl frowned. She hadn't told him about the day in Colombo, when a stone had been flung at her head, and he would not have noticed the scar unless she mentioned it. In different company she might have boasted jokingly of her "war wound" – but with him, she thought, this would only have caused embarrassment.

"I don't think Annabel feels threatened by anyone," she said. "She wanted to make a difference, that's all." Then, after a pause, "And so do I."

"It is far too great a task for an English lady to take on all alone."

"But I'm not on my own. I'm with you."

He was silent for several moments. "We do not need the English to help us," he said. "We have nothing to learn from the Empire about justice."

"I didn't mean it like that." Why must he be so quick to remind her of the differences between them? "Tell me, then: what is there for us to be afraid of?"

"Surely you can see for yourself." At last, he conceded a gentle smile. "Hollar's father must have feared him, or why else would he have fled?"

"But we don't know that he fled. Anything might have happened to him."

"Well, where is he, then?" Ganan glanced over one shoulder, and then the other, half joking. Then he leant back onto his elbows once more, lazily crossing one leg over the other. "He is not

here, and there is a reason for that: as far as the English are concerned, it is one thing to take a native mistress, but quite another
to admit to fathering her child."

Glen pondered this for a moment. "I've come to be friends
with a retired army captain who arrived in the area only recently
– Captain Emil Royce. Have you met him?"

"I've not had that honour."

"Well, he says that Hollar's mother was a Hindu. I suppose
Hollar must have told him that himself – or else it's common
knowledge at the guest house where he's staying."

"There you have it," said Ganan decisively. "To a Hindu, there
is no more exclusive stream of blood – and Hollar's blood is pol-
luted. He can never be one of them."

"But surely he would prefer to have the advantages of an English boy?"

Ganan looked up at her with wounded eyes. "That is neither
here nor there. Hindus are as particular about their blood as the
Jews. It is this pride that will be their undoing."

For an instant, Glen pictured the crooked wheel emblazoned
on Pieter's latest letter, and in the same moment she remembered
what he had said about the prison being laid out like a star, with
corridors leading away from the centre so that prisoners in one
wing would never know what might be happening in another.

"Glen?" Ganan laughed. "What is it?"

"You sound as if you've been listening to too much twaddle
from Mr Hitler..."

Her companion shrugged. "Hitler is a smart man, no? And
strong: he has led a crippled nation to greatness. He wouldn't
be fooled by Gandhi's sentimental trickery, as the British are. We
should be so lucky to have such leaders here."

Perplexed by his words, Glen did not notice the children running towards them.

"Seventeen," declared Althea with pride. Hollar returned the
pencil with a crumpled ticket stub on which he had recorded the
names. Ganan studied the list with a concentrated frown.

"This is very good," he said. "Very impressive, indeed. I've not
seen a hoopoe in a very long time."

"It's got a head like a woodpecker," said Hollar.

"Come and sit," urged Glen. "Mr Dharmasena is going to tell us all a story now." She shot Ganan a look as the children settled on the grass. "A folk tale, perhaps. Isn't that right, Mr Dharmasena?"

"Now that I can do," replied Ganan, with a conspiratorial glimmer. "It is a well-known fable in these parts, a story called 'The Blind Men and the Elephant'. Do you know it?"

They shook their heads.

"Well, it goes like this. A group of blind men was confronted by an elephant. Each man touched the elephant to try to discern what it might be, before sharing his opinions with the others. One man touched a tusk, and said that it must be a ploughshare; another man felt the tip of the tail and said it must be a rope. Then another felt the leg, and said it must be a pillar; the one who touched the ear said it was a fan; the one who touched the trunk said it was the branch of a tree. And the man who felt its side says it was a wall."

"And they were all wrong," smiled Althea.

"Well, they were all correct, in a way – but only partially so." Ganan straightened, becoming fully the schoolteacher. "What do you suppose the moral is?"

"That people should work together," chirped Althea.

"That there are different ways of seeing things," said Hollar.

"That all truth is relative," smiled Glen, with a mischievous glint.

Ganan nodded to each in turn. "You are already very wise," he said, and Glen noticed how his eyes seemed to laugh even when the rest of his face was serious. "The story does what the Cubist painters do, showing us all angles at once. I doubt that there is very much of consequence that I can teach you, after all."

"May we have an ice cream, Glen?" begged Althea, her attention swiftly diverted by the sight of a man steering a deep barrel trolley along the path.

"He is selling kulfi," said Ganan. "Do you prefer mango or pistachio?"

"Mango!" chimed both children.

"And you, Miss?"

"Pistachio sounds lovely," she said.

"Excellent." Ganan smacked his thigh and turned towards the *kulfiwallah*. "And when I come back, it will be Miss Glen's turn to tell us all one of her stories."

19

"You boys," sighed Mr Hendryks. "You grow too quickly."

We were searching the vestry for a spare surplice. Mine was now so small that it bunched up the armpits of the robe worn underneath. I looked like one of the sausages that you'd see discarded on the counter at the butchers' – the ones that had gone wrong, overstuffed into their stockings so that the filling spilled out at the top and bottom. For the last few months, the bottom of my surplice has been inching its way up from my knees to my waist.

"That's what Mother says," I replied. "That's what she used to say about Krelis. She had to keep letting out the hems in his trousers, until one day there wasn't any hem left – so Krelis had to wear Father's trousers to school. The other boys laughed at him."

"Now why would they do that?" asked Mr Hendryks, with a sad look.

"Because the trousers were ratty. They had oil stains on them and one of the buttons was missing, so Mother had to sew on another that didn't match. Like clown trousers."

"You're going to be tall like your brother," said Mr Hendryks. "I can tell."

"I'm only five foot two."

"You'll grow." Mr Hendryks pulled a bundle of robes from the chest he'd been rummaging through. "Here, try these."

When we had found one that fit, Mr Hendryks told me that he would take it home for his wife to iron so that it would be ready for church on Sunday.

"You don't need to do that," I said. "Mother can iron."

"Any way that we can help, we'd like to," explained Mr Hendryks. And because I knew that Mother would not miss the extra work, I didn't protest any further.

When we saw that the tearooms opposite Sint-Janskerk were still open, Mr Hendryks suggested a slice of *rijsttaart*. Knowing that there was a good chance Mother would have forgotten to buy food for supper, I agreed. We went inside and placed our orders with the waitress before sitting down to a table by the window.

"We missed you in church last week," said Mr Hendryks. "I had to tell Father Goossens that you were unwell." I didn't look at him, concentrating instead on pressing my fingernail into a groove in the table. "I know that was a lie, Marten. Where were you?"

I cut a vertical line across the horizontal one I was working into the wood. I could have told him the truth – that church was boring compared to the things Arend was teaching us; that I enjoyed shirking my duties because it was the last thing that anyone expected of me – but instead I just shrugged.

"Arend says that the Papist devil should be driven out of Flanders," I said.

Mr Hendryks looked startled. "Who's Arend?" he asked.

"The troop leader."

Mr Hendryks sighed. "Krelis never missed church," he said.

I glanced up at him to see if he was trying to trick me. But Mr Hendryks only looked sad.

"Krelis wasn't perfect, either," I said. "People don't know."

"Don't know what?"

I shrugged again.

"Tell me about this group you're in," said Mr Hendryks at last. "Are there many of you in it?"

"About a dozen in our troop," I said. "But there are other groups in the district, and hundreds in the region, and maybe thousands beyond that..."

"I got the impression that they move in packs."

"Not a pack, exactly. More like..." I gazed out the window, my eye caught by the flutter of rooks' wings. "More like a flock."

Mr Hendryks smiled. "Oh?"

"The way a flock moves, all balanced and ordered." I tried to show him using the plane of my hand. "You know why the patterns keep changing, don't you? When they're flying, and the formation looks like a blanket that keeps folding in on itself?"

"Why?"

"Because none of the birds want to be on the edges. When they're on the edges, they become targets for bigger birds. *Zap!*" I pinched my fingers like a beak at him. "If you're a bird, you're always trying to move to the centre, where it's safe."

"I didn't know that."

I remembered a trick that Pepijn had shown us. "It's like putting your hand through a flame. The middle part won't hurt you – you can put out a match with your fingers like that – but if you try to touch the outside bits, you'll get burnt."

Mr Hendryks nodded slowly. "So are they nice boys? Are they your friends?"

I considered the question. "Not friends, exactly. Comrades." And then, because I knew that this was what the Bolshevists called each other, I hastened to add, "Not comrades in that way, though. More like brothers in arms."

"In arms? Are you preparing for a war?"

"Isn't everyone?" I asked. The waitress arrived and slid two plates of *rijsttaart* onto the table. "Anyway, you'll be glad that we've been so prepared. If a war were to break out tomorrow, you'd be too old to join up, and it would be down to the youth to fight."

"Youth, eh? Is that what they call children nowadays?" Mr Hendryks speared the pastry with his fork.

"We're not like other kids. Arend toughens us up with circuit training and…"

"And what?"

"And tests of courage." I thought of the burn marks on Bastiaan's legs, the welts on Willem's palms. "Everyone gets broken down and built up again. Like taking a clock apart to find the bit that's going wrong and then putting it back together."

We watched a nursemaid walk past the window, leading six young charges. Each child was harnessed to a blue strap that the nursemaid had hooked around her wrist. Now and then she would give the strap a gentle tug to keep the toddlers from straying into the road.

"Man grows strong before he becomes good," sighed Mr Hendryks. "Youth doesn't know how to handle its strength. It is amoral – it thinks it can transcend God by defying His word."

"But it's not about morals, or God," I said, growing impatient. "It's not about any of that. It's about building character."

"Is that what Arend tells you?"

I shrugged, wondering how much Arend would want me to reveal to a non-member.

"Morality is something that you grapple with alone," said Mr Hendryks after a while. "No one can dictate it to you."

"Church dictates it, though."

"You take things too literally, Marten. Church offers us a code to live by; rules to help us rise above our baser instincts—"

"Arend says the rules are there to keep us lazy, so we'll stay weak. It only tells us what it wants us to hear."

"Oh? Such as?"

"Church tells us all about Hell, about mortal sins and venial sins, and eternal punishment and temporal punishment, and Purgatory and Limbo, and on and on." I took another bite, trying to swallow the frustration that was building in my throat. "But when you ask about Heaven, no one has any answers. 'It's a place so beautiful we can't even imagine it,' they say. Well, the Movement is different. It tells us exactly what we're fighting for. The troop is different, because it gives us respect."

"And hope? Does it give you that, too?"

"Of course."

"Really?"

I nodded. Mr Hendryks set his fork down and pushed his plate towards me. He'd not eaten half of his *rijsttaart*, although I'd already cleaned my plate of every last morsel. "Have it," he said. "After all, you're a growing boy."

20

He suggested that she join him at the Saturday market.

"I will be looking for a fish," he told Glen, as they left the Cinnamon Gardens.

"Excuse me?"

"To paint. You'll help me choose one?"

It was as unusual an invitation as she had ever received, and Glen had willingly agreed.

The market at Nuwara Eliya was one of the few local destinations that didn't pander to English conventions. It was tidy, to be sure – far more orderly than the heaving trail of street vendors that Glen had encountered on her arrival at Colombo – and there were, among the piles of avocados, pomegranates and star-shaped carambola, other more familiar products: Fairy soap and Radox salts, Cox's Gelatine and Cadbury's drinking cocoa – even Triumph bicycle wheels. The shoppers were almost exclusively native, however, and they haggled loudly in Hindi and Sinhala with stall holders resplendent in their market-day sarongs.

"The fish will have been brought up first thing this morning," explained Ganan. "That's why there is almost no smell. My mother always told me: a fresh fish should smell like cucumbers." A steely matter-of-factness belied his playful tone. "The English are too eager to smother fish in brine and batter. Here, you will see the real thing, as Nature intended."

He was in a fine mood today. Allowing herself to be led, the girl noted the way he seemed to carry himself straighter than everyone they passed. At last he stopped before the fishmonger's stall.

"Here we are." He planted both hands on his hips and considered the rows of glistening, scaly bodies. "What do you think?"

Glen found it difficult to see very far beyond the bloated puffer fish propped between mounds of crushed ice.

"Isn't it ghastly?" she whispered.

"Not quite the effect I was aiming for. But the others—" He guided her gently by the shoulders around one side of the stall, and Glen noted a pleasant sensation of being made to feel looked after. "You see, I was thinking of a still life. Scallops and cuttlefish, perhaps… and that red grouper for a little colour."

The girl pointed to a swordfish suspended by the nose from an overhanging branch. "He's a handsome specimen!"

"And far too dear for my limited budget," laughed the Indian. "I'm afraid we may have to limit ourselves to what's on the table."

"Oh, well… those yellow and pink ones are pretty. The little ones."

Ganan said something to the pin-eyed stallholder. "Snapper," he told her.

"One of those, then. Or the mackerel."

In the end, it was the mackerel that won: Ganan said that its silver-blue stripes would make for a fine study. "A watercolour etching," he said. "And *then* to my plate! It is a hard lesson for a fish to learn, that none of us can break out of our destinies."

"You believe in such a thing?" laughed the girl. "Tell me, then: what is mine?"

"To grow bored with this little island," he said, smiling. "To return home and marry a nice English boy with a respectable income. To bear him three plump, rosy-cheeked children and write a series of best-selling novels."

As they made their way across the road, a bicycle bell shrilled just in time for them to dodge its rider, a square-headed young man whose horn-rimmed glasses were a size too large and whose shirt clung wetly to his shoulders and back. Glen had opened her mouth to scold him for riding so recklessly, when Ganan opened his arms to receive the fellow in a friendly embrace. The two men exchanged words in a language Glen took to be Sinhala, while she waited patiently to one side, wondering when she might be introduced. The cyclist was stocky, with a beard that made him appear older than his years, and black eyes like currants set deep into his fleshy face. He wore a peaked cap similar to the one she had seen worn by Nehru in pictures and newsreels, although it was khaki, not white. As he erupted into peals of laughter, he patted his stomach and stomped one foot on the ground, propping his bicycle against the other leg.

At last, he seemed to notice the white woman, and passed a remark that made Ganan smile and shake his head. Glen thrust one hand towards the man, saying, "How do you do? Glynis Phayre."

"Glen – this is Roshan Samarajiva. We were schoolmates at the college." Ganan shifted his weight, glancing from the one to the other.

"A pleasure to meet you, Miss Phayre. I hope you are enjoying your little excursion?" Roshan's eyes twinkled as he shook her hand.

"It's been a lovely day." She glanced at her companion. "We've been looking for a fish for Ganan to paint…"

"Ah, yes: artistic pursuits!" Roshan said something in Sinhala, to which Ganan responded with a playful swipe. "Well, then I'll leave you to it. I hope we may meet again, Miss Phayre. You take care, eh, Ganan?" Laughing merrily, the man pushed off the ground with one foot, and wheeled himself through the crowd of shoppers, leaving them to wander back towards the drinks stand.

"What did he say to you?" she asked him.

"Nothing. Roshan has an unusual sense of humour. And he's not experienced at conversing with English ladies." Ganan sighed. "If you must know, he said he hadn't realized the market had become a safari park. He said a white woman must be careful not to creep too near the tigers."

Glen cast her gaze about the lazy procession of bullock hackeries, the freshly swept pavement, the elegant cornices decorating the pink stone wall that ran the length of the avenue. "As if I should be in any danger here…"

"Roshan knows of what he speaks. For too long we have been told that it is in our nature to be gentle." Ganan took her by the arm, pulled her out of the path of two boys on bicycles. "But those days are running out."

"He interests himself in political matters, I take it?"

Ganan smiled wryly. "As far as Roshan is concerned, in this country right now, there is only one political matter."

They bought some drinks and sat for a while on the steps of an unmanned ox cart to observe the market from a more comfortable distance. The coconut water had been sweetened with sugar and lemon juice and was a fine quencher.

"I hope you are writing another story," said Ganan at last.

Glen scraped the inside of the coconut with her straw. She did not want to admit that she had not written anything since the story she had shown him that day on the veranda – weeks ago now.

"I've promised my prisoner one, actually," she said evasively.

"Your prisoner?"

"A pen friend in Flanders. His name is Pieter. He's asked me to write him a story."

Ganan placed his coconut on the ground with a purposeful air. "What a wonderful thing," he said. "In all my life, I have only spent one night in a prison cell. But it was the loneliest I have ever felt."

Glen regarded him with amusement. "What on earth did you do to end up in prison?"

"Nothing remarkable," came the rueful reply. "I objected to being charged at by a couple of louts one night in Holborn. They had been drinking; I had not. I made the mistake of coming out of it in better shape than they did." Ganan offered her his hand as he rose to his feet. Glen accepted it and felt its strength.

"I don't suppose you'd like to come to a party?" she said, as they began to walk towards the bridge. The invitation from Douglas Brink had arrived only that morning. He had written the previous week to tell her that the culprit in the stone-throwing incident had been identified as a local street sweeper: *Mentally subnormal, by all accounts. He's been roughed up a bit, but shall almost certainly be released unless you decide to press charges.* Glen had thrown the letter into the grate without a second thought.

Ganan turned to her with a look of surprise. "A party?"

"In Matale. It's on the twenty-second. I'd love to go with you."

"I doubt I'll be able to make it, Glen."

She had no right to feel disappointed, Glen told herself, as they disposed of the coconut shells. Then, turning back up the main road, she noticed a white man in riding uniform cutting an imperious line through the crowd, trailed by a native assistant and a small child, presumably his daughter. White bloomers like cotton blossoms peeped beneath the little girl's smock, and women squatting by the roadside reached out to pinch her dimpled knees.

Her father had paused to buy a packet of cigarettes when the child's attention was attracted by the flute-player at the roadside – an ancient Vedda, naked but for a soiled loincloth and a knotted piece of string tied around one bony wrist, whose toes clutched the dirt where he squatted. When they had passed him earlier that morning, Glen noticed Ganan avert his eyes; he had shielded her from the old man with his body as if to protect her from something she wouldn't understand. It was only when the flute-player's tune ended in an abrupt, hideous squawk that Glen realized what had just happened. The child was hurried away by the attendant as the white man began thrashing the Vedda with his crop, ignoring his victim's pitiful wails and whirling arms.

Glen was waiting for a reaction from the crowd, but those shoppers and stall holders who had not simply carried on with their business watched on with blank indifference.

"Please," she whispered, turning to Ganan. "*Do* something."

But it was already too late. Whatever crime the Vedda had committed – enticing the white man's daughter with savage music? – he looked unlikely to offend a second time. As his assailant tucked his crop under one arm, drawing the back of one hand beneath his nose to wipe away the sweat, a pair of elderly women approached the crumpled figure on the ground. Gathering his head in her lap, one of them began to pull her fingers through his tangled hair; the other appeared to be checking for signs of life. Neither of them looked up at the purple-faced man who towered above them.

It was only as he turned to leave that the white man saw Glen. He seemed about to speak, but then he noticed Ganan. His gaze flitted between the white woman and the Indian man – once, twice – but he said nothing and, turning on his heel, he called after his assistant and left.

Ganan took her hand, lacing his fingers through hers.

"Thank you," she whispered, tightening her grip.

* * *

Until he took my hand, Pieter, I couldn't have told you what his feelings for me were. But in that moment I saw that he considers me his equal, and we have become united in our heresy against the old ways.

Is this love? There is something about him that gives me a sort of thrilling enchantment – something as ancient and wonderful as the green mountains that rise up all around us here, steadfastly guarding their secrets even as they seem to offer up an irresistible challenge – something truly alive, that I have never before seen in the eyes of an Englishman.

This land is deceptive, Pieter, and cruel in its deceptions. An ancient kingdom reduced to ruins where foreign tourists now picnic and snap photographs. No wonder he sought an escape: for a boy like Ganan must live a double deception, to his community and to the white man.

"Sometimes, their ignorance makes me afraid that I may one day do something I will regret," he told me as we left the market today. He said he would not want me to be a part of such a thing, whatever it may be. But now, how can I not?

No chance of sleep tonight! Our generator is running low again, and I promised Aunt Annabel that I would not keep my light on too late. More on the morrow…

21

I was halfway through her letter when I felt my stomach tear.

At least, I thought it was my stomach. There were only instants in which to hurl myself downstairs – through the kitchen, down the back steps, round the garden wall – before slamming the outhouse door behind me.

Afterwards, using a stick, I lifted my tapeworm from the bowl and examined it against the light that filtered through the outhouse walls. A white-yellow ribbon, about twelve inches long and so flat as to be almost translucent, coiled and flexed as I steered the stick towards the door.

My mother kept biscuit tins decorated with photographs of the royal family in the kitchen. My father used to joke that they joined us for coffee in the afternoons – even Princess Astrid, who had died in a car crash a year earlier. The pictures showed them playing in the garden, or posing in all their finery before the palace. Father would line the tins out along the kitchen table and ask if Her Royal Highness would mind passing the digestives, and if little Albert, with his golden mop of hair, wouldn't like some warm milk to go with his violet creams.

But with Krelis gone, we didn't have coffee together as a family any more, and King Leopold and Princess Astrid stayed with their children high up on the highest shelf, behind the sacks of flour and sugar that Mother didn't use because she no longer had the heart for baking.

Still balancing my tapeworm on the end of the stick, I climbed onto the kitchen counter, pulled down an oval tin with a portrait of Prince Baudouin on top and gently tipped the worm inside.

I took it with me upstairs, and returned to her letter.

There is one final thing that I must ask you, Pieter. Last night I could not decide if it was something worth mentioning at all, but in the bright light of day I have realized that I simply must.

I'm referring to the swastika with which you sealed your latest letter. Not to put too fine a point on it, Pieter, you simply cannot send things through the post emblazoned with such vile insignia. I dread to imagine what my poor aunt must have thought. I made my excuses, of course – but she has insisted that no such sign appear on any future letters arriving at Beulah Lodge, and any which do shall be immediately confiscated.

Perhaps, from inside your prison, it is hard for you to understand precisely the sorts of things we are hearing coming not only out of Germany these days, but England too – blackshirted gangs wreaking terror in the streets of London, of all places – and to appreciate the feelings that they stir up in families here and at home. You must take my word for it that whatever that sign represents for you, it has nothing to do with God-fearing, decent people of any nation or creed. I have no doubt that an intelligent and sensitive man such as yourself could scarcely support such a thuggish regime. I was hoping that our letters would strike a blow against selfishness and prejudice; I am not embarrassed to say that I even imagined that, should you one day be vindicated and released into the world – a hero, a prisoner of conscience who endured despite the odds – your letters would stand as a testament to the human spirit.

Please promise me that this shall be the end of any flirtation you may have with the agents of tyranny. Otherwise, I am afraid that I shall not be able to continue with this correspondence.

I blushed. This was not what I had intended at all. The only other person I had thought capable of making me feel this way was currently snoring loudly on the other side of the gatehouse wall.

Dear G.P.,

I will not include in this letter the sign that you call "vile". But you are wrong. It is a symbol of strength, unity and discipline. Pride, also. These are things that the English cannot understand, because England is a country full of Jews and communists. This is not your fault, of course.

I swallowed, torn between rage and humiliation. How dare she – she, who had written so proudly of heresy, of her love for a savage! Didn't she realize that these were tainted words?

Jesus said, "A house divided against itself falleth." Well, that is the way it is in your country – but not here. Tell me this: how can the Movement be bad if it makes us so joyful, if it fills us with hope?

Perhaps you don't realize that I am actually quite happy here. Sometimes I think that freedom is not such a wonderful thing, after all. At least prison keeps us safe from the people who would see us come to harm.

I returned to her letter, which included a brief description of a tiger hunt. Apparently, one of the men at the European Club had shot a male weighing almost thirty-five stone.

I enjoyed your story about the tiger, I wrote.

The only thing I can tell you about tigers is that you should always provide them with an escape route. If they feel trapped, they'll attack. A wounded tiger is much more dangerous than a healthy one.

I stuck my pencil between my teeth and prised open the biscuit tin. My tapeworm was curled up and looked much smaller than before. I replaced the lid and continued writing.

In fact, humans are a lot like tigers when they feel trapped. My friend Hendryks says that nowadays people are so busy watching their backs, they don't look where they're going. And that's when they become dangerous.

So dangerous that even God is afraid of us. That is when he starts to smite people, like spiders in the bath.

I tapped my pencil against the biscuit tin.

Did you know that baby cobras send out a nasty smell so that their mothers won't eat them? Imagine if you were that afraid of your own mother. Arend says that women should stay at home to look after their families. My girlfriend, Mieke, wants to be a doctor. Arend would say that she wants seeing to. Do you know what that means? Sometimes I would like to hurt her. Not in a bad way. Just to prove it. Do you understand?

Arend also says that we are descended from the Aryans, who came from India thousands of years ago. Arend says that Indians today have forgotten their glorious past. He says that the men have forgotten how to be men.

I read through what I had written so far. Almost as soon as I reached the end, I tore it up and started again.

Dear G.P.,

I'm sorry that it has taken me a while to write, but I have been unwell. I am sending you a gift. I'm sorry that it couldn't be a necklace, or flowers, but it is all I have.

Pieter

I passed by the Lekaerts' house on my way to the post office. In the front room, someone was playing a gramophone. I checked myself in case it was jazz, which Arend called a corrupting in- fluence. But the voice wasn't American at all. It sounded like Marlene Dietrich singing 'Ich bin die fesche Lola', and so I stopped to listen, resting my satchel upon the low wall.

They call me naughty Lola
The wisest girl on earth;
At home my pianola
It works for all it's worth.
The boys all love my music,
I can't keep them away,

So my little pianola
keeps working night and day.

Noticing a movement by the window, I pretended to rummage in my satchel. It sounded like Mrs Lekaerts, speaking in that gossipy voice women use when they're discussing things they know they shouldn't be talking about.

"That's just what I thought," she was saying to whoever it was in the front room with her. "No better than terrorists. I should imagine the poor man wishes he'd died with his comrades in the trenches… I mean, the *Kommunistische*!"

Bolshevists. Arend said that they were no better than common brigands – that come the day of reckoning they would try to snatch control of the Fatherland, and we must all be ready to defend Belgium against them.

I was straining to hear more when suddenly the window slammed shut, and the song on the gramophone disappeared into crisp silence.

22

"But what is it?"

Glen slid the piece of string back into the envelope and consulted the letter again. *I'm sorry that it couldn't be a necklace, or flowers, but it is all I have.* "He's very interested in natural science," she said. "I think it must be some kind of worm."

"I knew a little boy who used to eat worms," said Althea. "Boys are horrid."

"Pieter isn't horrid," replied Glen. And then, "The poor fellow – their prisons are far worse than ours. They corrupt innocent men."

Althea slid down from the bed and peered over Glen's shoulder into the vanity mirror. "Will you help me with my eyes now?"

Glen lined the child's lower lids with kohl, tapering the ends upwards like an Egyptian's.

"It needs to be darker," whispered Althea a few moments later.

Her cousin smiled, dutifully smudging darker shadow over her eyelids.

"Are you finished? Can I get dressed now?"

"Hurry up, then – your guests will be here soon."

The fancy-dress party for her eleventh birthday had been Althea's own idea. It did not matter to the child that she was a girl and that sultans were men, or that all the other little girls would be arriving as ballerinas or fairies. No pink tulle and ballet slippers for her, no tiara and bouncing ringlets. Black *shalwar* trousers borrowed from Jayanadani billowed over slippers that curled up at the toes. Her mother's burgundy prayer shawl, a souvenir from a honeymoon visit to the Punjab, had been transformed into a resplendent kaftan. Althea herself had painted an old pillowcase with a vivid Bird of Paradise motif to serve as a cloak. Her fuchsia turban sprouted an enormous peacock plume and black heron feathers that she had collected from about the estate.

"If only Mummy would let me wear a ring in my nose, like Jayanadani," she said, performing a turn on the landing as they made their way down to the garden – and Glen recalled the morning of her twelfth birthday, when her own mother had refused to let her wear one of Merle's evening gowns and instead pressed upon her a childish cotton frock.

"Is it all right? Do I look like a real sultan?" her cousin asked Glen again.

"Positively fearsome," smiled Glen. "Althea the Grim."

Mrs Cornish had arrived early to help Annabel decorate the garden with bunting. Her little boy – the indulged son-prince, six years old and small for his age – squatted on the garden step, sipping a glass of pink lemonade as the cousins emerged onto the veranda.

"What have you come as?" asked Althea.

"Tom Kitten," replied Penderel. He flinched as his ayah intervened to straighten his collar, grumbling when she reached to do up his top button.

"*Chalo*," smiled the ayah, ever patient.

"Tom Kitten? The one who was rolled in dough by a couple of nasty rats?" pressed Althea as soon as the nanny had retreated. Glen watched her tug the boy towards the table where ices were being laid out.

"Settling in nicely, are you?" Mrs Cornish beamed at Glen across the table of fairy cakes and petits fours, jellies and meringues, nudging a plate of lace biscuits closer to the majestic trifle that she had provided. "I don't know how your aunt manages, without proper help."

Glen sank into a planter's chair next to the phonograph. "Micah and Perdita provide all the help we need," she smiled, as she began to crank the handle, slowly teasing out the opening bars of a mazurka.

"Perdita's girls are like little dolls, aren't they?" cooed Mrs Cornish. "It's a shame to think they can't stay children for ever. I'd not grown up with servants myself, so I didn't know any better when Monty and I moved out here. Fell into the trap of thinking that I could confide in our girl, and how did she repay me? Got herself pregnant within the year and cleared off with two jewellery boxes." Mrs Cornish gingerly removed the capers from her sandwich before rearranging the salmon on the bread. "Now tell me," she continued, clearing her throat. "I don't suppose you've left a nice young man at home, have you?"

"No one special, no."

"Because Walter knows a fellow in the reserve army just your age. Not a military man, himself – he's a clerk. Lovely lad. Scottish, I think. A little shy, but you know his type. Monty and I would be more than happy to join you two at the botanical gardens some time." Her face became prim. "So many young people today think propriety is rather unfashionable, don't they? What with the King himself running off with that American hussy…" And she wriggled in her chair as if to release a crawling insect that had trapped itself in the folds of her dress.

"More tea, Cee?" Annabel inserted herself between her guest and Glen.

Mr Fenwick and Mr Childs helped to organize the tug of war that preceded the cutting of the cake, while Will Carney nursed a gin and tonic and watched his sons, dressed as pirates, playing at blind man's bluff with Hollar at the bottom of the garden.

"Splendid party, Annabel," he said. "Like something out of a storybook."

"Why thank you, Will," smiled Glen's aunt, making room for the cake. "It's just this blasted heat… the ice cream went a bit soft on one side, do you see?"

"Rather like me!" Mr Carney laughed, giving his wife's knee a pinch. "Isn't that right, darling?"

Fiona Carney gave a restrained smile.

"I hear you're a rather fine poet," said Mr Carney, flashing Glen a gleaming grin and winking like a schoolboy. "Lonely business, poetry."

"I've never thought of myself as lonely," said Glen.

"I shouldn't have thought so, either – a pretty girl like you!" said Mr Carney, laughing. His wife shifted in her chair. "Fi did some volunteer work with the local orphanage recently," he continued. "Turns out the old girl has a peculiarly poor sense of smell – isn't that right Fi? Meant that the other ladies were only too happy to let her care for the filthiest children. And believe me, some of them are proper little ragamuffins!"

"It's the least we can do," said Fiona. "First there was the drought, then the malaria epidemic last year…"

"That's right. Awful, awful. And those lot up north, banging on about self-rule – it's ridiculous. Eh? *In the land of the blind, the one-eyed man is king.* Eh?"

"As long as we're here, I think it's our duty to help," persisted Fiona. "So that when we go home—"

"But this *is* home, darling."

"You know what I mean," said Mrs Carney to her husband in a low voice.

It was six o'clock before the guests started to leave. Glen decided that she could still make it to the church in time – as long as Mrs Cornish didn't insist on staying on for one last sherry after the others had gone. But in the end she and Penderel left with the Carneys: the women cradling wedges of leftover cake, the children testing the noisemakers they had received as presents, sending a swelling rumour of sound into the valley below.

* * *

He was waiting for her when she arrived, hovering by the side entrance in the shade of a mangosteen tree, where it was not possible to be seen from the house. She noticed his bicycle first, chrome fenders glinting in the moonlight, before she heard his cough. Silhouetted against the luminescent green of the misted hillside, his figure cast complex shadows against the mottled walls.

The venue had been the result of a hasty but sagacious choice: Emil was spending the weekend with friends in Nanu Oya, and Hollar was taking his bath. None of the workers would dare visit here during the day, let alone at night. No one else would disturb them.

196

"I thought you might not come. Or that I had misread your directions."

"Is the door locked?"

"No." He moved aside. "Ladies first."

They seated themselves at a discreet distance in the last pew, and Ganan set a leather satchel between his feet. "Who showed you this place, then?"

"Emil." Clearly her companion did not recognize the name. "The English fellow who's been staying at the Burgher guest house in the village. Hollar's friend."

"The blind man?"

"Yes. He's a bit of a recluse, but in the nicest possible way."

Ganan smiled. In profile, his hawked nose, locked jaw and the stern ridge of his brow appeared severe, but front-on, his face was round and boyish. There was a softness to his gaze, an awkwardness to his expression, that reminded Glen of the beaming faces of children who chased after cars that rumbled through the village.

He reached into the satchel and carefully withdrew a folder. "Here: I made these for you."

Inside were three pieces of paper, each of which bore a portrait. The first two were of Tamil girls; the last picture was a fresh impression of the sketch from the botanical gardens: a dreamlike recollection of the reclining woman.

"I've never seen anything like it…"

"They are drawn with candle smoke. One catches the smoke by moving the paper overhead. In other words, the image is a carbon deposit."

"How clever!" *Like ghosts that have been pinned to paper*, thought Glen.

Ganan wiggled his head in a sideways nod. "It is quite a primitive technique. My fatality rate gets better with practice – there are not so many fire alarms nowadays."

Glen peered closely at the image of a child, where it was almost possible to detect the pattern of a flame repeated in negative light. She marvelled at the detail in the hatched creases of the jutting lip, the lines beneath the eyes. "They must be exceedingly fragile."

"Just as we are." He caught Glen's glance, held it long enough for her to shuffle the papers and return them to the folder.

"You should become an illustrator. Your talent is wasted teaching multiplication tables."

"I am working on a series of pictures to accompany a Sinhalese translation of the Mahabharata. Illustrations will never do justice to the Sanskrit, of course – how did the British judge describe it? 'More perfect than Greek, more copious than Latin, and more exquisitely refined than either'…"

"You do yourself a disservice. I think it sounds a marvellous idea."

"You know it, then?"

Glen tried to recall a picture book on Althea's shelf, filled with images of anthropomorphic heroes and multi-headed monsters. "It's an Indian myth, isn't it? Like the *Odyssey*."

"The Mahabharata is longer than the *Odyssey* and the Iliad put together. It is *our* story – it explains who we are." He studied her carefully. "Are you surprised that I am proud of these things?"

"Why should I be?" said Glen.

"Because before you sits Macaulay's Indian gentleman: English in tastes, morals and intellect. My own father died fighting for Britain in Mesopotamia. According to his comrades, he was entranced by the sight of a bird in flight when the bullet caught him in the back of the head." His expression did not soften with sadness: his tone was matter-of-fact. "It comforts me to know that his last moments were filled with beauty, with a vision of perfect freedom."

Glen pulled her legs beneath her, wondering what to say. She recalled the warmth of the stone grazing her skin that day in Colombo, the parrot outside the hospital window. "I'm so sorry," she whispered at last, reaching for his hand.

"My father gave his life for another man's ideal," he said, softly, as if testing her. "Maybe you would call it 'imperial tripe'."

"It must be awfully difficult," she ventured, "being torn between two allegiances. Like Mr Nehru."

The smile returned, and his voice became contemplative, less fired. "They say that the battleground between races is fiercest where the differences are least obvious. You cannot imagine that battleground within the soul of a single man." He smoothed a wisp of golden hair behind her ear, traced the curve of her cheek with gentle fingers. "The memsahib will call her servant a boy only until he gives her reason to find out that he is, in fact, no child. By that point, it is too late – for both of them..."

It was not too late just then. Too soon, perhaps, thought Glen, as she placed the collection of portraits to one side to allow him closer. The tips of slender fingers brushing her own, the incline of his head as she moved towards him – too soon.

And then she remembered Mrs Cornish pontificating about propriety and good form, and Will Carney pinching his wife's knee as he winked across the table. Suddenly it all seemed so trivial: their petty mores and indiscretions. Here, in the solemn stillness of the half-light, kneeling beneath a canopy of foreign sky, near the graves of little souls never destined to know this feeling, she recognized something different in the curl of his lashes gently brushing her cheek, something terrifyingly real.

Later, she would recall his awkwardness in those first moments – he was watching her, watching himself, chafing against the role in which he had been cast – and she thought of the party that she was missing at this very moment: the bright bodies of young girls swaying in the arms of clumsy boys playing at being men. She remembered Dougie's grenadine breath and the perspiration on his brow, the way he had called her "kid". And for a moment she felt the same rage that possessed the man who was kissing her now – angry, biting kisses – and she responded in kind, until at last she came to feel that he was fighting her and everything they held in common contempt.

Never had she known a man to struggle so violently with his passion, and she wondered if she had done enough to allow him to seduce her. Later, she would tell herself that it had happened quickly, urgently, but at that particular moment things seemed to move in dream-time, dream-slow.

She looked at her own hands, the colour of milk glass against his dark skin, and she wondered why he seemed less real to her now than the lover she had created in daydreams. Why did their bodies seem so suddenly foreign – his neck stained blue in the shadows, her whiteness brightly reflected in the moon's glow? Did he also feel the gazes of their ancestors, whose faces she imagined peering through the empty windows, sternly judging? Were these inherited fantasies, she wondered – the longing and fear of meeting flesh with a colour that is not one's own? Centuries of hypocrisy had led to this moment, centuries of bodies like theirs – native bodies, white bodies – being mutually forbidden, loathed and lusted after. When for a moment she opened her eyes, she saw both terror and joy in his face, a far-off look that wandered past her – through her – to a secret place. And then she realized that she was returning his naked stare, for he pressed her eyes closed with tender lips, as if to save them both from shame.

As she became aware of a half-imagined feeling, she told herself that they were Krishna and Radha: the clandestine lovers, the twice-enchanted. Yet why, at the same time, did she feel so strangely herself? *But of course, it's obvious*, she thought. *I've not loved like this before – because I've not existed like this before.*

Only then, at last, was she overcome with the sense that she had known him since the beginning, and the future was no longer a mystery.

23

Dear Pieter,

Well, where to begin?

I did say that I intended to bare myself to new experiences, although in all honesty I don't suppose this was quite what I had in mind. You remember the abandoned church I mentioned in one of my previous letters? Would it shock you to hear that in one night it has transformed from a rather sad and gloomy place to a lovers' bower? I didn't plan it that way, Pieter, honestly I didn't – and I'm sure neither did he – but now I really can't imagine how events could have unfolded any differently. I hope you won't think any less of me – I'm not a "loose" woman, Pieter – but it's all happened so quickly and yet somehow so perfectly…

Indeed, I see now that Ganan is unlike anyone else I have ever known, and yet he is just what I have always yearned for. He has a soft laugh and graceful hands, but his slight build conceals surprising strength. I saw something feral in his eyes when we first kissed: the hunger-mad look of a caged beast. And anger, too.

All of a sudden, I find myself envying Jayanadani and Nimali the hours they spend in his presence at school: I feel a frightening need to be near him, I cannot bring myself to think of the good Indian girl whom he must one day marry. But perhaps that need not be. Recently, I have enjoyed imagining what it would be like to bring him home to England, to our house, to Mummy and Pa.

Twice today I have contrived artful coincidences to see him about town – outside the school and in the bazaar – but perhaps he would be too shy to recognize me in public. I must be careful not to press him. Do you suppose he is worried about what his family would think? I should love to meet them, to prove to them that I am worthy of their son: I should wrap myself in a sari, keep my eyes lowered and kiss his mother's feet...

Afterwards, he said that we had been indiscreet, that we should proceed with caution. But I told him that it was too late for that, that nothing else mattered any more, that I only wanted to be with him. He seemed unsettled by this, and told me not to be foolish. Well, in that case I suppose I must be a fool!

I apologize for boring you with lovesick ramblings, but I simply had to share all this with someone.

Yours in exalted happiness,

G.P. (I suppose there is no harm in telling you my name; after all, I know yours. It is Glynis, but everyone calls me Glen)

P.S. I was sorry to hear that you have been unwell, and I do hope that you are feeling better by now. Thank you very much for the fascinating gift, and for not including any political insignia in your last letter. I do hope that there have been no hard feelings on this point, and that we can put our differences aside from now on?

In Krelis's room there was a box full of Harry Dickson serials going back to 1930, starting with *The Counterfeiter's Model*. I thumbed through the magazines, pausing over *The Girl Snatchers of Chinatown*. Krelis had kept that one hidden beneath a loose floorboard in his room until the day I discovered it by accident.

Issue 85 introduced Professor Flax's daughter, Georgette Cuvelier – aka "The Spider". Harry Dickson had a love-hate relationship with Georgette, whom I'd always imagined looking like Mieke but with black hair. I withdrew the magazine from the box and returned to my room.

Harry and Georgette kissed on page 14. He kissed her ruthlessly, as if meting out a punishment, but I wasn't sure what might have happened next, as the scene ended abruptly. I scanned the crucial paragraph for words that made me feel a little strange – words that I wouldn't say out loud, but that I could hold in my head next to the image of her in that dress, leaning over the map in the park.

Dear Glen, I wrote.
  Your letter reminds me of my own love-making (I swallowed and resisted the urge to cross out that word) *to my beautiful girlfriend. Pressing my mouth against her* (where was the phrase?) *sighing lips, I would hold her in an amorous embrace and* (clutch? wrestle? cup? brace?) *electrify her* (her what?) *heaving bosom with lustful caresses.*

I leant back in my chair and read what I had written. Immediately I tore it up and started again.

Dear Glen,
  You do not seem to be afraid of anything, but love frightens me. Love for money is a sin. Love for people who make you do bad things – that's also a sin. Unless they love you back. Does your gentleman love you?
  Self-love – now that is also a sin. Our talents are only given to us by God so that we may do good things on earth. Anyway, strength comes from working together, not standing out.
  When we go outdoors to exercise, they chain us together in groups. The group looks like an insect with many legs. The chains are long enough that it is possible to run a little, but not very fast. If one person goes too fast or too slow, everyone falls down. You do not want to be that person. You want to stay in the middle, and match your pace to the man in front of you. That is how you stay standing.
  Have you started to write my story yet? Perhaps you are finding it difficult. It would be best to start with the day my brother died. When my father heard that Krelis was dead, he went up to the gatehouse with a bottle of Westmalle and the family Bible and told me to go home. That was how it began.
  Now you can write the rest, please.

Love,

Pieter

203

P.S. If you can't read my brother's name, it is because I have written it in invisible ink! Hold a match under the paper to see.

* * *

Nijs and I had been friends since the day we both started at the kindergarten. Back then, school didn't mean lessons and red knuckles; it meant playing games with the nuns and learning songs beneath the lilac tree in the monks' garden.

The first time I noticed Nijs, he had his arms stuck out like a chicken. It looked as if he was trying to scratch a place on his back that was just out of reach.

"What are you doing?" I'd asked.

"Finding my angel wings," he'd replied.

"Your what?"

"When we were changing for swimming, Sister Bernadette poked my back and said, 'Look, Sister Clementine, little Nijs is starting to sprout angel wings.' And she's right: I can feel them coming in. You can touch them if you like."

He turned around.

"Those are your shoulder blades," I'd said. "They're not wings. Humans wouldn't have arms if they had wings. Look at birds."

"Insects have wings and arms," said Nijs.

"Insects are different," I'd said.

"Well, then so are angels," said Nijs.

And that's how we became friends.

I didn't see as much of him now. He wouldn't be convinced to give the Movement another go, so it was only on the way to school that we had any time to speak.

"I'm going to be a missionary when I grow up," I told him one morning.

"Not a zoologist?"

"Both," I said. "I'm going to go to the Congo and collect butterflies, and when I'm not collecting butterflies, I'll convert the natives."

"How do you do that?"

"You carry a big cross through the jungle. Like Piers de Jongh does in Mass." And I pointed my pencil at an angle, the way Piers de Jongh held the sceptre as he led the priests up and down the aisles.

"And that converts them?"

"And you teach them to read the Bible."

"Oh."

"Have you read this?" I pulled a yellow copy of *Ons Volk Ontwaakt* from my satchel and gently straightened its curling edges. The cover showed a picture of a boy our age, wearing a brown uniform and a kepi, giving the German salute. "Filip's father has a subscription. We're taking turns reading it. You can too, if you don't tell."

"Our Nation Awakes," read Nijs.

"Kuypers!"

I tore the magazine from Nijs's hands and shoved it back into my satchel. Then I turned around and saw that it was only Adriaan.

"This is for you," he said. His expression was stern, like the boy from the fulling mill who had come to tell us about Krelis. He didn't seem to notice Nijs.

He handed me a thin strip of paper covered in a jumble of letters. Nijs was peering over my shoulder to see, so I edged away.

"Thanks," I said.

"It's from Filip. Give it to Willem when you're done."

"All right."

Adriaan nodded and continued on ahead of us.

"What's that?" asked Nijs.

"It's a code," I said.

"What does it say?"

"None of your business," I told him. "It's members only."

Nijs tried to grab the paper from my hands, but I skipped out of reach just in time.

"What's so special about it, anyway? Some top-secret mission or something?"

"Actually, it is." I tried to ignore his doubtful look. "It's the kind of thing we could go to jail for if the wrong people found out. But you'll thank us when we've been victorious."

"You're a liar."

"No, I'm not. It's all part of Arend's mission to contain the Bolshevist threat." I pulled myself straight, tucking the paper into my shirt pocket and buttoning it securely. "They're our orders, if you must know."

"Read it, then."

"No!"

"Haven't you learnt to read German yet?"

"What does that have to do with anything?"

Nijs scowled. "It's only a stupid game, Marten. They're not real orders. Arend isn't some great commander. He's an idiot. And you're all idiots for listening to him."

When we got to school, I opened my desk as quickly as possible and pulled out a regulation yellow pencil. Making sure that no one was watching, I wrapped the paper tightly around the pencil, holding the end steady so that the letters would line up just so. It was a call to arms, I was sure of it; Adriaan's expression could only mean that the day of reckoning was nearing, and that we had been selected for a special mission.

A hand on my shoulder made me lurch forwards, bringing the top of the desk down hard onto my fingers. I let out a howl of pain.

"I just wanted to say sorry for calling you an idiot, Marten," said Nijs.

"Leave me alone," I huffed, and shoved my throbbing fingers into my mouth.

"Did you mean it, when you said you might go to jail?" For some reason his worried expression filled me with rage. I removed my fingers from my mouth and glared up at him.

"That's the problem with you, Nijs: you're just a big baby. Why don't you go and play with the nuns? The rest of us have more important things to worry about, like the Bolshevists and the Jews."

"I only wanted to say—"

"Are you a Bolshevist, Nijs? Well, are you?" I pushed my chair back, stood up and puffed out my chest so that it was touching his. A few of the other boys had begun to arrive for the first lesson, and they stopped to watch us.

"What's wrong with you, Marten?" Nijs looked at me with pity. "It's to do with Krelis, isn't it?"

It was the sound of my brother's name passing his lips that made me lunge. The other boys descended on us with whoops of excitement, chanting our names louder and louder. Nijs's mouth kept moving even as he parried my blows. Only when I landed a punch straight in his jaw did he relent – but by that point, it was too late. Mijnheer Vlerick tore me from the floor and cuffed me sharply, as the other boys scattered to their desks.

We were both kept back after school. Nijs's jaw wasn't broken, but his face was swollen and had to be covered in ice. We didn't look at each other once in the hour that it took to write out our penance to Mijnheer Vlerick. My palms still stung from the six strokes he'd given me for starting the fight.

Even before I reached the clearing, I could hear the shouts of the others ringing out through the crisp air. I arrived to find Arend presiding as usual, flanked by Dirk and Pepijn. Before them, Willem, Joos, Pim and Bastiaan crouched on the damp earth. Adriaan was sitting on a log next to Filip and Theo; I quietly slid in between them, keeping my gaze trained on the ground.

"You're late, Kuypers."

"Mijnheer Vlerick kept me after school."

"Why was that?"

"For fighting."

Dirk whistled; Pepijn snorted in amusement. I noticed that Arend was wearing brand-new rubber jackboots, and he smiled at me.

"I've just been telling the others about Staf de Clercq," he said. "Would you believe, Theo here says he's never heard of him."

I glanced over at Theo and shook my head slowly, the way Mr Hendryks did when he talked about people no longer believing in God.

"That's a real shame," I said. "Staf de Clercq is a hero."

"He is a true leader," said Arend. "He is an activist. A strategist, a warrior... he is the one who comes up with solutions to our problems."

"What sort of problems?" asked Bastiaan.

"Our country is hungry," said Arend. "Our people are tired, poor. And all because of others who work to undermine Dutch values."

We stared up at him.

"What sorts of people are these?" he asked.

"Bolshevists," I said, quickly.

"Who else?"

"The French."

"The Jews."

"Gypsies."

Arend nodded. "And what does Staf de Clercq propose we do about this?" he asked. The response was immediate.

"*Sla dood! Sla dood!*" yelled the other boys. They had been practising before I arrived. As soon as I could, I raised my fist and joined in.

Put them to death!

Arend laughed – a full-throated, manly laugh – and waved his hand to dismiss us. "Until next week, then," he said.

Filip called after me as we made our way home. I was walking with Adriaan through the flax field, telling him about that heathen Nijs.

"Wait up, Kuypers!" Filip shouted as he loped towards us. "Did you receive the secret message?"

I felt in my pocket, and then realized that I must have left the encoded strip of paper in my desk at school.

"I haven't had a chance to read it yet," I said.

Filip rolled his eyes. "Never mind. You're here now." He glanced at Adriaan as if waiting for him to leave. Adriaan didn't move. Filip rolled his eyes again and turned back to me. "You know Shimon Franck? Works at the Dijle pharmacy."

"Of course."

"Well, Willem lives two lanes down the road from the old man. Things haven't been right around there for a while now." Filip cocked one eyebrow, gauging our interest with his squinty eye. "Oh, yes. It's one thing that Franck's a Yid. But Willem's seen the book of spells he keeps under the counter at the pharmacy, and we have reason to believe that he's been practising the dark arts."

I swallowed. "Unnatural science?"

Filip nodded. "He has a cat – you've probably seen it – white, with pink eyes. An albino."

Adriaan shifted his weight with impatience. "So what?" he said. "Get to the point."

Filip narrowed his eyes at Adriaan.

"It's an aberration, that's what it is. Willem heard his mother say that that cat can predict death. When Sannie Huysmans passed away last month, the scraggy little thing had been squalling on her back wall for days. Last week Willem saw it sleeping outside the Marghem house... and you know what happened there, don't you?"

"Lise Marghem's baby," whispered Adriaan. "It went blue, they said. Meningitis."

"So you see, it's pretty obvious what's going on," continued Filip, hooking his thumbs through his braces. "And Willem and I think it's high time someone did something about it. We thought you might like to help, as you've got a cool head and a steady hand."

"Why didn't you ask one of the others?"

"Because Bastiaan's a sissy, Theo's as thick as a tree stump, and Pim will want to tell the whole world. We know we can trust you."

"So you, and me, and Willem..."

"That's right."

I shook my head, remembering what my lady writer had told me about groups of three. Cats were unlucky enough as it was. "Only if Adriaan comes, too."

Adriaan faltered. "Why me?"

"Because groups of three are unlucky."

Filip groaned. "Don't tell me you're superstitious, Kuypers," he said. "I'd have given you more credit than that."

"I think it's a bad idea," said Adriaan.

"Shut up," said Filip in a grim tone. "No one asked you."

"I'll do it if Adriaan comes along," I said.

Filip drew a heavy sigh. "Fine, fine," he said. "I'll tell Willem. Friday evening, we're meeting at his house. Make sure to wear dark colours."

When I got home, Aunt Marta was helping Mother to chop vegetables. My aunt was always in our kitchen nowadays, drinking her fruit beer, cooking and cleaning and putting things away in places where they didn't belong. I hated the way she managed our cups and saucers as if they were hers, the way she set the table with the knives and forks side by side. I helped myself to a carrot from the table and ducked out of reach as her hand swiped the air.

"Cheeky boy," she said. Aunt Marta's grey hair had turned yellow at the front, because she smoked so much. Her cuticles were yellow, too, and her fingernails dull and cracked as old ivory keys on a piano. But her teeth and the whites of her eyes were as clear and cold as frost.

"What do you know about Shimon Franck?" I asked, perching on a stool.

"Who's asking?" replied my mother, without looking up.

"Someone at school says he practises the dark arts. Unnatural science."

Aunt Marta sniffed. "If that's true, I wish he'd teach me some of it," she said. "His wife's the only woman at the market who never seems short of a franc. They've probably got the bank stitched up." She stopped chopping, then pointed the tip of her knife at me. "Nothing to do with science, Marten. It's all about canny greed, while others starve. You should pray that you'll never succumb to such greed."

And I did. That night, I knelt by my bed and prayed to St Bartholomew. *St Bartholomew, holy apostle of Our Lord Jesus Christ, who was also called Nathaniel, who tamed the natives in Africa and India, was martyred by being flayed and crucified head down, whose body was washed to Rome and rescued by the Holy Roman Emperor, even though it was too heavy to be carried by men, so that only innocent children could bring it ashore...*

I stared up at the ceiling. *On your festival day, grant me the courage to act like a man and the wisdom to see through the knavish deception of Shimon Franck's black magic. Amen.*

24

She watched the swift draw frantic circles overhead, skimming the vaulted ceiling with its tiny wings, ricocheting from one end of the building to the other and back again without so much as brushing the peeling plaster. Had it been in here before she entered, nestling in an invisible crevice and stirred by the sound of the door? Or had it swooped in behind her, lured by the draught and the sparkling glass? Glen imagined its heart thumping, its small brain struggling to fathom the difference between the air in which it flew and the blue sky so clearly visible through the transparent barrier, and she marvelled at the cruelty of its situation. Outside, a group of crows was perched on a disused telegraph wire. When she opened the door again, they were frightened away, but the trapped swift did not see that it had been offered an escape.

"You'll only tire yourself," she sighed, opening the book that rested in her lap.

It was the Ramayana that she had been thinking of when Ganan had described his illustrations to her – not the Mahabharata, after all. Althea had been only too happy to let her cousin borrow it.

"I've outgrown fairy tales," the girl had explained. "I prefer to read about real things now."

The story had been rendered for children and illustrated with lurid drawings of monsters, blue-skinned heroes and fantastical landscapes. Here is Sita, beautiful and brave. She is abducted by Ravana, the ten-headed demon who is as clever as he is cruel. Ravana is the king of Lanka and emperor over three worlds. He kills the eagle Jatayu and flees with Sita over the sea to his dark kingdom. But Rama will rescue his lover and slay Ravana – who may be immune to the blows of the gods, but cannot withstand an attack by a mortal – and the lovers will be reunited at last.

With Sita returned to him, however, Rama is overcome with the suspicion that she has been disloyal during her captivity. Outraged, Sita commands Lakshmana to build a fire. Declaring that she will burn only if she had sinned, Sita steps into the flames. For a dreadful moment, it looks as though she will be consumed alive – but by some miracle, she emerges unharmed. Seeing that she has passed the test of fire, Rama apologizes, and the flames turn to flowers.

She thought of Ganan's cinnamon taste, his square fingernails, the thick curls of black hair that teased his neck, behind his ears. He looked nothing like Rama, with his sloped forehead, bulbous eyes and full lips.

Was it only twenty-four hours ago that here, in this very spot, the world had changed? She wondered how it was that, even now, she felt so little shock about what she had done, what had happened between them. There was the act itself, which did not seem terribly remarkable in the scheme of things; and then there was the *significance* of it, the taboo, which was remarkable but which felt somehow unrelated to her, a thing apart from who she was.

The swift had ceased circling the rafters and alighted on a ledge high up in the apse. For the first time, Glen noticed fragments of decaying frescoes lining the perimeter of the ceiling. "I am the Lord; and there is none else" had been painted in thin, neo-Gothic script in one corner, Pompeian red letters against the grey. *How dare we insist on absolutes?* thought the girl, savouring the sensation of self-righteous disapproval. *How can we be so sure that our myths will not one day turn on us? What if we have imagined our god, the One God, incorrectly – with white skin, instead of blue?*

Outside, a dog yapped. Glen glanced back to discover the Captain standing in the doorway, pausing as if trying to identify a mysterious smell. "Who is it, Pepys?" he whispered. "Who is it, boy?"

"It's only me," said Glen, placing the book aside and rising to guide him to his seat.

"You're making a habit of visiting my hiding spot," said Emil, lifting Pepys into his arms.

"This is only my second time," said the girl. "It's a good place to think."

"Someone else has been here," murmured the man.

"Oh?"

"Pepys can tell. Look at the state he's in." It was true: as soon as he placed the dog back onto the floor, Pepys set off, stiff-legged, in pursuit of the rogue scent.

"Well…" Glen bit her lip. "I brought a friend here the night before last."

"A man?" he said.

"Does it matter?"

Emil grunted.

"Anyway, I'm glad that you've come," continued Glen. "I'd wanted to bring you some leftover cake after my cousin's birthday party, but your landlady said you had gone to visit friends."

"What about your admirer, then? Has he been here?"

Glen blushed. "It was he who came with me the other evening, after the party. To… talk."

"To *talk*?"

"I didn't know that you had friends in the area," Glen said, changing the subject.

"I was contacted by a colleague from the Ceylon Light Infantry reserves. He had something to give me."

"Oh?"

The Captain pulled a small leather-bound book out of his breast pocket. The spine was cracked, and bits of coarse binding fluttered at the joints. He passed it gently towards Glen. "It belonged to my father."

It appeared to be a journal or some sort of scrapbook. The pages fell open to where a photograph had been pasted onto one leaf, and she turned the book around to study the image. A boy crouched on the front steps of a whitewashed house, socks rolled about his ankles, squinting into the sun. Before him was a spaniel, which was being encouraged by its young master to look at the camera.

She turned the page. Butterfly wings had been pressed between the leaves; flower petals; a scrap of fabric stitched onto the paper.

Here and there were pages of notes, diary entries scrawled in spidery black ink. "Tell Boy to be good," read one. "And to look after Lucie until I return." Two veined dragonfly wings had slid into the crease.

"What a remarkable thing," she said.

"He kept it for me, apparently. While he was travelling to missions all over the country, crashing through jungles with his little retinue of Faithful. There was one year when my mother only had him at home for three weeks. I was at a mission school – the closest thing to a proper boarding school that we could afford – so I saw even less of him. Apparently, this was his way of making up for it."

"But you only just received it now…" She glanced at the date on the final page: *April, 1915.* "What happened in 1915?"

"There was a rebellion. Here, of all places. It isn't spoken of much any more – within a few years, the war rather overshadowed it. My father had just arrived when it happened."

"What kind of rebellion?"

"A religious one – Muslims lashed out against Christians and Buddhists, Tamils against Sinhalese, everyone against the English. It started at Colombo, but it soon spread into the villages. We responded heavy-handedly, as usual; introduced martial law, which only stirred things up further." He sniffed. "We show that we are civilized by being barbaric to the barbarians."

"Rather like the Indian Mutiny?"

The Captain smiled ruefully. "As children, we were told the story of two hundred English women and children that had been butchered and dumped in a well at Cawnpore; the tale of a captain's wife who was boiled alive in ghee. It gave us permission for unrestrained vengeance. But my father was not a vengeful man."

Glen stared down at the worn-out journal, filled with fragments of nature and memory. "What happened to him?"

Royce straightened in his seat and fixed her with an empty stare. For a moment Glen fancied that he could see straight through her.

"Have you ever wondered why this church is built of glass?"

The girl glanced around the cavernous shell, hearing for the first time the slow drip of water from one of the antechambers. The echo was almost imperceptible.

"I assumed that it was simply unusual," she said. "A folly."

"A *folly*." Royce spat the word, and Glen stiffened. "There was a fire during a service. A full service, at which my father was officiating. It just so happened that the doors had been bolted from the outside."

"I don't understand..."

"The entire congregation died. Sixty people in all, including twelve children. And my father."

"But who would do such a thing? "

"No group ever claimed responsibility. The rebellion was quashed on the same day, and there was no longer any honour in it." He stared up at the sky. "I had been offered a scholarship to King's – it was my one and only shot at a civilized education – but in the end I couldn't go through with it. There was my mother to look after, for one thing."

Glen nodded, waiting for the fist in her chest to unclench itself. She remembered what Perdita had said, about the coolies believing that the church was haunted, and shivered. The building that had seemed so perfectly designed for two began to feel crowded, teeming with ghosts. "I'm so sorry," she whispered.

"So now you know why I came here. I had never thought I would be able to visit this place – it was too monstrous, too awful to imagine. I'm glad that I don't have to see it now." Pepys had come to rest by his master's feet, and he fondled the dog's ears with gentle fingers. "And that he doesn't have to see me."

Not knowing what else to do, the girl reached down to scratch the whimpering dog behind the collar. Pepys yawned, shifting his bottom on the cool floor.

"I call it my fire-gazing time," said Royce. "After the hunt, the Rock Veddas retreat from the women and stare into the flames, so that they don't have to think or to answer questions. That's what I have done here. Perhaps it is time I stopped."

215

Glen shook her head. "Oh, no," she said. "No, you mustn't feel that you should. Not on my account. Not on anyone's..." She paused. "Does Hollar know?"

The Captain shook his head. "No. He has his own fires to contemplate." He closed his eyes, and indicated the book in Glen's hands. "Would you read me some? Please..."

There were several newspaper clippings folded in between the pages. She scanned the contents of one, which looked as if it dated from the end of the previous century.

The Wild Men of Ceylon are generally considered to be descendants of the aborigines of this island and are but a degree removed from wild beasts, although they exhibit a naive trust in their encounters with Europeans. Though they practice demon worship and demonstrate a moderate skill at archery, they are quite harmless, delighting in feasts of roast monkey and the smoking of ganja.

The girl turned to the next page, which was decorated with pen drawings. The text was dense but elegant, describing a visit to Varanasi. She read aloud:

Dear Boy,

I am now in the holiest city in all of India, called Benares. You will know from your little globe that it lies on the river Ganges, which the Hindoos consider to be sacred. Benares is known as the City of Light, and is most beautiful. The buildings here are made of sandstone, which gleams resplendent at the rising and setting of the sun. Broad stone steps lead from the riverfront into the water: these are known as "ghats". Doctor Jenkins and I have witnessed a number of cremations from the ghats, where the ashes of the dead are scattered into the river. This does not deter people from bathing in the water, as they believe that it will cleanse their souls, if not their bodies. There are many temples along the riverbank – Buddhist and Jain as well as Hindoo – but not so many churches...

She stopped. "I've not done this for ages. Read aloud, I mean."

"Kabbalah scholars read together so that they needn't confront the mysteries of knowledge alone."

She looked at him. "Who do you suppose will rule India when we are gone? The Congress?"

He chuckled, then said: "I could stomach Nehru, even if he is a socialist. But my guess is that Ceylon will go to the Japanese."

"How can you be so sure?"

"It is the worst that can happen, and I am a firm believer in anticipating the worst. Isn't there talk of a Japanese plane flying all the way to England any day now? The *Kamikaze*, they're calling it." A sad, slow shake of the head. "The calm we are enjoying now is only the eye of the storm. I hope that doesn't make me sound an awful pessimist."

"A realist, perhaps," suggested the girl.

"That's right." The Captain lifted Pepys onto his knee, and allowed the creature to lick his chin. "There is always the risk," he whispered to the little dog, "that the things we think we see are, in fact, only shadows on a wall. *Through a glass darkly*, and all that..."

* * *

For several days, Glen saw nothing of Ganan. She tried not to become vexed by his silence, reminding herself that it had never been his habit to see her during the week. Twice she collected Jayanadani and Nimali from school in the hopes of finding him there, to no avail. Both times, the girls informed her that he was busy with his drawing group, an after-school class for older students.

"Jayanadani wanted to go, but she is only in the third form," explained Nimali as they dawdled along the side of the road, swinging their satchels. "She doesn't even like to draw. It's only because she is in love with Mr Dharmasena."

"No, I'm not," snapped her sister. "And I do like to draw. You don't know anything."

"How many students are there in this class?" asked Glen.

"Three. Thilak is the only boy. Lakmini is very good at drawing, which is fortunate because she is not so intelligent and really very fat." Jayanadani spoke with no sense of irony: she had clearly given some thought to this already. "And then there is Amanthi, who is the opposite of Lakmini."

"Very intelligent?" said Glen.

"And not fat."

"She is beautiful," nodded Nimali. Jayanadani scowled.

"No, she isn't."

"Yes, she is. Everyone knows she is."

On the third day, the girls reported that the art class would be taken on a special field trip at the end of the week.

"It's not fair," pouted Jayanadani. "We should all be allowed to go."

"Why can't you?"

"Because Mr Dharmasena can't supervise everyone. There are too many children. Twenty-two in all."

Glen watched a leaf lift from the road, turning cartwheels on the breeze. "What if I were to come along – do you suppose that would help?"

Both girls brightened at the suggestion. "We could ask Mr Dharmasena," said Jayanadani.

"Ask him now!" said Nimali. And before Glen could stop them, both girls had spun on their heels and were dashing back up the road to the schoolhouse. After a moment's consideration, Glen decided not to follow them.

Within a few minutes, two figures returned bounding down the road, broad white smiles gleaming in flushed faces.

"At first he said no," said Nimali breathlessly.

"But then I said that we could ask other grown-ups to come, to make it easier," explained Jayanadani. "So finally he agreed."

"We have to be at school by half-past seven on Friday—"

"And we have to bring our own tiffins—"

"Well!" Glen wondered what this funny feeling was, this cross between anxiety and elation. "Well, what fun!"

The trip was to see the wall paintings at the nearby Sthripura Cave, where island lore had it that Ravana had held Sita captive.

The morning of the excursion, Ganan waited for all the students to load onto the bus before acknowledging Glen.

"It was good of you to offer to come," he said, in the professional voice of a teacher who is aware that his students are listening. He avoided her eye, and she noticed the colour rising above his collar.

"I was desperate to see you again. I was worried—"

"There is nothing to be worried about," he said with a stiff tone. And then, not wishing her to mistake his abruptness, he added, "I have had time to think. I did not mean to take advantage—"

She felt the tension from his body, the defensive stance of a cornered animal. "Why, don't be ridiculous!"

"You'll forgive me, I hope."

"But what is there to forgive?"

Ganan looked as if he were about to say something, but he checked himself – instead simply indicating that she should sit in the seat opposite his at the front of the bus. He followed her on board and introduced "Miss Phayre" to the class.

"Good morning, Miss Phayre," chorused the students, clattering their tiffin boxes. The youngest ones smiled shyly up at her; others stole conspiratorial glances, while some of the older boys craned their necks around those in front in order to catch a glimpse of the young white woman. She could feel their stares boring through the back of her head as she arranged herself in the front seat.

"Idols have been worshipped at the caves for centuries," Ganan explained to her, as the bus rumbled over the pitted jungle road. "But recently three were discovered which appear to be older than any of the others."

"Oh?" Glen listened absent-mindedly, too absorbed in his presence to pay much attention. Were those the same fingers, square-tipped and smooth, that had laced through hers when they first kissed? Were those the same tender eyes that had commanded her to submit by the light of the moon? The black curls that she had wound about one finger, the slender legs that had forced her against the pew – how different they seemed now. No longer connected to her, no longer hers.

"One is of Sita, the constant and pure, who was imprisoned in the cave. One is of Rama, her husband, who rescued her. And the third is of Lakshmana, Rama's devoted brother."

These were the only words that they exchanged on the way to the shrine. Ganan was preoccupied with his students; when he was not talking to a couple of older girls seated behind him, he peered out the window with a look of studious concentration. It was entirely unreasonable, Glen remonstrated with herself, to envy the girls their teacher's attention – especially as Ganan had so far shown no signs of jealousy or possessiveness where she was concerned. His students babbled happily behind them in their language, and for the first time Glen felt excluded by the strange music of words that meant nothing to her. Before long, she found that she was too self-conscious to raise her own voice in front of so many others – and so she, too, spent the journey gazing up at the seemingly impenetrable jungle canopy, studying it for occasional flashes of blue sky.

When they arrived outside the cave complex, they were greeted by a bandy-legged Sinhalese man with a face like a wizened apple and a tortoiseshell comb encircling his head. Once all the children had descended, chattering and laughing, from the bus, he introduced himself as Babiya and indicated that they should follow him. As he spoke, Ganan translated for Glen.

"He says that we are in the Ashoka forest – the same forest that is described in the Ramayana," Ganan explained. "That stream there" – he pointed – "is believed to be the one in which Sita bathed. On those rocks a shrine has been built to mark the place."

Babiya was now gesticulating at the water. His voice became shrill; twice he stamped his foot on the ground. Glen noticed that the children's eyes had grown large: the youngest ones stood with open mouths, transfixed by the old man's gestures.

"He says" – Ganan was struggling to iron out the crease of a smile – "he *insists* that at this point in the stream the water has no taste."

One of the older boys said something, eliciting sniggers from his companions. Babiya scowled at him, smearing the air in front of his face with one hand before barking a reply.

"What was that about?"

"Vidu asked if we could taste the water for ourselves. Babiya told him that the reason there is no taste is that this is the place that Sita cursed her captor. Only a fool would drink this water. We have to move further downstream if we are thirsty."

"Good Heavens."

They proceeded along an irregular path until at last Babiya brought the group to a halt.

"These are the caves," said Ganan. "The idols have been kept inside, to protect them from the elements." He addressed the group. "You have all brought with you your sketchbooks and your pencils. We will now spend some time making drawings of the idols and of the cave paintings. I will be checking on your progress." He turned to Glen. "Would you mind keeping an eye on the little ones?"

"Of course." She watched as Ganan left to inspect the paintings with his other students, then settled herself at the mouth of the cave. Within moments, a cluster of the youngest children had gathered about her feet.

"May we draw you, Miss Phayre?"

"I believe Mr Dharmasena intended you to draw Rama and Sita, not me."

"Please, Miss Phayre?"

"Oh, very well."

They were enchanted by her pale skin and fair hair. They marvelled at her shoes, the detail on her dress, the fine watch that encircled her wrist. Each student tried to capture the exact line of her brow, the curve of her mouth, and as they worked they stole glances to see who had managed to capture the English woman most truly. Eventually, one of the older girls wandered over to inspect their efforts. Glen hardly noticed her until she spoke.

"They think you are a princess." Glen met her with a liquid gaze. She was a young woman – not a schoolgirl at all, really – although her smile was almost childlike. Her eyes were like amber, her skin feather-smooth and fallow. A shapely black eyebrow arched in amusement.

"How ridiculous!"

"It's because you are so fair." She was winding the end of a lustrous plait with one finger, tugging it around her shoulder like a shawl. Thick lashes cast spider shadows across her cheeks.

"May I see what you have drawn?"

"The idols, Miss Phayre – Lakshmana and Rama." The girl spoke shyly, turning the page for her.

"These are excellent."

"It is thanks to Mr Dharmasena," said the girl. Then she noticed her teacher approaching and lowered her eyes. "Excuse me, Miss Phayre – I should finish them before he asks to see…"

She watched some of the smaller children follow the girl back towards the cave. Ganan smiled at them as he approached, touching one or two lightly on the head as they trailed past. When he was still some distance from Glen, he lowered himself to the ground.

"I suppose that was Amanthi, constant and pure?" Glen pretended to leaf through the pages of a child's sketchbook as the teacher lifted his head up.

"How did you know her name?"

"Jayanadani told me about her. She was right: she is very beautiful." Glen closed the book. "She was judging me."

"Don't be ridiculous."

"It's true."

"Even if it was, is that so strange? You judge everyone, Glen." He could see that she had no reply to this. "You are right to be angry with me," he said, in a low voice.

"You might have called."

"We have no telephone at the house."

"Well, a letter perhaps. You know where I live. Or you might have left something at the church…"

"I'm sorry."

"It's just," she said in a pleading tone, "it's just not the done thing, you know. The man always calls afterwards."

He shot a look at her. "Well, you're a clever girl, Glen. You found me." He reached for a couple of stray sketchbooks. "I know why you offered to come today."

"The girls didn't feel that it was fair to be excluded—"

"It had nothing to do with the girls." He began to pile the books. "You assume that other women are all like you, Glen: so totally defiant. Is it not enough that Jayanadani and Nimali are already so aware of their rights, of what is *fair*..."

"You don't approve of that?"

"Perhaps they don't realize how lucky they are. Ceylonese girls are freer than their Indian sisters. Those girls can look forward to universal suffrage; they will be spared child marriage—"

"Well, really!"

"You needn't try to make them like you, Glen. Stamping your little foot in indignation, so afraid of being taken advantage of! You make yourself ridiculous."

"You see us all as the enemy, do you? Even Jay and Nim?"

"Now don't be silly." He tried to make light of it. "Your aunt is renowned for her views on men."

"Now who's being ridiculous?"

"Oh, don't be angry. Please." His stern face softened, and she felt her frustration melt away.

"Darling..."

He warned her off with his eyes. But when he spoke, his voice was kind. "We are all the product of our times. Not so long ago, an emancipated woman such as yourself would have been a suffragette. A hundred years ago, a bluestocking. Before that, merely a harlot."

She allowed herself to laugh at this. "So you're saying that it was a harlot you pursued in the gardens? A harlot whose portrait you drew? A harlot who just the other night—"

"I wanted to know who she was. Just as she wanted to know what it would be like to kiss a coloured man – to write about in one of her books, right?"

"Don't even joke, Ganan!"

He registered her look of horror and began to backtrack. "And then, of course, I grew fond of her..."

"*Fond?*" She studied his face, but Ganan remained inscrutable. "It's almost as if you resent yourself for spending time with me, Ganan. For feeling something that's somehow *wrong*..." He composed his features into an ambivalent expression that made her heart sink. "But perhaps there's more to me than you think. If I had an opportunity to see you in *your* element, as you have seen me, to meet your people—"

"My mother would not take it well. What happened to Appah…" He shrugged. "Let's just say it did not leave her well disposed towards the English."

"Surely she knows that it had nothing to do with me?"

He stared at her blankly. "But you are one of them, Glen."

"No, I'm not!" And yet she felt the blow, knew that he was right, despite her best attempts to convince him – to convince herself – otherwise. "I'm on *your* side, Ganan." The girl was caught short by the beseeching note in her own voice, and something in her snapped. "Why must we always be the ones to apologize?" she demanded then, struggling to modulate her tone so as not to sound like Mrs Cornish. "I don't suppose you even know what happened in the glass church, do you?" She watched him falter. "No – not that. I mean the fire. The one *your* people started; the one that killed twelve children and Emil's father." Why this creeping guilt – it was true, wasn't it? So why shouldn't she speak of it? "You're not the only ones who have things to forgive," she said abruptly, and looked away.

She was so embarrassed by the outburst that she barely heard him get up. She only realized that he was sitting next to her when his voice broke the silence. "You're right, Glen," he said. His voice was soft, pleading. "I'm sorry." Then, seeing his students beginning to emerge from the cave, he rose with a sigh that could almost have been construed as an expression of relief, pausing just long enough to touch her hair. "Please, let's talk about this another time."

* * *

When we arrived back at the school, he dismissed each student individually before turning to thank me for joining them. Jayanadani and Nimali were inside, putting the sketchbooks in order, and so we had a minute or two alone in the shade of the neem tree. He said that he had been worried about seeing me again, before kissing me on the cheek, like a brother – no doubt out of decorum given our surroundings. And yet I felt a shudder of envy for that girl, his student Amanthi – the modest beauty representing everything that an Indian mother could want for her son. Isn't it strange how the dread of un-requited love makes us feel our emotions all the more keenly? For a terrible moment I recalled our night in the church and wondered if perhaps I had been the one to take advantage of him. Is that not a ridiculous thought?

Glen stopped to bite her pen, staring at the wall in her effort to retrieve the memory. She reread what she had written and considered starting again.

To answer your question: I don't know if he loves me. Perhaps he might. I do know that I love him; that I have a desperate need to love him, to love someone who deserves it as much as he does. But I shouldn't bore you with these silly worries. Emil is right: I think too much and feel too deeply. He should know. Blindness made him start to notice things that he had taken for granted: the shape of rooms, the density of walls – there are so many things we don't see until they hit us, and then it is too late. But when Emil lost his sight, he refused to be ruled by fear and shame and suspicion. Instead, he learnt to trust. So must I, now.

He has told me more about my aunt's little boy. Honestly, Pieter, the more I discover about Hollar, the more I realize we may never know. According to Emil's landlady, rumour has it that when Hollar's mother delivered him, her own mother insisted that she would not have a half-caste baby in the fam-ily home. The unfortunate woman was forced to take a poorly paid position many miles away, where her employer regularly took advantage of her and mistreated the child. After several years, when she could bear it no longer, she fled with the boy into the mountains, where they survived for some time with the help of a local tribe. But when malaria struck the village, she lost even their support. A mission doctor discovered her

*with the child – both were seriously ill by this point – and rec-
ognized that they were not members of the tribe. He brought
them to the hospital, where Hollar lived for almost a year before his mother died. I wonder now if it might have been the
same hospital in front of which I almost lost my scalp that day
in Colombo – Emil says that there are several native hospitals
in the city, so it's impossible to be sure. Hollar wandered those
cold corridors for several days before the Mission Society sent
him to a nearby orphanage. Another year passed before news
came that Annabel wished to adopt him. And then, his life
changed completely.*

*According to Emil, Hollar remembers all of this with the ex-
ception of his banishment from the family home. I remarked
on his fine memory, and Emil chastised me. "He is unable to
forget – that is not the same thing," he said. I think that he understands Hollar better than I ever will; he understands what
it is to be so close to one's mother.*

*Emil says that I must not pity him; that Hollar's skin is as
tough as an elephant's. But aren't elephants famously sensitive creatures, more attuned to kindness and cruelty than any
other animal? He smiled when I said this. There are stories of
elephants who have died of broken hearts, Pieter…*

25

The house at the end of Goswin de Stassartstraat backed onto the loading yard where Nijs and I used to dig for stones. A scrapheap had been piled against a brick wall which separated the yard from a row of private gardens; balancing on top of the heap, it was just possible to make out the dark outline of the bell within the square cathedral tower.

This evening, St Rombouts cathedral was decorated with yellow flags to mark the festival day. I'd had to explain to Mr Hendryks that I wouldn't be able to make it to Mass because I had promised to meet some friends instead.

"The same friends that gave you that badge?" he asked, poking his finger at my lapel.

"The Section Leader gives the badges," I said. "For swimming and archery and first aid…"

"But on St Bartholomew's day? I thought you were keen on St Bartholomew."

I narrowed my eyes at him the way Filip sometimes looked at Adriaan. "He's not my *girlfriend*, Hendryks," I said. Despite myself, I savoured the look of reproach that crossed his saggy old face. "St Bartholomew is dead. Skinned and crucified." I dropped a centime into his shirt pocket and tapped it the way I'd seen waiters getting tipped in the movies. "But you can light a candle for me, if you like."

When I told the others this, they laughed and clapped me on the back. They didn't know that Mr Hendryks was my friend: to them he was just an old man, not unlike Shimon Franck.

We spent several minutes admiring each other's night-mission attire: dark woolen knickerbockers and black school sweaters. Filip had brought a balaclava, along with a bag of supplies that he and Willem had collected in advance.

"What's in there?" asked Adriaan.

"Wait and see," grinned Willem. He had waxed his hair for the first time that day, parting it severely to one side just like the German Führer.

"So what are you going to do?" asked Adriaan. "Are you really going to kill it?"

"It's an aberration," said Filip, as if this was explanation enough. "A freak of nature. Of course, it's not the cat's fault. But the dirty Jew has been using it to cast spells on people. It has to be done."

"As quickly as possible," added Willem.

"How, then?"

"You could drown it," I said. Filip shook his head.

"We'd have to catch it first," he said, "and get it into a bag. Would you like to volunteer to do that?"

I shrugged, embarrassed by the fact that Filip appeared to have thought it all out. I was supposed to be good at planning things. The flying machine that Nijs and I had tried to build the previous year certainly didn't fail for lack of a good design. It had only failed because we couldn't find proper parachute silk for the wings.

"How about stoning it?" I said, determined to come up with an idea that might work.

"We can't be sure to get it right. Same goes for setting a dog on it, or staking it under an owl's nest. We can't give the old man time to find out, or else we're done for."

All this time, Adriaan had been very quiet.

"What about poison?" he said at last.

"We thought about that," said Willem. "But you can't force a cat to eat rat poison."

"Insulin," said Adriaan. "You could inject it with lots of insulin. It wouldn't hurt, and it would be sure to work."

"And where will we find insulin?"

"My Aunt Marta's diabetic," I said.

"You're hopeless," said Filip. "It's a good thing that Willem and I thought this out in advance, or we'd never get anything done. Look."

He tipped open the bag to reveal a fuel tin, some wire and a box of matches.

"We're not just getting rid of it," he said. "We're purifying it. Making sure that Mammon can't infest the remains. It's got to be done properly."

"You can't do that," said Adriaan, his voice rising shrilly even though I could tell he was trying not to look worried. "That's not purification. It's torture. It might not even work."

"It'll work all right," said Willem. "Just you wait."

Adriaan looked at me and stood up.

"I'm going home," he said.

"You can't defect," I objected. For some reason that I couldn't explain, I didn't want to be left alone with the other two.

"Let him go if he wants to," said Filip. "I never thought he'd be cut out for this kind of job, anyway." He spat at Adriaan's feet. "Go on, piss off."

"You don't have to do it, Marten," said Adriaan. "The Section Leader didn't order it. Even Arend didn't order it, and he's Troop Leader. It's not the same as defecting."

"Heads up!"

On the other side of the wall, someone had opened the kitchen door. Footsteps crunched towards us on a gravel path, and Filip hurriedly shoved the fuel tin, matches and wire back into the sack. Willem and I ducked behind the compost heap beside him, but Adriaan was too slow. While he dithered by the wall, furiously chewing one finger and staring at me with wide eyes, the garden gate swung open and Shimon Franck appeared.

In one hand he carried a bowl of pickled herring. The other supported a mewing cat, which was draped in the crook of his arm.

I had seen Shimon Franck in the pharmacy before, although never this close. Thin strands of grey hair were plastered to an enormous skull, and his watery eyes were protruding, but they didn't roll in their sockets or shoot fiery thunderbolts like you'd expect from someone who practises the dark arts. There were no toxic sweat stains under his arms, no book of spells, and although his shoulders were hunched, the bony hump on his back was not nearly as pronounced as I had remembered. He wore a hairy jumper and lambskin slippers. His lips glistened with saliva, flinching and wobbling – but when he spoke, his voice was soft.

"You gave me a fright," he said to Adriaan – but he didn't look frightened. In fact, he looked as if he was perfectly used to seeing Adriaan there. After gently setting the cat on its feet, Shimon Franck began to spoon bits of herring onto the ground and stroked the animal as it raced to gobble up the oily scraps. "There," he said, straightening. "That'll keep her happy for a while now."

For a few moments, he and Adriaan stood there together, staring at the cat. She wasn't mangy at all. Her white coat was thick and smooth, her tail straight, her whiskers tidy. Her eyes were pinkish rather than red, the same colour as her nose and her tiny, poking tongue.

Shimon Franck turned to go back inside, but stopped before he reached the gate. He looked at Adriaan, who was digging into the turf with his toe and staring intently at the ground. It looked as though Shimon Franck was about to say something, perhaps to call down fire and brimstone on the goy, but he didn't. Just a twitch of his eye – something that Adriaan must have noticed as well, because he immediately turned around and started stalking off across the yard without so much as looking at the rest of us. Once he was gone, Shimon Franck turned back towards the gate. Seconds later, the kitchen door was shut.

When we were sure that the coast was clear, Filip, Willem and I emerged from behind the scrapheap and stared down at the cat. It had finished the last of the herring and had begun to sniff about the garden wall for more.

"That Adriaan's a waste of space," said Filip, as he reached down to stroke her between the ears. "What a coward, running off like that. He should have stood his ground, showed the old Jew where to stick his herring bones."

The cat mewed hungrily.

"It doesn't look evil," I said, wishing that I had gone with Adriaan. But it was too late to leave now.

"Don't be fooled," said Filip. "The old man brought her out here on purpose. Who knows why, but he has his reasons." He lifted the creature from the ground and carried it across the yard. Willem and I followed.

"You're not really going to do it," I said – trying to sound as if I were making a statement rather than asking a question. It came out like a challenge.

"You think I'd lug all this junk out here just to talk about it?" snapped Filip. "Anyone can talk, Kuypers."

He stopped in front of a large tin drum that had begun to rust at the edges. He placed the squirming cat inside, and turned to Willem, who had begun to empty the contents of the sack onto the ground.

"How do you know you'll do it properly?" I asked. "If it's possessed, we'll need a priest to exorcise the demons." I glanced at Willem, who wasn't looking at me. "You can't just kill it. The demons might enter you."

The cat mewed, beginning to circle inside the drum.

"Don't be stupid, Marten." Filip spat into the barrel. "If you're going to be a girl, no one's forcing you to stay. You can run off home to your mum like that idiot Adriaan." He squinted at me. "It's not an exorcism, anyway – it's an execution."

I thought of the story that Glen had sent me, about the soldier who decided to risk execution rather than fight in the war. One of Father's friends had been a member of a firing squad that executed thirty men for abandoning their posts; afterwards, he said he'd always aimed just above the target's shoulder. I thought of the slaves who were executed after burying Attila the Hun, so that they could never reveal his resting place. I thought of Bastiaan and the Luger, and of the bloodthirsty rebels in Spain who would tie up priests' hands with their rosaries before killing them in the desecrated churches.

I watched Filip pick up the fuel tin. "How will you know how much to use?" I asked. My voice came out in a whimper.

"Enough to be sure," said Filip. "Fuel's not cheap, mind."

I peered into the barrel, where the cat was stretching itself against the tin walls, staring up at me with glassy eyes. She tried to drag her tiny claws against the metal, digging, digging. When she mewed I noticed pointy teeth rising out of speckled gums.

Filip unscrewed the fuel lid and eased it over the edge of the barrel. Yellow liquid splattered against the bottom of the drum until the earth inside had turned soggy and the cat's white paws were brown with mud. It mewed again, louder this time, and lifted its tail to piss. Willem and I had to hold our noses because the fumes were so strong.

"That should do it," said Filip, giving the tin a shake.

Willem wasn't smiling any more: his monkey mouth was clamped shut over buck teeth. He unclenched his palm, held out the matchbox. But Filip nodded towards me.

"Let Marten do it," he said.

"Why me?"

"Because you haven't done anything yet."

"I came, didn't I?"

"Are you a Yid-lover, then? A Satanist? You think the bitch has a soul?"

"No."

"Killing is part of a soldier's job, Marten. We all have to be prepared for it, for when we're called to defend Flanders."

"Of course," I said. "But soldiers kill other soldiers, not cats."

"You think it's easy to kill a man?" Filip smirked, his voice mocking and low. "This isn't anything like that."

"Go on," urged Willem. He must have known that if I didn't do it, he would have to.

I took the matchbox and slid it open. The first match took two strikes to light, and it quickly burned out. The cat cried again – a proper yowl this time, angry and shrill.

"Try again."

The next one flared beautifully. I held it the way Krelis had shown me, tipped upwards, so that the flame wouldn't travel as quickly and burn my fingers. I stared at the flickering sulphurous head: a miniature world ablaze. I was watching the smoke tendrils rise, curl and twist, puffing and streaming and then evaporating against the grey sky, when Filip snapped the match from my hand and sent it flying into the tin drum.

I heard the burst of flame before I saw it: a sudden explosion of heat followed by high, desperate peals from within the barrel. Frantic scraping. For a moment I thought I heard a baby cry, and then I realized it was not a human sound at all. It was a witchlike scream, the cackle of a she-devil. None of us moved as we listened to the snapping of bone, the hiss of air streaming through the cavities. I pictured the speckled gums melting around those pointed, pearly teeth; the steaming, sludging brains, the melting eyes.

I don't know how long we stood there. It felt like hours, but it could only have been a few minutes. I tried to imagine myself somewhere far away, but try as I might I couldn't summon Pieter van Houten's nerve – not with that noise and smell. At one point the screaming and the scraping got so loud that I wanted to cover my ears with my hands, bury my head under my arms and shout at the top of my lungs so that I wouldn't have to listen any more. But the other two were not doing this, even though Willem had turned very pale and was staring at the ground like you do when there's a scary bit at the cinema. Just when I thought that I couldn't bear the sound any more, the barrel stopped rattling, and it was clear that the little cat had finally given up. Perhaps she had been smothered by the smoke; perhaps she had simply resigned herself to death, like the Christian martyrs who burned at the stake. I remember telling myself that this was possible, even though I knew deep down that she had wanted to live.

Suddenly steam was rising from the barrel, white smoke, and I realized that Filip had poured water over our little inferno. Pinching his nose with an expression of giddy disgust, he leant over the barrel.

"Eugh!" He turned his face away, caught his mouth with his hands, composed himself, looked at me. "You've got to see that, it's disgusting. Willem, look…"

Gingerly, we peered inside. Splayed stick-limbs and a collapsed face, puckered and yawning. As if its body had been smashed, its spine twisted, and just the head – the senses, the brain, the knowing bits – remained.

My first instinct was to reach for it, to dust the silt and the soot with my sleeve. But Filip got there first.

"Come on," he said, using a piece of metal to pinch the carcass against the side of the barrel, dragging it out inch by inch and then tipping it onto the ground. "We'll have some fun now."

He tied it to the garden gate, using the wire to string its paws up in the air, tilting the screaming skull so that it looked like those tiger-skin rugs with the head still attached. Air breathed through the cavities, and a patch of white fluff fluttered from its belly. Willem and I hung back, sickened by the dead-sweet stink of burnt flesh. If it weren't for Filip, we probably would have run away then and there.

Once he was satisfied that the body was secure, Filip picked up a couple of stones from the ground.

"Not too big," he said. "Aim for the door, not the windows. When he comes out, make a run for it."

Willem and I did as we were told. When we each had two or three good stones, Filip launched his at the kitchen door. We pelted ours, too – mine hit the side of the house; Willem's took a chunk of paint off the skirting board – and when there were no stones left, we cast about for more.

Shimon Franck threw open the door just as the last of Filip's stones came flying towards him.

"*Godverdomme*—" He ducked, giving us time to scamper behind the scrapheap.

The Jew turned around to consider the damage, and muttered something under his breath. Slowly, sighing like an accordion that's had the air squeezed out of it, he bent down to collect the stones. Then he came towards the wall, I suppose to toss them back into the yard – there weren't any stones in his garden, it was all neatly mown lawn and pots of flowers – and that was when he saw it.

He clutched his chest with one hand and reached out to the splayed creature with the other, stumbling towards it – towards us.

"Geisha? My Geisha, is that you?" he wheezed, and tears started to stream from his eyes, disappearing into the folds of his old face. He gasped, his mouth opening and closing like that of a fish.

234

"Let's go!"

Shimon Franck looked up to where the scrapheap had come to life, just in time to see Filip and Willem bolt. I thought that he would chase after them, bellow at the top of his lungs, call down hail and brimstone on our heads – but he just stared, aghast, his fingers tightening around his breast.

And then he was looking at me, watching the darkness close in as I hit the ground, when everything went red and I could hear the *boom-ba-boom* of my clenching heart, the blood gushing between my ears.

I opened my eyes – was it only seconds later? half a minute, perhaps? – and there he was, right up close, but now he too was on the ground. With open eyes, watching me watching him die.

I scrambled to my feet and ran for it.

I must have cut my lip when I fell, or perhaps I had knocked out a tooth or bitten the inside of my cheek, because as I ran all I could think about was the copper taste of blood in my mouth and how to get rid of it. When I reached the town square, I made a beeline for the fountain outside the Schepenhuis and cupped my hands to catch the falling water. Gulping, spitting, gulping some more to eradicate the metallic taste, the rising bile, the thumping heat of my heart about to explode, wiping the threads of blood that trailed from my mouth. I started to cry, sticky tears blending with the crisp water as I doused my head, my neck, my hair, trying to erase the image of the man's face when he had discovered the burnt corpse of his cat – her little feline features screaming *why didn't you rescue me?* – the two of them together, wretched and alone. As I drank, a crowd began to emerge from De Kraan, where a radio was blaring loudly.

"A lousy two bronze medals, that's all we could manage," one man was saying.

"Trust the Germans to sweep the games clean," said another.

And then they were gone, as the bells of St Rombouts started calling the faithful to prayer.

26

I have a confession to make.

The girl paused, biting the pen. She breathed through the alien
gurgling of her stomach, inhaling the cool breeze that fluttered
through the window netting.

*I'm telling you because I can tell no one else. Not my aunt,
who has already suffered too much and would no doubt view
this as a calamity, a dreadful failure on her part. She is far
too busy, anyway – and in this case above all I know that she
would be utterly revolted by what I have done. I dare not tell
my parents, as they are too far away and would only fuss and
fret and beg me to catch the first ship home, which of course
is the last thing that I can do. Nor even Emil, because I dread
to imagine what he would think of me. I can tell you because I
know you will tell no one else, and because in a strange way I
feel that you will understand what it is like to find one's world
turned suddenly upside down against your will, even if you
yourself have been in some way responsible for bringing it to
pass.*

*There was a great commotion at Perdita's house yesterday,
when Nimali discovered a cobra in the kitchen sink. Word
spread quickly, and soon half the village was here to pay their
respects. They believe that the cobra came as a messenger.
Well, they may be right.*

*Pieter, I think I may be pregnant. It has been three weeks
since our tryst in the pews – early, I know, but they do say that
a woman can tell. It was only recently that I was going through
my journal, examining the bits and pieces I have collected
over these last few months – my little scraps of truth – and I*

wondered what it amounted to, what it meant. I looked inside myself, and I found nothing. But now it seems that this has changed...

I am going to tell Ganan this week. If he takes the news well, then we shall be a family, and a whole new adventure shall begin to unfold. But something worries me, Pieter. It sounds awful, but I have never been able to imagine myself giving birth to a healthy child: I know that something must be wrong with it. It will be a mongoloid, or have a cleft palate, or lack limbs; I am too weak, too insubstantial to contribute something strong and perfect to the human race. The other night, as I was watching Perdita chop vegetables, I discovered a second bulb growing inside one of the peppers. It made me think of a parasite, a sort of monstrous twin – and suddenly I felt so ill I had to run upstairs lest anyone ask me to explain my horror at something so silly.

What am I to do – take the local plumbago remedy? Trap a scorpion for its poison; crush peacock stones to make a lethal powder? I dare not seek the help of the native doctor – not only because I am far too frightened of what might happen, but because it would be impossible for my visit to pass unnoticed in the village. I have no hope of going to Colombo alone without rousing suspicion, especially not after what happened the last time; and I can't ask the local military surgeon, as there is far too high a risk that Mrs Cornish's husband, who is a medical offer, would find out.

And if there is more than one child? I once read of an Englishwoman in Jamaica who gave birth to twins: one black, one white. Do you think it could happen?

Write to me, soon. I need to be told that it is for the best.

Glen

As she stood up, her gaze came to rest on the smoke portraits tacked to the wall by the vanity mirror. Pausing to consider her own reflection, she tried to imagine her skin two or three shades darker; her lips more full; her hair coarser, black. Is that how he would look? For it would be a boy, certainly. He might even resemble her brother, with his tumbling curls and lopsided grin. But he would have Ganan's eyes, those long, thick lashes, the same stern mouth. And as for her? What attributes, tangible and essential, would she contribute?

She had slept through supper, and hunger was beginning to creep up on her. Tightening her gown, she made her way to the door and crept into the hallway. The house was asleep, switched off to the otherness of night-time. Feeling her way downstairs, through the corridor and into the kitchen, Glen spoke quietly to the smaller self inside her.

"Hungry, are you? Me, too."

"There's that roast chicken left over from earlier."

"Silly. You're only the size of my fingernail, far too small to eat chicken!"

There had been a time when she would only let herself write on an empty stomach, when she believed that physical hunger could whet her creative appetite. It all seemed hopelessly naive now. With a grunt, she heaved open the icebox door and took out the chicken leftovers. She did not stop to gather cutlery, or to make herself a neat pile of scraps with some sliced tomato for good measure. Rolling up the silk sleeves of her gown, she tore into the bird with her bare hands, greedily pulling the flesh from the bones, snapping the joints so that she could gnaw off every last scrap of sinew and skin and greasy grey meat.

As she stood at the counter, mopping up clumps of aspic with a piece of crisp skin, the shadows shifted softly in the moonlight and she was overcome with a sense of peace, fulfilment – and a sudden yearning for bed.

Everything will be all right, she thought, carefully returning the china plate with its remains to the icebox and wiping her fingers on a dishcloth. *These things have a way of sorting themselves out.* She did not need to settle into a life of triviality and self-regarding tedium: even marriage wasn't all that important. Ganan would keep her safe, would guard the parameters within which she could continue to be expressive and young and free. They would make a charming couple – a strikingly *modern* couple, people would remark in hushed, admiring tones – his strait-laced conventionality offsetting her modern womanhood. And the little one would inherit the best of them both.

* * *

She dreamt that there was no baby. Overcome by a delightful lightness, a blissful insubstantiality, she drifted through the walls of her aunt's house, across the valley and out towards the sea, snippets of verse circling in her mind as if unwinding on a spool. *Watch the wall, my darling, as the gentlemen go by...*

She floated over an expanse of black water and gazed down at the rippling waves that looked like so many wings flocking towards her; up, up from the heavy depths, up – growing lighter and quicker and stronger as they rushed towards the surface, racing to break through the shimmering barrier.

Then, a sudden, mighty crash: the sound of windows bursting in their frames, glass panes shattered to a fine dust by a scream binding many voices, a parrot's panicked squawk. The explosion came from deep down, sending a jolt of terror coursing like fire through her body, so that when she woke she was already sitting upright, damp sheets twisted around her legs, heart drumming in her chest.

And then, through the silence, the same words began to thread their way once more – louder and more insistent now, making her reach for the pillow so that she might smother them: *Watch the wall, my darling, as the gentlemen go by...*

27

The hour before dawn belonged to the birds. I would lie in bed listening to them bicker and cheep, barely noticing the light changing around me until at last it was morning.

That day, however, as I listened to the nattering of the lap-wings and sparrows, the crooning of the pigeons and the pretty song of a lark, I could not concentrate for long enough to match each bird to its call. The shriek of a barn owl, the brash cries of a wren and the flirtations of a thrush – for the first time, I could hardly tell them apart.

I was thinking about what it must be like to know that the thing you are looking at is the last thing you'll ever see.

I'll never know if Shimon Franck recognized me as the boy whose brother drowned in the river. Perhaps, in his final moments, he imagined that I was an angel, like the one Tobias saw. Or perhaps he thought that I was Death itself. This thought frightened me. I knew that a mortal sin requires a grave trans-gression, but I couldn't decide if what I had done involved full knowledge and full consent. After all, I hadn't actually been the one to throw the match into the barrel. And, if what Mr Hend-ryks said was true – that full consent means opening your heart to something without any doubts at all – I could probably be ex-cused on that count, too. Only a little part of me had consented to Filip's plan. Another part of me had shut off from what was really happening, like Father in the gatehouse, as soon as I saw the little white cat staring up at me with pink eyes as she lifted her tail to piss.

Then I remembered something else that Mr Hendryks had said, about people no longer believing in God – and for the first time I began to understand what that meant.

Someone still believed in me, at least.

Dear Glen,

Today there was an execution. When I hear footsteps walking towards the room at the end of my corridor, I count to twenty. If the footsteps stop after I reach twenty, I know that it is a dead man walking. Sometimes you can hear the prisoner praying, or making strange noises as if his tongue was stuck in his throat while the chaplain reads from the Bible. More often, though, it is very quiet. For the most part, people who are about to die do not scream. They are too frightened.

After the door closes, it is impossible to hear what happens on the other side. It is impossible to hear the bag going over the prisoner's head, the noose being tightened around his neck. All of this, you imagine. Then, at the very last minute, a hatch opens in the floor, and the prisoner falls through it. You do not hear the twisting rope, or snapping bone, or the creak of a body hanging by a thread. Only the bang of the trapdoor – and then nothing for a very long time.

I remembered what Krelis had told me about how war made people do crazy things, and tried not to think of the woman who had hanged herself in our gatehouse.

Your secret is safe with me. At least the baby's father is an Aryan, and not a Negro or a Jew. So you do not need to worry about your child being subhuman, even if he is not entirely perfect.

Jantje Meijer wasn't allowed to keep her baby after the police found out she was giving abortions in her back room to pay the rent. That was her punishment for committing a mortal sin. Do not let fear make you do something you will regret, and do not be too afraid of the pain. Arend says that all births are violent: of people, of nations. But doesn't the blood bear fruit?

Is it true that the English woman had a black baby and a white one at the same time? That is nature making a mistake. It happens sometimes. Take my brother: that was nature doing the right thing. And me: that was nature making

241

a mistake. Not the same mistake as Jews and Gypsies, but still a mistake.

I am looking forward to reading the story you have written about me.

* * *

I was walking home from my accordion lesson when I saw her.

It had been weeks since she had last spoken to me; weeks since I had retched in her arms and asked for the book on tapeworms. At first I didn't know it was her; all I could see was the yellow trim of her dress fluttering against his knee. Chinese yellow, it's called: the colour which, in China, used to be reserved for the Emperor's exclusive use.

They were standing against the wall of the Béguinage in an alcove that was set off from the street. Arend had his back to me, and it looked as if he was speaking into her ear. Mieke was holding his hands against her waist. I watched Arend press his face into her hair, and I felt my stomach lurch with a mixed sensation of awe and shame.

Pretending that I had discovered a problem with my accordion case, I knelt on the pavement to watch them from across the street.

Before long, Mieke started to wriggle about, and I realized that she wasn't holding Arend's hands so much as trying to peel them off her. He straightened, and I noticed a cigarette dangling from the corner of his mouth. Taking a step back, he removed the cigarette with two fingers before leaning in closer and blowing a puff of smoke into her face. She tried to push him away, but in that split second Arend's free hand shot to her throat. He seemed to push her into the wall with the ease of someone reaching for a tin of tomatoes, and I thought again of the woman in our gatehouse. Still, I did nothing.

The next thing I knew, Arend had released Mieke and was stubbing out his cigarette into the wall near her head. He pressed against her once more before pushing her roughly to the ground. As he turned towards the street, I began to fiddle with my accordion straps, praying that he wouldn't see me.

He didn't. As he rounded the corner, I heard him mutter something – "Commie slut", it sounded like – before disappearing down an empty lane.

I didn't stop to think that perhaps she wouldn't like me to see her like this.

"Are you all right?" I said as soon as I reached her, dropping my accordion at her feet.

Mieke's eyes were red, her mouth blotchy with what I supposed to be smeared lipstick. I saw that one of her barrettes had fallen to the ground, and I knelt to pick it up. When I offered it to her, she was staring up at me as if I was him.

"He's a monster," she said. "You're all monsters."

"No, I'm not," I said.

She snatched the barrette out of my hand and stabbed it into a clutch of hair.

"Yes, you are," she said. "That's what he does: teaches little boys to fight and fight and fight. He's obsessed with it, with being loved by little brutes. He thinks that death is beautiful."

"I'm not a little boy," I said.

I wanted to tell her that I was a political prisoner. There had been a mistake; I wasn't just Krelis's little brother any more.

"I'm a freedom fighter," I said at last.

Mieke laughed, but not in a nice way. "You've changed, Marten," she said. "I thought you were smarter than all that."

Then she stood up, and pushed past me before I had a chance to step aside.

28

The wedding celebrations carried on late into the night, filling the valley with the ringing of temple bells and trails of smoke from the oil lamps which flickered up and down the mountain ridge. Standing at the edge of the lawn, Glen and the children could feel the tremor of distant drums through the soles of their feet as they peered through the darkness at the far-off plateau.

"I can see the dancers," breathed Hollar.

"No, you can't," said Althea, without taking her eyes off the illuminated ridge. "You can't see them. You can hear them singing."

"Those are the *Jayamangala* girls," smiled Perdita, as she emerged from the servant's hut. "They are singing devotional songs." She gathered her sari around her and squatted on the ground, inviting the children to join her.

"Who's being married?" asked Glen. "Do you know?"

"No," replied the housemaid. "But it is a Sinhala Buddhist wedding, that I can tell." As if reading Glen's mind, she added, "The bride will be wearing a very-very grand sari, missy-mem. Gold thread, with pearls and stones and beads. *Padakkam*, you know – like a necklace, very heavy. And a *nalalpata* on the head, with gold and gemstones."

"A tiara," smiled Glen.

Perdita wobbled her head. "The wedding time is chosen according to the bride's date of birth, so it is an auspicious day, yes? The bride and the bridegroom pay respects on the *poruwa*, which is covered in flowers. Then the *Shilpadhipathi* leads the ceremony."

"Is it very long?"

"Very-very long, miss!" said Perdita, smiling. "First, there is the ceremony for the Seven Generations. Then the bride's uncle ties the little fingers of the couple with golden thread. Then the groom offers a white cloth to the bride, and afterwards she gives it to her mother. Also, the groom's mother will give a sari to the bride. The bride's mother gives her milk rice. They feed this to each other."

"Like a wedding cake."

"*Achcha*. When they leave the *poruwa*, the *Shilpadhipathi* cracks open a coconut. This is the time for the couple to light the oil lamp. And all the families give their blessing."

Glen tried to imagine what the bride must be feeling right now. The thrill of love, of a day devoted entirely to her? The weight of tradition and family expectations bearing down on her neck and arms like jewelled shackles? The joy and terror of giving herself entirely to someone else? Glen sensed all of these things as the tiny life within her hungrily insisted that she was now merely a means to an end, a vessel through which something – someone – else might thrive. She had invited Ganan to the church in order to avoid the engagement party in Matale – and look where that had led. Would Holly and Jim be married by now? Glen tried not to think of them, because thinking of them meant thinking of Dougie and Mrs Cornish and what people would say when they found out. Instead, she tried to imagine the couple on the hill circling their wedding flame, two lives joined as one. And then she realized that she herself had become two people: a self and a mirror self. Who was the stranger whose life had twinned so suddenly with her own? This dark little creature, conceived in a tomb…

As if sensing a change in the girl's mood, Perdita gently unfurled a corner of her shawl and cast it about Glen's shoulders.

"We are so pleased that you are here, missy-mem," she said.

Glen smiled weakly. "I only hope I've made myself useful," she said. "To the children, I mean. And Annabel." She looked across to her young cousins. "We do have fun, don't we? Even with our French prep."

"*Bien sûr!*"

Perdita tried not to watch her too closely, to wonder too long at the ways in which the English girl seemed somehow older. It was late, and the spectacle of the hilltop wedding was perhaps making her long for her old life – a life of cars and clubs and dashing young men. Perdita could not imagine what it must be like to be so far from home.

"You've seen Mr Dharmasena again?" she suddenly asked. Glen looked startled, and the housemaid worried that perhaps she had spoken out of turn. "Jayanadani told me that you have become friends with him, Miss. It must be good to have someone to talk to – someone who has also been to London, no?"

"Yes," murmured Glen.

"Look!" cried Hollar, pointing to the sky. Two swans had been cast into the air, set free to the joyous pounding of drums. Together, they swooped low into the valley before rising up across the mountain ridge.

"It is *hansa puttuwa*," said Perdita. "The symbol of marriage."

"Because they mate for life," said Hollar.

When Glen next looked up to the sky, both birds had vanished.

* * *

"It's the missy-mem! Hurry, Nimali."

Jayanadani slung her satchel over one shoulder – so hard it swung right around her body and banged against her hip – and rushed up the dirt road towards Glen. Nimali followed, black braids thumping wildly against her back.

"Did you come to meet us? Can we buy *kulfi* on the way home?"

"I got a ten in spelling, Miss Glen. Look…"

"Did Baba bring you in the car? It's so hot today!"

"Are you looking, Miss Glen?"

She peered over the tops of their heads at the figure emerging from the schoolhouse, shaking hands with each of his students as they filed outside. Had he woken this morning with any inkling that today would bring portentous news? By evening this would no longer be just another day of multiplication tables and recitation, chalk dust and bottles of pasteurized milk delivered by the local women's association – a day indistinguishable from all the others.

"Miss Glen, can we go now?"

"I just want a word with your teacher," she said, gently prising Nimali's hands from the folds of her skirt. "About the Latin books," she added, catching Jayanadani's eye. "If you start walking home now, I'll bet you anything that I still get there before you do…"

"No you won't!"

"Hurry, Nimali!"

She watched them until they disappeared around the bend at the end of the road, swallowed up by dervish clouds of red dust. Then she turned and walked towards the schoolhouse, her heart skipping at the sight of two local women sailing past on bicycles, their orange *dupatis* trailing in the breeze as they shielded their faces from the sun with black umbrellas balanced on the handlebars.

The teacher had returned to his desk and was forming neat piles of workbooks. Glen waited for the last child to leave before she approached him.

"Hello, there."

He glanced up, startled, and took what seemed to be an involuntary step backwards.

"I didn't hear you come in," he said, and indicated a child's desk in the front row. "Please, sit down."

She looked at the desk – the marks that someone had scratched with a compass, the inkwell caked with black crust, the groove in the wooden bench where bony bottoms fidgeted and squirmed through long lessons – and opened her mouth to speak.

"It is just as well that you came," he said, cutting her off. "I've had time to think, and I now realize that what I did was wrong – no, please let me finish." She recognized something familiar in his voice – that simmering adolescent rage, that impatience to be heard – and slowly sank onto the bench, feeling every bit the errant schoolgirl.

"Our talk at the caves clarified things for me. Too late, I fear, but that is why I feel it important to address these matters promptly." He cleared his throat. "Glen, I want you to know that I have every concern for your reputation – despite the fact that I have acted foolishly and with shameful self-indulgence." His gaze remained trained on the ground in front of his feet as he paced slowly from one end of his desk to the other. It was a half-prepared speech, that much was clear. "Not only have I neglected my personal and professional duties, I have allowed you to develop expectations that I, wretched creature, cannot possibly hope to fulfil."

Glen's heart began to race. No wonder he looked nervous! For surely this was nothing less than an elaborate preamble to a proposal: at any moment he might fall towards her on bended knee, forgetting whatever else he had planned to say in his desperation to hear her answer. In all her daydreams, never had she dared to imagine this moment.

"Is there somewhere else we can talk?" she asked.

He stopped and looked around the empty schoolroom.

"Perhaps the Club, for a palmyrah toddy?" she suggested. "You see, I have something to tell you, too – and it's something that calls for a little celebration, really."

Ganan straightened. "We don't drink during the full moon," he said.

"Who's we?"

"The Sinhalese."

"But Hindus don't go in for this *poya* business, do they? I thought you lot rose above all that."

"*You lot.*"

Mustering a small laugh, she said, "Come on, silly boy…"

"I am not a boy." This time, the edge in his voice was unmistakable.

"No, I don't suppose you are! Certainly not now that you're about to become a father—"

That was not what she had intended to say, or how she had intended to say it, and Glen realized that her words sounded cold, defensive. The statement rang out as an accusation, too late to withdraw.

He stared at her, grey-faced. "I beg your pardon?"

"I thought you'd like to know…"

"I see." He bent over his desk and began to shuffle papers furiously. He did not look at her. "How did this happen?"

Already Glen had begun to wish that she hadn't interrupted him, that she had allowed him to finish his piece first, to make his offer so that she might accept it before sharing what would have been delightful news. Embarrassed and irritated, she made no effort to disguise her petulant tone. "Well, there's only one time I can think of..."

"Don't patronize me, Glen."

"Look, I thought you'd be happy. If it's a problem I'll take care of it."

"Of course: as soon as the colony becomes a burden on the mother country, we tear it apart—"

"Hold up!" she protested, rather too loudly.

"Well?" He looked at her, and she realized that what she had taken for anger was actually fear.

"Actually, I had wanted to keep it," she said with a soft voice. "To share it with you."

He set the papers down once again, lowered himself into his chair. Resting his elbows on the table, Ganan steepled his fingers and peered up at her sternly, like a schoolmaster. But she could see the rising tides of panic behind his eyes.

"That will not be possible."

"Why not?"

"My family won't accept it: I will lose caste."

"Your own flesh and blood? They couldn't be so hard-hearted. And anyway, even if they did, what does it matter? You're a grown man, educated, a professional. These silly notions of purity..." A long silence ensued – and when she next spoke, there was desperation in her voice. "There's nothing to stop us being happy together..."

"But there is nothing between us."

It was the last thing she had expected to hear, and at first Glen put it down to his mercurial nature: a flight of passion, a momentary loss of reason.

"You don't mean that: just a minute ago, you were about to propose to me."

Now it was his turn to look flabbergasted. "I intended no such thing," he said.

"What?" she searched desperately for any indication of a smile, any note of tenderness.

"I don't know where you got that idea, Glen, but it could not be further from the truth." The ember light in his dark eyes had vanished. "We were friends – I hope that we might still be friends – but you must know that it can never be more than that."

"How can you say that, after all that's happened?"

"It was a flirtation with the impossible, Glen – surely you knew that all along?" He stood up and began pacing again, now with the restlessness of a caged tiger. "You were unlike any Englishwoman I had met before; I was charmed by you and flattered by your attention: I had never believed myself worthy of such interest." He stopped and shook his head, as if waking up from a dream. "And I assume you were also curious about a man such as myself. You made it clear from the outset that you did not share the bourgeois notions of your class, but were stubbornly modern, liberated, unsentimental." He stole a glance at her. "Foolishly, perhaps, I chose to believe this: I chose to think that things need not be complicated between us—"

"*Complicated*?" she snorted. "In other words, you saw a chance to sleep with a woman who'd ask for nothing in return?"

He became flustered, averted his gaze. "What happened in the church was a moment of indiscretion, nothing more. I thought you knew that."

"But I love you..." How weak, how pathetic those words sounded now!

"No, you don't." He spoke so softly that for an instant the girl thought she might have imagined his words. When she realised that she hadn't, she felt a new rush of anger.

"You are dismissing my feelings only because you cannot bear to be loved – you were everything to me—"

"I don't *want* to be everything to you. Or to anyone, for that matter." He wiped his palms on his thighs. "If you loved me, it was only because of who you thought I was. You must listen to me now. I don't think it's proper to make these matters public."

"*Proper*? I'm sorry – is that Mrs Cornish I just heard come in?"

"Don't be childish, Glen."

"Childish!"

Now it was his turn to plead. "Look: if there's anything you need, anything at all, I'll see to it that you lack for nothing. It is partly my fault, I know——"

"I don't need you to buy yourself a clean conscience."

"Well, what more can I do?" He pushed his fingers through his hair, scanning the desk as if searching for a hidden escape. "If I could turn back time, Glen, I promise you I would. I knew then that it was wrong – I wanted to explain this to you…"

"Explain what?" She let her hands drop to her sides. "The way you feel – or don't feel? Or what your family might think of a girl like me? A *gora*? White."

He would not look at her. "Perhaps it is a bit of both…" He swallowed. "I also need to prove myself, Glen. Last week I received an offer to study at the Government Law College. I was going to tell you…"

"Bombay?" she said. Her mouth was dry. "I thought you'd given up on the law——"

"I'd given up on myself, perhaps. But you helped me to change that, Glen." He faced her with what was perhaps meant to be a look of gratitude, and took her gently by the hand. "With any luck I will be gone by the time the child is born; there will be less gossip that way. Please, you must forget all about me."

She drew back, surprised by her sudden revulsion at his touch. Then, blinking back tears, she said, "And what of the poem, the picture in the park, the smoke portraits…" She fumbled for words, breath catching in a sob. "What was all that about?"

He shoved both hands in his pockets with a sigh. "It was art, just art. All art is quite useless."

"Don't say that!" The girl saw him contain his surprise at the passion in her voice with a look of cold composure. "You have nothing in common with the modernists you worship, Ganan. Cold, cruel art! You know that there is more to beauty than order, no matter what you claim…"

"Well, what can I say? What will satisfy you?"

"The truth!" She swallowed, tasting bile. "You told me that once we discover truth, we can't turn our backs on it…"

"I gave you my truth: there is nothing else to it, Glen." He had the crumpled look of a child about to cry: lost and bewildered. "I'm sorry."

Looking back, she could not remember how she got home. Almost certainly through sun-dappled jungle paths where monkeys screamed from the soaring treetops, across a creaking footbridge, up the dirt track – skidding, stumbling over loose slate and crumbling clay – to the high plateau where the paved road drove a straight line towards the Club, the station, the medical clinic. But she hurried away from those things, those people, into the valley.

The white gables of Beulah Lodge resembled the crest of a wave tumbling down the green mountainside amid an avalanche of clawing foliage. There was an explosion of feathers as Nuisance bowled through a cluster of Annabel's hens and shot towards her from across the lawn yapping, prancing, alert. Beyond him, she noticed Perdita's girls twirling among the root branches of the banyan tree. Sinewy tendrils grew out of the ground only to sprout limbs that drooped back to the soil: an endless cycle of birth and burial. She skirted the garden, keeping close to the side of the house. Casting the green netting aside, she ducked into the dim hallway, briefly dazzled by the neon blotches that pressed upon her eyelids. How bright the day was, even now. Clutching the banister, she pulled herself upstairs to the safety of bed: the soft eiderdown, the cool cotton pillowcase…

A letter had been left for her there. It bore an English postmark, and for a moment she wondered if it could be from her parents. She winced from a sudden searing pain: a dizzying loneliness and a desperate yearning for home, for Pa to gather her in his arms and envelop her in his peaty, fatherly scent and promise her that everything would be all right. What a little fool Ganan must think her: an ignorant, vain, deluded girl who could not be content with flirtation but had to fall in love with some silly idea. Oh, the exquisite agony! The perfect rage and humiliation of learning how she had looked to him! How could she have lost herself so easily to an obsession – for it was obsession, not even love at all – to abandon all pride and dignity in the name

of adventure? To have felt entitled to him without even considering what she might offer in return. Selfish creature, trapped in a
fool's paradise!

She sank onto the bed, studying the envelope through sore
eyes. Mummy would not type the address or send such a thin
packet – so clinical, so professional.

Inside, she discovered what looked like a compliment slip.

Dear Miss Phayre,

We regret to inform you that your correspondent, Pieter
van Houten, passed away on 1st September at Diegem
Prison, Machelen.

Thank you for taking the time to reach out to a fellow
in need. A new correspondent may be assigned to you on
receipt of the enclosed form.

Yours sincerely,

Dorothy P. Watt, Christian Women's Union

29

At the next meeting, Arend instructed us to turn in our badges.

"But why?" asked Filip irritably. It was he who had boasted to the other boys what we had done to Shimon Franck's cat almost as soon as the deed was done. At that point, he and Willem still had no idea that the old man was dead.

"Because a VNV badge was discovered near the dead man," snapped Arend. "Everyone must turn theirs in immediately."

All of Mechelen was talking about it now: the burnt cat tied to the gatepost, discovered by the owner, who had succumbed almost instantly to a heart attack.

"What's the world coming to?" Mr Hendryks had said to me at Mass the following Sunday. "That poor, poor man. His wife sent me a plum tart when I was in hospital – you're too young to remember."

I tried to imagine Shimon Franck in his kitchen kneading dough, pitting plums. "At least he died quickly," I said.

"A Jew," sighed Mr Hendryks. "That's what this was about."

"I heard it was because the cat was possessed," I said.

Mr Hendryks looked as if he was about to say something, but then the bells began to toll and it was time for us to lead the procession into the church. All through the service I couldn't stop thinking about the little white cat. She'd had a name, Geisha. Two images refused to erase themselves from my mind: when she was inside the barrel, lifting her tail to piss and staring up at me with pink eyes; then, minutes later, when she was no more than a blackened stump attached to a skull.

Usually I enjoyed the Mass and its rhythms: the way it belonged to the priests and the clergy and the altar boys. But today I made mistakes. I dropped the thurible during the reading; by the homily, I was still scrambling to secure the lid to stop it

bleeding clouds of incense. At Communion, my tongue refused
to take the wafer. It dropped to the floor, and Father Goossens
and I watched in horror as the fallen host was crushed underfoot by an approaching communicant. By then it was too late for
Father Goossens to do anything but offer me the wine and pray
that a suitable means of dispensing with Our Lord's body might
be found after the service. Later, as I watched him sweep up the
remains with more reverence than I had ever seen anyone handle
a dustpan and brush, he asked me if everything was all right at
home. I lied and told him that Mother and I were going to bake
a cake that afternoon.

Instead, I found myself in the wooded clearing, handing over
my VNV badge.

"The rest of the troop will not be punished for your stupidity.
A bit of mischief is one thing, but to leave your tracks uncovered
is an insult to me and the instructors who have tried to train
you properly." Arend turned to me. "Kuypers. You were a fool to
involve yourself in such an idiotic escapade, but I'm not going to
expel you from the section. I don't want to have to explain to the
District Officer why I've suddenly had to lose three boys. No one
shall mention this."

I looked at my badge: my mark of virtue and courage. The
sign of our patriotic brotherhood.

"I want to keep it," I said. "I'm not afraid. I'm proud of it."

Arend's mouth formed a grim line.

"Give it to me, Kuypers. For your own good."

"I'm not a traitor!"

Arend landed a vicious blow on my head. I doubled over, gasping, and let the badge fall to the ground. Dirk snapped it up
almost instantly and tossed it to our leader. I waited for Arend
to offer his hand. I didn't deserve this; he must have known it
wasn't fair. We were blood brothers, after all.

But Arend had already turned away.

I followed the river home that evening. As I reached a bend
just out of sight of the fulling mill, the thought suddenly struck
me that the past is like water: slippery, transparent, impossible
to pin down. Because a river has no memory, it is always surging

towards the present. It can't turn back on itself. It can't regret anything. It believes only in the future.

I found Adriaan behind the brewery. He'd not been at the meeting. The other boys had stopped speaking to him, like animals that can smell death on one of their own.

"You'll have to give Arend your badge," I said. "We all did. For the good of the troop." Like Petronius, who broke his signet ring before killing himself so that no one could be blamed for his murder.

"I've lost mine," Adriaan replied. He was poking at beetles with a long, crooked stick.

"Are you sure?"

"I can't find it anywhere."

I whistled.

"You'd better hope it's not the one they found near Shimon Franck's house," I said. "If it has your fingerprints on it, you'll be a marked man."

Adriaan just shrugged. Then he tossed the stick into a puddle, shoved his hands in his pockets and began to walk away. As I watched him go, I remembered something I'd read about bees. Everyone knows that when a bee stings you it dies. But not everyone knows that when it dies, it sends out a kind of chemical message to other bees to let them know where it is. Some people say that the chemical message is sent out so that other bees can come to die in the same place – but I'm not sure how true that is.

Before I could ask him what he thought, Adriaan was gone.

* * *

Sitting at my desk, I stared up through the window at the grey sky overhead. It was my favourite kind of sky, the kind where the sun is behind you and the clouds are ahead of you, dark and steely, but the sun lights up the leaves in the trees like hundreds of fluttering electric lights. The black clouds make them seem brighter, somehow.

Dear Glen, I wrote.

*Something terrible has happened. I'm writing to you be-
cause I can't tell anyone else. I know that you English have
bad things on your conscience, too, like the camps in South
Africa where you watched our Boer kinsmen starve to death.
So you will understand.*

That was supposed to be the easy part. But strangely, thinking
about little Boer children wasting away under an African sun in
another time, another war, only made me feel worse.

*I have blood on my hands. It was an accident, but that doesn't
make it any better.*

I bit my pencil. *He was a Jew,* I wrote. And because I couldn't be
sure what that meant, I erased it. But then I realized that I didn't
know how else to describe him, so I wrote it again.

*He was a Jew, but even that doesn't make it better. If he had
been a Bolshevist, he would still be dead. And the Bolshevists
are the worst, the people who go to Spain to join in the slaugh-
ter of helpless priests and innocent children.*

Don't get sidetracked. Don't tell her.

*My friends have abandoned me, and now I have no one but
you.*

And then, an idea: why hadn't I thought of it before?

*Do you think I could come to Ceylon? I could earn my living
by working on the tea plantation. You could help me – just like
the angel who delivered Peter from his prison cell (Acts 12).*

I would drink coconut milk and gorge myself on pineapples and
fish! I would learn the native tongue and convert the heathen –
become a boy martyr so that Mother and Father would be proud

of me. I would sleep in a straw hammock under the open sky, and my skin, now the colour of sour milk, would turn a healthy golden hue…

Or would it be better for me to kill my shame instead? I know about hara-kiri. You stab yourself in the stomach and twist the knife to make sure you die. But I think I'm too scared to do that.

I blinked, and realized that I was still staring out the window at the true light of a leaden sky.

I'm scared, I wrote. Was this perdition? I hadn't attended confession in a long time, and I was too scared to now. Perhaps I could redeem myself with acts of contrition instead. I could hold my hands under scalding water; I could rub nettles on my arms and legs; I could eat bad meat and grow another parasite, big enough to rupture my stomach.

Would this be enough?

Something inside me twisted and tightened, like my tapeworm but bigger – as if it was growing through my chest and up into my throat. There was a bump on my head where Arend had punched me. My eyes smarted; my palms were wet. I wondered if it was reasonable to feel lost in my own room. I thought of Leontius, who had cursed his eyes for their greed, and wondered if Filip and Willem suffered the same nightmares that I did, the same frightful visions of that little white cat.

I'm scared, Glen, because I bargained with the Devil and don't know what to believe. And without belief, a person is nothing. Some people believe in God, or in science, or in the Flemish Lion, or in Lenin. What do you believe in? Please pray for me, whatever it is.

And write soon.

Yours,

Pieter

30

She hadn't written his story in time, and now he was dead. Glen tried not to think how. Whatever the cause, life had run out before she could be bothered to spare the few moments that might have made him happy.

Over several days, she reread Pieter's final letter. Studying his words, Glen had wondered at the fact that he continued to speak to her from beyond the grave: here, on this page, Pieter seemed still alive. It struck her as a small miracle, like the banyan branches that returned to the soil only to regenerate themselves as roots for future saplings. She would breathe fresh life into him, her freed prisoner, whenever she read his words.

Something about that – the thought of breath, of breathing – finally made her reach for the matchbox on her dressing table.

Guiding the flame so that its flickering tip barely brushed the page, she turned the paper until traces of pale ink began to show themselves at the margins. And then, like flowers suddenly bursting into bloom, his illustrations revealed themselves: birds and trees and dazzling suns, sailboats and elephants, coiled serpents and snow-capped peaks. He had filled almost every available space with images of her life – that is, of an exotic life which he had imagined for her – and now the images seemed to shimmer on the page as if straining to make the final leap from fantasy to reality.

When she saw his drawings in all their simple beauty, she felt herself weaken. Perhaps it was the half-recognized feeling she had always carried with her: a sense of lonely void, complete and total emptiness.

For the first time in her life, Glen shed tears of pure grief, devoid of any self-pity.

* * *

According to family stories, her mother had not begun to show with Tully until the very end; in photographs, it was impossible to discern even the slightest swelling through tightly cinched corsets. But that had been in England: what chance did she stand here, in this cloying humidity, this sickening, dizzying heat? A gossamer blouse clung to the hollow space between her breasts and beneath her arms, plastered inside every crevice that caved and perspired.

And even if she could conceal it beneath sundresses and shawls – surely it was only a matter of time before someone noticed the rapidly diminishing supply of dry rusks that she smuggled to her bedside from the pantry every evening, to stifle the morning's creeping nausea – that sickness which would not limit itself to the early hours, but which struck at midday when the heat was fiercest, and sometimes in the evenings, too? Worst of all was the smell of frying coconut oil and garlic which emanated from the servants' quarters, wafted uphill by a warm breeze. Only a few weeks ago, the aroma had made her mouth water; now, she had to hold her breath whenever she passed through the garden.

If Annabel suspected that something was amiss, she didn't show it. But the children were another matter.

"Come and join me on the swings, Glen."

"Not now, darling. Just the sight of you makes me dizzy."

"Are you sure you're all right?"

"I'm fine, I'm fine."

"Glen?"

She removed her palms from her eyes and looked up. Hollar was standing over her, watching intently.

"What is it, darling?"

"What were you reading?" He pointed to the piece of paper that fluttered between her fingers.

"This? It's a letter. A very old letter, which fell out of an album that belongs to a friend of mine. I need to return it to him."

"Which friend?"

She waited for him to crouch on the step next to her before slowly unfolding the yellowed paper.

"Captain Royce."

Hollar's eyes widened. He sucked on his lip, hard.

"It's all right, darling. I know that you're friends with him, too."

Hollar stared at his hands, worrying a piece of skin that had begun to peel from one finger. "We talk about birds. When he was my age, he had his own falcon."

"I think this might have been something that he wrote as a child. Shall I read it to you?"

The boy nodded without looking up.

"All right, then. It's a letter from boarding school. He must have been... oh, six, seven? Can you imagine that?"

There was the flicker of a smile; Hollar shook his head.

"The spelling's preposterous. Here, look." She smoothed the paper. "Someone has blacked out parts of it, do you see?"

"What does it say?"

Dear Papa,

I am feeling better, thank you. ▮▮▮▮▮▮▮▮▮▮▮
▮▮▮▮▮▮▮▮▮▮▮ *I have not compland about the pohlio to any one and am trying to be brave like you said* ▮▮▮▮▮▮▮▮▮▮▮▮*. I wish that I could visit you some time and ride Jacks agan, he is so splendid but I dont know if I can now* ▮▮▮▮▮▮▮▮▮▮▮▮▮ *Sometimes I cry, but only when Matron isnt hear.*

That is all for now, Papa, as I am tyerd and must get rest. Please write to me.

Love, Boy

"What's *pohlio*?"

"Polio. I suppose that explains his limp." She ran a finger over the fragile scrawl. "Poor man. Poor little boy."

"Where did you find it?"

"On the footpath near the graves. Shall we take it back to the church and leave it there for him?"

"All right."

Hollar steadied her arm as they made the descent together. If she were to stumble and fall now, it might be dealt with quickly.

But how to be sure? Must one land heavily or simply at such an angle as to stun the thing inside? Would there be proof of it later; bleeding or cramps? It was common to miscarry in the early weeks, frighteningly easy.

She watched the boy as he helped her down the path with the sure-footedness of a mountain goat. Tiny beads of perspiration moistened his upper lip; his brown legs tautened as he gripped the rocky passage through scuffed plimsolls. One knee bore an irregular damson bruise: the badge of any self-respecting boy his age.

"Althea told me about your prisoner," he said at last, as they paused at the level space marked out by memorial stones.

She felt her pocket to be sure that the letter was still there: folded square, a child's plaintive cry. For a moment she struggled to distinguish them: Pieter, poor Pieter, now cold and dead in a grey prison morgue. And Boy, no less a prisoner in the military asylum – a purgatorial world of blazers and rugby caps, canings and first elevens. She studied Hollar's young face, earnest and questioning, and saw them both there.

"I should have written to him more often," she said at last. "Now it's too late – he's passed away."

The boy nodded. To talk about someone halfway around the world being dead was no different than talking about the same person being alive: neither made any immediate difference to them here, now.

"I'm sorry," he said. And he turned to continue the descent.

The side door of the church had been left open. Together, they proceeded up the aisle as far as the second pew.

"We were sitting just here," said Glen. "I'll leave it on his seat."

She paused at the spot, listening for the low echo of dripping water – but she could hear nothing. It hadn't rained in days.

"They wanted to send me away to school, too," said Hollar abruptly.

"Who, darling?"

"The people at the hospital, where my mother..." He dug his fingernail into a groove in the pew, staring at the slate floor, and Glen remembered the shuttered windows of the hospital in Colombo, the black tongue of the parrot rattling at the bars.

"Hollar? What is it?"

He looked up at her, holding her gaze. "You don't know?"

She shook her head.

"She committed suttee. There was a big iron stove in the hospital kitchens…" He looked up at her with clear eyes. "Someone passing outside the window noticed the flames. They wouldn't let me see her – I think she was cremated afterwards."

"Good Lord… when was this?"

"Before you came. A year, two years…" He was quick to reassure her. "But my mother wasn't mad, Glen. She was very, very pious. She wanted my father to come back for me."

"And when he didn't, you came to stay with Annabel?"

Hollar nodded again. She sat down.

"Is this what you think about when you come here?"

He shook his head, stared down at his hands in his lap. "I don't think about anything here. That's why I like it."

It was true: at that moment, she knew exactly what he meant. The empty church – the emptiness inside them both – was something fixed and dependable: a lonely fortress that kept those memories at bay.

"I like it, too," she said. "I wonder what it would be like to stay here for ever. Shall we try? You can run home and tell the others I'm not coming back: that I've decided to sit here, in this church, for ever." She forced herself to smile. "Until a handsome prince comes to rescue me, that is. Just like Sleeping Beauty."

As evening closed in, Glen felt herself growing queasy again. Suddenly, she was desperate to lie down, to breathe clean air through cotton bed sheets. She closed her eyes and swallowed the urge to retch. Hollar was standing at one of the windows with his back to her, gazing into the valley. As she doubled over, he turned around in time to see her cover her mouth with one hand, staring up at him with watering eyes.

"Are you all right, Glen?" He rushed to her side. She was breathing heavily through her nose, clutching desperately at the pew. Then, at last, through soft, shuddering sobs, she whispered words that he struggled to make out.

"I think it's time to go home," was all she said.

* * *

Two weeks later, it was confirmed: the baby would be born in May.

"Why didn't you tell me?" Annabel had begged. "I could have helped you!"

"How?" the girl replied through her tears. "By hunting him down and ordering him to marry me?"

She did not tell her aunt that she had wandered into the village several times in the last week alone, hoping to see him. Once, she had noticed Ganan waiting for one of the regular buses – juddering, spluttering people bearers, always overloaded, which turned up choking clouds of black dust in their wake. She had watched him, too frightened to call out, and briefly caught his eye. But he had only stared through her, as if gazing at a rather uninteresting shop window, before turning away.

"I still don't understand." Now her aunt, too, had tears in her eyes. "Why couldn't you trust me? What good am I to you, if you couldn't admit that you were in trouble?"

"I was ashamed," replied Glen. She did not say that she had not wanted to be implicated in Annabel's universal bitterness towards men; that she did not want to be subsumed into the false pride of self-imposed spinsterhood. She searched the room for a prompt, but all she saw were the usual things: the pretty white dresser, the mirror decorated with smoke portraits and Pieter's drawing, the slatted wardrobe, cotton curtains fluttering by the open window. Annabel had brought her squash and a cold compress, and was watching her niece from the foot of the bed with wide harebell eyes. Glen exhaled. "I thought that you'd see it as some kind of betrayal…"

"But that's ridiculous!" What was meant to be an expression of surprise and sympathy came across as a brusque chastisement. "Why should I feel betrayed?"

"Because it's a cliché, isn't it? *Young woman discovers the price of modern morals…*" Glen breathed deeply. "You know Mummy's dread of impropriety. First she had my brother's shame to live with, and now this…"

"Sylvia needn't know for now. No one else need know. Perdita, perhaps. We shall look after you."

"You don't have time to nurse me, Annabel – you're busy enough as it is."

"Twaddle. I'll tell you when I'm too busy." Her aunt briskly set about refolding the compress. "I suppose it's too late to stop your military friend scarpering back to India? I'd have thought he'd be far too old for such an escapade…"

"Emil?" A flush of colour returned to the girl's pallid cheeks. "No, no – it's not his."

"It's no use fooling yourself, darling. He doesn't deserve your protection."

"Emil doesn't even know about it!"

"Well, then?"

The girl turned her face away, focusing on the gnarled bough of the frangipani tree outside the window. On several occasions when she had forgotten to close the blinds, she had come into the room to discover her bed dusted with pink and yellow blossoms.

"Ganan." The word came out a whisper.

"Who?"

"The schoolteacher, Ganan." Her eyes filled with hot tears. "The one Jayanadani is in love with."

"Oh, Glen…" There was disappointment in her aunt's voice. "You don't do things by halves, do you? But how? No, never mind – I don't need to know." Annabel furrowed her fingers through untamed curls. "I should have seen that one coming."

"And to think, I actually believed that he…" She could not bring herself to say it. "I fancied that I was his muse – how foolish is that? And now that we've come this far, he wants nothing to do with me."

"Oh, my darling…" Annabel curled up next to her and took the girl in her arms.

"I thought that it would be different, that it would be *real* – better than stories, better than pretending that some boy I kissed at a May Ball could be anything but that, a silly boy." She suppressed a groan of self-disgust. "At first I pitied the local girls

– girls like Amanthi, his star pupil – because the idea of the dutiful wife seemed to me such a laughable thing. And then… then I saw that she would be able to have what I never could. And now I despise her…"

"I know. I do know."

Glen peered up at her aunt through sore eyes. "You can't."

"How do you suppose I feel about Hollar's mother?"

The girl had not prepared herself for this. "But why? What's there to despise?"

Annabel observed her niece: the child's stubborn chin, her wide, watchful eyes like those of a wounded animal. She opened her mouth to say something, but changed her mind. "You're right," she said at last. "Despising her would only have been pity for myself."

Glen was paying little attention. "I don't recognize myself any more," she mumbled. "I try to remember who I was before. And to think I believed myself in love." She rapped a clenched fist against her thigh. "Self-absorbed, self-adoring love!"

"Is there any other kind?"

"If only… if only he'd change his mind. He might, you know—"

Annabel resisted the urge to shake her. "But couldn't you see the *impossibility* of it, darling? How often do these affairs survive? In real life. I'm not talking about what goes on in story books." The girl was listening now, and she softened. "You'll keep the child."

"I couldn't live with myself, imagining it in an orphanage – or worse…" She gave a weak smile. "What on earth will Mrs Cornish say?"

Annabel rocked back on her haunches and shrugged. Now was not the time for half-truths. "I could tell you that it's none of her business – but that won't do you any good when the rumour mill gets going. Believe me."

"I know."

They sat together in silence, listening to the patter of feet in the room below, where Althea was busy building an obstacle course for her tortoise. Every now and then she would thunder upstairs to rummage about for something in her room, calling to Hollar not to touch her project until it was complete.

"I honestly thought that he understood me," said Glen at last – her voice, like her eyes, now dry.

"Let me tell you something," said Annabel. "None of us understands a thing – it's hard enough knowing ourselves, let alone knowing another person. Do you know what Ray bought me for my birthday, the year before he ran off?"

Glen allowed herself a small smile. "Oh, let's see – a sewing machine?"

"Worse than that: a pair of shocking-pink Schiaparelli heels." Annabel laughed, although Glen noticed that the smile failed to reach her eyes. "He must have blown three months' wages on those stupid things. What use would I have for such ridiculous shoes out here? Can you imagine me hobbling about the fields in Schiaparellis? And the worst part was, all I'd really wanted that year was a passage home, to see my sisters. But Ray said we couldn't afford it." Annabel pursed her lips, nodding in agreement with herself. "When he saw me cry, he thought that they were tears of joy. He was terribly pleased with himself. That's when I knew that he no longer understood me..."

31

One Saturday, Nijs and I had gone to the cinema to see *The Lives of a Bengal Lancer*. The newsreel before the main attraction was all about the latest troubles in India. While the other boys squirmed and chattered and flicked rubber bands at each other, I had paid special attention, scanning the crowds for my lady writer's face. But most of the people in this footage were Indians: marching in teeming human colonnades, pumping their fists in the air and carrying home-made placards covered in squiggly writing. White subtitles explained that the protest was part of a campaign for satyagraha, or "truth force". There had been a picture of a skinny, stooped little man with a shaven head and round wire spectacles sitting on a platform, and then pictures of Indian mounted police in smart uniforms looking stern because their British commanders wanted them to start clubbing the protesters, even though they were also brown-skinned.

Two nights after Shimon Franck died, I dreamt of a crowd like this one, full of men wearing saggy white trousers gathered at the crotch and stiff, oblong caps like the ones you'd expect to see on the waiters in an American soda bar. And then I noticed my brother among them. He was waving a sign that said *No God, No Country, No Master* and next to him stood Kurt Bokhoven, who had left school the year before and convinced Krelis to take a job with him at the fulling mill. Kurt had hollow cheeks and eyes that never blinked, as if he had the transparent eyelids that you find on certain reptiles. It was Kurt who had threatened to cut off my tongue if I told anyone about my brother; Kurt who had brought us the news that Krelis was dead.

In my dream, he had locked arms with my brother and a number of other men to form a human chain. Slowly, and from several different directions, the police began to close in on them.

These police carried guns, not clubs, and it was clear that they would shoot if the crowd didn't disband. I tried calling my brother's name, but no sound came out.

Then I noticed that there were monkeys frolicking in the streets, shrieking at the crowd and baring sharp, yellow teeth. They scampered between the legs of the police horses, and they clambered onto awnings and window ledges to hoot and howl at the chanting mob, their cries growing steadily louder until at last they resembled human screams. The protesters were so busy swatting at the monkeys that they hadn't noticed the police preparing to open fire.

I shouted my brother's name again, but still he didn't hear me. He was laughing, as if they were playing a marvellous game that the police would never win, and for the first time I realized how handsome he was. Standing next to Kurt Bokhoven, who was bow-legged and skinny, with a jutting scarecrow head and eyes that never blinked, Krelis looked like a young god. That was when I realized why he was laughing. He knew that he would be shot, a martyr to his cause, and it made him glad.

Suddenly the air was ringing with gunfire, and all the other noise – of screaming monkeys and horses' hooves and human commotion – ceased. A bit like getting blocked ears after swimming under water. But I could still see what was happening: the crowds dispersed by mounted police who felled the stragglers with swinging truncheons, crumpled figures like the bodies of petrified moths, the grimacing monkeys scattering, bounding over the bodies of the dead.

My brother lay in the middle of the road, and somehow I knew that he was counting the seconds until darkness fell. His eyes were the bluest I had ever seen them, like bits of shining sky. I tried to run to him but couldn't: it was as if a weight had been locked to my shoulders and my feet. When I looked up, I saw that Krelis was no longer there.

In his place lay four yawning tigers with thick, muscular necks, powerful claws and gleaming yellow eyes. One of them stood up and arched its back, before letting out a magnificent roar…

32

Now that Annabel knew, life became easier. No longer self-conscious about the time she spent alone in her cool, whitewashed little room, Glen sent off the form that had accompanied Pieter's death notice and began to plan a new story. This one, she decided, would be about her prisoner.

When the envelope with the Belgian postmark arrived in the second week of October, she allowed herself a moment to savour the promise of a new correspondent: a new voice, renewed inspiration. She unfolded the page – there was something familiar about the lined paper, torn from an exercise book – and began to read.

Dear Glen,

    Something terrible has happened. I'm writing to you because I can't tell anyone else. I know that you English have bad things on your conscience, too, like the camps in South Africa where you watched our Boer kinsmen starve to death. So you will understand.

She checked the date on the postmark: 14th September.

    I have blood on my hands. It was an accident, but that doesn't make it any better.

    He was a Jew, but even that doesn't make it better. If he had been a Bolshevist, he would still be dead. And the Bolshevists are the worst, the people who go to Spain to join in the slaughter of helpless priests and innocent children.

Where was the death notice? She reached for the drawer of her bedside table, rummaged about among sewing kits, powder puffs and yellowing magazine articles. At last she took out two letters: one, a card from Laurie from when she had first arrived in Ceylon, the other bearing the stamp of the Christian Women's Union. Postmark: 9th September.

My friends have abandoned me, and now I have no one but you. Do you think I could come to Ceylon? I could earn my living by working on the tea plantation. You could help me – just like the angel who delivered Peter from his prison cell (Acts 12).

Or would it be better for me to kill my shame instead? I know about hara-kiri. You stab yourself in the stomach and twist the knife to make sure you die. But I think I'm too scared to do that.

I'm scared, Glen, because I bargained with the Devil and don't know what to believe. And without belief, a person is nothing. Some people believe in God, or in science, or in the Flemish Lion, or in Lenin. What do you believe in? Please pray for me, whatever it is.

And write soon.

Yours,

Pieter

It took her several moments to convince herself of the impossibility of the paper in her hands. Had Pieter not died, after all? Continental bureaucracy was infamous: perhaps they had confused him with another man. But there was something new in this letter, a vulnerability that reminded her of the missive from the military asylum: something pitiful and naive, yet strangely – endearingly – hopeful. She read it through again, pondered the neat, square writing and the studied curlicues of the question marks. She smelt the paper: sweet, woody, woollen.

Glen found the Captain at the coolies' tea hut, on the fringes of the plantation near the road that led to his guest house. It marked the halfway point between Emil's temporary home and the glass church, and Glen had discovered that it was his habit to stop here with Pepys for some refreshment along the way. The first time he had come, one of the labourers had agreed to lead him to the church, and the Captain-*saheb* had memorized the route so that no guides were necessary on subsequent visits.

The tea hut was a makeshift affair, constructed of three bamboo walls and a coconut palm roof. In its shade, one of the workers' wives served tea throughout the day, boiled over a stone fire in a battered tin kettle. The glasses were smeared, and the seating arrangement was awkward – but the tea was pure and sweet, and its cooling effects unrivalled.

Her friend seemed surprised to be discovered here, but he welcomed the girl warmly, setting aside room on the rickety bench for her to join him.

"I've a little mystery that needs solving, Mr Holmes," smiled Glen, shuffling the letters on her lap.

"Have you, my dear?"

She told him everything: beginning with the initial advertisement in the newspaper, proceeding to describe the ensuing correspondence and the shock of the death notice – and now, Pieter's letter from beyond the grave. She was careful to skip over his comments about the pregnancy. Once or twice Emil stopped her and asked her to read from the letters – here she would describe the illustrations and newspaper clippings which Pieter had included with his missives – until finally he settled back in his seat with a thoughtful grunt.

"So what do you make of it?" she asked. "Do you suppose the death notice was a mistake? If he's alive, and is in trouble…"

"It wasn't a mistake," he replied simply. "No, I don't think it could be."

"Well, then?"

The Captain placed his empty glass on the ground. "Does it not strike you as strange that you should have been able to write to him directly?" he asked. "That there should be no filtering system in place? No central office, no censorship? I take it the letters haven't been tampered with? There are no prison stamps, for instance?"

The girl flipped through the papers, even though she knew full well that this was not the case. "No, nothing of the sort."

"He asks if you know how to use invisible ink, and this caused no alarm."

"Apparently not. It was Hollar he was asking about, really. I don't suppose he ever had any intention of using it for cunning purposes – it was just a bit of fun."

"Ah."

"You're thinking something, I can tell."

"The death notice – does it mention his town?"

"'Diegem Prison, Machelen'."

"Machelen, not Mechelen, where you sent all your letters."

"Yes."

Emil pursed his lips, pale eyebrows knitted in concentration. "Do you suppose political prisoners would be allowed access to newspapers?" he asked at last.

"I have no idea."

"It seems unlikely though, doesn't it?"

"Does it?"

The glimmer of a smile crept across his face, briefly filling his lifeless eyes with a mischievous flicker. "My dear, I think you've been duped."

The girl flushed to her ears. "Duped?"

"By a child. At least, that's my guess. You said he sent you some kind of natural specimen?"

"An insect of some sort, yes."

"In that case, I would go further. You have been duped by a boy young enough to assume that you would share his interest in beetles and invertebrates, or angry enough to wish to shock you. Possibly both."

"But why?"

"Think about it." Now he smiled, although she could not tell whether from delight at having solved a riddle or from amusement at her foolishness. "'When you have eliminated the impossible, whatever remains, however improbable, must be the truth.'"

She considered the letters again, seeing the careful cursive script with fresh eyes. How had he seen what she had not, after all this time? And then she remembered some of the things she had written to Pieter – about her brother, about her parents, about Ganan; intimate things which she had confided to him as if to a priest in a confessional – and she felt a rush of shame.

"Did you really never doubt him?" asked Emil, in a strange voice.

Glen opened her mouth to answer and shut it again. Only after he seemed no longer to be waiting for an answer did she reply, softly. "Perhaps I didn't want to. I wanted to believe."

He did not seem at all surprised by this. "You know, Glen, the Palace of Forty Columns in fact contains only twenty – but all around them are mirrors, which seem to double their number. It is a beautiful illusion."

Something about the phrase rang painfully true, and suddenly the girl realized that she did not know how to feel: torn between rage and disgust and awe and amusement, humiliation and despair, she finally blurted, "Well, then I shall tell him that I know!"

"No, you mustn't." His voice was soft, but firm. "The child will only panic. You'll have to be gentle with him, Glen. By the sounds of it, he is lonely and vulnerable, and you have been his confidant."

"He was supposed to be mine!"

"Be that as it may."

Despite herself, she knew that he was right.

* * *

She did not engineer the meeting; not consciously, anyhow. He was waiting outside the cricket pavilion, standing pointedly next to the sign that said "Whites Only", because he could, because a team of local men was permitted to practise here after the Saturday match.

Ray Moodie had been an avid cricketer, and Annabel had grown fond of the weekly games. "What's more, I don't need a husband waiting in the outfield to enjoy myself. All the ladies tart themselves up as if it were the Queen's Jubilee. The children get a taste of home, so that by the time they go to school it's not all completely foreign. And the sandwiches are to die for! *Do* say you'll come, darling."

Part of her hoped that he wouldn't be there, analyzing the English players, judging every error, every misfield. "He despises *slop-piness*, Miss Glen," Nimali had told her, whispering the dreaded word. It was true. Whenever she looked over at him, Ganan was following the ball with hawk eyes, his mouth set into its usual grim line, his fists clenched in both pockets. Every so often he would lean forwards, hips jerking, feet planted firmly. She could tell that he was desperate to run onto the pitch, to show them how to do it properly.

When the game ended, the players and their supporters mingled in the pavilion over cups of tea and cucumber sandwiches. Bone saucer in hand, the girl descended the steps and edged into the shade. He remained where he was, with his arms folded, peering out across the field where the crease was being swept and the pitch rolled.

"You must be melting over there," she said, noting the glint of pomade in his hair. "Come out of the sun."

He didn't move. "Did you find it entertaining?" he asked.

"Interminable, more like," she said. "To be honest, I was bored."

"They all are," he said, indicating the chattering masses overhead. "Boredom is a privilege of their class. These are trivial entertainments to them."

Glen rolled her eyes. "Come off it, Ganan – we both know you only loathe them as much as you want to join them." She tried to sound light-hearted.

"You presume to know me better than I know myself. But I am no self-hating Uncle Tom." His gaze roamed past her, proud and uninterested, and she remembered the triumph with which he had led her through the crowds of native shoppers at the market. He gestured vaguely towards the pavilion. "Who else takes exotic playthings to give a little more meaning to an empty, privileged life? The charitable ladies over there, yes." His mouth twisted in scorn. "You are no different, Glen. You deceive yourself if you think otherwise."

"Please, Ganan." She mustn't allow herself to get upset: not here, not now. "I didn't come here to defend myself. We've both had a chance to think things over; I thought perhaps we might talk civilly…"

For a brief moment, he looked as if he might accept the peace offering, but then the old defensiveness crept back in. "Do you think me such a pitiful creature that I would leap at your offer of a second chance?" he said.

"I expect no less of you than I would anyone else in your position." She took a deep breath. "In fact, I had thought you, of all people, would act with honour—"

"I honour my family. My reputation. What my students expect from me." He considered her. "The Empire's good name depends on the conduct of its women, no? Well, Glen. We are all free; we all have to earn our honour."

"Would you say this in the dock, if I were to claim that it was rape?"

There was a long silence. He despised her now, if he hadn't before.

"I am without guilt," he said softly.

"And full of shame." She brushed the crumbs from her fingers. They were not facing each other; a bystander would not think to count this conversation among the others. "Yes, you are, Ganan. Shame is what fuels your indignation with the world. Shame that your father died fighting for another country; shame that you couldn't hack it in London. You couldn't even bear to intervene when that poor flute-player in the market was being beaten to death in front of our very eyes. What held you back, Ganan? What prevented you from acting with any pride, with any decency at all?" Glen's cheeks flushed red, but still she did not raise her voice. "Your shame means that you won't accept anything from the Empire any more – not even one of its women."

Throughout this speech, the schoolteacher did not move. He stared out at the field, tight-lipped.

"Shame is a personal matter," he said at last. Then, as if to test her, he added, "You would know about this."

"Oh yes?"

"Giving yourself to men – so desperate for approval, so terrified of rejection, even while you profess to loathe dependency – and then expecting that they owe you something in return. Who taught you that? Was it your brother the coward? Your mother, the snob—"

"*Stop it.*"

"—your aunt, the pariah? Well, Glen? Tell me about your noble lineage, and then we can talk about shame!"

"Don't you dare," she said, "don't you dare speak of my family in that way. They are not part of this." She swallowed, set her cup and saucer on the ground and shot a dismissive glare at a couple of ladies who had turned to peer curiously at them from across the lawn. "I don't regret… it. Him, her – whoever it is." She pulled the corners of her blouse taut. "Don't worry, I wasn't serious about pressing charges. It would be too humiliating. I don't suppose you make a habit of it – it was your first time, wasn't it?" The knot in her chest tightened as she forced herself to laugh. "We made each other up, didn't we? You and I. Saw what we wanted to see." She swallowed again. "When the child asks, I shall say that you made an error. I won't cast you as the devil."

"The benign ruler," he whispered, "forgets that we do not make a habit of taking your women at the rate your men have taken ours."

"None of that is my fault."

He conceded the point with a tilt of the head. "Perhaps, then, we can agree that it is best to leave the past alone."

She glared at him. "I couldn't care less about the bloody Empire, and I won't be bullied into defending it, no matter how hard you try to make me. But *this*," pointing to her stomach, "this is not in the past."

She found that she could not bear to look at him now; as she turned away, Glen noted with some relief that they were no longer being observed. How funny to think that a few short weeks ago she should have flaunted her association with Ganan before the English ladies, laughed in the face of their disapproving stares!

277

At last, she was aware of him moving towards her. "I'm sorry," he said. There was bitterness in his voice.

"For what?" she bridled. "For calling my brother a coward, my mother a snob?..."

"For that, yes. And for creating... inconvenience."

"Inconvenience!"

"Come now – it is what you wanted all along, surely?" He glanced up at the stands, pretending not to notice Hollar and Althea waving down at them. "What better trophy than a little brown version of yourself – an *accessory* to your grand adventure in the Indies..."

"You know that's not true," she whispered. He did not seem to hear her.

"A souvenir, yes?" continued Ganan, warming to his game. "A little alien child to dress up as an English boy – like a Pekinese stuffed into tiny waistcoat and cravat!"

"Don't be ridiculous," she said. She was alarmed by the charge – angered by it, yes, but frightened, too. "If you really thought that – if you thought that I'd stolen something from you – you wouldn't wash your hands of it so easily. Who are you to talk of playthings, anyhow? The way you teased me with your drawings—"

"You extrapolate too much meaning, Glen."

"I expected to be told the *truth*."

Ganan shook his head. "Things changed," he said at last.

"*You* changed."

"I got more than I bargained for, Glen. I was reckless. I realized, too late, that you wanted me to be someone who I am not. By then I felt cornered; it was as if you were trying to shoehorn me into one of your stories—"

"I didn't make you a victim of you, Ganan." She drew herself erect, collecting her cup and saucer with as much poise as she could muster. "You did that to yourself."

They stood in silence as Ganan's teammates began to arrive. Both knew that there was nothing more to be said.

"When will you leave for Bombay?" she asked stiffly.

"At the end of the week." He looked at her, and for the first time Glen realized that she was not the only one to be afraid.

"Well, good luck."

As she turned to join her aunt again, she caught a glimpse of him as he tipped an imaginary hat – a boy mimicking his cowboy hero – and whispered words that would echo in her mind until the sound of his voice faded from her memory for ever. "A very good day to you, *memsahib*." The words floated on dry air before being consumed by the chatter of the ladies in the pavilion.

33

At first I didn't recognize the envelope in my mother's hand. It was only when she dropped it onto the kitchen table that I noticed the Ceylon stamp in the top-right corner.

"What do you suppose this is?" she said. "We don't know anyone called Pieter van Houten."

I took the letter from the table and pretended to study the writing. A drop of water had fallen onto Pieter's name, making it look as if the paper was weeping ink.

"It must be a mistake," I said.

I could see from her expression that Mother knew I was hiding something.

"Open it," she said.

"But it's not addressed to us."

"Open it, Marten."

I tore the envelope and slowly pulled out the letter. Glen had written two whole pages this time; between them was an extra sheet, smaller than the others. I held them tightly, hoping that Mother would not see beyond the first page.

"Well?" She peered over my shoulder, and for several seconds we were both silent. I stared at the writing before me without making sense of the words. At last my mother straightened, and out of the corner of my eye I noticed that her brow had puckered into a frown. "It's in English," she said.

I nodded. My mother hoisted her apron up around her waist, deep in thought. Just as I was about to admit everything, she asked, "What does it say?"

"*Dear Pieter…*" I stopped. "I don't think that we should read it. It's not addressed to us."

"Who is this 'Pieter'?"

My mother folded her arms. Her voice was firm and just a little loud. She never spoke like this when Father was around.

"I don't know, Mother."

"You do. Don't lie to me, Marten." She unfolded her arms, placed one hand on the kitchen table and leant down to look me in the eye, like Mohammed Khan in *Lives of a Bengal Lancer*. *We have ways of making men talk.* "Is he one of those VNV boys? Is he?"

I shook my head.

"You know what I think of those boys, Marten."

In fact, I didn't. Mother had never commented on my badge or my yellow scarf. I had not told her about the initiation, or the Luger, or the fact that Nijs wasn't allowed to come to the meetings. Still, I nodded.

She picked up the envelope once more. "*Ceylan*," she said, turning up the edges of the stamp with her fingernail. Something about this gesture filled me with irritation: the thought of my private world being rudely invaded, colliding with ours. I wanted to protect it. Perhaps that was why I said what I did.

"It must be for Krelis."

Suddenly Mother turned very pale. She looked up at me with eyes that seemed to droop with horror or disbelief – I couldn't say which exactly. It was as if my words had thrown her a million miles away, and she was peering out at me from some dark, distant place.

She could have asked why, or what it meant, or where it had come from. Instead, she said, "Who?"

So, I had lied. Now I must tell the truth. "He's not dead, Mother."

"Krelis?" She dropped to her knees, her head lolling forwards like a rag doll with the stuffing thinned out at the neck. I reached out to steady her, touching her gently on one shoulder to make sure that she hadn't fainted. After a moment had passed, she looked up at me with cloudy eyes. "But the accident... Kurt was there... he told us himself..."

"It was Kurt's idea," I said. "To pretend that Krelis was dead."

It seemed silly now. The little white cat was dead. Shimon Franck was dead. Dead meant the smell of urine and gasoline, the gushing of blood between my ears. None of that was pretend.

"But why? What's happened to Krelis? What does this letter have to do with any of this?"

As she spoke, I remembered what they had taught us about our Dutch cousins in South Africa: the surviving rebels who were banished from their homeland to live out the rest of their days working on plantations dotted about the Empire. And then I realized that there was a way for me to tell Mother the truth about Krelis without revealing my secret about Glen. Before I knew it the words were tumbling out. "It's from one of his comrades in exile, Mother." This was a lie, of course. "Krelis is alive. He's gone on a mission – not here, in Spain." This was true. "He wouldn't tell me any more than that. He's working with the communists to prevent another war. Kurt made me promise not to tell." I glanced down at the letter in my hand. "It's... it's a code. Pieter is his code name."

My mother's mouth fell open. She reached for my feet with white fingers and clasped my ankles tightly. "Read it," she whispered. "Read it to me, Marten."

I stared down at the page and picked out a line at random.

I know what it is to be scared, Pieter, I read, translating. *There are times when even adults feel like little children, overwhelmed and frightened and confused by the world.*

My mother raised a hand to her mouth. "Krelis!" she breathed. "My poor son – who are these people? What have they done to him, Marten?"

I dropped to my knees and forced myself to meet her terrified gaze. "Nothing, Mother," I said, in a voice that didn't sound at all like my own. How could I tell her what I did not know for sure, but what I had prayed for every night since the lie began? "He's fine. He's healthy. The others have called him a hero..." I scanned Glen's letter and landed upon another useful line. "See this?" I traced the writing with my finger. "*You are a wise and good man, Pieter.* He is fighting for a noble cause."

I watched the flesh around her mouth fall slack as the clouds in her eyes began to melt into tears.

"But why—"

"He didn't want you to know," I said. "He was afraid that you and Father would be ashamed. Because of the communists."

"Ashamed? No, no, Marten – we must tell Father at once—" She started to get up, but I stopped her.

"No, we can't," I said. My mouth was dry. "Krelis wanted to protect him." I crouched so that I was at her level. "If Father finds out that Krelis joined the *Kommunistische*, he'll go mad. The next time he drinks too much at De Kraan, he'll tell everyone. And then where will we be?" *If Arend finds out that my brother is a communist, he will skin me alive.* "Krelis wouldn't want that." I held her gaze, pleading with my eyes. "Please, Mother – Father mustn't know."

For several moments, Mother said nothing. Then, a little smile crossed her face: just the flicker of something – satisfaction, perhaps. She nodded. "Father will not know," she whispered at last. I was sure that I detected a note of triumph in her voice. "It shall be our secret, Marten."

Then, for the first time since Krelis's disappearance, she took me in her arms and held me very close.

* * *

As soon as I was on my own, I read Glen's letter from beginning to end.

Dear Pieter,

I really don't think that hara-kiri is a good idea, under the circumstances. Please promise me that you will not hurt yourself – I couldn't bear the thought of you coming to any harm. Will you promise me that, Pieter?

If what has happened truly is an accident, surely your friends will understand? Is there anyone at all that you can tell, someone you trust? I can't help but feel that you have already suffered enough – but then, it is not for me to judge these things.

You said that you lied to protect your brother. I think that this sounds very noble. Didn't Joseph's own brothers throw him into a pit and leave him to die, before deciding to sell him into slavery instead? Joseph spent years in prison, Pieter, but he never lost heart. And, if I remember correctly, he forgave his brothers in the end.

I know what it is to be scared, Pieter. There are times when even adults feel like little children, overwhelmed and frightened and confused by the world. Writing to you, I have sometimes felt that I have been writing to my younger self: the child who wished to be taken seriously, to be loved unconditionally. Hollar tells me that songbirds choose their mates by matching their melodies. In a strange way, I think that we were very lucky to have found each other, you and I.

You are a wise and good man, Pieter – that I know. You have a rich inner life: treasure it. You also have faith, which is something that cannot be easily created. I envy you that. It is this strength that makes it possible for the heroes of the Congress to endure years of confinement in His Majesty's prisons. For as long as the Mahatma and his supporters refuse to become demoralized or embittered by the experience, their oppressors cannot hope to win.

You are too kind to compare me to an angel. Most of us are blind most of the time; we fall in love with untested ideals, we tie ourselves up with deceits. We look at others and see only ourselves. I am as guilty of this as the next person. So focused on taming one who could never reciprocate, so mired in an elaborate fantasy of a tropical romance, so ensnared by Ganan's casual cruelty, I failed to see anyone but him – not even the blind man in his glass house, although he was staring out at me all along.

I see now that Ganan only loved me from a distance: an English girl sleeping in a garden, serene and unaware. Well, I have woken from that dream, Pieter. I have no use for it now.

Now, we must learn to live without absolutes and reach beyond the literal to what is grey and indistinct. You and I, or the man on the street... some of us will be lucky enough to learn to see the world for what it is. To see through the bad – in these dark times, it seems to me that evil has become mundane – and to discover the good.

You are always very welcome to stay with us if you ever come to Ceylon. I do hope that you will, one day. Of course, at times such as these, who's to say what will become of us all? The barbarians are at the gates, and it will fall to the little men to see that evil does not triumph. Perhaps, if there is to be war, we shall have to reinvent ourselves again. Perhaps war will give us all a second chance.

I had promised to write you a story, Pieter. Rest assured that I will. A novel, perhaps – for that is the highest expression of freedom. One day, you may even see it in a bookstore in Flanders! You have shown me that we are surrounded by stories: the trick, like reading invisible ink, is knowing where to look for them.

Take care of yourself, Pieter.

Love,

Glen

She had enclosed a scrap of paper which, unfolded, revealed the hazy image of a reclining woman. A portrait of herself, drawn in smoke.

* * *

Later that week, I returned to my safe spot in the woods. It was on a Sunday, when I knew that the troop would not be there.

There had been heavy rain the previous night, which meant that the ground was strewn with snails. They had come out to gorge themselves on sweet, damp mulch – but the rain had ended suddenly, and now they were stranded in the open like so many tiny shipwrecks. The first one I noticed split with a loud *crack* under my foot. Stepping on a snail is the worst feeling in the world. There is the sound of the shell breaking, and then the sickening squelch as the slug inside oozes into the sole of your shoe. I scraped my foot against a rock until all that remained was a small, wet stain, before carrying on through the forest.

The only sound was the clattering of leaves through crisp, still air. Near the clearing where we had learnt to fire Dirk's Luger, a fallen tree blocked my path. Perhaps it had upturned in the storm: its roots had been torn from the ground and now towered over the trunk. Squirrels had stripped away much of the bark, and apart from a few whorls and knots, the wood beneath was smooth and cool to touch.

I clambered over it and landed with a bump on the other side. Squatting against the curve of those thick roots, I took the letter from my pocket.

Dear Glen,

Will you forgive me?

My name is not Pieter van Houten. It is Marten Kuypers. I am thirteen years old.

I told you that I was Pieter because I had been lying ever since my brother left. My parents thought that he was dead. But there was no accident at the fulling mill, and his body was not washed away down the river Dijle. He went to Spain, to help the communists. It was Kurt's idea to pretend that he had died. I know it was wrong; I begged him not to go. But Krelis said that he would kill me if I told our parents. He said that he could fight for an ideal without shaming our family. Everyone is frightened now: of the past, of what will happen.

Once, the Rhineland stood between us and Germany. But when the Führer's soldiers rode in on bicycles and claimed it as theirs, King Leopold said that Belgium must remain neutral. That was when Krelis made his decision.

I told him that I would not lie, that I did not want to keep his secret and share his shame. He hit me and then he asked, "What will you stand for, Marten, when the time comes?" That was the last time I saw him.

Now that he has betrayed us, he can never come back. If he is dead, I won't see him in heaven, because he has abandoned God. My friend Mr Hendryks says that that is the price of freedom: you have to live with your mistakes.

If Father were to know, he would hate me, because it is wrong to lie to your parents. And he would be right to hate me, because it was my fault that the little white cat died, my fault that Shimon Franck fell over and never got up. Arend says that a good soldier feels nothing when he kills. I thought that I could be empty like that, but I was wrong. I'm not bad, Glen. Please say you believe me. I think that there is good inside me. I know that it is there, because it hurts.

Thank you for the picture you sent. You really are very lovely. Your Indian gentleman must be very clever to be able to draw with smoke. Whenever I look at your portrait, it seems a little different. Perhaps it changes when my back is turned.

I hope that you are feeling better, and that you will not hate me too much. I would still like to come to Ceylon one day.
From,
 Marten

P.S. Please do not kill the soldier in your story. I was wrong to tell you that he should be shot. Can you make him live instead?

I had not yet decided whether to post it. What if Glen wrote to my parents and demanded that I be punished for pretending to be someone else? But it had been her mistake to confuse Mechelen and Machelen; I had only done the responsible thing to protect her from disappointment.

A branch snapped, and footsteps followed the sound of a snail's shell rattling along the ground.

"Who's there?" said Adriaan.

I raised my hands in the air, like a surrendering redskin.

"What are you doing here?" he asked.

"It's a free world."

Adriaan leant over the tree trunk and pointed at the letter in my hand. "What's that, then?"

"Nothing." I folded it into a square and tore it once, twice, three times. "Nothing."

We sat there for a while, watching a magpie peck at something in the undergrowth. I noticed that Adriaan's bare legs had marbled in the cold. At last he looked at me and said, "Have you been coming to the meetings?"

I shook my head. The troop meant nothing now. "You?"

"No." Adriaan pulled his knees up to his chin. "Is it true what Pepijn said? That they're looking for a new group leader, because Arend is going to work for Staf de Clercq? He's not even going to finish the school year."

I dug my nails into the scar in my palm. "Who cares? I hate him. He's an idiot."

"Who – Arend, or Staf de Clercq?"

"Both."

He smiled, which meant that I did, too. Then I said, "You knew Shimon Franck, didn't you?"

I wasn't sure if Adriaan looked surprised or angry. The sun shone in his eyes, making the hazel flecks gleam like kelp floating in a deep sea. I thought of Glen's little half-caste cousin and wondered if there were any Jews in Ceylon.

"What do you mean?" Adriaan asked.

"He recognized you," I said. "In the garden, with his cat..."

"My father knew him," replied Adriaan. "But that's none of my business."

That was when I understood: he only wanted to be invisible. *What is seen is temporary, but what is unseen is eternal*, the Bible says – because life is no more than a prison for our souls. Perhaps Pepijn had told him about all the creatures that went extinct, and Adriaan thought that that meant humans, too. I could tell that he still had a lot to learn.

"Come on," I said. In my pocket I carried the origami crane that Glen had sent me; I had decided that I would give it to Mieke as a peace offering. "The Girls' League is exercising in the abbey meadow today – if the carillon school's empty, I know a classroom where we can watch them."

As we walked along the riverbank, I waited until Adriaan was a few steps ahead of me before dropping the scraps of my letter into the black water.

* * *

Observing the world from my room that evening, I studied the frost flowers that had begun to form in one corner of my window. If I closed one eye and peered through them with the other, the street below appeared as if through a kaleidoscope: broken up into shards of glass, like the geometrical figures we had begun to study at school.

Beyond my line of vision, a mussel cart clattered across the cobbles. I imagined steam rising from the pot into the ruddy face of the man who ladled a thin broth over the shells. The nights were closing in much earlier now; people huddled together outside the taverns, blowing into their hands as they discussed the possibility of war. I pressed up close to the window and gazed up at the sky, imagining the black outline of a Stuka overhead, like some dark angel. But there was nothing there – not yet, anyway. Below, weeds pushed through cracks in the pavement, reasserting themselves in their battle against concrete.

The previous night, a bird had become stuck in the chimney. I had lain awake for what seemed hours, listening to it trying to escape. In the end, it either gave up or found a way out, because I couldn't hear anything now.

Worse than war is the dreadful waiting for war: that's what Seneca wrote. Recently, the papers had been full of news about a Falangist attack on Guernica. Some people were saying that German bomb casings had been discovered at the scene; that the Luftwaffe had been involved in the raid. I thought of going to the park to see if I could find Guernica on the map of Spain – but then I decided it wouldn't make any difference.

Even though I knew, deep down, that I would not hear from my lady writer again, I continued to check the post as a precaution. I had rewritten my final letter to her, after tearing up the one Adriaan had found me with in the woods. The new version was very short, which I thought was probably for the best.

Mother and I did not speak of the letter that I had told her was for Krelis. Sometimes she would catch my eye and smile, as if she was enjoying our secret and the warmth it gave her to know that he was still alive, somewhere. I knew that this was a delicate lie, and any more letters from my lady writer might blow it apart: if that happened, Mother would never believe me again. So I waited, partly hopeful, partly anxious, undecided as to whether or not I wished Glen to follow my instructions. When no one was home, I would take all of her letters out from under my bed and arrange them on the floor around me. Perhaps I thought that I could summon her up that way, that all of these little pieces of her would somehow come together so that a living person would rise up before me, beautiful and whole.

For two or three weeks I waited, but her response never came.

My father still locked himself in the gatehouse in the evenings; Mother had to ask me to call him for supper. Tonight, I had discovered him with his head on the desk, cradled between his hands.

"Father?" I said.

He sat up with a start, and turned to look at me with the expression of a prisoner whose warden has just arrived to take him off for execution. He blinked in the light that cut through the dim shadows of the attic room.

"Yes, my boy? What's that?"

It was only then that I realized that he had been crying. He tried to conceal it – how many times had he told me, even as a small child, that I was too old to cry? – by rubbing his face roughly with both hands. But the skin around his eyes was bloated and glistening, his unbuttoned shirtsleeves damp with tears.

I swallowed, too embarrassed to console him. "It's time to eat, Father."

He nodded. "Yes. Is it, now? Of course it is…" He made as if to get up, but remained in his seat. "I'll be down in a few minutes. Tell your mother."

I left him there, still blinking in the half-light, too frightened to venture out of the darkness.

34

She arrived at the guest house shortly before three o'clock, as he had suggested. The clapboard bungalow was modest but tidy; the flower beds neatly trimmed, crisp lace curtains fluttering through an open window. When she rang the bell, a middle-aged lady answered: smiling and stout, with the leathered complexion of a Latin crone and the painted lips of a much younger woman.

"Miss Phayre? Please come in – Captain Royce is waiting for you in the sitting room."

Inside, Glen was struck by the strangeness of being in a home that was almost, but not quite, familiar. It was much smaller than her aunt's house, and more decorated; but there were the same hand-crafted tea chests in one corner, and a comforting sandalwood aroma. She followed the Burgher woman through to the front room and gratefully accepted an offer of some ginger cake.

"Ah, she arrives: the fair ingénue." The Captain pushed himself to his feet, leaning against the creaking arm of a high-backed chair, and received her with a kiss on the cheek. "Do make yourself comfortable. Mrs Martinus, some more tea would be lovely."

As they settled themselves by the fireplace, Glen took in the details of the room. Family photographs had been carefully placed along the mantle; a few in ersatz frames, others propped up on card holders, showing the faces of a man and a woman and three children. Two of the children were fair-skinned with thick, dark hair; the third took after his mother, with a swarthier complexion and fine russet curls.

"You've noticed the photographs?"

"Yes."

"There is a long tradition of mixed heritage on this island. And of tolerance, if one knows where to look for it."

Glen remembered what Mr Walsh had said about the Burghers: how they regarded the English as snobs. She smiled warmly as Mrs Martinus brought in tea and cake.

"Your children are lovely," she said.

Mrs Martinus paused, studying the pictures herself, and nodded proudly. "Yes, they are. Thank you, Miss Phayre," she said, before withdrawing from the room.

"Excellent tea," murmured the Captain.

On a side table, Glen noticed a large glass dome filled with flowers and stuffed birds suspended in mid-flight: a Victorian curiosity. Next to it was a gramophone and a pile of records.

"Shall we put one on?" she asked. "What have you been listening to lately?"

"Haydn," he said. "'Mass in Time of War'. I believe that I left it on the player…"

Glen set the needle onto a groove and waited for the crackle of sound before returning to her seat.

"Haydn composed this when Napoleon was twenty-six years old," said Emil. "He'd just assumed command of the Italian army and was assembling forces for an invasion. It begins serenely enough, but you'll soon notice a change…"

They listened in silence for several minutes.

"The bass solo in 'Qui tollis' is sublime. What a voice!" He breathed deeply, closed his eyes. "But there are menacing undertones – there, do you hear? More impassioned, more desperate, that plea for mercy. And now the drum rolls, as Napoleon's troops gather on the horizon…"

They were approaching the final section when a door opened suddenly. Without a word, a tiny woman – at first Glen thought that it might be a child – scrambled across the floor with a brush dangling from a palsied hand, twitching and flinching as if it were a spare limb. The creature was clearly the victim of a developmental condition: dwarfish, with a bug-like face, knotted mouth and leaking eyes, she scuttled up to the fireplace and swept around it in concentrated silence before ducking her head in apology to Glen and swiftly removing herself from the room.

293

"That would have been Alice," said the Captain calmly – so calmly, Glen thought, that she could almost be forgiven for thinking that he had seen her reaction.

"Is she not well?"

"She's never been better." He smiled. "The condition is genetic, and seems to be limited to a handful of families from villages in the north. It doesn't keep her from working."

Not for the first time, Glen was aware of a flopping sensation in her stomach: a fish out of water, twisting and turning and gasping for air.

"Are you all right?" he asked.

"I'm pregnant."

The Captain set his cup in a saucer. "Your friend?"

"Not any more, it seems."

"Ah. I'm sorry."

"Don't be. It's better like this, I think."

Emil placed the saucer on the table and placed his hands on his knees, palms down. "I should congratulate you: a child is cause for joy. More intelligent women should have children."

"At least I won't be on my own. Annabel has been marvellous about all this—"

"So you're staying here, then?"

"For the time being, yes."

The Captain nodded. "That makes one of us, then."

"You're not leaving, are you?"

"It is time. That's why I asked you here today."

"But why?"

"Because this is not my home," he replied.

"It's not mine, either," said Glen. "And I was hoping, with the way things have turned out... I could do with a friend, you know."

Emil's smile wavered. "I came here to pay tribute to my father. To see where he..." But he did not finish the sentence, instead reaching for a packet of cigarettes in his breast pocket. "I've been asked to take up a position training falcons at one of our airfields up north – the British base at Myitkyina. Some military brain has decided to deploy birds of prey against the pigeons that keep bringing down our planes. Bird strikes, you know." He lit a cigarette and tossed the match into the fireplace. "I need to move on, Glen: it's not healthy to live in the past. And anyway," he added, making an attempt at light-heartedness, "this is a hard place for a blind man to get about. I'm tired."

"But…" But what? She knew that there was no point arguing; that he owed her nothing. "It's so far…"

"Come with me, then."

"What?"

"You heard me." The Captain's expression gave nothing away; his voice was cool. Tendrils of smoke curled from his cigarette.

Glen's head had begun to swim. "But how?"

"The same way you came to Ceylon: for an adventure." He no longer spoke as briskly as before. "Perhaps, for love."

Glen's mouth felt dry. Why this sudden, sad tenderness for a man who seemed to know her better than she knew herself? He wasn't testing her: she was almost certain of that. Nor was this a sudden, uncontrollable expression of pity, or a selfless attempt to afford a haven for her and the child, to save her dignity. He had managed to make her feel at once exposed and rescued: and she wondered if perhaps he might be the only person in the world capable of seeing her as others couldn't. A hundred thoughts darted through her mind, charting invisible trajectories and bursting into light at the most unexpected junctures. How much she still had to learn about the love that makes no demands! What had she done to deserve this kindness? "I can't, Emil," she said at last. "I can't leave Annabel. And what would I do with a baby, all the way up there? Just think what a burden it would be…"

"Well, then." He did not sound too disappointed, and she wondered if perhaps she had mistaken his intention, if not the sentiment. For an instant, a crack had appeared in the marble: almost as quickly, it had sealed itself again. That was all.

She moved from her chair to be closer to that lone figure: taking his hand between hers, she wondered what she could say to express this confusion of emotions without embarrassing him. "I will miss you dreadfully," she whispered at last. "We all will." Then, something occurred to her. "What about Hollar?"

"I was wondering if you might give him this." The Captain reached into his pocket and withdrew the weathered journal. "I won't have anyone to read it to me where I'm going."

"Of course. He'll be disappointed that you couldn't say goodbye."

The Captain's expression darkened for a moment as he stubbed out the cigarette. "I'll come back," he said. "Tell him that I'll come back to visit."

"Emil?"

"Yes?"

She took a deep breath, glancing at the photographs on the mantelpiece. "Who is Hollar?"

He answered without hesitation. "A baroque etcher. Bohemian, I believe."

Was he joking? But there was no trace of a smile. "A baroque etcher?"

"Wenceslaus Hollar – probably best known for his maps and views of London. I believe there is one in Beulah Lodge."

Then she remembered it: a framed print that hung in a darkened corner leading to the kitchen, a view of London before the Great Fire of 1666. Below this elegant panorama of spires and domes jostling for space along the River Thames was an elongated double which indicated the positions of gutted buildings and smoking ruins, plotting the vanished docks and the scattered wreckage of churches and dwellings, factories and bridges and roads, outlining in painstaking detail the remains of once proud meeting halls, once industrious workshops. A bird's-eye view made the human lives below too miniscule to be counted: a disaster too monstrous to contemplate, forever frozen in the distant past.

"Hollar's mother had always admired the picture," Emil added, as if to fill the silence. "When the baby was born, she decided to name him after the artist."

"So his mother was a servant in the house?"

"She had been – when she fell pregnant, your uncle had her dismissed. She could not sustain a lie as easily as he could... shortly after the child was born, she went mad." He checked himself. "But this isn't something that we should discuss – not now, not in your condition..."

"Hollar told me what happened at the hospital. He called it suttee. He said that she did it out of piety."

"Perhaps she did," replied the Captain.

"But what about the father? Surely he doesn't deserve to be let off scot-free?"

"When your aunt heard that Hollar's mother had died, she must have seen an opportunity to make amends. Your uncle, I take it, had already left." The Captain paused to allow the girl time to deduce the rest. "Annabel was atoning for her husband's mistake, Glen. She decided to turn something shameful into something of which she could be proud."

"Uncle Ray?" The dashing young charmer who had swept Annabel off her feet at nineteen and spirited her away to a life of adventure? "But why wouldn't Annabel have told me? Surely the others must know – Micah, Perdita…"

"To protect her daughter, maybe? But that, I'm afraid, lies beyond my expertise." The Captain inclined his head, retreating from her into Haydn's music as it approached the final drum roll, the plea for peace.

* * *

Dear Sis,

Just received your letter. Delighted to hear the news that I am to be an uncle, even though it must have seemed horrid luck a few months ago. Rest assured that Mater and Pater really were none the wiser until your letter came, by which point it was too late for them to be anything but thrilled to hear that both of you are well. Just consider all the pretty lies that grown-ups tell their children, and you needn't feel any guilt for keeping it from them until the last minute.

It may interest you to know that they have sold the house – so if you were thinking of coming home any time soon, you might like to think again! At the moment they are staying with Merle, poor girl, and it sounds as if they could be thinking about emigration. Mummy has said that she'd like to know if there are many concert halls in Ceylon (joke).

I'm fine. Am considering taking up a role with non-fighting personnel at Bovington, but no guarantees yet.

For Heaven's sake, please don't do anything else too terribly foolish for a little while, at least. I doubt that my knitting skills are up to standard, so the diminutive one might have to wait while I search out an appropriate gift. In the meantime, I'm sure you would appreciate a bottle of something lovely – so let me know what you can't get there, and I shall have the chaps at Gordon's ship you a crate of it.

Look after yourself, sis. If I were half a brother I'd set sail immediately to set the rogue straight, but I know that would only embarrass you. Just say the word and I'll have Lord Linlithgow lock the fellow up with all the other scoundrels who bite the hand that feeds them.

Much love to Annabel and her brood,

Tully

She kept the letter tucked into the folds of her blouse for several days, imagining what her parents' response would be when they could finally meet their grandchild. She desperately wanted them to know her; she yearned to watch her father's face fill with delight at the sight of his granddaughter as she babbled and played on the reed mat in Perdita's house. She felt, somehow, that this tiny creature carried the promise of new hope for them all – hope for the future, folded into the tight threads of a *temari* ball.

And then, one morning, she received what was to be her final letter from Belgium.

Dear Glen,

I need to ask a very difficult thing now. I must do this to protect my family from any more lies. I wish that it did not have to be so, but it is very important that you do not write to me again. I am sorry. I will never forget you.

Thank you for everything.

Love,

Marten Kuypers

The girl traced his writing with one finger and smiled. It was a bittersweet sensation, this proud, gentle sorrow: like seeing her reflection in the shards of a broken mirror. She had been so desperate to love – and he, only to be loved. The name at the bottom of the page was new, but the person behind the words was the same: a strange and lonely boy who was learning to be brave.

"Marten."

The baby had begun to squall. Twisting in frustration, puckered face turning scarlet from the effort of crying, she reached out with curling, wrinkled fingers for her mother.

"I think she wants you," said Althea, trying to remain calm despite the piercing cries and violent wrestling of the infant in her lap.

Glen put down the letter to receive her child. They were sitting in cane chairs on the veranda, watching Hollar playing with Perdita's girls on the lawn. A knotted rope was being kept away from Nuisance, who yapped and snapped after the toy as it was tossed from child to child.

"Be careful," called Perdita from her spot in the shade, where she sat cleaning rice. "Don't make him angry." She shook her head. "It's all *haha-hoho* until someone gets bitten. The dog doesn't know it's a game."

That morning, they had gathered at the church for the naming ceremony. It had been Perdita who had suggested a *nam tebima*, a perfect compromise between Glen's desire to do something to confirm her child's arrival in the community and her ambivalence towards a formal christening. And so they had taken the infant to the glass church to be fed its first mouthful of rice in a brief ritual led by the local priest.

Mrs Walsh had arrived with a fruitcake, and Mr Walsh had dandled the baby on his knee with such innocent delight that Glen temporarily waived her resentment towards those who treated her child as a public plaything. The Cornishes had made their excuses. Mrs Cornish did not seem to have decided her response, and had yet to call at the house. This did not disappoint Glen. By her seventh month, word had spread at the Club of *a rooti in the apakah* at Beulah Lodge, but to date no one appeared to have connected the schoolteacher's departure with the birth of a half-caste child. The idle and curious had popped in with gifts of knitted caps and blankets, which the girl had accepted with good grace; they cooed over her child and described it as only they knew how: "dusky", "placid", "old soul". Glen knew that her daughter was more than the sum of these things, but she agreed with them for politeness' sake. She now felt more confident than ever that she must stay here, to show them what a fine person her daughter would grow up to be.

The servants needed no such convincing: a steady stream of coolies came to pay their respects, led by the plantation manager and a number of Annabel's senior workers. Glen could see Perdita's mounting impatience with the gushings of her social inferiors, the tea pickers, but the girl would not have her impose any restrictions on their visits. Both Micah and Perdita were proving to be fiercely protective of the newest addition to the household, as were Jayanadani and Nimali. But no one was as enchanted with the infant as Hollar.

It was he who got up with Glen in the early hours to sit with the baby when she cried; he who folded her blankets with obsessive precision; he who stood by with clean nappies to hand while she was being changed; he who held her for hours while she slept, humming a soft tune while he stroked her downy black hair. His love for the child had taken them all by surprise.

Only Emil considered it unremarkable. "They are alike," he said to Glen outside the church that morning. The Captain had returned without warning, carrying an overnight valise in one hand and a small wooden box in the other, as surprised to discover a party gathered at the church as the celebrants were to see the khaki-clad figure and his dog emerging from the valley's green gloom. Pressed to explain how he had managed to secure leave so far from the airbase, the Captain had referred vaguely to a mission in the Andaman Islands, where Nicobar pigeons were being considered for airfield use. Only after the ceremony, as Glen helped him lift Pepys into the car that would take him to Colombo, did he ask her to give the box to her cousin.

"I could not have come back empty-handed," he said. "I promised him that."

The ashes of Hollar's mother: retrieved from the hospital, where they had been saved from the rubbish heap by a worker who had remembered her son.

"What shall we do with them?" Annabel asked the boy that evening.

"Scatter them outside the church," Hollar had replied. "Into the valley, so that she can be everywhere."

The baby had begun to hiccup, and Glen bounced her on one knee. They had nicknamed the child Turtle, as that was what Althea said she most resembled. Her skin was the colour of dark honey; her hair was black, although in some lights the fine down on her temples showed an auburn tinge. Her eyes remained a piercing, cobalt blue. Every morning her mother checked them for any sign of change, although by now it seemed unlikely that they would darken. It seemed a miracle to her that such a tiny creature could reinvent herself every day; each morning, a new little person greeted her from the cradle. This filled her mother with pride, but also with sadness. *You did this to me*, thought Glen, looking at the stains on her shoulder and the red-faced putto who put them there, recalling fretful nights just a week earlier when the colic had struck. *You made me this way: nervous, protective, unashamed. I wasn't always like this.* But although she grieved for the person she had once been, she could not be angry. Her life had become a new life: a remarkable thought. Glen's own mother had always provided the impetus for her actions; every rebellion had been a challenge to maternal hopes and expectations. Here, at last, she had discovered something better: an answer to the emptiness that she had once strived to fill with adventure. Perhaps it could be put even more simply than that. She now knew what it was that she most wanted, and that was to succeed for her daughter.

The child had been born on the first day of the monsoon. Over the weeks that followed, Glen had begun to rediscover parts of herself that she had thought were lost to time: childlike wonder, an overwhelming urge to demonstrate love. And then, as life began to return to some kind of normality, she began to write again.

There existed only scraps of scenes at this stage – what little she could manage between feedings and nappies – and she had already decided that the gestating tale would be a novella. Nothing as ambitious as a novel, but more than the empty poetry she had written back in England. The story would be about a man called Pieter who flees his life in Europe to start afresh in the tropics. He had already provided her with a first line – the rest, she trusted, would follow in time. For now, she was holding it in her mind, nurturing its potential, waiting for the right moment to breathe life into it. This, she knew, would be a tale to surpass all her previous attempts: a story that was beautiful in its simplicity, which would make people yearn to know each other better. A story so real that readers one day would wonder whether the tale could possibly be true.

Antwerp, 1960

From my desk, I can trace the swell of bruised clouds through the open skylight. I see quite well after a good night's sleep. By this evening, it won't be so easy: my eyes will start to itch again, and before the light begins to fade my eyelids will feel heavy, will clamp together like wooden shutters snapping on a latch. A powerful thing, the human eyelid. Sheer will alone won't force it to budge if the brain dissents.

This is what I told the girl when we met. Muscles are instinctive, I said. There's no reasoning with a dying muscle, even if the rest of the body is still young and healthy. It will do what it has to do, like an animal that disappears into the forest to die quietly.

The girl asked me why it had to happen that way, and so I told her about my injuries – the knock I had taken from a German customs official during the war, the explosion that sent me crashing through a florist's window. Perhaps I did this to impress her. Then I told her what the doctors had said, that it was more likely a case of premature blepharospasm, and too much reading was the cause. I have your mother to blame for that, I told the girl, trying to make a joke of it.

From what I could see, she was a small, tidy creature. Dark, of course, like her father. The first thing I noticed was the way she seemed to hide behind a curtain of black hair, thickly draped to obscure her eyes and much of her face. It was a sign of shyness, and as soon as I recognized it I felt a sudden tenderness towards her. Her eyes were a lighter colour – green or grey, I can't say for sure, but bright as water. She spoke with an antipodean lilt, although from time to time her intonation would curl around itself in a manner that harkened to her island origins. She had brought me a bouquet of wild flowers, which she arranged in a vase by the window while I set about pouring mugs of black tea.

She had grown up with my letters, she said. Her mother used to read them to her at night, instead of fairy tales. For as long as she could remember, she had known my name.

I placed her mug on the table and reached for my own. She had begun to rummage in her shoulder bag, by turns pulling out several pens, a city map, a wallet, a dog-eared paperback... and then a book crammed with yellow paper. She handed it to me.

"They're all together, at the back," she said.

The lock was broken, but stiff to release. Inside, many of the pages were blank. Here and there were sentences scribbled in an impatient, girlish hand, but more than anything the journal seemed to be a repository for ticket stubs and sections torn from magazines and newspapers. Her little scraps of truth. Where the binding forced the pages to part, she had inserted an advertisement.

Anonymity guaranteed. Details of participating offenders available upon request. Box 7339.

I turned to the bundle of letters at the back, tied with kitchen string. One or two were still in their envelopes.

"It can't be..." I slid a single folded sheet out at random. The page was smaller than I remembered, the ruled lines a darker blue. In my astonished hands the paper felt as vulnerable as a little bird.

Some days, we are put on half rations; other days, we do not eat at all. Often the electricity is switched off so we are without heating or light.

I read it through once, twice. Then I took out another page.

We want to say: so-and-so died on this day; that is the end of it. But that's a lie. Death is a lie.

With unfeeling fingers I untied the kitchen string. Released from the bundle, one of the envelopes fell to the floor. I picked it up, and pulled out the letter within.

Dear Glen, Something terrible has happened.

The paper trembled in my hand.

"Here," she said, passing me the mug of tea. Her eyes were gentle. I returned the letter to its envelope and placed it on the coffee table, wiping my palms on my knees.

"Please, tell me about you," I said, hearing my own voice too loudly in my head. "About what brings you here."

She was pursuing research in Amsterdam, where she had been granted special access to Vrolik's zoological collection. Her dissertation was to do with pathology and congenital malformation, because she was interested in nature's mistakes. She said this with a smile, and waited for me to take the bait. When I didn't, she asked me why I had come to Antwerp. I told her that the city was more conducive to writing, and that it had a fine zoo. Well, she said, I must visit her before her year in Amsterdam was out, and she would show me around the Artis gardens.

She had written to me on a whim, using the old address. Mother told her where I lived and provided directions to my apartment – no doubt hoping that at last I would heed her advice that no man should enter his forties still a bachelor. My initial reaction to the news had been one of terror: undiluted fear of being known, of facing the humiliation of childhood lies. It is not easy to invite one's doppelgänger to tea. I had thought about phoning the girl, trying to persuade her that I was in no state to be seen, that I had closed a door on the past. But then I had wondered if she, too, was alone.

"Your family..." she said at last, glancing at the bundle of letters which sat between us like an accusation.

It was a question we had all learnt to ask without asking.

I told her that my Father died of typhus three days after the Nazi flag was raised over the palace in Brussels. "But he was already a broken man." I watched her sip the tea, waited for her to swallow. "My brother fought in Spain for almost a decade. In that time, I received one letter from him: in 1944, just before the invasion of the Vall d'Aran. Soon after that, he was captured with a guerrilla regiment and executed."

"I'm so sorry."

"To think, in the months after he left I felt only shame. I wish I might have had the courage to be proud, instead…" She was waiting for me to continue, and so I rushed the story to its inevitable conclusion. "I don't know if he was shot or hanged. He could have been drowned in a tub of ice water, for all I know…"

The girl did not flinch, as I had expected, nor did she offer any further gesture of condolence. I decided to fill the silence by saying that I had thought of her mother often.

The girl nodded.

"Your mother wrote that war might give people a second chance," I said. The foolish words of a foolish girl: I could see that now. Terrified of her mistake, of the little stranger she would bear. "Did it?"

"After what happened in Singapore, we decided to move to Australia." I waited for her to continue, trying to imagine her mother's anticipation of a fresh adventure, of a new life for her young daughter, in a suburb by the sea. No storms or pirate attacks, she had written of that long journey that started it all, nearly thirty years ago. "I say 'we' – I mean Mummy and Aunt Annabel. I was only five. There didn't seem any point in returning to England by that stage. We – Mummy and Annabel and my cousins – left Ceylon in 1942. Two days into the journey, our ship came under fire from Japanese aircraft."

"Your mother—"

"She was on the open deck when the first bomb hit – that was the last anyone saw of her. My aunt and her two children took me into a lifeboat. We drifted for a day before rescue came." She set down her cup. "I don't remember it, really. When I smell salt water, I think there are perhaps snatches of memory which come back to me – bombs like tiny black droplets suspended in the sky; the sight of a dead fish, belly-up alongside our boat…"

Now it was my turn to say I was sorry. "Her siblings…"

"Uncle Tully was working in the Central Telegraph Office when it was hit by an HE bomb. My other aunt kept her family out of London for the duration of the war and reclaimed the family home in Wiltshire several years ago. She paid for my education."

"And your cousin – a boy—"

"He works in the Currumbin aviary, in Queensland."

The girl's expression gave little away. It occurred to me that she was harder to know than her mother, despite being physically here, flesh of her flesh, drinking tea in my sitting room. Why couldn't I feel more shocked by the news of her mother's death? Perhaps because she had always existed mostly in my imagination, and always would; perhaps because, to a child, death is something that afflicts only old people, and she would remain forever young...

The girl had noticed the records on the table. "Poulenc?"

"The Concerto for Two Pianos." I took the teapot through to the kitchen. "Better than rock and roll."

When I returned, I asked her what had become of her father. She told me that she didn't know. "I received a birthday card from him the year before we emigrated – I suspect Mummy wanted to give him another chance to know me, but by then it was practically too late. Later we heard rumours that he'd sent donations to the Azad Hind government in Singapore. If it's true – if he had any hand in the Japanese invasion – I don't want to know." There was a pause. "My father's loyalty was always to his colour. For her part, my mother was only capable of loving one person at a time, and better that it was me. She never got used to the idea of giving love away for nothing. My father was handsome, of course. But I think it was the idea of him that she fell in love with. It's harder to fall out of love with an idea in which you've invested so much."

This was the most I'd heard the girl speak all afternoon, and it wasn't immediately clear who was more startled, she or I.

"We all lost a little faith along the way," I said. "My father crumbled when he lost his. Every day I thank God that I lost mine."

I could feel the girl watching me through her curtain of hair. Suddenly self-conscious, I reached for the paper bundle on the table between us. When had my handwriting ever been so neat?

"Your letters meant a lot to my mother," she said. "I think we all have someone we'll always love, even if it's not meant to be.

You know how they say that every man has three women in his life? Well, my mother had three men. My father, my godfather... and you."

"Your godfather?"

"Emil Royce. I never met him – he was still in Burma by the time we emigrated. When Aunt Annabel tried to trace him after the war, none of the leads came to anything."

"The letters gave the impression that he was a good friend to her. I'm sorry that I don't have any of them here – they must still be in a box at my mother's house..."

"It's all right." She shifted, her thoughts already elsewhere. "In one of your letters, you wrote that you had blood on your hands." She gave a half smile. "You can imagine my curiosity, even now, to know: do you still?"

"We all do," I said. "That's the saddest part of all."

You can't kill a book, Adriaan had said. On the morning after our final exams, he and his family disappeared onto one of the trains bound for Poland. I hadn't realized until that moment how many relations he'd had. They said farewell to Mechelen on a day of glorious sunshine. From the train, he would have seen fields of daffodils stretching for miles, the flowers jostling in the breeze like an advancing yellow army.

"But you didn't fight." It was a statement from which I was supposed to infer a question.

"No." I wrote pamphlets, while Nijs grew angel wings on the Eastern Front.

I felt the weight of her gaze lift and travel across the room.

"You've written many books?"

"A few." Why did this feel like an admission of guilt? "Writing is just a noble fantasy."

"My mother wanted to be a writer."

"I remember that."

"But she wasn't very good."

From the kitchen came the sound of clattering dishes, cutlery hitting the linoleum floor.

"Will you excuse me for a moment? That will be Miep..."

The cat had overturned a plate of meatballs. She had already chased several into the sink, where she batted at them like so many cornered mice. I lifted her from the counter and carried her into the living room.

"That's half of dinner gone. You're welcome to stay for some *stoemp*."

"That sounds lovely – can I help?"

"It's mostly done. Won't be a minute."

The cat hadn't touched the potatoes. Tipping carrots and leeks from the steamer into the pot, I remembered the bacon that was still sitting in the fridge.

"I hope you don't mind – this is real bachelor food. Belgian bachelor food."

"It smells delicious."

We ate in silence, watching Miep slink about our feet in search of titbits. At last the girl set her plate on the floor, smiling as the cat began to lick away the last traces of cream.

"It was good of you to answer my call," she said. The curtain of dark hair made it difficult to tell whether she was still watching the cat or looking at me. "A lot of people don't want to discuss what's past. I was afraid I might remind you of something you'd rather forget."

"The Germans have a word for that: *Vergangenheitsbewälti-gung*. I tried to make my voice sound light. "They have a word for everything, the Germans – whatever else one might say, you've got to give them that." I began to collect the plates. "We spent so long looking forward – I remember my own impatience to grow up, to put aside childish things – and now it seems we are forever looking back." I stood up. "Perhaps that is simply down to my age."

"But you're young!"

"You're kind."

I returned from the kitchen to discover the girl examining the contents of my bookshelves. Running one finger along the spines, she stopped when she reached the mantelpiece. Lifting the envelope from where it stood propped between the iron candelabra, she murmured the name I had written in pencil.

"*Miss Phayre.*"

"Open it." I waited as she prised open the envelope, taking care not to tear the paper. Inside was a single blank page. She did not hesitate, as I had expected, but said, "Do you have a match?"

I passed her a box from the tin. Wordlessly, she struck a match and raised it to the paper. It was a practised gesture; I did not need to tell her to find the watermark, to hold the flame some distance from the page. She drew the match backwards and forwards, tilting her head like some small, dark creature whose curiosity has been aroused, and then she let out a quiet grunt of satisfaction. Tipping the match into her empty glass, she turned to me in triumph.

Translucent ink revealed the lines of a reclining figure: a woman, deep in sleep, her head angled slightly towards the viewer.

"She always said that she felt terribly guilty for never writing your story." The girl fingered the paper, creating shadows through the ink.

"Perhaps, then, I shall write hers. Both of ours." A flicker of interest, like the flutter of bird's wings caught out of the corner of one eye. Still the letters waited between us. I lowered myself into my chair, indicating the typewriter at the window. "With your permission, of course."

Acknowledgements

Thank you to Diane Victor for her expertise on creating smoke portraits, and to Jane Hoskins for her colonial reminiscences. The article on the Rock Veddahs is based on one published in *The Graphic* in June 1884. Grateful thanks also to the BELvue Museum and the Museum of Army and Military History in Brussels, and to the Jewish Museum of Deportation and Resistance in Mechelen.